STARS AND BONES BOOK V

Witch in the Wylds

BEATRICE B. MORGAN

AUTHORS 4 AUTHORS PUBLISHING
Marysville, WA, USA

Published by Authors 4 Authors Publishing
1214 6th St
Marysville, WA 98270
www.authors4authorspublishing.com

Library of Congress Control Number:

E-book ISBN: 978-1-64477-188-4
Paperback ISBN: 978-1-64477-189-1
Audiobook ISBN: 978-1-64477-190-7

Edited by Renee Frey
Copyedited by Brandi Spencer

Cover design ©2024 Practically Perfect Covers. All rights reserved.
Interior design and map by Brandi Spencer.

Authors 4 Authors branding is set in Bavire. Book title is set in Allura and Bilbo Swash Caps. Series title and other headers are set in Cinzel. All other text is set in Garamond.

STARS AND BONES BOOK V

Witch in the Wylds

BEATRICE B. MORGAN

Authors 4 Authors Content Rating

This title has been rated 17+, appropriate for older teens and adults, and contains:

- Brief sex
- Graphic violence
- Moderate language

Please, keep the following in mind when using our rating system:

1. A content rating is not a measure of quality.

Great stories can be found for every audience. One book with many content warnings and another with none at all may be of equal depth and sophistication. Our ratings can work both ways: to avoid content or to find it.

2. Ratings are merely a tool.

For our young adult (YA) and children's titles, age ratings are generalized suggestions. For parents, our descriptive ratings can help you make informed decisions, but at the end of the day, only you know what kinds of content are appropriate for your individual child. This is why we provide details in addition to the general age rating.

For more information on our rating system, please, visit our Content Guide at:
www.authors4authorspublishing.com/books/ratings

DEDICATION

To those who get that tingly feeling in your
ribcage when you pick up a new book.

Me too.

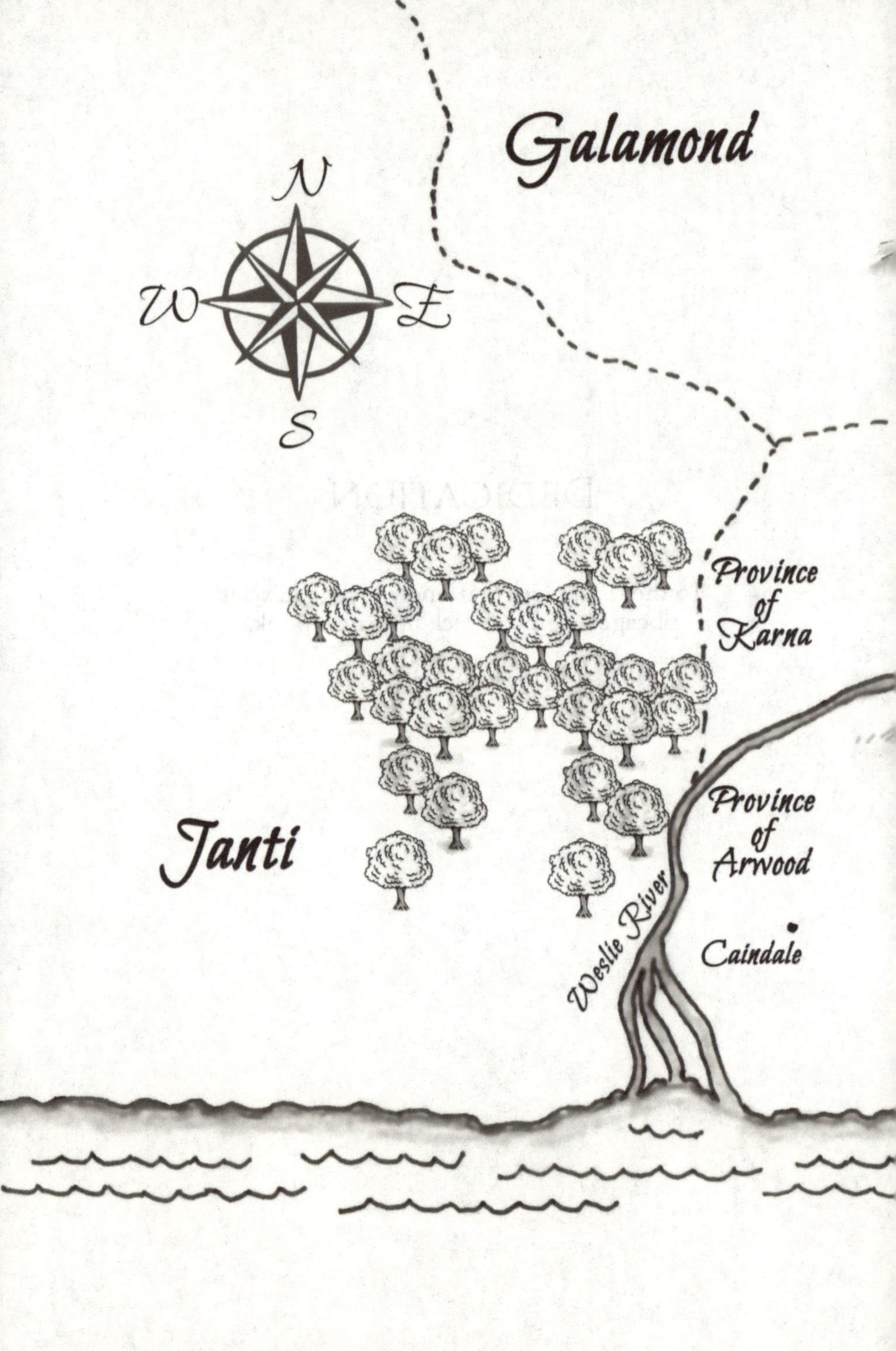

N
W
S
E
Galamond
Province of Karna
Province of Arwood
Caindale
Weslie River
Janti

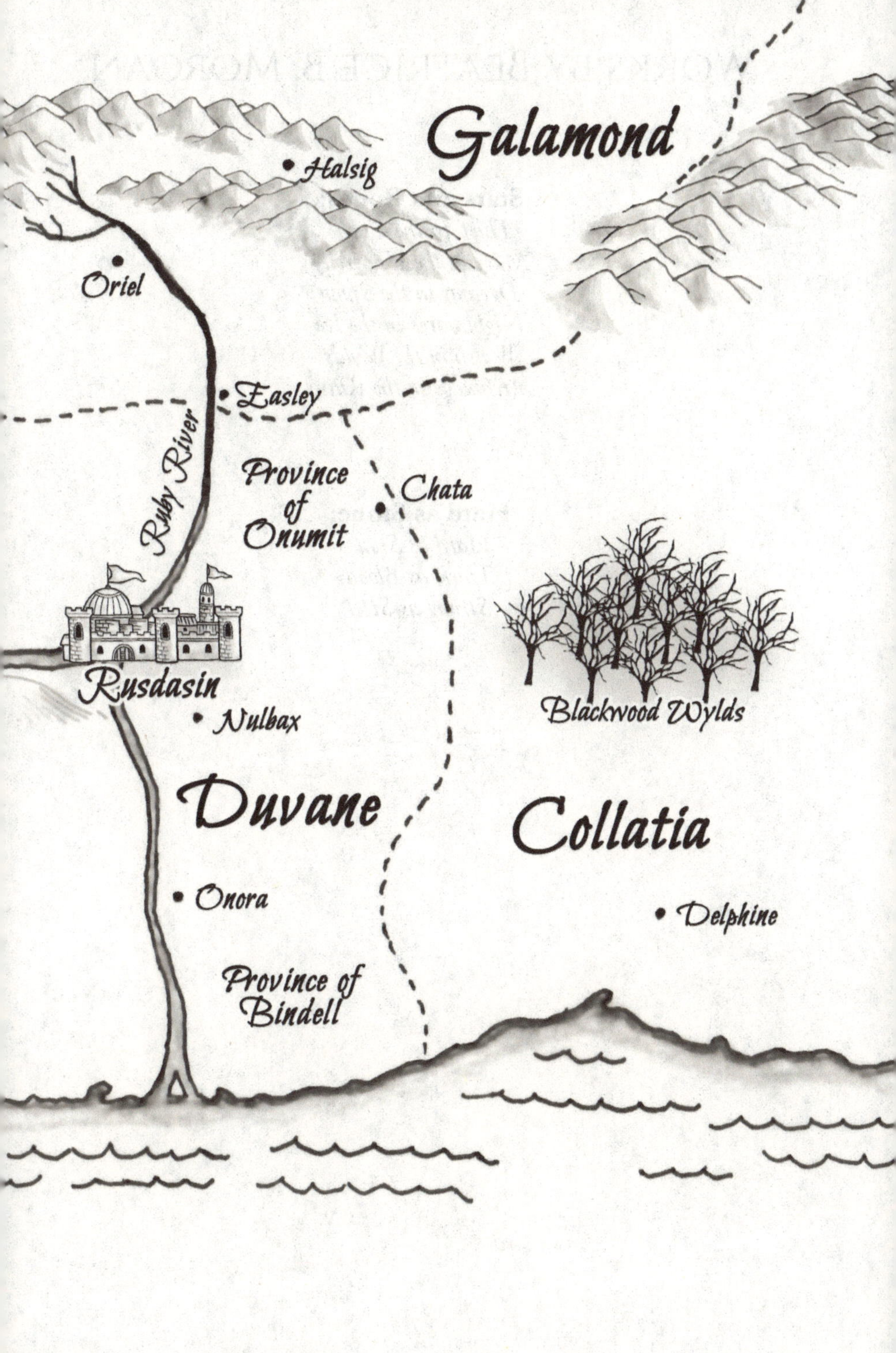

Galamond
Halsig
Oriel
Easley
Ruby River
Province
of
Onumit
Chata
Rusdasin
Nulbax
Blackwood Wylds
Duvane
Collatia
Onora
Delphine
Province of
Bindell

WORKS BY BEATRICE B. MORGAN

Stars and Bones:
Thief in the Castle
Mage in the Undercity
Dreams in the Snow
Nightmares in the Ice
Witch in the Wylds
Archmage in the Ruins

Hard as Stone:
Hard as Stone
Thick as Blood
Strong as Steel

Table of Contents

CHAPTER 1

Juniper Thimble had never given credence to the term *weary traveler*. She had grown very weary in the two months. Her back ached, her legs hurt, her head throbbed, and her stomach demanded something other than unseasoned fish and water. How people traveled for a living, she would never understand—between sleeping on the hard ground and picking bugs out of her hair and half washing in streams and ponds, her mood had turned sour.

What she wouldn't give for a proper mattress!

Her horse snorted, and she imagined he agreed.

Sir Isaac Pinul rode in front of her, and Sir Reid Sandpiper rode behind. The narrow and winding mountain pass did not allow for two horses abreast and, in some places, barely allowed for one. The route Isaac had chosen was the reason it was taking so long. The mountain pass was far less traveled than the main roads, and they could not afford to be seen. At times, the path was too treacherous for the horses, and they had to be led. A run-in with bandits had cost them at least half a day, though they had gotten a few rations out of it. A rockslide had cost them another two or three days.

Juniper wished they had time to stop and rest, even for a few minutes. Her sense of urgency faded with every sunrise. They had fled Rusdasin, royal city of Duvane, in the middle of the night for Delphine, royal city of Collatia. On the surface, they were ambassadors seeking aid from Collatia for the recent siege in Rusdasin. Secretly, they were looking for the Archmage of Fire, who had supposedly allied himself with the Collatian crown.

The Archmage of Fire was their only lead to finding how the archmages had defeated Nexon a thousand years ago, and how they might do it again before Nexon and his army of black-magic-wielding apostates and thralls took over the realm.

Juniper sighed at the thought.

"Are you all right?" came Reid's quick response, just like every time she had made even the slightest of noises along the journey.

"Yes, I'm fine," Juniper said just as quickly.

She didn't have time to list her worries to Reid, and even if she did, she didn't want to.

The coolness of the spring nights had lessened with each sunset until the summer heat penetrated even the shadows. Her magic confirmed it; summer was around the corner. Her ice huddled deep within her, recoiling at the warmth of the air and length of the day.

And traveling had given Juniper far too much time to think.

The truth of herself kept resurfacing, jabbing her thoughts like dull knives. Isaac and King Bentley Bradburn believed her to be the lost princess of Collatia, Isolde Balendin. That in itself felt beyond ridiculous, but on top of that, they also believed her to be the subject of a one-thousand-year-old prophecy that claimed a princess would return to stop Nexon from returning to power. Juniper didn't fully believe the princess part, and she didn't believe the prophecy part at all.

What was she supposed to do against Nexon, Archmage of Earth, who had a thousand years of experience and skill against her?

It rattled her nerves and twisted her stomach into knots.

The mountain pass widened as it entered a forest of ancient oaks with leaves of deep green. A stream babbled somewhere unseen. Birds chirped madly in the full branches, fluttering back and forth, taking flight as others landed. Between the oaks, Juniper spotted the biggest blueberry bush she had ever seen—it was as large as a small house and thrice as tall as Reid. Little reddish-purple berries bloomed on every branch, and bees buzzed between the white petals.

Reid nudged his horse to ride beside Juniper. She felt his stare and considered ignoring it.

No, the journey had made them all grouchy. She met Reid's honey-brown eyes, and something tight unraveled in her chest. Reid looked at her as if the kingdom didn't rest on their shoulders, as if she had never done a thing wrong, as if she were important.

"I'm fine," she said, answering his unspoken question. "Just tired and sore and hungry."

"And cranky," Reid added.

"Oh, like you can talk."

He smiled, though it didn't hide his exhaustion. The days in the sun had warmed his bronze skin, though it had left her pale skin an unflattering shade of pink. She'd never taken the sun well.

Reid wore his silver knights' armor—as did Isaac. An owl and chain adorned the breastplate, signifying them as knights of the Order, even though the Order had fallen into shambles. Reid and Isaac were two of the fraction of knights who remained.

The path narrowed, and Reid slowed to ride behind Juniper. The trail angled downward through a series of stone monoliths, six on either side. Engravings had once decorated the stone but had long since been dulled by weather and time. Moss and vines had taken over most of the stones. Juniper tried to get a better look at the language underneath the moss, but a snake uncoiled from within the vines, and she decided not to.

The mountain path rose up and down, around and around, and then steadily angled down. Finally, after what seemed like hours of feeling like she would fall forward, the path met a road of packed dirt and gravel. The path leveled. The mountains lessened. Gradually, the trees thinned.

They reached the outskirts of Delphine as the sun began its downward descent. Fields of tilled soil and planted fields stretched over the countryside. Ranches of sheep, cows, and pigs spotted the spaces between the fields, flourishing the scent of manure. They passed through a small farming village. Southern Collatia had a warmer climate than Rusdasin, and it showed in the homes and cottages. Many had open courtyards in the center of the home—the traditional style, according to Isaac, which also included breezeways, verandas, and timber arches.

The village smelled strongly of livestock, but underneath it came scents of dinner—spices and sizzling meats and sugary breads. Many of the homes had their kitchens and a firepit in the open courtyard. It made Juniper's stomach growl.

Night fell, and they camped in a grove. They sat around the campfire in sullen silence and ate the last of their provisions. Their grueling pace had exhausted them all, and no one had the mind for conversation. Juniper slept fitfully and woke to the same sullen silence.

The villages grew closer and closer together, until the farmland between them vanished. All the while, the city of Delphine grew larger.

At last, they approached the city gates.

A wall of pale red stone circled Delphine. According to Isaac, it had four gates, one for each cardinal direction. They approached the West Gate, an iron lattice masterpiece that remained closed and guarded. Two guards stood outside the gate, and more patrolled the battlements. The guards wore simple, sturdy armor of iron and steel. Their helmets bore plumes of red feathers, and the royal seal of the Balendin crown gleamed on their breastplates—a crescent moon surrounded by a laurel wreath.

A guardsman halted them at the gates. "We're not taking any more refugees. You'll have to go to the North Gate. They've a camp here."

"We are not refugees," said Isaac.

"What business do you have in the city?" asked the guardsman, doubt in each word.

"I am Sir Isaac Pinul, ambassador from Duvane, returning home after business in Rusdasin. I have brought friends with me. They are no refugees. They will have a home with me in the city."

The guardsman frowned. "A knight, eh?" He half laughed. "You'll have to go to the North Gate."

Isaac sighed through his nose. "Let me speak to your commander."

The guardsman straightened. "There's no need, you'll have to go—"

"Your commander, soldier," Isaac demanded.

The guardsman studied Isaac with dislike. "Very well, *sir*." He turned and called up to the battlements, "These travelers want to speak to the commander."

The guardsman atop the battlements did not guffaw or roll his eyes. He turned at once into the tower. A few moments later, a guardswoman appeared atop the battlement, her armor decorated with red and white details. Her helmet bore a plume of gold.

"What's all this?" she shouted to the guardsmen below.

"Commander, Sir Isaac Pinul wishes to speak with you about entering the city," said the guardsman.

"Is that so? Hold the gate. I'll be right down."

The commander vanished from the battlement and reappeared through a side door on the ground level a few moments later. She marched to Isaac with authority and looked over their party—her eyes lingered on Juniper, and something frighteningly like recognition flickered over her eyes. The commander stood tall and proud. She had the pale golden skin of southern Collatia, and dark hair braided behind her head. Juniper wanted to look away, but she forced herself to hold the commander's gaze. Looking away would make her look guilty.

"It's commander now? You've been busy these few months, Sandra," said Isaac.

"As have you, I see," said the commander.

"Rusdasin has made me long for home," Isaac said. "I don't remember the mountain pass being so unforgiving."

"Aye." The commander stepped closer and lowered her tone. "Forgive my men for their suspicions. We've had refugees spilling over the hills, claiming to be everything from royalty to priests."

"Of course, Commander," said Isaac.

"What news do you bring?" asked the commander.

"Rusdasin has suffered an attack," Isaac said lowly.

The commander's stoic face flinched.

"Bradburn Castle was taken, but the king yet lives. He has mounted a resistance within the city and has struck the enemy a blow. We have come seeking aid from Collatia."

"The queen needs to hear of this." The commander turned and shouted, "Guardsman," —He jumped into a straight-backed pose—"ready my horse. I will escort Sir Pinul into the city."

"At once, sir." The guardsman ran to the stables.

Juniper unclutched the reins. She'd held them tight enough to leave indentations on her palms. She hadn't anticipated not getting into the city. Of course, she'd never let something so rudimentary as a wall stop her. She had overcome far more complicated and well-guarded obstacles.

The West Gate opened with a sigh of well-oiled hinges. The commander and Isaac rode through first, and Juniper and Reid rode behind. The guardsman did not look happy about it, and his glare lingered on Juniper. She forced herself to stare at the commander as they rode through the shadowed gatehouse and into the sunlit city of Delphine.

CHAPTER 2

Juniper had lived in Rusdasin all her life. She knew little of other cities, and while Delphine had buildings and streets, it looked like a different realm. The cobblestone streets were wide, the sidewalks glittered in the early morning sunlight, and the alleys held few shadows. Homes rose three and four stories tall, with open shutters and arched dormers and verandas. Many roofs were gabled and ended in spires, decorative weather vanes, and sparkling globes in gold, cerulean, sage, and every color imaginable.

They passed a market teeming with booths, carts, and shops, all packed with trinkets, food, baubles, and things she hadn't the time to see. Spices and herbs scented the air, and it made her mouth water. The city rang with voices, bartering and laughing and chatting. Somewhere in the market, drums and strings and woodwinds dotted the air with a happy song. She imagined people dancing in the street, even though she couldn't see them.

She spotted a corner shop with three floors of dresses in shades she had never seen. One window held vibrant blues and purples, another held sizzling reds and oranges, and yet another held bright pinks and yellows. The roof vaulted and ended in a golden weather vane shaped like a ballgown.

Reid caught Juniper's eye and frowned.

She could hear his grouchy reprimand, *That's not why we're here.*

The commander escorted them straight to the palace at the city's southern edge. The grand palace of pale stone sat on a hill, higher than the city around it. A wall of the same pale stone surrounded it, and guards patrolled the battlements and watched the party approach from the turrets.

Delphine had not been the royal city for very long. Balendin Castle had been the royal center of Collatia for hundreds of years, until the civil war. The remaining members of the royal family relocated to the summer palace in Delphine to rebuild—Juniper remembered that much of history.

The outer gates of the palace opened at the commander's order. A well-trimmed garden of fully bloomed roses and vibrant lavender greeted them, scented with the sweet floral of magic. Juniper thought nothing about the garden until she spotted two mages tending to the rose bushes on the far side, their fingers working over the smaller blooms and buds. They were using magic to tend the garden. Her surprise melted as she remembered Collatia did not hold the same iron grip on its mages as Duvane. Juniper glanced at Reid, but he held his stare ahead of him. By the unreadable coldness—a knight greeting a foreign entity.

A cobblestone path led to the front of the palace. An arcade stretched around the garden, and water flowed over a channel on top—forming an aqueduct. Excess water cascaded into shallow pools lined with blue stones. In the angled sunlight, the blue stones glittered.

The garden ended at a set of large oak doors carved with blooming flowers, trees, whorls of vines, and a glorious depiction of the moon. The doors were closed, and a line of guards in white and gold blocked the procession. Each wore a red sash and a dark gold scabbard.

Standing in the center of the blockade was a young man with dark hair and pale gold skin. He wore the white and gold armor of the others, but he also wore a golden cape and a decorated scabbard. The Balendin crest adorned his breastplate. As the party came to a halt, the young guard set his hand on the pommel of his blade.

"General Balendin, sir," said the commander. "Sir Isaac Pinul seeks an audience with the queen. He brings urgent news from Rusdasin."

Isaac nudged his horse a step forward.

General Crespin Balendin, the former king of Collatia, eyed the party with a suspicious scowl. He reminded Juniper of Reid's uncle, Captain Sandpiper. Crespin's gaze lingered on Juniper, and though her hands shook, she held his stare.

If she were Isolde, Crespin would be her cousin. His father and her father would be brothers. His father had stirred civil war and then murdered her father, and the rest of her family, in an attempt to grab the throne. He had failed, and his son had taken it—Crespin was the only living heir, besides his younger sister.

"My sister will want to hear what you've to say. I will escort you. My men will see to your horses and goods," said Crespin in a harsh voice—one used to shouting.

With a few quick commands, stable hands and servants took the horses and their gear, including several of their weapons.

Standing in front of the palace gates, Juniper felt small. She felt…like an imposter.

The oak doors opened with a hushed sigh of metal on metal, and General Crespin led them into the palace.

They walked through a grand foyer of pale white stone and glittering tiles of purple, blue, and green. The silvery yellow ceiling domed, like a miniature moon. Crespin led them into a sunny corridor. Through the tall windows, Juniper spotted a courtyard of shimmering pools and marble. Everywhere she looked, Juniper spotted another splash of color, shades between blue and green and purple.

Sunlight poured from the tall windows, sparkling over the colors and marble and glinting off veins of gold and silver in the white stone.

"The Summer Palace is quite remarkable," Reid said conversationally. "I had hoped to see it one day. If only it were under better circumstances."

"I'm fond of it," said Crespin in a tone that implied the opposite. "We've had to make adjustments over the years to accommodate its use as the primary palace, such as the barracks for the Royal Guard, the guest wing, and the library." Crespin glanced back at Juniper, his stare cold. "We build as funds allow."

The civil war had devastated Collatia's economy. They were still recovering almost twenty years later. Juniper didn't remember it; she had been an infant when the war ended. Crespin would have been old enough to remember.

Crespin led them into the throne room, a grand circular space of blue and white tile. Golden pillars spiraled to the ceiling, and hanging brass lanterns held sparkling white-gold magelights. The dome of the ceiling was etched with blues, greens, and gold—a mural of stars, humans, and bones. It took Juniper a moment to realize she had seen it before, at the crown of the world, in the garden of the gods.

In the instant she realized it, in the space between heartbeats, she understood something she had never understood before, something grand and beyond herself—and in the next moment, that understanding fled.

Juniper blinked away her stupor—she had paused to look at the ceiling, and the others had continued walking.

She glanced up at the mural. What just happened?

"Jetan," Crespin barked at one of the guards. "Take word to the queen. Sir Isaac Pinul has arrived with urgent news from Rusdasin. It cannot wait."

A guardsman ducked through a curtained doorway on the other side of the throne room.

Crespin led Isaac, Reid, and Juniper to the center of the throne room, within a puddle of magelight that seemed brighter than the rest of the room. Juniper felt something shift in the air—she suspected magic at work. Royal guards stood at intervals around the throne room, watching them from every angle. Somewhere nearby, water trickled. Jasmine grew in golden pots, and their perfume scented the air. She felt terribly exposed.

No one spoke.

She felt morbidly out of place, more so than she ever had in Bradburn Castle. She did not belong in the summer palace and never would, but knowing that she could have inherited the throne, the kingdom—it unsettled her and made her stomach twist.

Footsteps approached. Several sets. Jetan returned through the curtained doorway and took up a post beside it, his face impassive and alert. A young man in gold and white armor came next; the decorations on his pauldrons denoted a higher status than the common guard. His light brown hair was immaculately trimmed and combed to the side. He marched to the throne and stood beside it, hand on his pommel.

Next came an older woman in blue robes. She wore her silver-streaked blonde hair in a tight braid and upon her face a permanent frown. She strolled to the throne and stood on the side opposite the guard. Her pale eyes scanned the visiting party. A sensation raked over Juniper's body, subtle but there—magic. The older woman was a mage.

By the way Reid's fingers curled into a fist, he had felt the sensation too.

The curtain swished aside once more, and a pretty young woman with pale golden skin and dark auburn hair glided into the room. The silver of her crown caught the magelight. Queen Myrisha Balendin.

"The herald hadn't yet announced you," Crespin said at once, nodding to the young guard beside the door, who'd paused mid-breath.

"Oh," said Myrisha. She paused a step, then continued to the throne. "Next time I shall remember."

Juniper stared at the young queen—they could have passed as sisters. Juniper did not have the golden skin tone of her cousins, but they shared a face, dark blue eyes, and auburn hair.

Myrisha walked with natural grace to her throne. She wore silken robes of vibrant blue and gold, elaborate in its drapery. She sat on her simple wooden throne and took in her visitors. Her gaze lingered a moment on Juniper, yet they lingered on Reid too.

Crespin marched to the throne, gave a curt bow of his head, and took up a post beside the older woman.

"Sir Pinul," said Myrisha in greeting. Her voice filled the throne room, but she lacked her brother's powerful cadence. "I hear you have a story to tell me. Please, go ahead."

CHAPTER 3

Queen Myrisha Balendin revealed nothing of her thoughts as Isaac told her about Nexon, the siege of Bradburn Castle, and the growing resistance. Isaac held himself like a knight—stoic and calm despite the dire news. He did not sugarcoat it. He identified Nexon as the Iluvin Archmage of Earth.

Juniper stood slightly behind Reid and held as still as possible. She didn't want to draw attention to herself.

The decorated guard standing by the throne noticed her. Juniper met his calm gaze, and his brows furrowed. Juniper looked away and took the smallest steps behind Reid, hiding herself from the guard's direct view.

As Isaac spoke, Myrisha listened intently. Crespin scowled. The odd feeling of exposure in Juniper's gut remained.

Finally, Isaac's story came to an end. A heavy silence filled the throne room, and Juniper peeked around Reid's shoulder. Myrisha wore sympathy in her fine features, but also a steadfastness.

"You say Nexon has returned?" Myrisha asked, her voice steady. "And you believe this Iluvin mage to be the same as the mage defeated a thousand years ago in the Great War?"

"Yes, Your Majesty," said Isaac. "He revealed himself during his siege."

Myrisha leaned toward the older blonde woman. "Lenette, fetch Delmont. He needs to hear this."

Lenette glided away through a curtained doorway behind the throne.

Juniper held in her surprise. Delmont Thacket—the supposed Archmage of Fire. He was here, and they hadn't had to ask for him.

"A word of caution," said Crespin to Isaac. "Our forces are not what they used to be."

"Our neighbors have come to us in their time of need," Myrisha said to her brother. "We must answer their call however we can."

"And expend our own forces?" Crespin said to his sister. "We send soldiers to Duvane, and then our own defenses will be weakened. Nexon will know that. What's to stop him from attacking when we're weak? It would be foolish to protect another at the expense of yourself."

Myrisha frowned. "So, you would have me do nothing?"

"If all this is true," Crespin said, agitation eating through his words, "we are dealing with an ancient, angry mage with an army of rebel apostates and enthralled knights and demon beasts—and we are sorely outnumbered, even without sending part of the army west."

"Just yesterday you were bragging about your battlemages being second to none, General," Myrisha said, her tone sharp on his title.

Reid flinched at the mention of battlemages. Juniper could only imagine what he gleaned from that information. Reid, like most in the Order, held magic within extreme suspicion and caution. He likely despised the idea of battlemages, but Juniper thought it wonderful. Mages were wicked useful.

"We have less than a hundred battlemages," Crespin argued.

"Less than a hundred *fully trained* battlemages," Myrisha said. "More still in training. And I believe it was you who said one battlemage equals one hundred soldiers."

"One hundred regular, non-magical soldiers," Crespin said through gritted teeth.

"Enough," Myrisha said, though her voice lacked authority. "We will not argue in front of our guests."

Crespin's frown deepened. Myrisha took a calming breath, and her irritation vanished. Just like that, the argument dissolved in such a way that only came between siblings having had a lifetime of arguments; Crespin and Myrisha had apologized silently and instantly.

If Juniper had grown up with them, would she have joined those arguments?

Myrisha's gaze returned to Isaac, then grazed over Reid and Juniper. "You have not yet introduced your friends, Sir Pinul."

Isaac hesitated, warranting a curious look from the queen and a suspicious scowl from the general. A silence befell the room, and it thickened with every moment.

Isaac cleared his throat. "My apologies, Your Majesty. These past few weeks have been most trying. I have brought with me Sir Reid Sandpiper and Juniper Thimble."

"The thief?" spat Crespin, eyebrows nearly to his hair. His glare turned murderous. "The one who tried to kill Adrian Bradburn and then saved him?"

Every eye in the room turned to Juniper.

Isaac tensed. "I see word has reached here."

"One of those is true," Juniper muttered.

Myrisha raised a brow.

"The saving part," Juniper quickly added.

"You bring a thief into our kingdom, into our palace?" Crespin asked, his voice rough.

"Crespin," warned his sister. "I am sure Isaac had a very good reason." Myrisha turned her own glare onto Juniper, then onto Isaac.

"I did," said Isaac. "She has proven herself in the eyes of His Majesty, King Bentley Bradburn, and now acts as his ambassador."

The silence churned, and Juniper felt the scowls and anger. It had been easy enough to ignore them back in Rusdasin, but she had never felt so exposed as she did standing before the Collatian throne.

"I believe you, Sir Pinul," Myrisha said, much to the annoyance of her brother. She stood. "It will be a few hours before Lenette returns with Delmont, and you look like you could all use a rest and a warm meal. It's amazing how a warm bath can lift the spirits."

Juniper fully agreed.

Myrisha stepped down from her throne, her robes shimmering in the magelight. "Sir Pinul, I invite you and your guests back to the palace for the evening meal. Delmont will be present. I also have something to ask of you."

"Anything, Your Majesty," said Isaac, bowing.

"I need you to speak with Commander Yorlan and report back to me regarding the state of the Sentinels," Myrisha said. "Have a report when you return this evening. I apologize for the short notice. I know Reese has missed you dearly. She and Connor are more than welcome for the meal, of course."

Isaac bowed deeply. "Of course, Your Majesty."

Understanding slapped Juniper—Isaac had been an ambassador to Collatia for years. He had lived in Delphine. He had worked closely with the dead king and queen. He likely had friends here, including whomever Reese and Conner were. By the look on Isaac's face as he left, he had missed Reese as well.

"Will your friends require housing? We have room in the guest wing," Myrisha said.

"That would be most gracious, Your Majesty," said Isaac.

Juniper's heart jumped into her throat. Isaac had said they would be staying with him, and Juniper had expected it. Reid looked as surprised, though it quickly vanished from his face. She hadn't missed Myrisha's subtle tone on *friends*.

More likely, they wanted to keep an eye on them.

"It is an honor to house ambassadors," Myrisha said, though the word ambassadors lacked assurance. "I will escort you to the guest wing. This way, please."

The young guard walked beside the queen, a hand on his sword, as she led them through an adjoining corridor. Several of the Royal Guard followed.

"This is Captain Ryland Bellamy, of the Royal Guard," Myrisha said.

"It is a pleasure, Captain Bellamy," Isaac said.

"It is mutual, I assure you, sir," said the captain in a smooth and articulate voice. "I've a sister in the Sentinels, and she holds you in high regard."

"That is good to hear," said Isaac. "I look forward to seeing what Commander Yorlan has accomplished in my absence."

The queen and her captain led them to the guest wing, an assortment of chambers surrounding a simple courtyard. It resembled the rest of the palace with its golden-veined white stone pillars, tiles of blues, greens, purples, and shined wooden doorways and arched doors.

"Please, make yourselves at home," said Myrisha. She spoke mostly to Reid, though she tried her best to make eye contact with Juniper. "If you need anything, please let a servant or a guard know. I will have servants assigned to the guest wing."

"Thank you, Your Majesty." Reid bowed his head. "Your graciousness is beyond words."

"Before we part, I must congratulate you on your coronation." Isaac bowed again to Myrisha.

"Many thanks, Sir Pinul." Myrisha nodded slightly toward him. "I trust you to see them to their rooms."

Myrisha and her captain left the guest chamber. Several royal guards had stationed themselves in the guest wing. Juniper had the feeling more lingered beyond her sight. Not that it mattered; they were guests, but Myrisha would be a fool to trust them blindly—especially knowing who Juniper was.

He led them onto the veranda bordering the courtyard, off of which were identical pale wooden doors. Birds fluttered about the courtyard. Jasmine and lemongrass grew in wild bunches, and the sun glinted off an overgrown bush with glossy pink leaves. Fresh, damp soil scented the air, and underneath it, the subtle scent of magic persisted. This small garden was not as well-kept as the roses in the front garden, and by the smell, someone had quickly fixed it up for guests.

"The chambers are all identical," Isaac started. "I will not be far. My quarters are in Eldridge Hall, on the other side of the palace."

"This will do." Reid paused beside one door. He set his hand on the handle and looked back to her for approval.

She hesitated. Her skin flashed hot then cold. "There are more rooms," she said in a small voice. "Would you rather have your own?"

Reid wore no easy emotion. "Would you rather have your own?"

It took her a heartbeat to answer. "No."

Reid let himself into the room and left the door open behind him.

Isaac cleared his throat, eyes elsewhere. "If you need anything, there are servants a mere moment away. There is a bell at the end of this corridor that will summon someone at any hour. They will answer questions or fetch tea or send word to me. They know where to find me."

"Thank you, Isaac," Juniper said.

He lingered, and his stoic expression slipped. He wore a fatherly face underneath it.

"We'll be all right," she assured him. "Myrisha was right about a warm bath."

Isaac nodded and left. Juniper watched him go, and as he rounded the corner, she met the eyes of the nearest royal guard. He wore the same unreadable, cold mask as Bradburn's guards.

No, she didn't want to sleep alone in a strange room in a strange palace in a strange kingdom. Not if the option to sleep in the same room with Reid existed. They had shared a bed, but never a room. Her chambers at the castle had been hers, and he'd had his own. Even in the king's house in the Undercity, they had separate rooms. She glanced down at the moonstone ring—her engagement ring. She supposed she would have to learn to share everything with him, even her space.

And…she could learn to do that. Probably.

Juniper walked into *their* room and shut the door behind her.

CHAPTER 4

The suite was moderate, though smaller than her chambers at Bradburn Castle. Brass folding screens divided the room into sections: sitting room, bedroom, and bathing room. The walls were the same white stone, and the floor had a pattern of sky blue and pineapple yellow tiles. Juniper strolled into the bathing room. A narrow window of leaded glass allowed just enough light to illuminate the copper tub and matching vanity. A circular mirror with copper edges hung on the wall—Juniper avoided her reflection. She didn't want to know how disgusting and greasy she looked from sleeping outside and washing without soap. Her water magic allowed for mildly better washing, but it did not take the place of soap.

The tub did not have a faucet, or tap, or any way that she could see of turning on the water.

"Reid?" Juniper asked. His booted footsteps approached. "Do you know how to turn on the water?"

He motioned to the stone spout, then pulled a chain that vanished into the ceiling. Water gargled within the wall, then gushed out the spout and into the tub.

"Where is it coming from?" Juniper asked. She could hear the water moving through the walls. She could feel it too.

"The aqueducts," Reid said. "They surround the palace and catch rainwater. I've only ever read about the system. I've never seen it in person. It's ingenious."

Juniper eyed the basin, the spout, the seemingly seamless construction. Curious, she felt along the water as it flowed. It came through perfectly formed pipes in the walls; there were no leaks or even seams. She ran her fingers along the stone spout, perfectly formed and delicately carved.

"It's all made of stone?" Juniper asked.

"Looks like it." Reid frowned at her. "Why?"

"Because this was obviously made by magic."

Reid didn't answer. He gazed out the window.

Water filled the tub, and Reid released the chain. This time, Juniper heard the clicking of whatever mechanism stopped and started the water flow.

Reid meandered around the folding screen and Juniper dropped her dirty traveling clothes onto the floor. She took quick stock of the soaps and body tonics—minimalist and unscented. Juniper chose at random and lined the bottles on the edge of the tub. She heated the water until it steamed and submerged herself. Oh, the water felt marvelous! She felt the water all around her, confined by metal and stone, held in place. Water was made to flow, to move, to churn, to always be moving. She felt it—that yearning to flow.

She washed and relished the feeling of clean skin.

"Bradburn Castle was better stocked," she said playfully. She relaxed against the tub.

"King Bradburn also has more gold in his treasury," Reid said. "We are lucky Queen Balendin allowed us to stay. If her brother still wore the crown, he would not have. We would either be staying with Isaac in the Sentinel Hall or staying at the cheapest inn we could find. Or worse, in the refugee camp."

"Why does he not like us?"

"There is animosity between Duvane and Collatia because Duvane waited so long to aid them during their civil war," Reid explained. "It is thought that if we would have intervened sooner, not so many lives would have been lost."

Including her family. Isolde's family.

"Why didn't we?"

"That is a question for King Bradburn."

She hummed as she considered that question and quickly pushed it aside. "I have another question. What is a Sentinel?"

"They are essentially knights," Reid said. "Isaac helped organize them after the civil war, in an attempt to ward off future uprisings and such disasters. They learn much of what knights do, but they do not align themselves with the Order."

"And the Order is okay with that?"

A beat passed. "The Order isn't fully aware of what Sentinels are. I wasn't either. Isaac informed me only this morning."

Juniper could hear the scowl in his tone, the one that came from uncertain disapproval.

"Oh?" Juniper grinned, though Reid couldn't see it. "You mean Isaac has been secretly sharing the Order's secrets with another secret group of anti-magic warriors? Scandalous!"

"I would have thought the same, but our circumstances have changed that." Reid sighed, then added, "Because they are not connected to the Order, they have escaped Nexon's control."

"And we still have anti-magic warriors on our side," Juniper finished.

"If Myrisha allows us aid," Reid said, the words mildly bitter.

"You mean if Crespin allows her to allow us aid," Juniper corrected. Reid huffed, and she could picture his face—brows furrowed in disapproval mixed with his weary traveler attitude.

A knock sounded on the door, and Reid moved to answer it. Juniper climbed from the tub and magicked water from her skin and hair.

"Thank you," came Reid's voice, and the chamber door closed. His footsteps headed back across the tiled floor. "That was a servant. She reminded us that we are to dine with Her Majesty, Queen Myrisha tonight. She also delivered fresh clothes."

"What color?"

"Does it matter?" Reid asked dryly.

Her slight humor vanished. "No, I supposed it doesn't."

Juniper stepped around the folding screen and into the bedroom. Reid sat on the bed, gaze unfocused on the opposite wall. She recognized it as his thinking face, marred by relentless exhaustion. Still, his lack of interest bothered her. She stood within his view, naked and clean, but his eyes remained elsewhere. She hesitated a moment more, but his eyes didn't so much as flicker in her direction.

The servant had delivered two sets of clothes for the both of them, traditional Collatian robes that consisted of a unfitted floor-length dress, tunic, and a sleeveless vest that reached to her knees. Juniper had seen the style in shop windows in Rusdasin, in all manner of exotic style and patterns and colors—hers were pale blue and off-white. However, their dinner with the queen wasn't for a while, so she pulled the loose sleeping shirt over her head instead. It looked like a man's shirt; the sleeves billowed to her elbows, and the hem reached mid-thigh. It was ridiculously soft, so she couldn't find it in herself to complain.

"You should bathe." She climbed into the soft bed, intent on a nap. "It will make you feel better."

Reid sighed and vanished around the folding screen. She listened to him undress, his boots hitting the floor, the buckle of his sword belt, the swish of his shirt. She had the thought of joining him, but her limbs had gone leaden against the soft blankets. She hugged one of the pillows to her chest. The headboard had been carved with curvy spires and painted a lovely gold, like a fantastical landscape from a story.

It was easy to imagine herself a princess instead of an ambassador begging for aid.

Reid didn't take long, or she might have dozed. She didn't know for certain. Reid climbed into the bed with her and reclined against the pillows with a sigh.

"Feel better?" Juniper whispered.

"Yes."

A few moments passed, but neither fell asleep. The sunlight streaming in felt far too bright and happy for sleep.

"Do you think the king will build a new palace somewhere, like the Balendins did, rather than rebuilding his castle?" Juniper asked.

"Why would he not return to Bradburn Castle?"

"A lot of it was destroyed."

"Not all of it is ruined," Reid said. "Much of the structure still stands."

"I couldn't tell. There was a lot of smoke."

Reid inhaled slowly and released it as slowly. "More than just Balendin Castle was lost during the civil war. The royal family was slaughtered, and thousands of people died in the years following. There are still people in Rusdasin, and our king yet lives. We will return and take our castle back. Bradburn Castle isn't just a throne room or a fortress. It is a home. To the king, to the guards, and to the staff. They didn't lose a castle; they lost a home."

She caught the bitterness and rage in those words.

"As did you," Juniper whispered.

Reid looked away, but the answer shone in his eyes. "Yes, I lost my home. As did my uncle, my aunt. Everything they had, gone. Forced to flee for their lives and hide."

The inflection on his tone grated her nerves. "And I can't possibly understand what that feels like," she added.

Judging by the subtle flicker of guilt in his eyes, he did think that. She rolled over onto her other side, facing away from Reid.

"Jun," he started, exhausted.

"Take a nap," she said. "You're being grumpy."

She shut her eyes. She needed a nap too. After a few calm heartbeats, she felt the tug of sleep, of a much-needed rest.

Movement stirred her from her almost-sleep—Reid slid his arm around her middle, the other under her pillow. He cradled her body with his. His warm breath grazed her neck.

They hadn't touched each other during the journey. They hadn't the time or the energy, and the bedrolls hardly provided privacy. She'd missed the comfort of his body against hers, a ward against the dark.

Chapter 5

Reid held Juniper against him. Her breathing slowed as she fell asleep. Despite the harrowing journey over the mountains, he couldn't sleep. The panic and guilt of leaving his home and his family in a city stolen by Nexon caught up with him. It was easier to ignore while moving, when he had something to occupy his thoughts. Now, lying awake, he couldn't escape it. Nexon had stolen his home, banished his family to the Undercity, and nearly killed them all.

Again, mages used their magic to kill and raze and threaten. Again, mages took his home. Juniper was right—she didn't understand.

He still didn't know how many of his friends in the Royal Guard and Order had died since the siege. He might never know. He had survived and hidden and fled. Now he slept in a bed in a palace, holding the woman he loved. How many had lost loved ones that day? How many now slept alone? He hugged Juniper closer.

A second home, ripped away by apostates.

Reid fell asleep amid his unhappy thoughts.

The sun shone through the open shutters. Baking bread filled the small cottage with the scents of butter and herbs. Reid watched his father whittle a piece of wood into something lovely—his father sold figurines of animals and people to travelers. One day, Reid would whittle just as good.

"Every stroke counts." His father motioned to the knife. "Against wood to create, but also against another man. Don't ever take up a blade without the intent to use it."

Reid took in the words.

The cottage door opened. Reid's older brother carried in an armload of wood for the stove. He walked into the kitchen without looking at Reid or their father. He had been moody since he'd met that girl down the road. Reid went back to watching his father whittle. Whittling made much more sense than girls, anyway.

Slowly, the figure of a woman carrying a jug of water emerged from the block of wood. The woman was no bigger than Reid's curled fist.

"What's her name?" Reid asked his father.

"She doesn't have one yet. What shall we name her?"

Reid had never made such an important decision as naming someone. But it didn't take very long.

"Mariana," Reid said.

His father's brows rose. "After your mother?"

Reid nodded.

The door to the cottage opened, and Reid's mother hurried inside. She shut the door and fumbled with the lock.

"Mariana?" asked his father. "What's wrong?"

"Trouble." She looked at her husband then to Reid. The sunlight caught the moonstone in her ring as she slid it from her finger.

Reid's father stood, setting the wooden woman on the table beside his whittling knife. He went to the window and looked in the direction his wife had come. His brows furrowed. Reid didn't know what was happening or what his father had seen, but he knew something was wrong.

Reid's father went into the kitchen. His mother closed the space between herself and Reid, knelt down, and took his little hands in her own.

"Reid, this is important, listen to me, okay?"

He nodded.

"This ring," she said, pushing her moonstone ring into his palm, "is more important than anything else. Go into our room, get under the bed, and stay there. No matter what. Do you understand me?"

His mother spoke with a strong voice, one of a woman who knew everything—and Reid nodded. He clutched the ring and did as his mother had instructed. He hid underneath his parents' large bed. The shutters were closed, leaving the room in shadows.

The cottage burst open, rattling the paintings. He jumped and clutched the ring to his chest. Blood pulsed through his ears. He watched through the open door of the bedroom. He recognized the voices, the mages his parents had let stay in the barn.

"Where is it? Where is it? Where is it?" one of the mages demanded, again and again. Lightning crackled and whipped.

His mother screamed.

Reid clutched her ring as tight as he could, her last words playing over and over: *Stay under the bed. No matter what.*

His brother screamed, and then his father screamed.

Reid had never been more terrified. His father collapsed onto the floor, his eyes lifeless and staring into Reid's hiding place. Another thump followed—his brother.

And his mother screamed again.

Reid knew what he had to do. He was a knight! This is why he had become a knight—to rid the world of mages like them, who thrived on causing pain and misery. Reid crawled out from under the bed and ran into the main room.

The mage held his mother above the floor, twisting her body with his vile magic. Reid knew what to do—he'd gone through years of training for this, sat through grueling lessons, studied and studied and studied. He grabbed the mage's wrist.

He felt the magic coursing through the mage, and he shredded through it. The magic scattered and receded. The mage screamed.

"Stop! Stop! Stop!" pleaded the mage.

Reid didn't stop. This mage had hurt his mother, hurt his family. He would not let it stand. This is why the Order had been formed.

But his mother still screamed.

Everyone was screaming.

"Stop, stop, stop," Juniper pleaded, tears clogging her voice.

Reid's dream shattered.

Juniper clawed at his hand that clutched her wrist. Her pleading became incoherent. She wriggled under his arm, awake and crying. Tears streamed down her cheeks.

He felt it—the scattering of her magic. Reid yanked his hand from her.

"Juniper?" Reid asked, but she didn't answer.

Juniper rolled onto her stomach, near the edge of the bed, gasping for breath. Her entire body shook. Her arms and legs trembled as if in a fit. Under her gasping, panting breath, she pleaded, "I'm sorry, I'm sorry, I'm sorry."

Thunder crashed—rain beat against the windows of the palace. If not for the storm, the guards would have heard her scream.

"Juniper," Reid gasped, reaching for her.

She flinched away. His heart sank, heavy with guilt. He looked at his outstretched hand, his treacherous hand. He had caused her tears, her cries. He had hurt her. Intentionally or not, he had done this to her.

"I can help," Reid said, though his voice came out weak and strained.

He flattened his hand on her back, but the material of her sleeping shirt blocked the technique. It worked best when skin-to-skin. He pulled her sleeping shirt up and flattened his hand against her bare back, over the scarred flesh where

Maddox's brand had once been. He felt the knotted magic, a tightly coiled bundle deep within.

According to the Order, knotting a mage's magic would not only disrupt their ability to use magic of any kind but also cause every muscle to seize. He had knotted Juniper's magic enough to paralyze her.

He began to unknot her magic. He felt it within her, gentle and cool as a winter breeze. The worst knot was within the stomach, and he started there. He massaged his hands along her skin, outward from her stomach, coaxing her magic to unravel, and soothing the kinks. He had never attempted the technique, and his reversal showed it. Some of the kinks refused to untangle. A knot in her thigh took considerable care to undo. He worked the magic back down her legs, into her feet and toes, and down her arms, into her palms and fingers.

Gradually, Juniper stopped shaking. She stopped crying. The storm continued to rage, banging against the sky and the palace walls.

He helped her roll onto her back, and he continued unraveling the magic.

"Knights are trained to disrupt magic," Reid explained. "The technique I…used on you is known as Suppress and Dissipate. I…didn't mean to. I was dreaming, and I… I'm sorry, Juniper."

She didn't answer. He didn't know if she could. Her expression had gone unreadable and cold. Tears linger on her lashes.

A vicious clap of thunder shook the palace walls.

Having any other magic so close would have unnerved him, but Juniper instilled nothing of the sort. Her magic reacted willingly to his touch, friendly—it knew and trusted him, just as Juniper did.

She trusted him, and he had hurt her.

He unknotted her magic as much as he could—until exhaustion and the expenditure of energy tugged. He sat back on the bed.

"Are you all right?" Reid asked.

Juniper pushed herself into a sitting position, keeping her back to him, and set her bare feet on the floor. "I think so," she said, her voice weak.

Reid reached out to her but hesitated to touch her. Would he hurt her again?

She straightened her sleeping shirt and stood. Her knees gave out. Reid jumped across the bed as she collapsed into the skewed blankets. She tried again to stand, and Reid stood right behind her with his hands outstretched. He didn't touch her. She wobbled, but she didn't fall. Taking small steps, she started for the bathing room.

Reid stayed within arm's reach as she washed her face and dressed in clean robes. Her movements were shaky and slow. She wouldn't look at him.

She hobbled into the sitting room and sat in the only chair not within the sunlight. Reid opened his mouth to speak, but a knock sounded at the door. He went to answer it.

The kind-faced servant girl from before stood on the other side, her lavender robes simple and trimmed with silver. Her light brown hair was tightly braided and twisted into a bun. Behind her, rain fell over the courtyard.

He feared the guards had heard Juniper screaming—but no guards stood on the other side. They remained where they were. They stood in sight of the door, and he prayed that the storm had blotched out any sound she had made.

"I am to remind you of your dinner with Her Majesty. It is in an hour." The servant girl gave him a curt nod of her head.

"Thank you," he said.

"Is there anything you need, Sir Sandpiper?"

He almost said no, then thought of Juniper. "Tea, please."

"Right away, sir." The servant girl bowed slightly. She hesitated like she might say something else, but her eyes darted over his shoulder. She left.

Reid shut the door. He turned—Juniper wore a vicious look.

"You know," he started playfully, "If you keep glaring at her, she won't be inclined to like you."

"I don't see why I would need her to like me," Juniper said bitterly. "She seems to like you enough for several people."

Reid's brows rose. "Is that jealousy? You're being ridiculous."

Juniper gave no other retort, and Reid knew he had made a mistake. She did not feel well—thanks to him—and she wouldn't for a while. Her playful mood from before was gone. They sat in tense silence, listening to the storm. He could think of nothing to say that he hadn't already said, and Juniper offered no quips. The servant girl returned with tea for two and arranged it for them on the sitting room's table.

"It is a special blend," said the servant girl. Her eyes flickered to Juniper several times, who continued to glare daggers. "A Collatian specialty."

She made a cup and handed it to Reid. It smelled like roses and honey. It tasted much the same.

"It's delicious," he said.

The girl smiled. She then made a cup for Juniper, who took it with shaky hands.

Juniper took a small sip. Weakly, she said, "I agree."

The servant lingered another moment, during which she looked at Juniper— who wasn't looking—with a cautious curiosity. "Would you like me to do your hair, miss?"

Juniper's eyes snapped to the servant. The girl paled, though she held her ground. "Fine. Might as well. I can't."

Her words barbed his heart, but he held his gaze steady.

The servant moved around Juniper and went to the bathing room. She returned a moment later with a bottle of tonic and a bone brush. Juniper did not object as the girl massaged tonic into the tangles, brushed it out, and tied half into a braid and left the rest around her shoulders. "There," said the servant girl. "You look ready to greet the queen."

Juniper remained quiet and sullen as the girl replaced the things in the bathing room and gracefully made her way back to the door.

Reid stared at Juniper, imploring her to say something to the girl.

"Thank you," Juniper said at last, her voice mirroring her gloomy expression.

"My pleasure, miss." The girl curtsied. "I will return to fetch you for dinner."

Reid nodded, and the servant girl left.

Juniper sipped her tea loudly.

"How are you feeling?" Reid asked.

"Like someone twisted all my bones in the wrong direction."

Her words hurt, but he deserved it. "I am sorry, Jun. I…I didn't mean to do it, but I did, and I am sorry."

How could he explain it? Fleeing his home, leaving his friends, and the journey had spurred the dream—it was the feeling of having another home ripped apart by magic, the fear of losing those he cared about most. When his uncle had been injured, Reid feared the worst. He feared losing his uncle like he had lost his father. When his aunt's fate remained unknown, he feared he had lost her. He feared being unable to do anything, unable to help, unable to protect those he loved. It made him feel like a helpless child, hiding under his parents' bed while they were tortured and killed.

He had felt such ripe anger in his dream, and he had unknowingly turned that anger on Juniper.

Reid readied for dinner while Juniper sipped her tea. Neither spoke. The robes he had been provided fit loosely, a step from his usual shirt and trousers. The thinner material fit the warmer air, though it did not grant him the opportunity to wear his armor over it. Though, in a show of civility, he didn't need his armor.

A knock came to their door, the signal for their dinner with the queen. Reid stood first and held his hand out for Juniper. She hesitated—that feverish stubbornness of hers wanted to prove she didn't need his help—but she took his hand. He took it to mean some part of his apology had been accepted, or she couldn't stand on her own and didn't want to fall and prove him right.

He liked the first option much better.

CHAPTER 6

Juniper and Reid followed the annoyingly pretty servant girl into the dining hall. Juniper had to put more effort into walking than she had in a long while—since she'd been poisoned by Nexon's beasts. She didn't know how Reid had done whatever the hell he'd done, and at that moment she didn't care. She was tired, hungry, and in pain.

The dining hall was an arcade of pale stone. The arches had been carved in a blocky style, but somehow retained the elegance of the palace. Royal guards stood at intervals around the room. Rain whisked against the arched roof, and lightning flashed on the other side of the high, pointed windows. Warmer, humid air whistled through the drafts.

Juniper sat—rather ungracefully—and Reid sat beside her. He tried to catch her eye, but she pretended to be more interested in the silverware.

Servants stood in the almost-shadows of the arches, diligent and patient. Juniper couldn't see the annoyingly pretty girl, but if she were in the room, she'd be making her stupid moony eyes at Reid.

Juniper had plenty of words for her. None were kind.

Jealousy. The very word was stupid, but as much as she could deny it to Reid, she couldn't deny it to herself. The girl hadn't even done anything, but she annoyed Juniper. How dare she make moony eyes at Reid when he was clearly sharing a room with another girl—his betrothed.

Isaac joined them, and he came alone. He sat across from Juniper and offered a kind smile. "I hope you both got some much-needed rest."

"Yes," Reid answered. "How are the Sentinels?"

"They are progressing very well," Isaac said. "They are an efficient force and well-disciplined. I want to introduce you when possible."

"I would like that," Reid said.

Not a moment later, a door in the center of the arcade opened. Crespin marched into the room, hand on his pommel, mouth in a scowl.

Myrisha and Captain Bellamy walked in after him, side by side. Myrisha's golden gown shimmered in the magelight. Lenette came after, followed by a handsome man with dark brown skin and fire red hair. Black tattoos lined both his arms, whorls and curling lines. He wore robes of deep crimson and a sash of gold.

He looked no older than forty and carried himself with a superior air—that irked Juniper. He eyed the visitors with weary suspicion.

As was custom, when Queen Balendin approached the table, her guests stood—Juniper with mild difficulty. When Myrisha sat, the rest of them sat.

"Thank you for joining me," Myrisha said to her guests. She looked at the red-haired man. "This is Delmont Thacket, my magical advisor. Delmont, these are my guests, Sir Isaac Pinul, Sir Reid Sandpiper, and Juniper Thimble."

Quick greetings passed, and the food was served by silent servants in pale yellow uniforms. Juniper watched the dishes as they arrived—steaming rice, buttery vegetables, and mixed fruits. Her stomach threatened to claw its way out of her throat and devour everything in sight. It smelled amazing!

Juniper selected the proper fork—wouldn't Reid be impressed?—and her grip slipped. The fork began to fall, and Reid's hand grasped hers. To anyone else, it appeared that he had simply caught her fork and gave her an affectionate squeeze, but Juniper felt it—that strange sensation of his energy unknotting the clogged magic in her fingers, loosening her fluidity, all so she could hold a damn fork.

He let go, and she continued her meal as though it hadn't happened.

Halfway through one of the most delicious rice casseroles she had ever had, she caught his eye. She hadn't meant to, but she had. He watched her every move with an expression darkened by guilt.

Waiting to be the hero, likely.

She had the urge to accidentally knock her entire plate into his lap. She didn't. She was too hungry.

She stole her attention and thoughts away from Reid and his strange knight-powers and focused instead on the archmage sharing their meal. Delmont Thacket kept his eyes on his plate, adding little to the conversation that passed between Myrisha and Isaac. He mostly listened and observed.

After the meal, a dessert wine was served—another Collatian tradition—and Juniper felt remarkably better. The wine tasted like strawberry pastries.

Myrisha took a sip of her wine. "Delmont, my guests have brought me an interesting story. They claim that Nexon, the Archmage of Earth, has not only returned but taken over Bradburn Castle and infiltrated the Order of the Knighthood."

Delmont sighed. "Why is it that every time you invite me to dinner, you give me bad news?" He had a deep, pleasant voice.

"Softens the blow," Myrisha said.

"At least you waited until after dinner this time." Delmont took a long drink of his wine and looked at Isaac. "Is this true?"

Isaac nodded. "I'm afraid so."

Delmont hummed a disapproving note. "That's not good. I heard Nexon was moving, but I didn't think it would come to this, or so soon."

"You knew about Nexon?" Isaac asked, though he didn't sound surprised.

Delmont hesitated a moment before answering. "Yes. I have received word from trusted sources regarding Nexon. Tell me what happened."

Isaac told the tale again. Juniper tuned him out. She had lived it, and listening to it yet again felt utterly exhausting. She focused instead on her knotting magic. It felt…congealed, like water trying to flow out of a half-frozen spigot that was also filled with leaves and twigs.

She didn't know when it had started. She'd been dreaming, and then pain shattered everything. She had never felt such pain. It radiated into every bone, every hair, every nerve, contorting her magic asunder. She had become aware of the source—Reid's hand—only a few moments before he woke. In those long moments, she couldn't do anything but scream. Her body did not obey her. Her hands had gnarled, her toes had curled, and her bones felt like they might snap.

She had thought, shamefully, that Reid had done it on purpose, that she had done something to warrant his defense, that she had accidentally used her magic on him while she slept and he had acted appropriately for being attacked.

Then he had apologized and explained. She had not attacked him. He had attacked her.

That a knight could do such a thing to a mage—through touch—terrified her. She never wanted to feel that pain again, or the vulnerability of being entirely helpless.

She could feel her magic slowly unknotting itself from the coil Reid had tied it in. How long would it take?

Isaac's story ended, signaled by the sudden silence and refilling of wine glasses. Juniper declined a refill.

"Nexon has made his move and is no longer hiding," Delmont said, leaning back in his chair. He accepted a refill. "It's troubling, indeed. You have those loyal to the Order and this small army of criminals and apostates. We have the Collatian Royal Army, including a handful of Battlemages and Sentinels. It is not a staggering number of soldiers, but our odds depend on how large of an army Nexon has managed to build."

"We have friends currently trying to find out," Reid said. "They are on their way to Baxion, where we believe the horde of Nexon's followers to be."

"Baxion?" Delmont's brow creased. "I've never heard of such a place, but Nexon wouldn't hide somewhere easy to get to. Do you have a plan from here?"

Silence fell. Reid nudged Juniper. Delmont and Myrisha were looking at her—the first curious and expecting, the second just curious. Isaac tilted his wine toward her.

Ah, he wanted her to explain the next part.

"We find the other Iluvin archmages," Juniper said. "They defeated him a thousand years ago, and they might be the only ones capable of doing it again."

Delmont's curious gaze shifted. He beheld her as if he hadn't seen her properly before. Juniper held his gaze, daring him to deny it. She felt the eyes of Myrisha and Crespin, but she focused on Delmont.

After a long moment, Delmont broke his gaze to take a drink of wine. "And you came here to see me, I take it?"

"A trusted source informed us that you would be of help," Juniper added, choosing her words carefully—she didn't want to outright accuse him of being an archmage.

"A trusted source?" Delmont chuckled. "I know who you're talking about, or at least I have a very good guess."

"Then you are?" Juniper asked. To Delmont's raised brow, she added, "An archmage?"

If her accusation surprised anyone, no one showed it. Myrisha observed the interaction with a calm curiosity. Crespin analyzed it with a frown. Captain Bellamy held his face in a perfect stoic mask. Delmont's curious stare turned a shade vicious, and though his body appeared relaxed, his eyes wore a challenge. Juniper met that challenge with her own.

A heartbeat, and the air shifted. The room superheated, and it felt like she stood beside a massive oven. Sweat gathered under her hair and between her back and the chair. Still, she held Delmont's gaze.

A drop of sweat ran down her neck and into her robes.

"I take that as your answer?" she asked, grinning.

The heat vanished as quickly as it appeared. Delmont's vicious stare melted, and a mad grin stretched across his lips.

They had found the Archmage of Fire.

CHAPTER 7

Juniper held Delmont's mad stare with her own.

"I am," Delmont said. "I do not, however, know how the archmages of old defeated Nexon. My great uncle did not share the knowledge with me, or anyone as far as I know. I know what the rest of the world knows."

Juniper's hope dwindled. That foolish part of her had hoped Delmont would have the exact answer they needed. *Maybe*, said that dwindling hope, *he's lying*.

"As far as the other archmages," Delmont added, "I am uncertain. I am here, Nexon is in Rusdasin, and the last I knew, the Archmage of Energy was somewhere in Duvane."

"The Court Magician of Duvane," said Isaac, his words tainted with grief. "Mason Hobbs. He was the reason we were able to escape Nexon's siege unscathed."

"Mason Hobbs," Delmont repeated with a snap of his fingers. "That was the name. That just leaves the Archmages of Water and Air. The old Archmage of Water died a few centuries ago, before I came into possession of the title. Gods only know where the new archmage is. Could be anywhere in the world. The last I knew of the Archmage of Air, she went into the Blackwood Wylds, but that was…about five hundred years ago. I barely remember her. I was a child. My father said she'd gone mad. If she is still alive, she would be the one to ask. She was there when they fought Nexon. She was a girl, but she was there."

The Blackwood Wylds—tainted land that stretched along the center of Collatia. According to history, that was where the final battle of the Great War took place. According to legend, it was where the archmages defeated Nexon, and the expenditure of magic tainted the very earth.

"We can't send them into the Blackwoods." Myrisha frowned. It's far too dangerous. We've lost too many scouts to the Wylds as it is."

"But if there is a chance the Archmage of Air is still here," Reid started.

"And if she knows how we can defeat Nexon," Juniper added on the heels of his words. "We have to try to find her. We need to find her."

Delmont nodded. "That is possible. She is the only person left living who was present when it happened, and unless the other archmages passed down the secret, she is the only one who knows how they defeated him."

"But to go into the Wylds?" Myrisha asked, aghast. "It feels like too much to ask."

"It is a dangerous and hostile place," said Crespin, eyes pinned on Juniper. "Only monsters of darkness and tainted magic live there now. No plants will grow. No man can live off the ground. But if that is where you wish to go, I will not stop you. I can only warn you."

Myrisha did not look happy about his answer.

"One of Nexon's minions mentioned that he is looking for the final piece of something that will restore him to power," Juniper said to Delmont. "Do you have any idea what that means?"

Delmont shook his head. "I don't." He took a drink of wine. "I assume you know about the prophecy as well?"

She felt the blood drain from her face, and he noticed.

"We do," Reid answered for her.

"Speaking of," Isaac started. Juniper shot him a warning glare, which he ignored. "There is something I must admit, Your Majesty. It is about Juniper."

Myrisha set down her goblet of wine, giving Isaac her full attention.

Bellamy, Delmont, and Crespin looked at Juniper, and she looked down into her empty wine glass. She should have accepted that refill.

"Most of the world knows her as Juniper Thimble, the thief, but that is not her real name."

Juniper felt the floor shift under her feet. The impending announcement of her heritage coupled with the stiff magic in her bones churned her stomach and darkened the edges of her vision. Reid's hand landed on her knee, his grip sure. She set her shaking hand over his, pleading silently for his steadiness to seep into her.

"She is Isolde Balendin," said Isaac from somewhere far, far away.

Silence fell, thick with disbelief. The darkness receded, and Juniper dared to glance down the table. Myrisha wore surprise—her brows rose as she took in Juniper with fresh eyes. Her brother did the same, though malice laced his intrigue. Bellamy did not look angry. If anything, he looked as though he had suspected it.

"Isolde?" Myrisha whispered. "She is alive?"

"Impossible," Crespin spat. "I don't believe it."

"I admit," Juniper said, her voice mirroring her shaky nerves. "I don't fully believe it either."

"I remember Isolde," Crespin spat. "I held her when she was but a few hours old." His hands moved inward, as if to cradle a newborn. "You mean to tell us you've kept our uncle's daughter hidden in your kingdom all these years?"

"That was the initial plan," Isaac admitted. "Your uncle sent me away with the child. I took her to King Bradburn. She was supposed to grow up in the Royal Greenhouses, but rebels found her. To make a long story short, she ended up in the Undercity working as a thief."

"And you found her and brought her here?" Delmont asked.

"Another long story," Juniper added. "If you wish to hear it, I suggest you call for more wine."

Delmont chuckled, but he was the only one.

"She does look a great deal like you, Myrisha," Captain Bellamy said.

"She looks even more like the late queen," said Delmont. "She has Lenora's northern skin and the Balendin eyes, like Sebastian."

"She does," Crespin said, though disbelief hung on every word. "That doesn't mean I believe it. There are mages out there that can change a person's appearance. It could be a ploy to ally with us, or to claim the throne."

"I do not want anything of your throne," Juniper said bitterly, meeting Crespin's glare with her own.

"And Lenora's attitude," muttered Delmont. He held his wine to his mouth, taking in the scene with devilish glee.

Crespin started to say something else, but Myrisha held up her hand to silence him. He pursed his lips.

"There is a way to know for certain," Myrisha said, her voice calm and strong—the voice of a queen. She held her dark blue eyes on Juniper. "We will send her to the Spirit Gate."

"The what?" Juniper asked, her voice thin.

"There is a pool in the heart of the Singing Garden where the magic is thickest," explained Myrisha. "The Spirit Gate is a place where the veil between our world and the Otherworld is thin and communication between is possible."

"The Otherworld?" Juniper repeated, the word a wisp. It left a sinking feeling in her chest. "Who would I be speaking with there?"

Myrisha shrugged, a graceful motion on her shoulders. "The dead, the gods. Whomever answers your summons. It depends on the magic and the spirits."

"Spirit Gate?" asked Reid. "I've never heard of such a thing."

"It is old magic," Myrisha said.

"Some of the magic the Order decided shouldn't exist," said Delmont. He spoke the words lightly. "Makes you wonder how long Nexon has been messing with the Order."

"What do you mean?" Reid asked. His hand on Juniper's knee twitched.

"Is it not obvious?" Delmont asked, a brow raised. "The Order has systematically been hunting mages and locking them up, making it easy for Nexon to sort out possible inheritors of the archmage powers and easy for him to groom rebels of the Order, thus making it easy for him to harness those rebels and form them into his own apostate army while eliminating anyone who could rival his power."

"And he's made sure there's no one to oppose him," Juniper added. Also, by hunting down princesses.

"Nexon has been planning his return for centuries," Delmont added, though he didn't sound surprised.

"Shit," Reid mumbled, low enough that only Juniper heard.

It was another blow to Reid's ideal of the Order. Juniper tried to squeeze his hand, though her hand didn't cooperate.

"Who I am changes nothing of why we're here," Juniper said, shifting the subject away from the Order. She met Delmont's gaze. "We still need to stop Nexon."

Delmont parted his lips to speak—

"Who you claim to be changes things if you are indeed the heir to the throne," Crespin growled.

"Not for me," Juniper growled back at him.

"I want to know," Myrisha added, her tone light but firm. "Don't you want to know the truth of who you are?"

Juniper had no answer ready. She did, but she didn't.

Delmont sipped his wine loudly.

"Jun," whispered Reid. "It would put an end to your doubt."

"Fine." Juniper sighed. Reid was right. She knew he was right, and she did not feel like arguing. "I'll go to this Spirit Gate."

Myrisha nodded. "Someone will escort you there first thing tomorrow—"

"—tonight," said Crespin. He stood. At his sister's disapproval, he added, "I will escort her. Right now."

Myrisha frowned. "Crespin, they have had a long journey. They need rest and a good meal."

"It's fine." Juniper stood. It took considerable effort not to fall back into the chair. She met Crespin's scowl with her own. "Better to get this over with now."

Myrisha looked like she wanted to argue, but she didn't. "Very well."

Crespin started for a door on the far side of the arcade. Juniper followed, albeit awkwardly on sand-filled legs. Reid stood and in a few quick steps, appeared at her side.

They would put an end to the doubt, one way or another.

CHAPTER 8

Juniper and Reid followed Crespin into the palace's central courtyard. Two royal guards dutifully trailed behind. The storm had dulled, leaving the evening sky streaked with bubbling storm clouds. The storm ushered in warmer, humid air. A drizzle continued, speckling Juniper's cheeks. The magelights, safely tucked into an open arcade that circled the large courtyard, glowed molten gold.

A tree grew in the center of the Singing Garden, the biggest tree Juniper had ever seen—its trunk was as thick as a house, its boughs were thick with leaves the size of her head, and its branches stretched wider and taller than the palace. The drizzle struck the leaves, a sound as massive as the tree. Bushes with leaves of pink, gold, and purple spotted the garden in artful arrangements, and shoots of bright white and silver dotted the spaces between. Vines grew along wooden trellises and up stone columns, blooming with vibrant orange and spring green.

Under the smell of rain and mud was a floral scent, sweet and subtle. Juniper had never smelled magic quite like it. Was that how old magic smelled?

Crespin led them along a stone walkway toward the tree. The path diverted around the tree, but Crespin did not follow the path; he climbed down through the roots. The roots had grown in such a way that mimicked stairs, and those stairs led underneath the tree and to a narrow hall made of roots. Juniper followed Crespin, her steps cautious—the tree itself seemed aware of her, and she didn't like the feeling.

"What is this?" Juniper asked. She stepped into the hall. The sound of drizzle through the leaves echoed.

"One of the last of its kind," Crespin said with reverence. The drizzle had left a sheen on his dark hair. "A singing tree. Something else the Order has tried to rid the world off."

"Another reason to rid the world of that monster." Reid entered the hall. He turned sideways to fit his shoulders better.

Crespin didn't say anything. He held Reid in his cool gaze. Reid hadn't worn his silver armor to dinner, yet he had been wearing it when they arrived. Crespin knew Reid's connection to the Order.

Without the rain clogging her hearing, she could hear something else—a whispering, melodic and wispy. A thousand voices singing at once, an otherworldly choir. She couldn't understand the words, but somehow she knew she would if she listened harder and longer.

"Jun?" Reid asked, bringing her out of her thoughts.

Reid and Crespin were both staring at her. She opened her mouth to ask if either of them heard it, but Crespin cut her off, "Let's not waste any more time."

The hall ended at a simple wooden door. Crespin opened it without hesitation, but Juniper lingered over the threshold. She had the strangest feeling of being submerged, enough that she took a sharp intake of breath.

Reid appeared at her side, eyes questioning. *Are you all right?*

Had he not felt it?

She nodded. She didn't want to say any more with the guards listening. She followed Crespin through the door.

It led into a temple. The roof vaulted, and stars had been etched into the white stone. The floor had been etched with bones, skulls and hands and feet and bones she didn't recognize. There were no magelights or torches or channels of natural light, yet the temple glowed. Juniper scanned the ceilings and walls for the light source but saw none.

But she felt it. Magic. It flowed through the air here, thick and free. Juniper had felt it before, when she entered the garden of the gods. Magic, untouched and untainted. Pure.

A priestess in indigo met them just inside, her dark hood shading her face.

"This girl wishes to visit the Spirit Gate," said Crespin. All arrogance and suspicion had gone from his voice. He spoke with respect and reverence.

The silent priestess nodded. She motioned for Juniper, then started down one of two narrow halls that curved and angled further into the ground.

"Follow," Crespin said to Juniper. She took a step, as did Reid, but Crespin stopped him. "You don't."

Reid started to argue, but Juniper stopped him. "I'll be fine," she said.

He didn't look happy about it. She squeezed his hand, then followed the silent priestess down the curving hall. The ceiling was carved with stars, ancient and faded. The occasional tree root wound in through the stone and then back out. The hall ended at another wooden door. The priestess led her through and into a small room with double doors on the opposite side. Ancient tiles lined the floor and walls, and the stone ceiling depicted a mural of the gods, arranged in order of their seasons.

The priestess pointed to a stone bench, on which sat a few sets of silken robes of white. The priestess said no words, but a strange understanding came over Juniper. She undressed completely, underthings and hidden daggers included, and pulled on a white robe. The priestess then led her through the second set of doors.

The illumination was brighter on this side; the air itself glowed. The room was circular. An arcade lined the outer wall. The dark blue ceiling held stars of white and yellow and blue; the tiled floor rippled with etched bones of gray and white and green. In the center of the chamber was an obsidian pool. Instead of water, it held a thick purple substance.

Magic. Juniper's breath evaporated in her throat. Magic so thick it swirled like water. The air glowed with it, reeked of it. Flecks of gold flickered within the purple, like embers, like the last few blinks of a star before dawn. The magic moved gently, tendrils curling around one another endlessly, never ceasing. Always flowing.

Whispers rose from the magic, voices both known and strange, in words she almost knew and words she did not. It was the same voice she heard in the courtyard.

Enter, it said. The voice came from within her mind, from within the pool, from nowhere and everywhere at once.

The voice did not frighten her. It filled her with a sense of peace.

Juniper stepped onto the obsidian edge—at the touch, the magic seemed distant. It rallied in the air, against her skin, and in the stone, but the obsidian hushed it. It held the thickest magic within the pool. Juniper took a deep breath and stepped into the magic. Her foot vanished and met a smooth surface not far below the surface. The magic was not cold, or warm, or wet. It didn't feel like water, or anything she had encountered. She felt it against her skin—a tingle, a breath, an energy. It flowed and thrived, aware and awake.

She couldn't see her foot below the surface, though the magic rose only to her ankles.

Magic at its thickest, Myrisha had said. A thin point between worlds.

She took another step, and then another, and another, until the magic reached her thighs.

Spirit Gate. What did Myrisha want Juniper to gleam from this place? Juniper didn't know if she wanted to speak with the dead or the gods; both options filled her with dread. She had done plenty to aggravate the gods, and she had a long list of dead people who might want revenge.

She took another step into the magic, and another and another, until it reached her chin. She took a deep breath, and then submerged herself.

The moment her head went under, everything changed. The floor fell away, and she tumbled deeper into the magic. She took a gasping breath of surprise and found herself able to breath. It was not air that filled her lungs, but the energy of the magic—magnified air, imbued with magic. Somehow, her body knew how to use it just the same. She could not see walls or the edge of the pool, or the bottom or surface. Swirling purple mist surrounded her in every direction, never-ending and flecked with gold.

She tried to swim, but she couldn't tell if she was moving or staying still.

Was she supposed to do something? Myrisha had called it summoning. She needed to summon someone. But who?

She thought of the couple she had grown up thinking of as her parents, but they were likely still alive, unless Rusdasin had burned to the ground after they'd left. Not that her fake mother would be happy to see her—Juniper had been sent to replace the infant she had lost. That woman had never been kind to Juniper. Her tutor had been far more of a mother.

She thought of her kind-faced tutor, but no one appeared through the mist. She hoped it meant her tutor was still alive.

She floated for a long moment.

On a whim, she asked, "Blugo?"

Her voice did not echo.

No one answered her call.

"Hello?" she called a little louder.

Still, no answer came. No one appeared.

She started to swim. Maybe she was in the wrong spot. It felt a bit like flying, or how she thought flying would feel.

"Hello?" Juniper called again.

A shimmer—a woman appeared. She wore robes of smoky black. She had moon-pale skin and raven hair. She had dark, clever eyes that watched Juniper from underneath a large hood.

"You don't know me," said the woman in a voice of black velvet, a dark caress. "I know you. I know all my children."

Juniper blinked at the stranger. She looked familiar, but Juniper couldn't place her. Yet, as odd as it was, the woman's presence felt familiar.

"We've met before, but briefly. My temples are few, especially in Duvane. My few shrines are scattered and often ramshackle. No, the finery and sanctity are reserved for Bala and Espone."

Juniper's heart skipped a beat. She knew who stood before her—Bera, goddess of shadow, patron of those who dwell in the dark, and notoriously, thieves.

"Ah," Bera said, a clever smile on her lips. She had the natural beauty of a moonlit lake. "You do know me, then."

"But…why?" Juniper asked, her voice a whisper of itself.

"Why?" Bera asked in return, her smile straightening from her lips, but not her eyes. "Why what?"

"Why have you appeared to me? I was born under Blugo's stars."

"You think so?" Bera's brow rose. "Juniper Thimble might have been born under Blugo's stars, but Isolde Balendin was born on the longest night of the year, when my stars outshine his."

Juniper's heart fell into her stomach at the same time it jumped into her throat. "So, it's true?" she whispered. "I'm really her?"

Bera nodded. "Isolde Anita Balendin, the princess born on the winter solstice, in the time of shadow." Her humor faded, even from her eyes. "From the moment you were born, your father knew what would become of you. He knew you were the one."

"The one?" Juniper choked on the words.

"The one the prophecy spoke of," Bera said. "A thousand years ago, it was foretold that a princess born in the time of shadow would rise against the foul archmage and prevent him from repeating his reign of terror."

Juniper's vision tunneled and her skin went clammy. She would have fallen, had the magic allowed no such sensations.

The *one*.

"You're still surprised?" Bera asked. Her brows rose. "I thought you knew? Was it not obvious from the moment you discovered your heritage?"

Juniper pressed her hand against her heart. It thumped madly. She hadn't wanted to believe it. She wanted Nexon to be someone else's problem. She didn't believe herself capable of the feat.

"How… What can I possibly do to stop him?"

"What do you mean? You have already done more than anyone else," Bera said. She counted on her slender fingers. "You halted his experimentation with those vile transformations. You saved Ison Rolin from his control and in doing so took Nexon's puppet, forcing him to find another which allowed Mason Hobbs to detect him. You interrupted his plan to steal Prince Adrian's body and rule in his stead. You alerted the remaining Iluvin of his movements. You've begun the trek to find the archmages to defeat him once again. If not for you and your intervention, Nexon would have gone unknown."

Even as Juniper heard the charges, it felt unreal. She shook her head. "I'm just a thief," she whispered.

"Just a thief, she says." Bera laughed, an eerie, melodic laugh.

A fierce chill wrapped around Juniper's spine. She had heard that laugh before. In the temple of Blugo—when she had begged him for help, when she had thought him her patron, *Bera* had laughed. Bera had been the one to help her? And then again, Bera had led her to the abandoned house she used to get into Bradburn Castle and save Glenda Sandpiper and all those servants.

"Do you honestly believe that is all you are?" The goddess tilted her head at Juniper, rattling unseen jewelry. "We are all many things, both good and bad and somewhere in between. We are all capable of horrible things, just as we are capable of great kindness and wonderful things. You might have been a thief, but that doesn't mean you can't become something else. A worthy princess, perhaps? A good wife or mother?"

Those words—*wife* and *mother*—drove a certain nail of worry far deeper than it had been. She hadn't had time to think about being a wife in weeks, and even before, she had shoved those thoughts aside. But…being a mother? The thought slid down her spine, cold and slimy and viscous.

Juniper met Bera's knowing gaze. "I wanted Myrisha to be the one the prophecy spoke of."

"Why?"

"Then she would carry the burden of stopping Nexon, not me. It would be her responsibility, not mine."

"As would the risk of failure," Bera added.

Juniper nodded. Yet both burdens had fallen onto her shoulders.

"Do you want to see them?" Bera asked.

Juniper met the goddess's gaze with confusion.

"Your parents," Bera clarified. Juniper struggled to answer, but Bera spoke again, "They want to see you."

Before Juniper could answer, the goddess of shadow burst into a cloud of blue fog. Within that fog, two figures began to form. As the fog solidified, Juniper's heart stopped and twisted in her chest.

Her parents.

CHAPTER 9

Ison Rolin had not missed the long days on horseback. He and his friends had been traveling for days, sunup to sundown through endless hills and forests, surviving off dried meat and canteen water, relieving themselves behind trees and bushes. They were heading to Baxion, a settlement somewhere in the northern hills of Collatia. They had crossed the border between Duvane and Collatia the day before, and the forest looked the same. Trees, rocks, trees, wild brush, and more trees.

Ison rode behind Mabyl. She had the better sense of direction. They followed no known path or road—it would make them far too obvious—and they trekked through wild weeds, overgrown brush, and through shallow streams. One of Nexon's former followers had provided them with a drawn map to Baxion, which served as their only guidance.

Mabyl guided her horse up a hillside, and Ison rode a few steps behind. A warm, humid wind hissed through the trees. It layered an uncomfortable layer of sweat under his woolen tunic. He could cool the air against his skin, but it would take too much energy and he would have to do it constantly.

"Look at that," Mabyl said. She paused at the top of the hill.

"Is something on fire?" asked Xavier. He rode behind Ison and didn't bother to mask his exhaustion and irritation. Xavier had never left Rusdasin, and he had never traveled—it had put him in a bitter mood.

"No, it's the Wylds," Mabyl said.

Ison crested the hill after her. It didn't take long to see what she saw. The forest stretched horizon to horizon, dotted with small mountains of gray stone. While the forest to the north and west grew healthy trees and fresh greenery, the forest to the east darkened into terrible shades of black and charcoal. The Blackwood Wylds. The deadened heart of the forest. The trees of the Wylds bore no leaves and had shriveled and withered. Ison's stomach clenched. He hadn't realized they would be so close. Even from this distance, he felt the utter wrongness of the Wylds, like some ancient beast would snatch them in its jaws if they wandered too close.

"So, we have options," Mabyl said. "We either pass through the northern edge of the Wylds, or we skirt them. It'll take longer to skirt. What do you say? Power through or cower around?"

Ison knew what he wanted—he would rather ride a week out of his way than tread too close to the cursed forest—but he looked at the others. Mabyl stared down at the Wylds with a mixture of curiosity and madness. With the leaves and twigs that had gotten stuck in her messy blonde hair, she looked every bit mad. Of course she would want to jump headfirst into a cursed forest.

Xavier guided his horse beside Ison's. The assassin had kept quiet through most of the journey. He looked at the Wylds with a masked expression. Ison couldn't tell if it came from indifference or uncertainty. Bois rode with Xavier. Her glassy eyes did not see the Wylds; she was blind. She used her air magic to sense the world around her, and the Wylds would be too far. She hadn't complained, though exhaustion pulled at her pleasant face. Finn guided his horse to a halt on Mabyl's other side. He eyed the Wylds with fascination.

"What does everyone think?" Ison asked.

"We are already on a tight budget when it comes to time," Xavier said grimly.

"It can't be all that bad," Finn said. "It's just the edge."

"I will be able to sense anything coming," Bois added. "Nothing will sneak up on us."

"All right, through the Wylds it is," Mabyl said. She started down the other side of the hill.

Ison sighed in resignation.

They continued their northeastern trek through the forest. The closer to the Blackwood Wylds they rode, the darker the trees, the paler the leaves, the dryer the dirt, until ghastly vines snaked over the narrow path, deadened trees leaned precariously over the path with bare branches the color of soot and ash that looked like claws ready to grab unwary travelers from their horses. As they rode underneath the reaching branches of one such tree, a caw unlike anything Ison had ever heard screeched from the darkness of the Wylds.

Ison couldn't imagine what the Wylds were like deeper within. He had heard too many horrible stories about them. Monstrous creatures with vicious jaws and insatiable bloodlust, birds the size of cows, and demons disguised as brambles.

As they trekked eastward, they passed fewer healthy trees and more dead, gangly trees and thorny brambles and strange shrieks and caws. More than a few times Mabyl burned through the brush to allow their horses safe passage. As the sun lowered, bugs chittered and chirped. The humid air turned cooler and dry, and Ison pulled his red scarf tighter around his neck.

A shriek tore through the air—Ison jumped and ducked. A massive blackbird flew overhead and vanished into the Wylds.

Behind him, Xavier muttered, "I hate this place."

Ison did not argue.

They rode through the edge of the Wylds far too long for Ison's liking, and as the deadened forest diminished and the healthy forest returned, he was able to relax.

Evening approached, and Mabyl led them to a relatively secluded spot, and they stopped to camp. Ancient oaks shaded them from the sky. Ison and Xavier saw to the horses, Mabyl burned the brush away, and Fin erected stone huts for each of them. Bois wandered the perimeter, her glassy eyes unseeing, her magic sensing anything nearby.

After a dinner of dried meat and nuts, Ison collapsed into his stone hut. His bedroll barely softened the stone. Ison pressed the balls of his hands into his eyes.

During their travel, they had taken turns going into villages. They had bartered for supplies—or stolen them—and listened for gossip. Word had spread of the unrest in Rusdasin. The siege of the castle had left a feverish uncertainty in the kingdom. Some whispered of the king's death, others whispered he had gone into hiding, and others still whispered of the king's forces marching back to Rusdasin. On one of his turns, Ison had pretended to be a shopkeeper from Rusdasin. He had spread rumors of the king's escape and resistance. The villagers had drunk his words eagerly.

He had started a dangerous game with his rumors, one that could get them exposed, but the sliver of hope he planted felt worth it.

The sun rose, and their routine started over. Finn flattened the stone huts, Mabyl boiled river water for them to drink, and Ison and Xavier readied the horses. They shared few words. They all felt the pull of exhaustion, though no one complained. They trekked through the forest, up and down small hills, over fallen trees, through streams, around lakes.

The sun crossed the midday point, and bruised thunderheads bubbled to the northeast. The storm pushed warmer, humid air through the forest. Sweat gathered along Ison's spine.

"We'll need to find camp before that storm reaches us," Ison said.

"It's still half a day away," Xavier said.

Xavier was almost right. The clouds thickened and rose taller. A few hours later, Ison heard the first clap of distant thunder. He saw no lightning, and they had a few hours of daylight left, so they kept moving.

Lightning appeared an hour from sundown. They crested a short hill, and in the illumination of the lightning, Ison spotted the pale gray of stone on the next hill—a village. Relief spread through his chest like a warm drink. Maybe they would find an inn or a barn to sleep in tonight, out of the rain. Or at least a few provisions to keep their supplies from dwindling.

They rode a little faster. The storm quickly approached.

Only, it was not a village.

They had reached the outskirts of a city. Stone buildings jutted from the ground, and old cobblestone streets ran between them. The silence of the outskirts unsettled Ison, and in the lightning that followed, he saw the truth—the city was abandoned. The structures were in partial states of collapsing, and vines and brush and trees had poked through the stones and taken over.

With each flash of lightning, his horror tightened. Cobblestone streets stretched as far as he could see, row after row of homes and buildings, left to the elements—a city large enough to have once held hundreds of thousands of people.

"Gods," Ison muttered, his voice lost in a low roll of thunder.

"What happened here?" asked Bois, her soft voice lined with the same unease.

"Are there any people here?" Ison asked her.

"No," she answered at once. "I don't see anything but ruins. Mice and a few cats, I think, but no people."

"That means we've got our pick of the rooms," Mabyl called over the thunder. She and her horse strutted ahead of them.

The others followed behind. Xavier eyed the shadows wearily, as did Finn.

The city was daunting, to say the least. Every structure lay in ruins, empty and cold. Life had been absent for a long time. Walls had collapsed, windows had shattered, doors rotted away. Moss and vines grew between the stones, slowly breaking apart the mortar. Signs of violence remained—some structures had fallen over time, but others looked to have been knocked down. The further into the city, the greater the violence—more than a few structures were gone entirely, leaving only a darkened dent on the ground. He spotted scorch marks on fallen stones and places where the ground had opened to swallow buildings whole.

The sun edged toward the other side of the world, pulling shadows deeper and darker, and the storm edged closer. Thunder rumbled and lightning flashed. Still, they made their way through the city.

At the heart of the ruined city, they found a truly awful sight: an abandoned castle. Its gardens were gnarled and unsightly, full of thorny bushes and wild vines and twisted trees. The iron gates had been blasted open, leaving one on the ground and the other hanging by a hinge, both overtaken by thick vines.

"Prime real-estate," Xavier mumbled.

Thunder cracked in tandem with a searing bolt of lightning, momentarily brightening the devastation of the castle.

"Right now, I don't care," Ison said. "I do not want to be outside when the storm hits."

They started through the broken gates. The castle loomed toward the sky, its towers dark and its windows empty. Parts of the battlements had crumbled, and several turrets had collapsed. Mabyl led them up the wide front steps and into the vestibule—the front doors had been blown apart. Once, the vestibule had been beautiful—pillars of marble, amber trim, water-clogged portraits, all covered in dust and ash and age. A chandelier had fallen to the center of the vestibule, the crystals crushed and cracked.

"Do you know where we are?" Mabyl whispered. She glanced at Ison, her mad eyes full of bright and fierce wonder.

Ison swallowed. "I have a strong suspicion."

He had known from the moment he saw the castle.

Lightning flashed, cleaving the vestibule in two. Thunder cracked. Then the vestibule felt utterly silent.

"Feel like sharing?" Xavier glanced sideways at Ison.

"The Dead City," Ison whispered. "Once the royal city of Collatia. Destroyed during the civil war. Home now to only ghosts. This is Balendin Castle."

"I say we camp inside. If this thing's survived twenty years of storms, it'll survive this one," said Mabyl.

Ison followed Mabyl through the vestibule. Their horses trampled over the bits of broken crystal and shattered tile. It smelled abandoned, like stagnant water, mildew, and dead rodents. They turned down a corridor, and the first of the rain splattered through the broken windows.

Thunder and lightning crashed together—a fearsome blast of light and sound, shaking the stones they illuminated. The summer storm ushered in a warmer wind, and that wind whistled against the castle's fallen towers and empty windows. It filled the halls with a warm, wet air.

Mabyl turned down a windowless corridor and summoned a magelight to brighten the way. The rain thickened and fell harder, blanketing the air in a loud, constant hum. Mabyl wandered deeper and deeper, away from windows and broken doors and drafts. At last, they came to an intact chamber that looked to have once been a lounge, but the furniture had long since been broken or plundered.

It didn't take long to set up camp. Finn didn't have to make huts, so they laid out their bedrolls on the floor. Bois saw to the horses. Mabyl gathered kindling for a fire in another. Ison whisked the smoke away from them, through the door where a draft caught it.

Rations and water shared, they sat in moderate silence around their fire. Outside, the storm raged. Had it sounded like thunder when the city fell? When the rebels brought down entire buildings and homes and burned everything else?

"Rest up," said Mabyl as she reclined on her bedroll. "We've got another wonderful day of travel ahead of us. Best to be well-rested."

Ison agreed, but he couldn't find sleep. He lay awake, listening to the storm and the others' breathing. He couldn't stop thinking about the castle, about the horrors that had led to its decrepit state, the death the stones had witnessed.

Is this what they would find when they returned—if they returned—to Bradburn Castle?

CHAPTER 10

Juniper's breath hitched. Through the fog, King Sebastian Balendin and Queen Lenora Balendin appeared. They looked as regal as any king and queen. He wore a finely made house coat of dark blue and silver, and she wore a lovely dress of purple silk that draped from her bare shoulders. A ghostly crown set upon each of their heads.

And then Juniper knew. Bera spoke the truth. She was Isolde, and she was looking into the faces of her parents.

She looked like her mother. They had the same auburn hair, heart-shaped face, and pale skin. Juniper shared her father's midnight blue eyes and pointed nose.

"My baby girl," said King Balendin. His blue eyes went misty. "I'm glad to see you alive and well. And grown. I'm sorry for putting this burden on your shoulders. I would take it from you if I could."

Juniper felt something tighten in her chest. His deep, somber tone struck her mind, the place where half-forgotten dreams and fuzzy memories lurk. Whether she had dreamed the voice or remembered it from so long ago, she didn't know.

"We didn't realize Nexon was behind the uprising," said Queen Balendin. Tears lined her eyes. Where her husband's voice was strong, hers was soft. It did not lack strength; each softly spoken word had the strength of steel. "We knew of the prophecy and feared someone might make an attempt on your sister's life, like they had in Janti. We tightened security of the castle."

"And when you were born on the solstice, we knew," added her father. "Someone would come for you, thinking you were the one destined to rise."

"And the state of our own kingdom grew more unstable," said her mother. "Your father and I had to send you away. We had to hide you, protect you, before an assassin slipped through our defenses."

"Now I understand," said her father. Regret darkened his eyes. "Nexon had caused the uprising. He used my own brother as a lever to do so, and he sent him to kill an infant out of fear."

Juniper's breath hitched. "Nexon used him?

"Sabian is my older brother, and he was not pleased when Father named me his heir," her father said, distaste and regret mingling on his words. "Nexon twisted Sabian's jealousy into hatred, and used him as a tool to rid the Balendin line from existence, because he feared our lineage. We have strong roots in the Iluvin. Nexon is the reason Collatia is in the state that it's in. He is the reason my children were murdered, and my nephew was forced to kill his own father to save a crumbling kingdom."

Juniper shuddered. Nexon had caused the Collatian civil war? All because he wanted to make sure there would be no princesses to stop him.

"Do not hate your uncle," said her father. "Sabian was not himself that night. His eyes were not his own, nor were his words or thoughts."

Possessed. Just like Penet and the advisor.

"I don't," Juniper whispered. "He took a friend from me the same way."

She remembered. When Nexon possessed Ison, nothing about him was the same. His eyes were the cold blue of Nexon's, and his mannerisms and expressions were arrogant and mean. She had known instantly that Ison wasn't himself. Penet had been the same; the moment Nexon took him, she had known.

"You understand it now," said her mother. "What that monster of a man has caused. Not only for our family, but for the entire realm. So much destitution and death, as a means to secure his own power."

"I thought Bentley would be able to protect you," said her father. "I sent you away for your protection. To save not only you, but untold numbers of people that would die if Nexon fully rose to power again. I…do not regret sending you away. You would have been killed in your cradle if we hadn't."

"We wanted to send your sister too," said her mother. "We ran out of time. Your brothers refused to abandon their kingdom and their people, even if it meant their lives." A fierce pride came over her mother's expression, mirrored by her father's.

"Bentley kept his word, though he had help," said her father. "He is a good man. Remember that, Isolde."

"I know," she said, her voice weak. She knew King Bradburn to be a good man.

Hearing that name on her father's lips sent a strange wave of nausea through her knees and into her stomach.

"Or would you rather be called Juniper?" her father asked, raising an eyebrow.

"I don't know," she whispered.

"An honest answer," said her mother. "You're confused."

"Who am I supposed to be?" Juniper asked.

"You are supposed to be exactly who you are," said her mother.

"That doesn't make any sense," Juniper said.

Her mother motioned toward her with a graceful swish of her hand. A few golden flecks followed the motion. "Who do you think you are?"

"I…" She didn't have an answer. Not one that made sense. "I'm me. I don't know what that means. I've always been Juniper. Isolde feels like…someone else."

"Then be Juniper," said her mother. "The name of a thing doesn't change the nature of the thing. You are still you, regardless of what name you answer to."

"Your grandmother wanted to name you Olga Vendasa," said her father with a chuckle. "Luckily, your mother and I agreed it was a terrible name. We named you after your mother's great-grandmother, Isolde, and my favorite aunt, Anita."

Her parents shared a knowing look, and something silent passed between them—a shared memory of a life past.

"But…" Juniper started. She felt too much to make sense of it all. Isolde Balendin felt like someone worthy of existence, someone raised in love and taught compassion. Juniper Thimble had been raised in a pit of wolves, taught to steal and lie and kill.

"And if you had been raised differently, you would not be the person you are today," said her mother.

Juniper's eyes widened. Had she said that out loud?

"Things work differently here," her mother said, her eyes soft and kind. "You have seen the worst of Rusdasin, and you have seen the best. You have been thrown down, and you have learned how to pick yourself back up. You have witnessed poverty and desperation, and you have witnessed luxury and wealth. You have learned to value friendship and loyalty, and to fight not only for yourself but for those you love."

Juniper felt shame—her face heated. "You know about all of that?"

Her mother nodded. "Death does come with perks." She winked. "As much as I abhor people like Maddox Hawk, he did teach you independence, intelligence, and strength."

"And neither of us would change a thing about you, dear," said her father. He closed the space between them and put a firm hand on her shoulder. She felt the weight of his hand, felt each finger, and felt the metal of his wedding ring. "I'm proud of who you've become. Regardless of how you got here."

"And you have done well for yourself." Her mother glided to her husband's side. She cupped Juniper's cheek. Her fingers were slender, and the touch was delicate. Her eyes twinkled. "Reid is a fine young man."

"He has a good head on his shoulders," said her father. "Stubborn and a bit foolhardy, but then so was I at his age."

"That implies you are no longer those things," said her mother.

Her father laughed, a deep laugh that warmed the space around them.

Her parents. Juniper had never felt a longing like the one that tore through her chest. For her parents, for the siblings she would never know, for the life that had been ripped away before she knew it. Tears pushed against her eyes, harder and harder. She didn't want to cry, but being there, in front of her parents, a glimmer of the life she would never know, the tears fell. Her mother hugged her close, and her father embraced them both.

How long she cried into her mother's shoulder, she didn't know. Slowly, the tears came to a stop. Her father pulled away first, then her mother.

"And now you must throw yourself into danger once more," her father said grimly.

"Danger?" Juniper asked. "Do you mean the Blackwoods? Is she there? The archmage?"

"We can't say for certain," said her mother. "The Blackwoods are a very strange place. The magic there is wild. It is a glimpse of what magic once was."

"I want to tell you not to go," said her father. "The Wylds are dangerous and full of strange things. But you've got the notion in your head, and if you're like your mother, nothing I say will change your mind."

Her mother frowned, though not scornfully.

"If we knew who the archmages were, we would tell you in a heartbeat," said her father. "Death does not equate to being all-seeing. We can learn only selective things."

"And we chose you," said her mother.

"But if anyone can find the archmages, you can," said her father. Juniper doubted that and started to object, but her father stopped her. "How, we don't know. That is yet to be decided by you, dear."

Juniper sighed dramatically.

Her mother laughed and playfully smacked her father's arm. "She takes after you."

Her father said, laughing, "I was about to say the same thing."

A shimmer came over them, rippling through their beings like light through water. Juniper's heart trembled. She had nearly forgotten they were dead. She had a million questions to ask them, about death and the beyond, about magic, about her siblings, about Collatia, about her family—but the words refused to come. Panic and dread and fear scrambled her thoughts too much for her to pick just one.

"Our time here grows short," said her mother quickly. "Remember, Juniper, we are always with you. Even if it doesn't feel like it."

"We must go," said her father. "We love you."

"More than you know," said her mother.

Her father kissed her temple. Her mother kissed her cheek. And—before she could speak—her parents faded back into the fog.

WITCH IN THE WYLDS

And again, Juniper floated alone in the void.

CHAPTER 11

No one else appeared through the mist. Both her parents and Bera had gone. Juniper started to swim toward the surface, but she couldn't tell if she was moving. She didn't feel the movement in her limbs or see it in the magic around her.

She swam for a while, but nothing happened. She did not reach the surface. She hadn't gone that far into the magic, had she? Had she slowly been sinking while she talked to her parents? A seed of panic grew in her chest, and it grew larger with every stroke of her arms and kick of her legs.

Out, she thought. She wanted out.

And the magic answered her—her hand broke the surface of the pool. Cooler air graced her fingers, her palm, and the world tilted sideways. She fell into the obsidian edge. Touching the obsidian calmed a whirlwind of magic within her. She could feel the pool, feel the edge of it, feel the world on the other side—and for a frightening, fleeting moment, she thought she felt the presence of another world, larger and shadowed, just beyond her reach.

A hand grabbed onto hers and pulled. Her head broke through the surface, and she fell into the owner of the hand; they tumbled onto the floor. Her breath evaporated on impact, and he let out an *oof*.

For a heartbeat, she was aware of the smells of the temple, of the world, of the stone; she *felt everything*. The Spirit Gate had lacked the smells and sound and feeling of the world. The air was too thin, the stone too hard, her flesh too heavy—it was all at once overwhelming and familiar. She took a gasping breath, and the feeling vanished. The strangeness of wearing flesh and bones vanished too. The ache in her blood returned, albeit lessened.

"Juniper?"

Reid grasped her shoulders. His honey-brown eyes implored into hers. She rolled off him and onto the floor—the motion triggered a strange tilted feeling in her bones, like the world had gone crooked. She shut her eyes and took a steadying breath.

Reid knelt beside her and brushed her hair out of her face. His steadiness flooded into her cool skin.

When the world righted itself, she opened her eyes and found his again. He no longer wore the robes from dinner. He wore Collatian robes of pale red and yellow.

"I saw them," she whispered. Her breath felt too thick for her lungs. "I saw them."

"Who?"

"My parents." Her voice broke. She sucked in her next breath. Her lungs stretched as though she hadn't breathed in days.

Understanding washed over Reid's face. "Your parents? King and Queen Balendin?"

She nodded. Tears threatened to return.

Reid helped her to her feet. She felt awful, like she had slept too long. Her muscles complained, her back ached, and her thoughts scattered. She stumbled—Reid caught her. She felt bruises forming along her body from the obsidian stairs.

"You're readjusting," came a soft voice. It was Myrisha, wearing flowing robes of soft pink. She observed Juniper with a weary warmth. "The Spirit Gate takes a lot out of a person."

"Is that why everything feels so strange?" Juniper asked.

The queen nodded. "I didn't get the chance to warn you. Crespin was so adamant about throwing you in as soon as possible. He's impatient, my brother." Regret shadowed her face. "Time does not exist the same within the gate as it does here. You've been gone for almost two days."

"Two days?" Juniper repeated. She looked at Reid; he nodded.

She put a shaky hand to her temple. Again, she had crossed into another realm and returned days later.

The queen said, "It's best to return to your chambers and rest. I will have something to eat brought for you, as well as some tea. Any special requests?"

Juniper shook her head. Her stomach did not want to think about food.

Myrisha left through the double doors, her robes flowing like sunset waters behind her.

With Reid's assistance, Juniper shed her white robe and redressed. She leaned onto him as they retreated from the temple and into the twilight courtyard. The storm had moved on, leaving the sky periwinkle blue and the sun brilliant gold. The magelights didn't seem as bright now, not after the temple. The garden burst with colorful flowers and blooming bushes, some she knew and others she had never seen before, and the air smelled of pollen and nectar and damp soil.

Without the rain, the singing was louder. She could hear the otherworldly voice, the strange and familiar language.

"Can you hear that?" Juniper whispered.

"Hear what?" Reid's brows rose.

"The tree."

"Can I hear the tree?" He repeated in a tone that suggested he did not. Understanding smoothed his features, and he added, "Myrisha mentioned the trees don't sing as loud as they once did. Maybe your magic allows you to hear what I cannot. Is it pretty?"

"In a haunting kind of way."

He hummed. "I'm not sure I want to hear that."

"Think of it like a haunted children's choir."

Reid frowned. "That doesn't sound good at all."

"It is…" she started, then paused. "But it's distant."

Back in her chambers, Juniper started a bath.

"While you do that, I'm going to send word to Isaac that you've returned," Reid said. "I won't be gone long."

Reid's footsteps marched across the chamber and into the corridor.

Juniper held the chain with her magic and looked through the vanity while the tub filled. She found a small glass bottle of bath salts. She emptied the bottle into the water. The churning surface fizzled and hissed; the water turned a bright, milky pink. An overpowering scent of roses and sugar filled the chamber.

Juniper washed the empty glass bottle under the faucet and dried it with her magic. She set it on the vanity. From within her robes, she took out a small orb of cloudy blue ice. Inside, she held a small amount of the Spirit Gate. The purple swirled like smoke, constantly flowing. She held the orb of ice over the mouth of the glass bottle, and opening a tiny hole in the bottom, she allowed the magic to flow out of the orb and into the bottle. It plumed against the bottom like heavy fog.

She wrapped the bottle in an old pair of socks and tucked it into her satchel. She doubted Bera would mind. She was the patron of thieves, after all.

No sooner had she lowered herself into the bath than Reid returned. And he wasn't alone.

Juniper caught the chime of the pretty servant girl over the pouring water. She released the chain and halted the flow.

"…delightful time of year. I hope you are still here for it."

"It sounds marvelous," Reid said. "I've never been the one for balls, but Prince Adrian and Lady Roslyn adore them."

"The summer solstice is nothing like a ball," said the servant girl. "It is out in the streets. Girls wear crowns of flowers and bright dresses. There is barefoot dancing and a different tune being played on every street. Vendors sell sweets and iced juice from every corner."

A tray was set down, and china and crystal gently rattled.

The servant lingered, and an awkward silence settled.

"Thank you for the tea, Jana." Reid said.

"It is my pleasure, Sir Sandpiper," said the servant, her words honeyed.

And…she lingered. Juniper's good mood crumbled.

It would seem that while Juniper had been conversing with the dead, *Jana* had had time to introduce herself.

"I—" the servant started, but Juniper spoke louder, "Reid, love, would you bring me a cup of tea?"

"Of course," came Reid's swift reply.

Jana the servant bid a quick farewell and left.

Washed, dried, and with a fresh cup of tea, Juniper reclined on the bed. Had it been this soft before?

"The whole chamber reeks of flowers," Reid complained. He pushed open the narrow shutters on the window. Floral scents from the garden whisked inside, along with the stench of sun-warmed dirt and stone. "Did you have to use the entire bottle of salts?"

"I didn't know it was so potent." Juniper sipped her tea loudly. "Weren't we supposed to get food along with this tea?"

"Jana said it would come later," Reid said.

"Who?" she asked innocently.

"The servant who brought the tea."

"Oh, you've already exchanged first names? You're moving fast."

Reid frowned. "We've bought a house in town and plan to wed in the autumn."

Juniper toyed absently with the moonstone ring on her finger. "Have you told your uncle yet? I want to be there when you do. I've always wanted to see him smile."

Reid looked up from the cup of tea he was making for himself. "I was joking, Juniper."

"As was I."

"No, you weren't. I've heard you joke. That was far too bitter for—"

A knock sounded on the chamber door, and Reid left to answer it. By the warm scents that wafted through the room, the promised meal had arrived.

It felt odd—Juniper sauntered across the room on legs that still felt like sand, while Reid stood over a group of servants as they arranged a meal in the sitting room. The servants left in silence, and Juniper plopped into one of the chairs.

"Just like old times," she mused.

Reid sat across from her. The servants had brought dishes for two, yet Reid didn't eat. He had likely eaten earlier. The food smelled amazing—buttery and cheesy and perfectly seasoned! She ate, Reid drank tea, and neither spoke. Reid wore his thinking face and stared into his tea.

Halfway through her meal, another knock sounded at the door. Reid stood to answer it just as Crespin let himself inside, looking like someone had stepped on his toes. His glare found Juniper at once, seething with hatred and fury.

CHAPTER 12

"Yes, general?" Juniper asked dully.

"You may have convinced Myrisha that you are Isolde, but I need more proof than your word," Crespin said. "For all we know, your tale of meeting the dead king and queen was just another lie."

"And what would you want as proof?" Juniper leaned back in her chair. She was too tired for his attitude. "I have no family jewels hidden away, birthmarks, or passwords. Until today, I was as skeptical as you are. Trust me, I wish it were a lie."

Crespin curled his fingers into fists. "I was there that night. I held Myrisha as the castle burned, as servants and guards were slaughtered in the halls, as my own father proclaimed change and necessary bloodshed. We have struggled to hold this kingdom together, defend it, keep its streets and roads safe, and you think you can just walk into the palace and—"

"You killed him," Juniper whispered, her father's words resurfacing.

Crespin fell silent. His lips pursed. "What do you mean?"

She met this burning gaze. "You killed your father that night."

Crespin paled, and his hatred melted into confusion, then shock. "No, General Rorick struck him down."

"My…father," Juniper said with difficulty. "He told me you were forced to kill your own father to save a crumbling kingdom."

Crespin wobbled, then grabbed the back of a chair. He guided himself into it without taking his eyes off Juniper.

"History tells a different story," Reid added.

"The only people who knew what I had done are dead," Crespin whispered. "Not even Myrisha knows. You…" He shook his head. "After the siege of the castle, my father wanted to search the entire city for newborns, anyone younger than three months, and put them to death. I didn't understand his reasons, but I…I didn't want any more bloodshed. I was a boy, not even old enough to grow a beard, but I knew my father needed to be stopped. He had killed our family. He nearly killed Myrisha and I until she called him Father, as if he had forgotten us. His people had killed our mother, and he acted as though it didn't bother him. He…" Crespin buried his head into his hands. His stony exterior trembled. "I took the king's sword, and I thrust it into my father's back with all the strength I had."

"General Rorick?" Reid asked, his tone softer.

"He claimed to have done it," Crespin whispered. "He told me that if I were to be king, the people could not know I had killed my father, who had, that same night, killed his brother. He was the only one who knew, as he took the secret with him to the grave not two years later." Standing, Crespin sighed through his nose. His stony exterior returned, reinforced. "You say your father told you this?"

Juniper nodded. "He did."

Crespin sighed in resignation. His gaze had lost its burning hatred, though he still did not look kindly upon Juniper. "You may be my cousin, but that does not mean I trust you."

Footsteps filled the corridor. A knock sounded in the room. Crespin answered it, and Myrisha glided inside. Her pink robes fluttered around her like pedals. Her guards—including Captain Bellamy—stationed themselves just outside the door.

"Oh, I didn't expect to see you here," Myrisha said to her brother. Her brow furrowed. "Not being mean, are you?"

"Not at all," Crespin said, though his tone lacked force. He bid farewell, then let himself into the corridor.

A heartbeat passed, then Myrisha sat in the chair Crespin had just vacated.

"I told him about you," Myrisha said sheepishly. "I told him not to do anything rash, but it would seem he has ignored my advice. Again." She sighed. "I hope he didn't say anything nasty."

Juniper shook her head. She thought about telling Myrisha what had transpired, but she held her tongue. Crespin's secrets were not hers to share.

"How are you feeling?" Myrisha asked.

"Better, thank you."

A beat passed. Juniper glanced toward her forgotten plate and brought a forkful to her mouth. The food had gone a tad cold.

"It's true, isn't it?" Myrisha asked. "You are Isolde Balendin?"

Juniper's next bite lodged in her throat, and she took a long drink of tea to force it down. "I am," she whispered.

Reid's brow rose slightly and his lips twitched—a subtle expression he quickly banished into neutrality.

"I knew there was something about you when I saw you in the throne room," Myrisha said. "You were conveniently standing behind others"—she motioned to Reid—"so you would not be noticed. Captain Bellamy noticed you first. He's quite observant. My brother is just stubborn. He remembers what it was like before the war, before our family was massacred. He was forced to carry the burden by himself. He'll come around."

"I'm still grappling with the truth," Juniper admitted.

"That is understandable," Myrisha said. "It's not every day a girl discovers she's a princess. A queen, if the law is to be abided."

"You are queen," Juniper said firmly. "You are far better at it than I could ever be. I wasn't lying when I said I didn't want the throne. I have no interest in ruling or being in charge of other people. I can barely handle being in charge of myself."

Myrisha chuckled. "Oh, I'm not in charge of myself. I have other people to worry about that."

"That sounds tiresome."

"It can be," Myrisha said. "Ruling is not for everyone. Take my brother. Everyone thought he should rule because he was the oldest heir. He is a great general. He knows strategy and combat, but he rules with that same iron will and commanding presence. He knew it too. I didn't want to be queen, but I knew that I would have others to help me. So, when Crespin told me he wanted to step down and make me queen, I accepted."

Juniper made another cup of tea. Her hands grew less shaky with every passing moment. The knots Reid had tied in her magic had faded too.

"The question everyone will ask is what you will do from here," Myrisha said.

Juniper sighed. That was why Myrisha had come—to gather information. Fine. Juniper would comply. Tea in hand, she recounted what she had seen in the Spirit Gate to Reid and Myrisha.

"Your father told you to go to the Blackwoods?" Myrisha's voice was distant with worry. She leaned onto the table; a delicate golden chain around her neck caught the magelight. "The Blackwoods are dangerous."

Juniper nodded, struggling with the words *your father*. It felt so strange to think of them. He hadn't outright told her to go there, but he had implied it. She wanted to go there, and if thinking the dead king agreed would help Myrisha understand, it was a lie Juniper was willing to tell.

"How are they dangerous?" Juniper asked.

"People vanish if they get too close, including my trained and experienced scouts. The few scouts that make it back report strange sounds and shadows and mangy beasts. They've found entire villages swallowed by the Blackwoods, the ruins hundreds of years old. The plants and animals have died, leaving the earth barren and inhospitable." Myrisha's face turned grim. "According to legend, from the tainted earth grew tainted trees that produced tainted fruit that tainted the people and animals. Many horror stories exist about the Wylds, about the monsters lurking in the dark, about the abominations that were once men, about the witches that come to steal naughty children."

"And we have to go there?" Reid asked Juniper.

Juniper met his gaze. *We*, he said.

A fine young man with a good head on his shoulders, albeit stubborn and foolhardy—Juniper had not told them what her father had said about Reid. It felt too personal.

"It's not a good idea," Myrisha said, standing. "But I will inform my council of your identity as well as your desire to venture into the Blackwoods. Until then, you need your rest. The journey, if you undertake it, will be long. Not as long as the one you took into the wilderness of Galamond, but dangerous all the same."

"You know about that?" Juniper asked.

Myrisha nodded to Reid. "We had plenty of time to speak while you were in the Spirit Gate. Don't worry, he told me good mostly things." She started toward the door, but hesitated. "I know it must be hard for you, knowing who you are and who your parents were. Your parents, like mine, were killed in the civil war, though people remember yours fondly. If you need to talk, feel free to send for me."

Understanding warmed Myrisha's eyes, a mirror of the longing Juniper felt to have known her parents, for a life that she might have had. In that other life, Juniper and Myrisha would have grown up as family. She was family—cousins.

"Thank you, Your Majesty," Juniper said. And she meant it.

Myrisha rejoined her guard in the corridor, and the horde of them retreated down the corridor.

"I like her," Juniper said to Reid. "I thought she was a bit stuck-up at first, but I like her."

"I agree," Reid said. "On both accounts." His soft expression hardened into a frown. "Juniper, are you certain about going into the Wylds?"

"Yes. If the Archmage of Air is there, and if she is the only one who remembers how they defeated Nexon, then we need to find her."

"But you heard Myrisha," Reid argued. "People don't live in the Wylds. Food can't grow. Even the animals are tainted monsters. If the archmage went into the Wylds centuries ago, she won't be there now."

"My father told me to go there," Juniper countered, though it was a lie.

"Yes, your dead father," Reid snapped, and immediately pulled his lips against his teeth. "I'm sorry, I didn't mean—"

"If *your* dead father would have told you to go somewhere, you wouldn't have even taken the breath to tell me about it," Juniper snapped back at him. "And you are welcome to stay here."

She stood. She didn't feel hungry anymore. She marched around the folding screen and threw herself onto the bed.

Reid came around the folding screen. "Is this because you're tired, or because you think I'm seriously considering letting you wander into a cursed forest alone while I stay here and marry a flirtatious servant?"

She mumbled unintelligible threats into the pillow.

He sighed. "Go to sleep, Juniper. You're being grumpy."

Reid pulled the blankets over her, and she fell into a strange sleep filled with purple smoke and blurry figures she thought she knew but couldn't get to. She woke sometime in the middle of the night; the magelight had taken on a sinister glow. Reid had joined her, but he slept with a space between them wide enough for another person.

Of course, considering the last night they had shared, the space didn't seem like a bad idea. She'd rather not wake up with her magic twisting her bones into new shapes again. Though she craved his touch, she stayed away.

CHAPTER 13

Juniper sat on the bed in a puddle of buttery morning sunlight, absently brushing her hair, when a knock sounded at the door. Reid answered it, and when Crespin's dry tone said her name, Juniper slid off the bed and around the folding screen. Crespin's dire gaze snapped to hers.

"Myrisha informed the council of your existence this morning," Crespin said. "They are overjoyed that you are alive, and they wish to meet with you."

A lump formed in Juniper's throat, and her voice came out a croak, "When?"

"Immediately," Crespin said. "They are waiting in the council chamber."

That would explain why he looked so dire. Her knees felt weak. She leaned onto the folding screen to hide it.

Juniper wasn't given a choice. Crespin stepped aside, and servants hurried into the room. Reid and Crespin lingered in the sitting room while the servants dressed Juniper on the other side of the partition. They helped her into a fresh set of coral and ivory robes, brushed and fixed her hair with pearl-tipped pins, and touched powder to her face and color to her lips. Her stomach churned the entire time, and she fought the urge to vomit. A buzzing started somewhere in the back of her mind, and it grew louder with each heartbeat. Reid and Crespin spoke quietly—she didn't hear a word of it.

The servants stepped back to admire their work, and Juniper's heart tumbled at their awed faces.

Reid walked beside her as Crespin led them through the palace and into a circular room with a high ceiling. Sunlight streamed through the leaded windows. The council members sat along a crescent shaped table of pale wood. Incense flavored the air with bright citrus. Granted, this room felt far less dark than the one in Bradburn Castle. It looked more like a lounge they had repurposed into the council chamber.

Which, given the history of the palace, it might have been.

As Juniper entered, a hush fell. Every pair of eyes landed on her. Studying. Gawking. Disbelieving. It felt far too much like a trial—the nightmare she often had where angry judges listed her crimes one by one, while the hangman lowered a noose around her neck.

Crespin led her to the middle of the room, equidistant from every council member.

"I present, Her Highness, Princess Isolde Balendin." Crespin gave a modest bow in her direction.

Hearing the title aloud made Juniper feel like emptying her stomach. Reid must have suspected it, for he stepped slightly closer. Crespin remained on her other side, gaze impassive and alert. He stood tall and proud, like a general.

Whispers surged around the room.

"Can it be true?"

"She looks like Lenora."

"Myrisha spoke the truth."

"By the Gods."

The edges of her vision darkened.

Then a councilwoman held up her hand for silence. The others quickly obliged. The councilwoman said softly, "You look remarkably like your mother. I admit, I doubted Myrisha's tale. Yet here you are. Alive and well. Isolde, I know I speak for us all when I say how wonderful it is to have you back."

Juniper forced herself to meet the eyes of the woman. She had weathered, dark brown skin. Her pale brown eyes were misty. Silver streaked her dark hair.

"I served under your father," said the councilwoman. "Before that, I served in the Royal Guard. Many others here can tell you similar stories. We thought you dead, and here you stand. The gods have been merciful."

A round of agreement went through the chamber.

"Our queen tells us that you do not wish for the throne?" said the councilman on her left, his words less welcoming and motherly than the first. "Admirable, if not questionable. Why return if you wish not for your birthright?"

The councilman had not spoken it as a question; he had stated it.

A silence settled, and she realized they were waiting for her to speak. Crespin gave her a slight nod of encouragement.

"That is true," she said meekly. "I don't want to be queen."

"And you spent the last several years as a thief, correct?"

Juniper swallowed. "Yes."

A sinister whisper resounded, one of doubt and skepticism.

"And you now work as an ambassador to King Bradburn?"

"Yes."

"That is quite the career shift."

"It was."

Silence settled once again, this time thicker.

"Our queen also explained that you wish to venture into the Blackwood Wylds," said another councilman. His eyes were misty too, yet he beheld her critically. "To find a missing archmage. I wish to hear your reasons from your own mouth."

She swallowed. Her voice did not come as confident as she would have liked as she said, "I need to find the archmage to learn how they defeated Nexon a thousand years ago, and the only archmage remaining who might know vanished into the Wylds."

Murmurs echoed through the chamber.

"Nexon?"

"Archmages?"

Question after question came at her, and she ignored them all. Their doubt fueled her anger, and when silence settled again, she found her voice.

"Nexon is no myth. He has been gathering an army of apostates and black magic for centuries," Juniper said firmly. "He attacked Rusdasin, took Bradburn Castle, and threatened me and my friends countless times. We must stop him."

Should she tell them about the prophecy? She inhaled to use it as a reason, but the words didn't make it to her lips. They died on her tongue.

A part of her didn't believe it, and it sounded silly enough out loud when other people talked about it.

"You want to venture into the Wylds looking for someone who vanished hundreds of years ago?" asked the councilman. The mist had gone from his eyes. Confusion replaced it.

"It is my only lead," Juniper reasoned.

"It is preposterous," he said. "We cannot allow such a thing."

"Scouts do not return," said another. "The Wylds are vicious and dangerous."

"The Wylds aside," said the first councilwoman, "There is the matter of your return. This will not stay secret. The people of Collatia deserve to know you did not perish that awful night. Since you never received a proper investiture, we must hold one before you are legally and officially recognized as a princess of Collatia. We begin planning immediately."

"We will need to appoint a planning committee."

"We should appoint the same as for Myrisha's. They did a wonderful job, and they did not overspend."

Juniper blinked. As the council talked over party details, her rage boiled hotter.

"What about the Wylds?" Juniper blurted, silencing their discussion. Again, all eyes turned to her, and she had the feeling of having spoken out of turn. "We don't have time to waste on parties. Nexon must be stopped!"

Eyes bore into hers, and she faced them fearlessly.

"We will discuss your proposal," said the councilman in a tone that meant they would discuss, not plan, and do so without her.

"Do you not care about the innocents?" she asked, trying her best to sound like Myrisha. "The innocent men and women and children who die every day at his hands? At the hands of those who follow him?"

A gentle murmur started and ended too quickly.

"We will discuss the matter," said the councilwoman dismissively. "In the meantime, it is good to have you back, Isolde."

Crespin nudged her arm. Her time with the council had ended. As the council began to mumble, Crespin led her back into the corridor. She fell into step behind her cousin, and Reid kept close at her side. On the way back to the guest wing, she fell into a dismal daze.

"What is an investiture?" Reid asked.

"It is a coronation of sorts," Crespin explained. "It's a ceremony during which a person is announced to the public. It's a stuffy old tradition. Typically, it is when someone accepts a title or a higher station. Normally, they don't last very long, but when you're royalty, they tend to be…tedious."

Juniper felt a pit open in her stomach. She hardly listened as Crespin talked about getting her chambers in the royal wing, finding her a suitable wardrobe, and arranging a tour of the kingdom.

"There will be hands to shake and babies to kiss," Crespin said listlessly as they entered the guest wing. "The committee will plan it. They will take care of everything. All you have to do is show up and look like you want to be there."

Juniper let herself into their guest room. A tray of steaming tea had arrived. Juniper plopped into the chair and poured herself a cup with shaking hands. Reid sat beside her.

"When will all this start happening?" Reid asked.

Crespin shrugged. "Likely within the week, if the investiture committee is chosen today."

Footsteps, and then a hasty knock at the door. Crespin answered it. Servants glided inside with a tray of breakfast. They flourished the lids as they uncovered the eggs, sausages, and fruits.

"Is there anything else you require, Your Highness?" asked the servant with a gentle bow.

Juniper's fingers twitched on her teacup. "No, this is wonderful. Thank you."

The servants blushed and left.

"This smells delicious," Reid said. "Will you be joining us, General?"

"No, I have a meeting. I will see you this afternoon."

Juniper heard her cousin's footsteps, the door open and close, and Reid's gentle words. She barely registered what he said. As he filled his own plate, he spooned a bit of everything onto hers.

Her limbs felt like warm lead and her gut had knotted itself into an impossible shape.

Your Highness.

CHAPTER 14

The council's decision came before Juniper had finished her eggs. Crespin delivered it himself. The council refused to allow Isolde to venture into the Blackwood Wylds. Juniper gawked at the news. Crespin didn't seem at all surprised.

"They all agreed that sending you into the most dangerous part of the kingdom is a terrible idea," Crespin said dully. "However, they have agreed to discuss aid for Duvane."

"Do they not care about the fate of the kingdom?" Juniper asked. "We don't have time for this."

Crespin held his hand up. "They will arrange for a party to venture into the Wylds after your official announcement. Until then, you are not to leave the palace without an escort. Word of your return is spreading fast. The council suggested the summer solstice was the perfect time to announce you to the people."

"A proper escort?" Juniper laughed bitterly. "Do they know who I am? I am perfectly capable of handling myself. Against man or beast."

"It is true," Reid added dryly.

"Be that as it may," Crespin said through gritted teeth—not a man used to being questioned. "The council has made its decision. You will stay here until told otherwise."

"They are not in charge of me," Juniper said.

"The law says otherwise," Crespin added. "You are a Balendin, the rightful heir to the throne, and by sacred oath are bound to adhere to the council's decisions."

"I took no oath."

"Your ancestors did."

Juniper seethed but held her tongue. She had never let something like laws or sacred oaths get in her way before. She didn't feel like starting now. Or ever.

Crespin took a calming sigh. He tried to speak pleasantly, but the words came out forced. "The investiture committee has been chosen, and they will meet with you shortly. It is in your best interest to stay here, cousin. I will see you at dinner."

Cousin tumbled ungracefully from his lips.

The general left before Juniper could complain or argue. As the door opened and closed, she spotted more royal guards in the corridor than there had been before. She snorted in disgust. They obviously cared more for their lost princess than they did a stray thief.

"An escort," she muttered. She set her fork aside. Her feeble appetite had vanished.

"I thought you enjoyed playing a lady?" Reid took a bite of toast.

"Playing is fine," she said. "But I'm not some doll to be put on a shelf! I will not be locked in a palace like some ninny that can't hold her own. I can! I have for the past ten years!"

"Crespin knows that," Reid said calmly. "I know that. I suspect Myrisha knows as well. But the council? If they are anything like the council in Rusdasin, they see royals as figureheads, not as people, and see Isolde as something to covet. The princess they all believed dead."

Juniper huffed. "I'm no princess," she whispered, more to herself than to him. "I'm a thief. There are no walls that can hold me."

"You are not just a thief anymore," Reid said, more firmly. "You are also Isolde Balendin, and like it or not that name comes with…"

"Shackles?" Juniper added.

Reid frowned. "I was going to say restraints."

"Same thing."

Juniper sulked while Reid finished his breakfast. Thoughts rolled through her mind, one after another. She twisted her finger around a lock of hair, twirling and twirling. Thinking. By the time Reid set his fork aside, she had reached a conclusion.

"We could take a walk," Reid suggested. "Get some fresh air and sunshine. Isaac tells me the southern garden is one of the most beautiful he's seen."

She doubted that—she had walked through the garden of the gods. She would never see a garden more splendid.

"Or," Reid started. "You can come with me to Eldridge Hall. Isaac invited me to train with the Sentinels while we're here."

She considered it. She wouldn't mind seeing the Sentinels. She also wouldn't mind a long bath and time to herself.

"If you don't, you'll only be sulking around here," Reid said.

She let out a long, grievous sigh.

Reid donned his armor as she sipped another cup of tea. He lingered by the door, looking at her expectantly.

"Fine," she said. She set down her tea, smoothed wrinkles from her robes, and followed him into the corridor.

At once, the guards stood straighter.

Reid offered her his arm, and she took it. They started through the guest wing. Juniper felt the eyes on her, servants and guards. She pretended not to notice.

"Why did you leave your sword?" Juniper asked Reid. He had not donned his Mage's Bane.

"The Sentinels don't use the bane as a weapon," Reid said quietly. "They also have little of it, considering the Order's secrecy over the exact recipe and making."

She harrumphed. Good riddance, she thought.

Eldridge Hall was on the other side of the palace. It sat within the wall but separate from the palace. It was made of the same pale stone and blocky style, only it had red shingles and pointed dormers topped with golden spires. Even from the outside, the sounds of clanking armor and steel echoed. The inside glowed with magelight. The back of the hall held a mural of lapis and limestone, a stylized circle with half being the sun and half being the moon. Laurel leaves surrounded it, a nod to the Collatian crest.

Reid led her through the main hall and to the yard between it and the palace wall. A group of Sentinels in dark silver armor had gathered there. Their breastplates bore the same symbol as in the hall. As Reid entered the yard, their conversation halted.

"Reid," said a broad-shouldered man with dark brown skin and short black hair. A scar traced the left side of his face. He clapped Reid on the shoulder. "I was hoping you'd come today. I want to show you my ward."

"He thinks it's better than it is," said a tall girl with a playful, husky voice. She flashed an infectious smile. She had deep golden skin and short caramel hair.

"And this must be the girl we've heard so much about," said the man with the scar. He stepped in front of Juniper, pressed his palm to his heart, and bowed deeply. "Princess Isolde, it is an honor. I am Sentinel Calvex Hutton."

"Sentinel Rue Bellamy." She bowed too.

"This is Captain Bellamy's sister," Reid added.

"Older sister," Rue added.

Juniper swallowed. They stood, and Reid gave her arm a little squeeze. She blinked at him. Was she supposed to say something? The longer the silence went on, the more nervous she became.

Calvex and Rue looked at her as one might look at a freshly revealed portrait, and she hated it.

A shout came from the other end of the yard, saving her from words she didn't have. At once, Calvex and Rue jumped to attention. Reid stood a little straighter too.

A tall, lithe woman with light brown skin and black hair marched across the yard. She held herself like a soldier—shoulders back, chin up, arms constantly held at an angle from which she could unsheathe the sword at her hip.

"Commander Yorlan," Reid whispered to Juniper. "She leads the Sentinels."

A few steps behind Yorlan, Isaac marched in Sentinel armor. Sentinels marched into the yard from the hall, and Juniper released her hold on Reid. She found a spot to sit—a low wall that surrounded a swallow cerulean pond with tiny silver fish. Reid stood to the front of the yard, beside Yorlan and Isaac, as the Sentinels lined the yard in even rows.

They did not have the same menacing presence as the knights of Duvane. They could do many of the same things, yet these anti-magic warriors radiated with something warmer.

"You've had time to practice your wards, now let's see them," Yorlan ordered. Her voice rose over the entire yard, yet it didn't sound as though she was shouting.

The Sentinels took a stance, and at once they drew their hands inward and then out again. About a third managed to summon a ward—a shimmery wall of magic that would deflect incoming magic. It also could rebound magic onto a mage, which Juniper had learned firsthand when helping Reid practice his ward.

Reid and Isaac walked the yard, correcting stances and watching those who had not managed a ward. Yorlan stood at the head of the yard, watching from afar, but Juniper doubted she missed a thing.

"Princess," came a familiar and grating voice. Jana, the annoyingly pretty servant girl, flashed her hapless smile at Juniper. "I've been looking for you."

Juniper sighed. "Why?"

"Her Majesty wishes to see you in the guest wing lounge." Jana gave a curt bow of her head.

Her eyes roamed over the yard, and they snagged. Juniper glanced in the same direction. Jana had been looking at Reid. He stood by Rue, instructing on the proper ward technique. Anger burning, Juniper jumped down from the wall and busied herself brushing wrinkles and dirt from her robes.

"Let's go," Juniper said with as much as a superior drawl as she could muster.

Jana led her out of the yard and back through the hall. Two royal guards fell into step behind her. One she recognized from the guest wing, the one stationed outside her chambers. Juniper fumed. *Juniper* hadn't been guarded, yet *Isolde* warranted two guards. Jana led Juniper back to the guest wing and to double doors carved with stars. Four royal guards stood in the corridor, including Captain Bellamy, who opened the doors for her.

"Thank you," Juniper said.

Captain Bellamy closed the doors behind her.

Two women waited for her. Myrisha and a blonde stranger. At the sight of Juniper, the blonde woman rose from her seat with the grace of a swan.

"Ah, Princess, it is an honor to meet you," she said, bowing. She had an accent, but Juniper couldn't place it. Her sunny complexion suggested south. "I am Coraline. My queen has asked me to make a few new garments for you."

"She is the best seamstress in Delphine," Myrisha added.

Juniper sighed. "All right, let's get this over with."

Coraline instructed Juniper to stand on a stool while she took measurements; it felt familiar yet strange. Juniper had enjoyed being pampered in Bradburn Castle, but it had been a game. She had known from the start it wouldn't last. It had been a vacation from her thieving and the Undercity.

Myrisha and Coraline talked all the while, about dresses and colors and fabrics. Juniper half-listened.

The lounge had an overwhelming number of pillows and colorful throws, and yet somehow everything went together—it matched the colors of the rest of the palace. The few windows allowed glimpses of the darling blue sky.

Finally, after what felt like hours of being poked and prodded, the seamstress took her notes and left.

"You look exhausted." Myrisha offered a warm smile and patted the couch beside her. "I suppose the council has that effect on people. Besides that, is everything all right?"

Juniper collapsed onto the couch beside Myrisha. The couch was stiff, and the cushion barely hid the hard wooden frame underneath.

She inhaled and held it—pausing for dramatics. She released her breath in a huff. "Everyone is treating me differently."

"That is expected," Myrisha said. "When I became queen, everyone treated me differently. Even people I had known for years, even Coraline. Only Crespin treats me the same, like his little sister. It is both irritating and refreshing."

Juniper did not like the sound of that. She didn't want to be treated like a girl made of glass who couldn't lift a finger for herself.

"Would you like a tour of the palace?" Myrisha asked. "I have no meetings this morning, and it will give you something to do other than sit in your room until the committee descends."

She didn't like the sound of anyone *descending*.

"That sounds lovely," Juniper said.

Myrisha gave a regal smile. "Wonderful. Let's get started."

The queen drank the rest of her tea in a single swig and stood. Juniper didn't bother with her tea; she had had plenty before the meeting. Myrisha offered

Juniper her arm. Juniper hesitated, then slid her arm through the queen's. Myrisha guided them into the corridor.

"I am giving Isolde a tour of our palace," Myrisha said to Captain Bellamy.

She wanted to correct her, *Call me Juniper.*

Myrisha paused, giving him the opportunity to object, but he did not.

Juniper felt a hot anger. Did Myrisha have to ask the captain's permission to give someone a tour of her own home?

Myrisha started through the guest wing. They made their way back to the vestibule, and the tour began. Bellamy walked a step behind, vigilant and silent.

Juniper felt curious stares every step of the way. Servants peered around corners and in doorways. One servant polished the same spot on a golden vase as Myrisha and Juniper passed. Guards watched her too.

Their gazes were often accompanied with quick whispers, *Isolde, Isolde, Isolde.*

The Summer Palace had been finished five centuries ago and started at an unknown date. It had been built as a summer home for the royals—the Summer Palace reflected a summer night while Balendin Castle had reflected a winter night. In the grand ballroom, the ceiling had been painted in shades of gold, and ivory stars mimicked the midsummer constellations. According to Myrisha, the grand ballroom in Balendin Castle had reflected the midwinter sky.

Isolde. Isolde. Isolde.

Myrisha led her through the library—small compared to the one that had been left in Balendin Castle. A few of the scholars had escaped the slaughter, and they had been hard at work the past twelve years, replacing and rewriting what had been lost. Juniper picked out a few books to read, relishing the feeling of adventure in her arms.

Isolde. Isolde. Isolde.

Myrisha walked her through arcades, courtyards, and a few towers. No space had gone to waste, not like Bradburn Castle with its empty lounges, sitting spaces, and rooms of relics. Captain Bellamy's constant presence behind them reminded her of Reid, and it gave her an odd sense of comfort mixed with annoyance. His armor even clicked, though Bellamy stepped lighter than Reid.

Isolde. Isolde. Isolde.

CHAPTER 15

They stopped for lunch in a sunny parlor with copper pots of leafy ferns and daylilies. The oak table had been set for six, and food for as many was arranged. The parlor overlooked the yard where the Sentinels trained. Most had left for lunch. A few lingered, including Reid, Rue, and Calvex. Juniper was watching Reid demonstrate his ward when she noticed a few servants watching—including the annoyingly pretty Jana.

The door to the parlor opened.

"I am glad you could make it, Sir Pinul," said Myrisha.

"It is an honor, Your Majesty," said Isaac.

Juniper turned in time to see Isaac rise from a bow. He hadn't come alone. A woman stood beside him, in her forties and kind-faced. At the sight of Juniper, the woman coughed on a sob and rushed to wrap Juniper into a tight embrace. Isaac did not look surprised. If anything, he looked pleased. Juniper was about to tell the woman to get off when she stepped away of her own accord. She held Juniper at arm's length, and Juniper got a better look at the woman's face—her heart jumped into her throat.

It was her tutor, or the woman Juniper believed to have been her tutor. She was older, but there was no question.

"Isolde," the woman breathed. "It is you. All grown up."

Isaac appeared at the woman's side. "Isolde, this is my wife, Reese. She was your nurse when you were a babe."

Hearing that name on Isaac's lips stirred something unpleasant and cold, counteracting the warmth of seeing her tutor again.

"My tutor," she whispered.

"It sounded better than *guard*," said Reese. She stroked Juniper's cheek, and that's when Juniper noticed the boy standing beside Isaac. He looked no older than ten.

"Our son, Connor," said Isaac.

Juniper wasn't quite sure what to think. All this time, Isaac had a wife and son in Delphine. He had left them behind to answer King Bradburn's summons, to venture to the edge of the world, and serve for an untold time a kingdom away from his family. The very idea that he had left them felt so…strange.

Isaac, Reese, and Connor joined them for lunch. As they ate, Reese told Juniper how she and Isaac had carried her across the border, through forests and over mountains with only the stars to guide them. She had stayed with Juniper at the greenhouses as a keeper. She had taught Juniper to hide her magic in fear she would be found. And then Juniper had vanished. Reese believed herself a failure, and when Juniper could not be found, she had sought Isaac's help—they had returned to Delphine together.

"We hadn't spoken to each other before that night. One thing led to another, and here we are," Reese said. She cast a loving look to Isaac, which he returned. Connor pretended not to notice.

"Why did you never mention your family?" Juniper asked Isaac. He'd had many chances along the way to Galamond and back.

"Few in the Order knew," Isaac admitted. "Others frown upon marriage between a knight and a mage, especially a mage of a foreign kingdom."

Juniper caught Isaac's subtle inflection—marriage between a knight and a mage. Had Reid thought of the Order when he had proposed to her?

After lunch, Isaac and his family departed and Myrisha and Juniper continued their tour.

Whispers of *Isolde, Isolde, Isolde*, followed them down every corridor.

"According to legend," whispered Myrisha as they meandered down an interior corridor of the royal chambers, "The paranoid king ordered the architect to build secret passages throughout the palace. However, no record of those secret passages exists. The only clue comes from the architect's journal."

"Are they real?" Juniper whispered to Myrisha.

Myrisha gave her a mischievous grin and winked. She led Juniper into an alcove that housed a gold and blue tapestry. Juniper blinked, at first concerned, but then Myrisha pulled the tapestry's thick fabric aside—and revealed a lightless secret passage.

Juniper couldn't help the smile that crept over her face.

"Come on," Myrisha whispered, and tugged Juniper into the secret passage. She pulled a mage stone from her pocket. As the stone met her skin, it began to glow a warm yellow.

The dark passage connected with another, and Juniper spied another intersection further down. A network of secret passages. It gave her a fierce tingle of excitement, the kind that came from slipping around unnoticed. Myrisha tugged her to a tight spiral staircase that led up into a sunny tower. Books and half-finished artwork scattered the steepled room. It smelled of paint and charcoal and warmth. Sunlight spilled through the arched windows, setting every dust mote aflame. A desk with paint splatters and ink stains set against one wall underneath two unlit lanterns. A mattress lay on the floor on the opposite side, shaded by a delicate folding screen with a rose pattern. Several mismatched pillows and blankets scattered the bed, and by the glimpse of the skewed sheets and pillows, two had been sharing it.

"This is my favorite place in the palace," Myrisha said. She guided Juniper to an arched window. It overlooked the city. The sun glinted off weather vanes and shop windows, and dots of color flashed as people moved about the streets. "It reminds me there are people relying on me, who are affected by my decisions and actions."

"It's cozy," Juniper said. It was a hideaway. "Is this supposed to make me feel better about being trapped in the palace?"

"That feeling comes and goes," Myrisha said grimly. She sat on the cushioned window seat. The sunlight warmed her pale golden face. "I remember my mother talking to your mother. It's one of my earliest memories. Your mother, the queen, told my mother that the crown is heavier than it looks. It took me a long time to realize what she meant. The day of my coronation, they set the crown on my head and I thought, 'this isn't that heavy.'" Myrisha lifted the silver crown from her head and held it in the light. "It wasn't the metal or the gems she was talking about. It was everything that comes with the crown. The public appeal, the approval, the decisions."

"Being a queen." Juniper's throat constricted at the mention of her mother. "Not just wearing a crown and looking pretty."

Myrisha replaced the crown on her head. "Exactly."

"I still don't want the crown," Juniper said. A little less now.

"I would be lying if I said I wasn't a little disappointed," she said, a laugh on her tongue. "I had hoped you would take the throne and the crown, and I could be Lady Myrisha again. I could sleep in, take walks through the city, and just…be me." Myrisha released a slow, dignified sigh. "Are you sure you don't want to be queen?"

"I'm sure."

"We could share," Myrisha said. "We look enough alike that most people wouldn't tell us apart. I'll be queen for a week, then you could be queen for a week, and so on."

Juniper laughed. "As appealing as that sounds, I don't think I would be very good at making decisions for an entire kingdom. I'm far too selfish and apathetic toward strangers, especially the stupid ones."

Myrisha laughed.

Captain Bellamy shifted, stealing both girls' attention.

"Your Majesty," he said tentatively. "You have a dinner meeting with the Market Association. It would be wise to be prepared."

Juniper wanted to tell the captain that it would be wise not to tell the queen what to do, but she held her tongue.

Myrisha sighed. "Yes, yes." She turned her pleading eyes onto Juniper. "Are you sure you don't want to be queen? The Market Association is quite riveting."

"Your lack of desire to go implies exactly that," Juniper said.

Myrisha laughed. "Very well, if you insist. We will escort you back to your chambers. Do we have time, Captain?"

Bellamy shook his head. "I would recommend being early. The Market Association gets cranky if they have to wait, even if they arrive early." To Juniper he said, "I'll have one of my men escort you, Princess."

Juniper bristled at the title. "You're so generous," she deadpanned.

Bellamy frowned, and Myrisha tapped the back of her hand on his armored shoulder. The two of them shared a look—one Juniper had seen before, a private look of silent communication. She had seen it pass between Captain Sandpiper and Glenda, Adrian and Roslyn, between Xavier and Ison, and between countless others. And…the skewed sheets, pillows for two… Standing in the secret tower with Myrisha and Bellamy gave Juniper a steep sense of intrusion.

And she understood why Myrisha had brought her to this tower. It hadn't been just another stop on the tour. This tower was a private place for Myrisha, and bringing Juniper into it was a show of friendship, a token of trust.

And it made Juniper feel like she had swallowed rocks.

CHAPTER 16

A royal guard escorted Juniper back to the guest wing.

Isolde. Isolde. Isolde.

A servant stood in front of Juniper's door. To her dread, the investiture committee was waiting for her in the lounge. She heaved a sigh. Her long, warm bath would have to wait. She marched to the lounge—guard right behind—and found a team of three chatting in the lounge. As she entered, they each jumped up.

"Isolde, it is wonderful to meet you."

"Oh, you darling, welcome home."

"You look just like your mother."

The meeting that followed made Juniper's dread and anger curl together until she couldn't tell them apart. The committee talked about a parade, what dress she would wear, what food they would serve at the grand dinner, if they should have a ball, and which nobles she should meet first. They chattered like birds about all the things she must do, will do, and all the people she must meet; and parties and events she must attend or host. Juniper had little to add, not that they left room for her to speak.

Isolde. Isolde. Isolde.

"You would look lovely in indigo, Isolde."

"Isolde, what do you think?"

"Myrisha has told me about you, Isolde."

Isolde. Isolde. Isolde.

At last, the meeting ended. The same guard guided her back to her chamber on the other side of the veranda. Before he could speak, Juniper muttered a quick thank you and shut herself in her chambers. The guard lingered on the other side of the door, then marched away. Juniper took a deep breath. Reid had not yet returned, and she had the room to herself. She meandered to the bed and threw herself onto it.

Is this what being a princess would be like? Being followed and watched every moment of every day? She rolled onto her back. Too much had happened in such a short amount of time, and her body and mind hadn't done a good job of keeping up.

❋

Three weeks.

Three weeks of putting up with the chittering, talkative committee who fawned over Juniper like a newborn animal. Three weeks of servants and guards bowing, whispering *Your Highness* and *My Princess* as Juniper passed. Three weeks of being escorted by a full retinue of royal guards. Three weeks of meeting arrogant nobles, captains, and generals.

Three weeks of *Isolde, Isolde, Isolde.*

Three weeks for Nexon to have done gods only knew what to the realm.

Thoughts of Nexon swirled with her agitation and fury and regret as a retinue of royal guards escorted Juniper back to her new chambers within the royal wing. She hadn't wanted to move into the royal wing, but no one had listened to her.

Two guards posted themselves on either side of the double doors, and Juniper let herself in and slammed the doors behind her.

She allowed herself a moment of silence and privacy.

The new room was larger, but it did not feel as comfortable. It reminded her of her room in Bradburn Castle, of being locked inside, of the guards who stood outside the door to make sure she did not escape.

She crossed to the bathing room. The tub was twice as large, and a selection of perfumed salts and soaps lined the shelf above it.

"This seems more to your liking," Reid had said on the first night in the new room, motioning to the bathing room.

His attempt at humor hadn't made a dent in Juniper's dread.

Everyone wanted her to become Isolde and acted as though she were mad for pretending otherwise. She didn't want to be Isolde. She wanted to be Juniper.

She washed her face in cold water. Summer in Delphine was warmer than in Rusdasin, and the heat pressed against her magic. The cold water refreshed not only her spirit but also her ice.

Muffled voices sounded in the corridor. The voices came closer, and she recognized Reid's somber tone.

He said something too muffled for her to hear, and then a girlish giggle followed.

A burning rage flashed under her skin, and as the door opened, she sat straight as an arrow. Reid's armored footsteps entered the chamber, and the trailing end of Jana's giggle died away. Jana's featherlight steps crossed the sitting room, and the soft *ploosh* of clean laundry sounded.

"Good day, Sir Sandpiper," Jana said. The door opened and closed.

Reid walked into the bedroom and began the odious task of removing his armor, piece by piece. Juniper dried her face by magic and sauntered into the bedroom. She leaned against the decorative arch that separated the bed from the rest of the room.

"How was your dress fitting?" Reid asked without looking at her as he added his greaves to the stand.

"Boring," Juniper deadpanned. The committee had fussed and fussed over what dress Isolde would wear for her announcement, and then settled on periwinkle and gold without asking Juniper what she thought. "I think you ought to be proud of me for not strangling them all today."

"Is that so?" Reid mused.

His nonchalance irked her. Reid had spent most of his time with the Sentinels, training and getting to know the commanders.

"What was she giggling about?" Juniper asked flatly.

"I was talking about training for the Order," Reid said as he unbuckled his breastplate. "How we had to survive in the woods for three days before becoming a squire, and how the Sentinels require five days."

"That's not funny."

"I didn't say it was. Most end up with some form of disease or sickness, either by drinking stagnant water or eating strange leaves. A few unlucky ones end up with parasites." Reid hung his breastplate on the armor stand. "I managed to survive with minimal damage. I grew up in a rural village and knew things others didn't. Henry had a parasite that took a month to get rid of, with magical healing."

"That's disgusting," she said.

Reid half-laughed. "Then I won't tell you where it came out of."

She pretended to gag. "Your little friend laughed at that? That's disgusting, not funny. You'd think she's trying to get on your good side."

He frowned. "Or maybe she is being friendly."

"I've seen friendly, and I've seen flirting," Juniper said flatly. "That was not friendly. That's the type of fake giggling a girl does when she wants something."

Reid's frown became a scowl. "And what do you think Jana wants from me?"

"I don't know." Juniper crossed her arms. "You should ask her. You two seem comfortable enough. With the moony eyes she keeps making at you, she'd probably tell you anything."

"You make her nervous," Reid said quietly.

Juniper scoffed. "She confessed this to you?"

"She did," he said. "First you were a thief, now you are her princess. And you're always scowling at her like a pissed off dire wolf."

She huffed. "Reid, we don't have time for this."

"The council sent a contingent of soldiers and battlemages to aid Rusdasin, and Myrisha has sent scouts to assess the situation," Reid reminded her. "We have done what we set out to do, which was broker an alliance."

"With me as the bargaining piece," Juniper muttered.

Reid frowned. "They have promised more aid if the reports call for it. Right now, there is nothing else we can do."

"We should be halfway to the Wylds by now," Juniper said.

"Hunting for an archmage who may or may not still be alive," Reid countered.

"And who may be the only person who knows how to defeat Nexon."

"I don't understand why you think we can't defeat him with magic and steel." Reid set his final piece of armor on the stand, then straightened the pieces. "You are being unreasonable. These people have extended their home to us, and they are treating you as family, as royalty."

"I'm being unreasonable?" She snorted. "These people have locked me in this palace, stationed guards to keep me *safe*, and ordered me to stay indoors. They're planning the rest of my life with very little input from me. They've amassed a list of people I am to meet, people I am to swoon, and people I have to avoid. I am not some lost little girl in need of coddling!"

"Think of it from their perspective," Reid argued. "They suffered a vicious civil war that they believed stole their entire royal family. Now here you are, the last remaining fragment of that family. Isolde is a sign of hope for them. That is what they need you to be."

"That is not what I need me to be," she said bitterly.

Reid took her hand in his and lifted her chin with the other. "Isolde, these—"

Her anger seared white-hot. She ripped her chin from his grip and yanked her hand out of his. "Do not call me that," she hissed. "My name is Juniper."

Reid stumbled over his next words. Confusion and worry passed over his knightly expression. Whatever he had meant to say hadn't worked as he had intended. It didn't matter.

Whispers seized her thoughts. *Isolde. Isolde. Isolde.*

Everyone was ready for Juniper to vanish from existence, because Isolde was more important. Beloved, where Juniper was abhorred. Even Reid and Isaac seemed ready for her to vanish.

And hearing that name on Reid's lips tore through her chest. It opened a bottomless abyss, and she tumbled straight down. Tears pushed against her eyes, but she refused to let Reid see them. Instead, she let her anger burn hotter. She stormed to the cabinet, grabbed her satchel, and tossed it onto the bed. She hastily gathered her things.

"What are you doing?" Reid demanded.

"I'm packing," she said, shoving clothes and things into her satchel a bit haphazardly.

"Why?" Reid stomped to the edge of the bed.

"Because I'm not staying in this room," she spat. She didn't buckle the satchel; she tossed the strap over her shoulder, grabbed her library books, and stormed into the corridor.

The royal guard standing across from their door jumped. He quickly bowed his head and placed his open hand over his heart. "Princess Isolde."

Juniper ignored him. Hearing that name said with respect and reverence struck a nerve. Hearing it directed at her struck something quite different. A livid rage worked its way up from her stomach, heating the surface of her skin like fire.

Reid dashed after her. "Stop this. You're being childish."

She ignored him until she reached the small lounge where she and Myrisha had taken tea that afternoon. She spun on her heels, and Reid halted within a hand's reach. "You've done just fine without me so far. I'm sure you'll be fine for a night. Why not ask your pretty little friend for company? I'm sure she'd love to. Just remember *her* name."

She slammed the door behind her, rattling the paintings of the lounge and the silver vase by the window. She stomped across the room and set her satchel on the sofa and plopped down beside it.

Reid lingered outside the door. She imagined the royal guard staring at him, wondering what could have happened, and Reid making the awkward walk back to their room. After several long moments, he walked away.

The whispers remained. *Isolde. Isolde. Isolde.* Only this time, the whispers spoke in Reid's voice.

Juniper pulled a book into her lap, reclined on the sofa, and began to read.

Or she tried to.

Reid's absence left a gaping hole beside her. His use of that name made everything worse. He had turned from her. As had Isaac. Without either of them, she had no one in Delphine. Everyone wanted Isolde, the lost princess. No one wanted Juniper.

A guard's calm footsteps sounded in the corridor. He stationed himself outside the lounge.

Guarding *Isolde.*

Juniper's anger burned. Isolde might have needed protection, but Juniper Thimble did not! Isolde might have been a placid lady that allowed guards to escort her from one room to another, who enjoyed planning parades and parties, but Juniper Thimble did not take orders.

Her mother's words returned. Maddox had taught her to be strong, independent, and smart.

She made her own decisions. She protected herself with ice and steel.

And Juniper Thimble would do just that.

CHAPTER 17

When Ison was small, before the knights took him to the Marca, he had lived in a small town. His parents ran the only inn, and Ison remembered playing up and down the steps with his older brother, Idel. A guest from Rusdasin had stayed there, and Ison had asked him about the castle. Ison had never seen a castle, but he had heard stories of how big and grand they were.

"They're big and grand, all right," the traveler had assured him. "But they are old and filled with dark corridors and ghosts."

The memory had churned into a whimsical dream, one in which the traveler wore a pointed emerald hat and spectacles that magnified his eyes. He carried a satchel packed to bursting with books and scrolls.

The traveler had laughed, then his horse spouted wings and flew away.

Ison woke with the traveler's maniacal laugh echoing in his head. The others were still asleep. The storm had moved on, leaving the castle dripping and silent. The magelight had faded to near darkness, and through the corridor, Ison spotted a faint blue glow—dawn. Giving up on finding any more sleep, Ison stood and crept into the corridor.

He started forward, opposite the way they had come. He followed the glow to a corridor lined with windows. The glass had long since shattered—save for one window near the end. The wind whistled through the drafts, turrets, and battlements—a ghostly hissing. Humid air whisked inside. Puddles gathered under the windows and between the stones, and water streaked down the walls and windowpanes. Blue dawn glowed in the cloudless east.

Balendin Castle looked as big as Bradburn Castle, but where the castle he knew had been filled with life and torches, this castle held darkness and ghosts. So many rooms and passages left to the elements, so much forgotten furniture left to decay, so many paintings whose surface had molded and cracked. So many forgotten memories.

Juniper had been born here, as had her siblings and parents. They had died here too.

Ison continued down the corridor. A crawling sensation on his neck sent gooseflesh down his spine—he spun to look behind him. He saw nothing but puddles and shadows. He started walking again, and the feeling persisted. It felt like the darkness was moving when he wasn't looking. He felt eyes in every room, every corridor.

He reminded himself that he could blast any attacker into the stone walls hard enough to crack skulls, or slice right through them with a blade of air.

Although, he didn't know if it would work on ghosts.

When the dark grew too thick, he summoned a forever flame. The bluish white light banished the closest shadows.

He passed through a grand set of moldy, broken doors and into a grand ballroom. Stone pillars lined the room, carved to look like twisting vines. Iron chandeliers hung along the domed ceiling, each capable of holding several magelights. The ceiling had been carved and painted to look like the night sky. If Ison remembered his astronomy, the stars depicted the sky in midwinter. The floor had been tiled in faded colors of gold and blue. Archways led off the ballroom, the curtains rotten and filled with mildew and dust.

What must this place have looked like twenty years ago? Fifty?

His footsteps echoed off the tile as he crossed the ballroom. Shadows stretched from side to side, parted by his forever flame. He chose a doorway at random and followed it through a grand corridor, up a wide staircase, into an old servants' passage, and up a narrow staircase. He continued moving up until he came to a set of tall, dark wooden doors that had been blasted inward. The Collatian royal seal had been engraved onto the wood. Scorch marks still blackened the stone walls.

The Royal Chambers.

Many of the chamber doors had been blasted apart. Ison glanced through each one. The destruction behind each door made his stomach clench, but it was the beautiful bassinet turned over on its side with an old blanket strung across the floor, that stole his breath. The rest of the room looked to have been scorched, the furniture charred, the stone blackened.

Juniper had escaped, he reminded himself.

Ison wandered into a grand room, larger than the others. A dark stain marred the stones of the sitting room—blood. Ison felt his skin go clammy. King Balendin had been slain in his own chamber. By his brother. Right where Ison stood. The queen had died in the bedroom.

Ison didn't want to see any more bloodstains. He walked into the room opposite the bedroom. It was a grand study, twice as large as Mason's. Broken windows had left the space musty and dank. An old wooden desk took up much of the space. Mold grew up the sides. The hearth had long since been cold, the logs turned to mildew and compost. A rug had once covered the floor, but time had worn the color to grays and browns, and mildew grew among the threads.

On the far side of the study, an archway led into a circular chamber. An iron staircase circled up the center of it, all the way to the top of a tower. No windows illuminated the tower. In the light of his forever flame, Ison saw markings on the walls. He brightened the flame and held it higher. He had first thought the marks to be a map, but they were not. Dots and vines weaved a family tree that reached the very top of the tower.

Ison gripped the rail of the spiral staircase. It seemed sturdy enough. He lifted his foot for the bottom step.

"Are you sure that's smart?"

Ison jumped, lost his footing, and stumbled backward into the wall. His flame went out on impact. A tall, narrow figure stood in the archway between the study and the tower, shadowed by the sunlight spilling in.

"Xavier?" Ison gasped. He leaned forward on his knees, willing his heart to slow. "Shit."

Xavier chuckled and brought his own magelight to life. Unlike Mabyl's, which burned with yellows and reds, Xavier's burned gray. A ghost of his shadow-colored energy magic. It cast a strange light on the family tree.

Xavier glanced from the tree to Ison. "Did I scare you?"

"Of course not," Ison said, brushing dust off his pants. His cheeks flushed.

"I thought you heard me following." Xavier shrugged. "I wasn't trying to be quiet."

"Stomp next time," Ison said. "Or whistle, or speak, or something. Gods."

Xavier glanced at the tower. "So, what did you find?"

"A family tree, I think." Ison reached again for the stairs.

Xavier stood at the bottom of the stairs as Ison slowly made his way up. The iron creaked but held. The center support for the stairs remained intact, as did the stone around it. When the stairs did not come crashing down, Xavier started up too.

Ison summed his flame back to life and held it out to scan the hundreds of names etched into the stone. There were no dates, only names. He followed the lines and names all the way to the top of the tower, and gasped.

Xavier quickened his pace to the top. The iron barely creaked.

At the very top of the tree, at the top of the tower, five names were carved into the panels of the vaulted roof. Each of the five panels had a name, a god, and that god's corresponding element. Ison could hardly believe his eyes.

"Are those…" Xavier paused, standing close behind Ison on the stairs.

"The five Iluvin families," Ison gasped. "I…thought this was a legend."

"What legend are you talking about?"

Ison followed the panels to the very top of the tower. It looked as though something had once been set into the center, but it had long since fallen or been stolen. Around the indentation, gold paint flaked and cracked.

"Legends say the gods bestowed magic to five Iluvin, creating the first archmages. All mages are descendants of those first mages. These are them, those first mages, and this tree…their descendants."

Xavier let out a low whistle.

And above those five names were the five gods of the elements. Blugo, god of winter, had gifted water. Bala, goddess of nature, had gifted fire. Boxel, god of the harvest, had gifted earth. Rappa, god of strength, had gifted energy. Espone, goddess of merriment, had gifted air.

The beginning of magic.

The names of the first archmages were circled in gold, and Ison scanned the rest of the tree—a few other golden rings scattered the tree.

"Look," Ison said. "These golden rings must indicate an archmage. This tree tracks the archmages."

"And we might be able to find the next one," Xavier added on the heels of his words.

Ison blinked, his mind jumbled. He hadn't even thought of that, but they could! They made their way down the tree, searching for golden circles. Ison traced his eyes over the vines. They crossed between families, split into dozens of children and grandchildren.

"The Iluvin live longer than normal humans," Ison explained as they searched for golden rings. "That's why the archmages are so spread out."

He slowly made his way down the stairs. Names mixed and families married, until few had the original family name.

"Look," Ison said, a gasp on his tongue. "There's Mason Hobbs."

Indeed, the court magician's name had been circled in gold. One level from the bottom of the tower. According to the tree, Mason had children. A son and a daughter, who then had a daughter. Mason had grandchildren? Ison had never known. Mason had never mentioned a family.

At the thought of the court magician, something in Ison's chest squeezed enough to cork his next breath.

If he ever saw Mason again, he would ask about his family.

"If those are his only children, then wouldn't they be next in line to be archmage?" Xavier asked. "Mason doesn't have any other close relatives."

Ison had noticed—the families had thinned in the past several generations. Fewer children.

And it clicked. "Nexon has been weeding the Iluvin families," Ison said.

Xavier chuckled darkly. "And if he knew about this tree, then he would know exactly who might be a candidate for the archmage powers."

"And he could hunt them down and kill them before they could stop him," Ison said. "Do you think he took the castle just to find this?"

"People have killed for much less," Xavier muttered.

Ison moved further down the tree. If he could find the names of the current archmages, maybe he could find a way of getting those names to Juniper. He found Delmont Thacket's name, circled in gold.

He found Angyla Ohnen, but the vines made it hard to know what she was the archmage of.

"Mason is the Archmage of Energy, Nexon is the Archmage of Earth, and Delmont is the Archmage of Fire," Xavier mumbled. "That leaves air and water. This Angyla could be either one of those."

"So that leaves one," Ison said.

He and Xavier took turns moving about the tower, looking for golden rings. Ison couldn't believe he traced the lineage of the Iluvin. There were hundreds of descendants, yet few golden circles. There were more golden circles near the bottom—when Nexon had started his hunt. The tree ended at the generation of the civil war, when the city had fallen.

"I'll be damned," said Xavier.

"What did you find?" Ison said, staring at a name he couldn't pronounce. It looked Jantian.

"A mutual friend," said Xavier, his tone dark but humored. "One you'll want to see."

Ison pulled his eyes from the Jantian name and joined Xavier on the other side of the tower. He followed Xavier's pointed finger to the name, and Ison's breath tumbled ungracefully from his lips. And for a long moment, no air would come back in.

"It looks like we found the Archmage of Water," Xavier said, loosely crossing his arms. He tilted his head to Ison. "Think we should send word to Jun?"

They had indeed found the Archmage of Water.

It was Isolde Balendin; a golden circle bordered her name.

CHAPTER 18

A knock sounded at the door. Juniper lounged on the couch, dangling her feet over the arm, propping a book on her thighs.

"Princess?" came a tentative voice. "I have come to escort you to dinner."

"I will take dinner in here," Juniper said. An order, not a request. "Alone, please."

The servant lingered at the door, and Juniper feared he would object.

A long moment passed. "Of course, Princess."

The servant started away. Juniper smiled to herself.

Not long after, a timid servant delivered dinner for one. He arranged it neatly on the table, poured her a glass of wine, then bowed himself out of the lounge.

If this castle operated like anywhere else, everyone would have heard of her spat with Reid by now.

Juniper took a sip of wine first, then began to eat.

She ate her fill, and the servant returned to remove the dishes. Before he left, he quietly asked if she would like another room prepared for the night.

"This is fine," Juniper said, pretending to be angry. "A blanket would be lovely."

The servant blinked at her, then bowed. "At once, my lady."

He returned later with a soft blanket large enough for three.

Juniper reclined on the sofa, book in hand, blanket over her legs. The evening light faded into twilight shades of amber and plum and then indigo as night fell. Her magic strengthened with the night—like she could lift seas and command storms. Juniper summoned a magelight to read by.

She waited until full dark.

She set the library book on the table beside two notes, one for Reid and one for Myrisha. She pulled on her cloak, secured her satchel, and glided across the room to the tapestry she had given little thought to during her tea with Myrisha. It hadn't been until the queen showed her the way into the secret tower that Juniper suspected something else. Indeed, as Juniper pulled aside the heavy fabric of the tapestry, the shadows went farther in—a secret passage.

Normally, Juniper would have spent days or weeks planning a route into and out of a heist, including contingency plans in case of unfortunate situations. For high-security or important heists, Maddox would have double-checked her plans, routes, and research. This time she had only herself, but as Maddox had boasted and as Juniper had proven time and time again, she was the best the Undercity had. No castle or palace or prison could keep her in.

But that underlying sense of doubt remained, as it always did. There were many things that could go wrong. Unforeseen obstacles. Hidden guards. A nosy servant in the middle of the night.

Juniper lifted the hem of her robes and ducked into the passage. She couldn't have dressed in her traveling clothes without looking suspicious, so she wore a set of indigo robes. They were impractical, but she hadn't anything else to wear. The tapestry swished behind her, shutting her in darkness.

It took a heartbeat, but her eyes adjusted.

She crept down the dark chamber, turned left at an intersection, and to the heavy iron door she had found earlier in her exploration of the passages. Water gushed and dripped on the other side, and she could feel it—the water's power and movement.

The door led into an aqueduct room. A pale magelight glittered near the ceiling. Water fed into the room through two main channels on either side, and that channel fed a series of smaller channels that fed the stone pipes in each guest room. A wide grate on the floor caught the excess. Juniper had felt the extent of the aqueducts during one of her long baths—on a whim, she had cast her magic along the water and found this marvelous room. That it was also connected to the secret passages had been a bonus.

She knelt beside the grate. The excess water dripped onto stone far below. Juniper lifted the grate with her magic and sent a tendril to the bottom. It wasn't far.

"What's this?" came a disgruntled male voice.

Juniper's heart skipped a beat. She spun. A guard stepped around a large tank. He stood mostly in shadow, but it did not hide his scowl.

"You are not supposed to be here," he said. "This area is strictly—"

Panic surged, and ice encased the guard. She did not kill him. She dissolved the ice and lowered the guard's unconscious body to the floor.

It would seem that being a princess didn't allow her to wander through the dark passages of the palace, at least without an escort.

She spat a silent curse. This guard would alert the other guards, cutting her escape time down considerably. She could kill him, but that would make it much worse.

Juniper jumped through the dark hole. Her feet landed on wet, angled stone. Tendrils of magic carefully set the grate back into its place. A heartbeat, and her eyes adjusted to the dark, dank passage. The stone walls were magically crafted and seamless. A slick channel in the middle of the floor angled downward into darkness, guiding the excess water along.

She started along the channel. At least she wasn't hunting demons this time.

The channel merged with other channels, the flow increased, and by the time she reached the center of the channels, she waded ankle-deep in cold water. The center was a square room with four channels flowing into it. The water vanished down a drain in the center of the room.

She heaved a sigh that echoed. Of course it went down. No escape tunnel ever went up.

Juniper used her magic to lift the grate. She felt the water flowing on the other side; it was much deeper than her ankles.

Her planned route suddenly seemed terrible.

But she either had to jump in and find out where it led, or head back to the lounge and find another way.

Juniper felt along the water. It wasn't moving fast enough to sweep her away. It steadily angled down, further and further. She felt the stone walls on either side, ushering it along. Finally, at the end of her sight, the water tumbled freely.

It led out. Where it led to, she couldn't tell.

She jumped. Cool water rushed up to meet her, rising to her chin. She grappled with her footing but steadied herself.

She walked with the water, down the dark tunnel. The cool water soaked her to the bone and splashed with her movements, and it didn't take long for it to soak her hair. The cool water against her scalp sent a shiver down her spine. Juniper cast her magic through the water around her. She would be able to detect anything within it—no dark, amphibious monster would sneak up on her.

The tunnel opened into a dark room. A grate on the far side let the water flow out and down the cliffside—she had reached the far southern edge of the palace. Juniper climbed out of the channel and onto an angled platform. A set of stone stairs spiraled up and out of sight.

Juniper whisked the water out of her clothes and hair. She shuddered as the cold water left her person. Dry, she started up the spiraling stairs. They seemed to go on forever, until at last, she reached a chamber. Plain wooden doors on the far side of the room likely led out, but she hesitated; a figure lounged against the wall beside the door, nearly hidden in shadows.

"I figured you'd go this way," said Crespin, his voice dry and bored. "Isolde."

"Oh, you did?" Juniper challenged.

Crespin pushed off the wall. The ambient magelight warmed half his face. He set his unamused gaze on Juniper. "Because you're a water mage, and what better way to sneak out than through water? You're going into the Wylds, aren't you?"

"Are you going to tattle?"

Crespin shrugged. "Probably not until Myrisha finds out. She'll tell the council; they always liked her more than me."

"I can see why," Juniper mumbled.

Crespin scoffed. "Because she follows the rules, and I would be doing exactly what you're doing had they denied me."

Juniper blinked. "You'd crawl through a waterlogged tunnel?"

"I would take it upon myself to do what I thought was right," Crespin elaborated. He crossed his arms and stepped aside, giving her a path to the door. "If Delmont is right, and you are the one the prophecy spoke about, then we're fools for locking you up."

"You'd be fools even if I wasn't," she added.

Crespin's straight-line mouth twitched into a grin. "Get out of here before I change my mind, cousin."

The door led into the yard between the palace and the wall. Juniper navigated between the patrolling guards on the grounds and to the western wall. Getting over the wall proved tricky, but with patience and luck, Juniper slipped through the guards and into the streets of Delphine. She followed shadowed side streets and alleys and slipped into a few wealthier establishments to retrieve necessities for the journey, including clothes, food, and first aid. She also snatched a map of Collatia she hadn't realized she might need. She snatched a horse from a busy tavern's crowded stable. She took the North Gate out of the city—getting through the gate took a small bag of coins and a tired guard.

The refugee camp reinforced her decision. Hundreds of people were living in lean-to shacks and tents, washing in rain barrels, and cooking over campfires. These people had fled Nexon's destruction, out of fear and safety. And while Nexon terrorized, the council wanted to talk about parties.

She followed the northern road out of Delphine. According to the map, it went north then curved to the east. Once, it had led from the Summer Palace to Balendin Castle. Without the castle, she didn't know where the road ended. It didn't matter. The road skirted the southern edge of the Wylds, and that is where she would go.

She rode steadily through the night, and as the sun broke over the eastern horizon, the unease in Juniper's stomach had softened. She crested a hill and glanced back at the city of Delphine, a spec on the horizon.

A voice whispered, *It could still be yours.*

It could. She could be queen. But she didn't want to be queen. She didn't want to be in charge of a kingdom. She could barely keep up with herself.

She guided her horse north. She didn't know how far she would have to travel. She had minimal supplies, but she would make do.

She had her magic, and she could find food and make shelter. She would handle the Archmage of Air, then Nexon, and then she would think about playing princess for a while—when the fate of the realm did not rest on her shoulders.

CHAPTER 19

Juniper rode through the night and into the next day. She kept one eye ahead of her and the other behind. Her flight from the palace would have been discovered by now, and she didn't want to think about the panic she'd caused. Reid would be furious.

She stopped by a stream to let the horse rest and eat. She caught fish and cooked them over a fire. Her sleepless night had caught up to her, and exhaustion and irritation tugged at her thoughts. Yet—the clear skies, the warm breeze, and the crackling fire relaxed her.

This felt right. This is what she wanted—to do something. She knew in her gut she had done the right thing, yet it stung in her heart. She had hurt people in the process.

The breeze picked up, jostling leaves and whispering through overgrown grasses. Juniper pretended she didn't have a realm to save or kingdom relying on her or an archmage bent on her death. For a few moments, she was a weary traveler pausing in a meadow.

But she had little time to waste on fanciful thoughts and daydreams. When she had picked the fish bones clean, she returned to the road.

Over the next few weeks, she kept a steady pace. She passed through dozens of towns and villages. She kept her hood up. She looked far too much like the queen, and it would not do to be recognized. News had spread of the siege in Rusdasin. Many took it as a bad sign. Townsfolk whispered of another war. They also whispered about Isolde.

It all unsettled Juniper.

She traveled through summer-parched forests, up and down and around small mountains, and around vast lakes of deep green and gray. As the main road curved to the west, she kept north. The villages became fewer and fewer. The forests grew unruly and overgrown. The road narrowed. The air grew imperceptibly cooler with every league. Juniper spotted plants she had never seen before, including a tree with sapphire bark and snow-colored leaves. A group of bushes had blossoms the size of her hand with pointed buttery pedals.

She didn't have the time to stop and gawk. She kept her pace steady and quick.

Every night, as she unrolled her stolen bedroll, she thought about how much better the trek would have been with Reid. She hadn't spent so much time alone since she met Reid, and to be alone again felt… She didn't like it. She missed having a presence beside her as she slept.

Every morning, her apprehension twisted anew. With every turn in the road, with every hill, she didn't know what to expect. The unknown kept her nerves knotted.

She crested a hill.

"Gods," she whispered.

She had reached the edge of the Blackwood Wylds. The forest behind her was thick with summer-parched leaves and thick brush, but the forest ahead of her bore no such color. The trees faded into shades of black and gray. The bleakness of the cursed forest stretched to the horizon, blackened trees and silence. A stark line separated the Wylds from the rest of the Blackwoods—one side grew healthy, the other grew in a nightmarish tangle of dead trees and thorny brambles.

The forest was dead. She didn't know what she expected, a scary forest filled with shadows and beady-eyed monsters.

Which, she supposed, it was.

Juniper hadn't the words. The Wylds gave her a horrible sense of apprehension, and she understood why it had become the subject of horror stories and legends. Even her magic sensed the wrongness of it, the silent warning to stay away.

It's not too late to turn back, she imagined Reid saying.

"It's too late for me," she whispered back.

She straightened her shoulders and nudged her horse forward. Might as well start in while she had daylight left to see by. She would rather not wander the Wylds in the dark.

Her horse stepped over the boundary of the Wylds. At once, she felt a shift. It was subtle, like stepping through a cloud of steam or slipping beneath the surface of a calm lake. The air pressed against her magic. The pressure was bearable, though unpleasant. It felt like a heavy blanket.

The dirt road looked the same—scarcely used and weedy, only the weeds were brown and twisted and angry. Overgrown brambles stretched over the dirt, curved thorns ready to grab and tear. Blackened vines crisscrossed over the road and around dead trees.

Juniper slowed her pace in the Wylds. She didn't want to injure her horse or herself, and she didn't know exactly what she was looking for. Where would the Archmage of Air have gone? The Wylds seemed endless. She wouldn't be able to remain in the Wylds for very long. She had limited supplies, and by the looks of the place, she wouldn't be fishing or picking berries. She wouldn't trust any food she found in this abysmal place.

She traveled deeper into the Wylds. The road narrowed. The air cooled. Trees clustered around it, shading it with their barren limbs and crooked shadows. She saw few animals—only scurrying creatures with beady, rabid eyes. She spotted a few plants that grew fruit, but the fruit was dark and shriveled. The ground was hard, pale brown and gray—the color of the land during famine. Most of the trees looked like stone, the bark sharp and spiked. Angry greenish black vines snaked around trees and through brambles, slowly bending the trunks to their will. It smelled like decay, like withered vegetation and compost, like dried and weathered wood. The few streams she saw were the color of mildew.

Cursed—it was the only word Juniper had to describe the Wylds.

As she traveled deeper, the subtle shift of the air thickened. The air was different. Heavier. It weighed on her magic. The deeper into the Wylds she rode, the heavier the weight. It pushed against it, not violently like Reid's technique, but enough that she felt it.

In the early evening, she came across an abandoned village. Only the stone remained; wooden or thatch roofs had long decayed. The street had once been cobblestone, but a layer of dirt and blackened vines and ugly tree roots had clogged the stones. Most of the stone buildings had collapsed.

She guided her horse through the village's widest street. Her head told her that she should make camp here. The daylight was fading, and she had little time to find another spot. Her gut told her to run the other way; the thought of staying in this place unnerved her. What if she woke up with blackened vines squeezing her throat? She didn't want to close her eyes for too long.

She found a stone house with four standing walls and a partial stone roof that might have once been a second floor. As good a spot as any other. She tied off the horse and quickly set up camp in the stone house. Finding dry wood was easy. She focused—she snapped a tiny flame to life on her thumb.

It took a lot of her concentration to spark a flame—to control unnatural magic when there wasn't much here. Her tiny flame died out quickly.

The smoke slithered up and around the partial roof, a thin white line trailing to the sky. She fed the fire twigs and sticks, and as the trail of smoke thickened, so did her unease. The heat radiated off the fire and fought the strange chill in the air.

A sinister caw sounded in the trees above, followed by a chaotic flapping of wings.

The twilight diminished, and the fire grew brighter—letting anything and anyone within the dark forest know a stranger had entered. The glow would be visible for leagues in the still air.

She gathered her magic and doused the fire. Cold darkness engulfed her, and she immediately felt better.

Without the crackle of the fire, she could hear the whispers and barely-there sounds of the Wylds.

She imagined Reid asking, *Are you all right?*

Her stomach quivered. A nervous ball rattled in her chest, threatening to untwine in a feverish fury at the first snapped twig in the dark or licking of jaws.

Using her night sight, she carved runes for protection and warmth into each wall. The barrier rose around her, and her unease lessened. Only slightly. She nibbled on her rations and kept her back to the south wall—the only wall without windows—and kept her eyes on the darkened village before her.

Despite her magic, the runes, and the daggers on her person, she did not feel safe in these Wylds.

Chapter 20

Juniper unrolled her bedroll on the smoothest piece of ground she could find, then pulled her legs to her chest.

She missed Reid.

Hell, she'd even take Crespin's company over this silence.

Something moved at the edge of her vision. She jerked her attention sideways, to the house across the street. A tree had grown through the house, and its branches and roots had slowly disassembled it, holding the walls at strange angles and pushing up the stone floor chunk at a time.

She didn't see anything. Her heart still pounded.

Juniper hadn't seen many animals on her trek through the Wylds, but things had been chittering and scurrying since full dark. Juniper wasn't inclined to meet any creature that called the Wylds home. Just in case, Juniper cast her magical net onto the house. She felt nothing alive, nothing moving. Twisted vines, old stone, and knobby tree roots slowly uprooted the entire house. Nothing lurked. Nothing stalked.

It didn't settle her unease.

She settled onto her bedroll, but she didn't fall asleep at once.

As she lay there, a fat spider the size of her hand crawled along the edge of the barrier. It hesitated, then started away.

Something stalked through the dead brush, its footsteps padding between her heartbeats. She reminded herself of the runes, of her magic.

She needed rest. Her body craved it, but her mind refused it. The wind sighed through the dead trees, and it made a menacing whisper. She would rather ponder the idea of all the horrible monsters lurking in the Wylds' lost villages from the safety of the summer palace. She had read plenty of fantastical stories to dream up a few monsters of her own.

As she fell asleep, her imagination dreamed up a creature of stony-steel scales, a snout wide enough to swallow a human whole, curved horns for ramming and tearing, and four eyes like fire. It snapped its three rows of yellowed teeth at her. Juniper ran through the Wylds to get away, the beast gained on her. It jumped— she felt its talons rip into her skin.

She woke with a violent start, and at once reached for the brown eyed man at her side.

And found the space beside her empty.

Her panic escaped her throat in something like a sob.

The longing for him widened into an endless abyss. She brought her hands up to her eyes. Her heart beat too fast, her breath came in gasps. She willed her heart to slow, then lowered her arm. She glanced around the Wylds, yet nothing looked at her from the darkness. Nothing had crossed the barrier.

When had she become so dependent on Reid?

She reclined onto her bedroll and comforted herself with the fantasy of slaying the monster from her dream. It hadn't stood a chance against her. She would hang its horns above the hearth in her new house, the one she and Reid would share.

Juniper struck camp before dawn. She had slept terribly. Things scurried just out of sight, snapping her away from the blurry edge of sleep. She had barely slept at all, and she felt the lack of rest pulling on her limbs. The horse seemed much better rested, and he eagerly continued their journey north.

The deeper she rode into the Wylds, the stranger the sounds and darker the shadows. The brambles grew in tangles taller than the horse. The trees grew as tall as the singing tree at the summer palace and just as wide, their roots thicker than homes. In several places, she had to forego the road in favor of smoother terrain around tree roots. They passed up and down gentle hills, through crags and cracks in the stony ground, around sharp bluffs and steep cliffs, all deadened and gray.

The odd pressure on her magic continued. More than once, she summoned a handful of flurries just to make sure she still could.

She tugged the horse to a halt just after midday. Gods, she was exhausted. She set up a quick camp in a grove, and she passed out before her head hit the bedroll.

She woke to a horse's fearful whine. Juniper cracked her eyes open. The sky burned with the silvery shades of late twilight.

A terrible roar echoed through the Wylds.

Panic surged through her bones, and she jumped to her feet. She saw immediately what had scared the horse. A monstrous beast ambled toward them. Once, it might have been a bear. Matted brown fur covered the beast. Its massive jaw split and pointed teeth snapped at Juniper.

Juniper let out a roar of her own and sent a wall of ice crashing into the beast. It flung backward. Before the beast could rise, she sharpened the ice into twin blades. One blade pierced the cursed bear through the throat; another struck the chest. It tumbled backward, paws scratching at empty air.

She took a breath, then her heart skipped a beat.

A grayish fog rose from her ice, slithering out of her control. It was the same subtle shift that smothered her magic. It was a leeching, a strong wind whisking her magic out of her hands. The grayish fog thickened and churned, turning darker as it curled toward the ground.

And before her eyes, the darkness within birthed into a cursed bear. It rolled onto the ground, eyes yellow and bloodshot, brown fur matted and patchy, its jaw too wide, and its teeth too sharp. Its beady eye settled on Juniper at once.

That monster had come from her magic. She felt a sliver of it within the bear, but it did not listen to her.

The beast let out a fearsome growl. Juniper hesitated. If she used her magic, she would only create another.

She pulled her steel dagger from her waist.

The bear swatted and she dodged. She struck it—but it also struck her. As her steel bit into its thick hide, its claw sliced through her side.

Unnatural pain seared across her side—she screamed.

The world shifted, and the ground rushed up to meet her. Rocks smacked against her hip and shoulder. Her raw, torn flesh burned, and her stomach churned at the feeling of blood flooding from her body. She rolled onto her back. The bear lurched over her, as if it knew it had won.

It padded closer and stood on its hind legs. It sneered down at her with mad eyes.

Her heart pounded, faster and faster, like rushing footsteps. The world darkened at the edge, pulsing with her breath.

A horse screeched. The bear roared.

A silver tinted shadow rose in front of her, and the bear's talons met steel. A masculine roar, a slice, and the bear thumped on the ground.

She blinked.

The bear was dead.

Her stomach threatened to send her meager rations back up. She closed her eyes. The air felt too silent, too still, as if the Wylds were watching. Waiting.

Her heart thudded too loud.

A huff—someone else was breathing. She opened her eyes in time to see the monstrous bear crumble into a dense mist of inky blacks and sickly greens. The mist settled on the ground and sank into the dead soil. The silver tinted shadow stood between her and the bear. The dim twilight glinted off his silver armor.

Reid sheathed his Mage's Bane and turned his unreadable mask to her.

She could barely choke out his name.

In that moment, she didn't care about whatever lecture he had planned or how many things she had done wrong. She only cared that he was there.

"Gods, Juniper," Reid said breathlessly. He knelt at her side and placed a hand against her stomach, eyeing the wound. "It's not deep, but…it doesn't look good."

"I've got…bandages," she managed to say.

Reid rummaged through her supplies and returned to her side with ointment and bandages. He pulled the tattered fabric away from her skin and used his dagger to remove the ruined tunic from her person. He spread a stinging ointment over the wound and wrapped her middle. His warm, calloused fingers grazed her skin only as much as he needed to.

Pain radiated from the wound, even with the ointment, as if the edges were burning. Chills began in her arms, and soon her entire body shook.

Reid helped her to her feet, then pulled a clean shirt over her head, then a heavy cloak over her shoulders.

"You're here," she managed to say.

He didn't say anything. His gaze remained unreadable.

Reid helped her onto her horse. Night was quickly overtaking the Wylds, and she saw only muddied shadows. She latched onto the saddle and focused entirely on remaining upright as Reid hoisted himself behind her. His arms came around her and grabbed the reins.

"I rushed through the Wylds. Barely stopped to rest. Then I heard a scream," came Reid's familiar voice in her ear. His warm breath greeted her scalp. Despite the pain in her side, an effervescent joy pulsed deep inside her chest. "I have a small camp in a grove nearby."

Reid took Juniper to his camp, no more than a bedroll and campfire. His horse, a lovely chestnut, was tied to a tangle of roots. Its black eyes took them in as they approached. Reid helped her off the horse and to the fire. He unrolled her bedroll next to his own.

"I'm sorry," she whispered.

He tilted her chin up. His eyes remained unreadable. "You need rest. We'll talk in the morning."

She hadn't the strength to argue. She reclined—pain shot through her side— and a painful sleep took her almost immediately. She fell asleep with Reid in her view. He sat on his bedroll, staring into the fire.

CHAPTER 21

Morning came with an overcast sky and unnatural chill. Juniper took a breath—and pain seized her entire body. A gasp escaped her lips, and the day before came rushing back.

Reid appeared in her view. Despite the pain and his unreadable expression, she felt joy.

"Can you stand?" he asked.

She struggled, and he helped her to her feet. He uncorked a canteen and handed it to her. She took a long drink while he added a handful of twigs and kindling to the embers of their campfire. Reid ate from his rations. She didn't feel remotely hungry, and her rations remained in her satchel.

"Lucky you arrived when you did," Juniper said lightly, her voice scratchy. "I would be in worse shape."

"You'd likely be in the stomach of that bear," Reid said flatly, eyes on his dried meat. "Or whatever the hell that thing was."

"Cursed," Juniper whispered.

"You should be fine. Just don't move any more than necessary for a while. Until it heals." His tone held plenty of accusation.

She couldn't blame him. She had done it to herself. Guilt and shame settled on her bones, masked partially by the pain and oppressive air.

"Myrisha was upset," Reid whispered.

Her guilt tugged a little harder. "I suspected she would be."

"Yet you left anyway."

"Because I don't take orders," Juniper said in a single breath. Her next breath hitched, as did the breath after. Breathlessly, she added, "I don't have time to play politics."

Reid's gaze bore into hers. Underneath his mask, anger burned. "What was your plan? Run into the Wylds and search blindly and hope a dire wolf shows you the way?"

That stung, and she didn't bother to hide it. "What would you have done otherwise?" she spat. "Unless the council has hidden maps of the Wylds no one knows about."

"They know more about this place than we do," Reid argued.

"Yet they refused to share any of that information."

He seethed. He huffed, and his next breath lacked the worst of his anger. "And now you're injured, and we're leagues into the Wylds."

She felt his anger, felt it in every word. She knew she deserved that anger, but it still irritated her. She wanted to argue how stupid his lack of a plan was to her somewhat plan, but the pain in her side and the grimness of the Wylds reminded her that he was right. She just didn't want to admit it.

"Your recklessness nearly got you killed," Reid said, sounding just like his uncle. "Depending, it still might."

She wanted to prove him wrong, but she felt something worming through her blood. Something foreign, something dangerous and dark.

"One more day," she said. "We ride further in, one more day. If we don't find anything, we turn around."

Reid frowned—he wanted to argue.

"One more day," Reid said. "We have enough supplies for that long."

Reid struck camp and readied the horses. Juniper did little. She didn't want to agitate the wound, and any time she moved, Reid's eyes would flash to her, reprimand at the ready.

They continued north. Juniper, determined to prove she didn't feel as bad as she really did, rode her horse. As they rode, Juniper told him about how the second bear had materialized out of her magic, and the odd pressure she felt. Reid's scowl deepened, and he wore the same look as when he disapproved of magic. It was a mixture of appalled, disgusted, and afraid.

"Have you ever heard of that happening?" she asked. Being a knight, Reid had learned all about magic—especially the dark variety—in his studies.

He shook his head. "There is something wrong in these woods. That much is certain. There is magic in the air, but it is…dark and twisted."

"Cursed," Juniper added.

Reid nodded.

They rode for a while in silence. Juniper hated it, but she rode slower. Her side hurt, and the pain hadn't eased. . It wasn't healing like it should. Her magic wasn't stitching her body back together. The curse of the Wylds must have interrupted her magic. Every bump and jostle felt like her skin was ripping further, a little deeper. The odd feeling of invasion slithered further and further.

The road wound to the north, then to the east, and then to the north. By the time the sun tilted for its downward descent, she no longer cared about the Wylds or the archmage or the realm. Pain sucked every thought. She rode behind Reid, but she refused to bother him with it. She would rest when they camped.

And…they hadn't seen anything. She heard plenty. Scurrying. Skittering. Rumbling. Whispering. But no sign of life.

Darkness ebbed at the edges of her vision. She focused on Reid's silver armor. He guided his horse up a narrow incline lined with knotted roots. Juniper followed. The sun broke through the overcast, glinting off his armor. With every clop, her side ripped. She squeezed her eyes shut, trying to block out the pain.

"Look at that!" Reid said.

She opened her eyes. Reid had stopped at the crest of the hill. Her horse paused beside his.

Green.

She blinked in disbelief, sure the pain was causing hallucinations.

The green remained. A splotch of green grew in the middle of the cursed Wylds. Green stretched out before them, tucked within a timber wall. Chimney smoke puffed from the stone and timber buildings within.

"A village?" Reid asked.

"I don't trust it," Juniper breathed.

Reid glanced at her. His frown deepened. "You need a healer, Jun. We don't have a choice."

"Who or what would live in this nightmare?" Jun asked, hating how pitiful she sounded.

"It doesn't matter," Reid said. "Come on."

They started toward the village at a careful walk. With every step, the darkness encroached on her awareness. Juniper focused on not emptying her stomach on her horse.

The outer wall of the village was made of a mixture of healthy and blackened timber, kept together with a brownish paste that had dried into stone. Battlements circled the top of the wall, manned by patrolling guards. As they approached the gates, the decaying scents of the Wylds mixed with the smells of freshly turned soil, fruit trees, and blooming flowers—and something earthy Juniper didn't recognize.

As the path neared the gates, it widened. The trees and brambles had been cleared a good distance away from the wall, making it harder for anything to approach unnoticed—including Juniper and Reid. Sentries gathered on the battlements above the closed gates. Each wore patched leather armor spotted with iron plates. Each held a spear and stood tall and lean.

"Halt," said the sentry in the middle. He held out his free hand. He looked a shade green, or maybe it was the angle of the sunlight.

Juniper and Reid halted.

"State your business, stranger," said the sentry. A strange accent tilted his words.

The two flanking sentries looked young, maybe fifteen or sixteen. Each stood stone still and gazed down at their visitors like the worst sort of monsters.

"We travel from Delphine," said Reid in a commanding voice, regal and knightly. "We are ambassadors of Her Majesty, Queen Myrisha Balendin. Please, my friend needs a healer. We were attacked."

Another sentry appeared on the battlement, older than the others. He had the same sickly green look about him. Words passed between them, too low to hear from the ground, and then the older sentry approached the edge of the battlement.

"You may enter," bellowed the sentry, his voice deep and strong. "Do not draw your weapons, or you will not make it through the gate."

Juniper blinked. Her eyelids didn't want to open again.

"Jun," Reid breathed.

She forced her eyes open.

The thick wooden gate began to open with the heavy *clunk, clunk, clunk* of old gears. Voices came from the other side, too far to hear. Reid took the reins from her hands, and the horse followed him through the gates.

Juniper fought for each breath. The gates began to close behind them—*clunk, clunk, clunk*. As the darkness submerged, Juniper saw a thousand shades of green. Then only darkness.

CHAPTER 22

Juniper felt a steady warmth. It soaked into her skin, her bones. With each breath, awareness settled. She was laying on something soft. The heat came from a crackling fire. The flames flickered on the other side of her eyelids. It smelled like fresh, rich earth and rosemary.

She heard muffled voices.

She opened her eyes. She was in a narrow wooden-walled room.

The ceiling arched, and a bundle of green herbs hung from the central beam. An iron lantern held three lumpy candles of varying sizes and shades of white. A small hearth of brown stone burned in the corner. The room had a single window at the far end. Pale sunlight slipped between the uneven slats of the shutters.

She was lying on a bed of mismatched furs and faded wool blankets. She pushed herself into a sitting position. A pain struck through her side, and she fell back onto the cot.

At the thump, the voices silenced.

Footsteps sounded, then a curtain swished. A shrunken old woman entered the room. Her brownish-green skin looked like tree bark. Pointed ears poked through her loosely braided white hair. Her bright gold eyes darted over Juniper with clinical disinterest.

"Ah, the sick one is awake." The old woman's voice grated like a crow's caw. She loomed over Juniper's bedside. With her came the sweet scent of tobacco. "You're lucky that boy of yours got you here in time. Another day, and you would have been too far gone to save."

Juniper blinked. She vaguely remembered the village. A splotch of green in the middle of the dead Wylds.

"How are you feeling?" the old woman demanded.

"Where am I?" Juniper asked.

"Oh, it's worse than I thought."

Juniper didn't laugh.

The old woman's slight smile curved into a frown. "You're in Sinjon, girl. You arrived yesterday evening. You fell unconscious soon after arriving. I am Enna, and my granddaughter and I have nursed you away from death's claws."

"Reid—"

"Your friend is fine," Enna said. "He is resting in the next room."

Juniper had never heard of Sinjon. She pushed herself into a sitting position. This time, she was ready for the pain and pushed through it. She wore nothing but stiff, fresh bandages around her middle. Her wounded side tingled.

Her boots and her satchel rested on the floor by the wall. She spotted the hilt of her dagger sticking out of one of her boots.

The odd pressure on her magic was gone. Still, her body felt weak and wobbly like she had slept too long.

A second pair of footsteps sounded, softer than the old woman's. A tall, lean girl with skin the color of summer leaves and bright gold eyes entered the room. She carried a wooden tray with a small earthen teapot and a single cup. Like the old woman, she had sharp pointed ears. Two dark braids hung over her shoulders. A hemp necklace coiled around her neck, on which hung a yellow gemstone.

The granddaughter.

The girl set the tray on the table beside Juniper's cot. She poured a cup. The tea was pale and smelled like grass.

"Ah, thank you Lilianna," said Enna.

"The man is awake as well," said the girl in a somber voice.

"Go tell Jarek. He'll want to see them."

Lilianna nodded and left. She moved with strange grace.

The man—it took Juniper a moment to realize she meant Reid.

Enna poured a cup of tea and handed it to Juniper. "Drink the whole thing."

Juniper did not drink it.

"The Wylds are a dangerous place," said the old woman. "You are lucky to have survived as long as you did. The creatures out there are cursed, and that curse spreads. Now drink the tea. It gets the medicine in you faster than creams or ointments."

Juniper felt the water in the tea; she didn't feel anything that shouldn't be drunk. She sipped it. It tasted like grass too. Under Enna's watchful stare, Juniper forced the tea down.

Green skin. Pointed ears. The girl and her grandmother were druids. Juniper hadn't paid much attention when Maddox taught her about druid culture and history. Druids were older than the Iluvin, and notoriously reclusive. What little she knew about druids came from books, and she had lumped them together with dragons and dire wolves—ancient and gone. Druid clans once dotted the thick forests of the realm and had a strong affinity for the earth. That is likely how they were able to survive in the Wylds.

Tea gone, Enna gave her a scratchy tunic and woolen dress a few sizes too large. Juniper did not complain. It was better than wandering the village naked. Juniper dressed, then Enna led her through the curtain and into a hallway lined with similar curtains. At the end, a door led into a hearth room filled with hanging herbs, old rugs and furs, woolen blankets, and wooden furniture. Everything looked old and well-used. It was…cozy.

Reid sat by the hearth. At the sight of Juniper, he stood. Rather than his armor, he wore mismatched woolen garments similar to her own. He looked better rested than the last time she'd seen him. Juniper sat on the fur-draped bench beside him. The hearth warmed her face and stole the chill from her skin.

"How are you feeling?"

"Better," she said.

Enna set a large tea kettle over the hearth and filled it with water from an earthen jug.

"It'll be a while until the curse is out of your system," Enna said casually. "A few days, maybe a few weeks. It depends on your body. We tend to recover fairly quickly, but I don't know about outsiders."

Enna made them both a cup of tea, just as bitter and grassy as the one before. She lingered in the room, tending to the herbs that hung from the ceiling and grew in pots scattered around.

Halfway through the tea, a door opened—the one in the hall. Heavy footsteps sounded across the wooden floor. A hulking man appeared in the doorway. He wore a heavy, tattered cloak. He had dark brown hair braided behind his head and skin the color of leaves about to turn for the fall. His ears were slightly pointed. His bright gold eyes took in the two of them.

"You must be the visitors from Delphine," he said in a thick voice. He sat in a wooden chair. It gave a vicious squeak under his weight. "Sent by our queen."

Juniper bristled at his dismissive tone on *our queen.*

"Chief Jarek Hamish," he said, patting his chest. "Welcome to Sinjon, though I'm not sure how much welcome there is to be had. I won't lie to you, I am surprised you made it to the gates. We haven't had visitors for decades. Some of our children have never seen strangers. The forest is not kind."

"It was not the friendliest," Juniper admitted.

"That is an understatement," Jarek said. "The woods beyond Sinjon are cursed. Tainted with magic."

Juniper curled her fingers toward her palm. Jarek spat *magic* with enough hate and distrust to rival most knights.

"Now, tell me, who are you and why are you here?"

Reid sat a little straighter, and before Juniper could speak, he said, "I am Sir Reid Sandpiper, and this is Juniper Thimble. We are ambassadors sent by Her Royal Majesty, Queen Myrisha Balendin."

Juniper caught the slight alteration in Reid's tone—he was lying. Myrisha had not sent her, and she had not sent him.

"Ambassadors?" Jarek asked, his tone suspicious. "Why would our queen send ambassadors now? We haven't had contact with anyone from the royal family for fifty years. I can only assume the Wylds have gotten to anyone foolish enough to enter."

Juniper swallowed a gulp of tea with difficulty.

"Civil war tore the kingdom apart. It ended nineteen years ago," Reid said. "The royal family has relocated to Delphine in the south and are still putting the pieces back together."

Jarek hummed a note of disinterest.

"Her Majesty has lost scouts to the Wylds," Reid said, his tone curt yet underlined with knightly authority. "It worries her."

"Few last in these woods," Jarek said. "There are monsters out there, tainted by magic. Just like the bears you encountered. They are twisted versions of the creatures they once were."

Juniper looked into the dregs of her tea. Cursed was the only word to describe those monsters. Enna said that curse was in Juniper, that it would take time to flush out. If left untreated, would she have turned into a nightmarish version of herself?

"The curse is what kills the forest," Jarek said grimly. He motioned to Juniper. "Had you not arrived in time, the curse would have stolen your mind."

"And I thank you," Juniper said. "I would much rather keep my mind the way it is."

Jarek did not smile. Enna, however, glanced over her shoulder with a slight curve on her wrinkled lips.

"But be lucky it was just a bear," Jarek said. "There is far worse out there."

"Worse?" Juniper managed to ask.

Jarek's expression darkened. "We call them Shadows. They appeared centuries ago and have been scaring our hunters and scurrying through the dark since. They have…increased in these past few years. They are the reason few can journey through the Wylds. The forest is treacherous even for our seasoned hunters. The Shadows lurk in the darkest parts of the Wylds, and mostly leave us be. We have survived long enough while our queen has abandoned us."

Jarek's dismissal of Myrisha irked Juniper. She snapped, "I can guarantee our queen doesn't know the extent of your troubles."

Jarek's gaze bore down on her, but Juniper had never been the one to back down from a glare.

She continued, "She has an inkling that something is wrong. The few scouts who managed to make it back bring scattered stories. No one knows there is a village out here. No one has been able to get close enough."

Jarek huffed, or it might have been a laugh. "Between the curse, beasts, Shadows, and witches, few can survive. Only the foolish attempt the Wylds unprepared."

"Witches?" Juniper repeated.

Jarek stiffened, and Enna glanced from the hearth to Juniper. Her golden eyes were shadowed.

Juniper had the sense she had said something wrong.

"Yes," Jarek said. His tone was grim. "They are not like us. Not anymore. The curse has turned them into monsters, mad with darkness. They created the Shadows, and now command them like foot soldiers. They were once druids, like us, but have lost their humanity and see only destruction."

"If those witches are the problem," Juniper started, "why not hunt them down and put an end to them?"

"We have tried." Jarek's heavy hands curled into fists. "They have powerful dark magic on their side, while we have a band of sentries and hunters with dulled swords and patched armor. We do what we can to maintain life here."

"Maybe Reid and I could dispatch this threat for you," Juniper said.

"No," Jarek barked. "We do not antagonize the Shadows or the witches. Even if you could find them, you would not survive the encounter. I have seen what magic can do. It tears through the body and mind as easily as the wind through the trees. They leave us alone, and we leave them alone. As chief, I forbid either of you from seeking the witches. While you are here, you are guests. You will respect our laws."

Juniper held Jarek's warning glare.

"We understand." Reid looked pointedly at Juniper.

She understood, but she did not agree.

Jarek leaned back—his chair gave a fitful squeal of protest—and rubbed his temples. "Forgive me," he said, his voice softer. "These past few years have been especially trying. Less game, longer winters, shorter summers." He heaved a sigh. "Tell me, ambassadors, how have you survived the Wylds, yet scouts could not?"

"We are no scouts," Reid said.

"Reid is a knight of the Order," Juniper explained. "Trained to combat magic. He is also among the finest swordsmen in Duvane and Collatia."

Reid wore his mask well; she couldn't read his face. She suspected it would take many more compliments before he forgave her.

"And you?" Jarek looked her up and down. "You don't look like a soldier."

"I'm not," Juniper admitted. "I…have a different set of skills best suited for questionable situations."

Jarek frowned. "You're a mercenary?"

"I used to be a thief, but now I work for the crown," Juniper lied, the words slipping off her tongue as smooth as any truth. "Queen Myrisha is most understanding and forgiving."

Jarek hummed a disapproving note at Juniper. "I expect you to keep your head on straight while you are here."

"Of course, Chief." Juniper laid her hand over her heart. "I am here on my queen's orders. I would never think of defying her."

Reid's fist curled into a fist, then relaxed. Juniper did not look to see the disapproval on his face. She knew her lies would stir his agitation, but right now, they needed Jarek to like them. They needed Sinjon's supplies and shelter.

Jarek eyed them for a moment longer, then stood. "Very well. You will need housing while you are here. I have a spare room in my house, and you are welcome to it, Reid."

Reid glanced at Juniper. "I would prefer if we stayed together," he said to Jarek.

"You'll be staying here with me, girl." Enna refilled Juniper's tea. "You need to heal before you do anything else."

"Enna is the best healer we have," Jarek said proudly. "You will be in good hands."

Reid looked like he wanted to argue. Juniper felt the inkling to—she didn't want to be separated in this odd druid village. Yet, she knew that as soon as they had a moment alone, the lecture would start.

She wouldn't mind putting that off for a while longer.

"Thank you, Enna," Juniper said. "That is gracious of you."

Enna snorted a laugh.

"Now, the midday meal isn't for a while, and you are both welcome at my table," Jarek said. "My wife is a fine cook, and you both could use a warm meal." Jarek stood. The chair gave a squeak of relief. "Before that, I would be honored to give you a tour of our village. Juniper, do you feel well enough?"

"Yes," she said at once.

Enna frowned, looking at the tea.

Juniper drank the rest in a few gulps, then handed the empty earthen cup back to Enna. She stood, albeit ungracefully.

Jarek led them through the narrow hall and to the main door of the healer's hut, as he called it. Juniper kept her eyes averted from Reid. She knew what he would say once Jarek couldn't hear, that she had defied Myrisha's orders by going into the Wylds, that her net of lies would strangle her sooner or later, and surely something about Jarek's distrust of magic. But she pushed those thoughts aside. They had made it into the Wylds and found a promising start. She considered it a small victory.

CHAPTER 23

Jarek guided Reid and Juniper out of the healer's hut and into the morning sunlight. Juniper shielded her eyes—it took a moment to adjust. Sinjon was an oasis. Green, vibrant life thrived between the walls. Bugs and birds chirped and chittered. Even though summer neared its end, the trees bore succulent fruits and bright green leaves.

Enna's hut sat within a thick garden of herbs, flowers, and bushes. The air was drenched with the heavy scents of herbs and fresh soil. Morning glory twisted up the north wall of her house, making it look as if the stones were held together with vines. Roses in red and yellow climbed over the wooden fence. Smoke puffed out the chimney. On the other side of her garden, sheep meandered through a shady paddock.

As wonderful as this oasis seemed, it made her skin prickle. It seemed too good to be true.

Jarek started through the village with Reid and Juniper a step behind. The dirt streets had long since been stomped into a hard matte. The main streets had paving stones, but most were dirt and patched with grass. The village was made of stone and timber, held together with brown mortar and thick vines. The gentle hum filled the air, voices and footsteps and the thrum of life. They passed through farms that grew wheat, grapes, and things Juniper didn't recognize; she heard the bleating of sheep and goats, the mooing of cows, and the snorting of pigs. Smoke puffed from a smithy, where a broad-shouldered man with pointed ears hammered white-hot metal against an anvil. They passed an apothecary with hundreds of vials and bottles and pouches, a candle maker, a butcher, and a shop full of colored yarn. The air smelled like soil and herbs and livestock and woodsmoke.

Most of the druids had a green tint to their skin, varying from pale olive and grayish sage to rich emerald and deep pine. They were mostly tall and slim, though some were broad, like Jarek. Those with greener skin and pointier ears were taller and slender, while those less green in their skin and rounder ears tended to be wider. Most looked at Juniper and Reid as if they had never seen someone without green skin and pointed ears. According to Jarek, some of the younger druids hadn't. As the chief guided them along, eyes of gold and amber followed them with uncertainty and childlike wonder.

Jarek led them to a large structure built into the side of a cliff face. Four carved pillars flanked the entrance, and wide steps led to a set of wooden doors twice as tall as Jarek. The floral carvings on the pillars looked suspiciously like runes, but unlike any runes Juniper had ever seen. They were curvy and nonsensical, yet elegant. Three mossy bridges led to the structure; they arched over a clear river. Juniper gawked; the water was pristine. Fish fluttered about underneath.

The doors opened to a large chamber. Thick stone pillars held up the ceiling, each carved with a different pattern of flowers and trees. Torches hung in iron brackets, shadowing the chamber in reds and oranges.

A few druid women were scrubbing the floor with what smelled like fresh soil and mint leaves. At the opening of the doors, their quiet conversation died. Their curious gazes washed over Juniper and Reid.

"This is the Great Hall," Jarek said. "It is the oldest building in the village. It has withstood centuries of storms, hosted weddings, funerals, celebrations, and feasts."

Juniper eyed the strange runes again. Reid did the same. He likely thought the same—magic helped keep this place standing.

Jarek led them to the northern side of the village, to a house set on a hill. It was set apart from the other houses, and from its front step, most of the village lay in view. Like the other buildings, much of the home was made of timber. The roof arched and curved, like an upside down boat. Moss and healthy vines grew along the sides and the roof, spotting it with pale blue blossoms.

"This is my house," Jarek said.

He led them through the wide front door and into a cozy hearth room. An iron cooking pot bubbled over the fire. A well-used table and chairs set to the side, beat-up pots and pans hung from the ceiling, earthenware bowls, plates, and cups lined wooden shelves. Spices were drying on a rack, and a few fresh herbs grew on the windowsill.

"Ingrid?" Jarek called to the empty hearth room. He hung his cloak beside the front door.

As Jarek closed the front door, the back door opened. A slender woman with dark brown hair and sage skin walked inside. She set a basket of herbs on the table. She blinked once at the strangers, and then her face smoothed into a motherly grin.

"Who's this?" she asked.

"This is Sir Reid Sandpiper and Juniper Thimble of Delphine," Jarek said. "They have traveled to Sinjon on request from Queen Myrisha Balendin. It would appear our queen has not abandoned us."

"That is wonderful news," said the woman, though she wore the same cautious curiosity as the rest of the village.

"This is my wife, Ingrid," Jarek said to Juniper and Reid. He set his hand on Ingrid's shoulder.

"It is a pleasure to meet you." Juniper nodded.

"A pleasure, ma'am," Reid said.

"And they have manners!" Ingrid said excitedly.

"I've invited them for a warm meal," Jarek said.

"He bragged about your cooking," Reid added.

Ingrid blushed, but a proud smile stretched across her face. She brushed chopped herbs into her boiling stew. The strange herbs added a flavor to the air that made Juniper think of bright greens and vibrant blues.

"Jarek told me about the bear that attacked you," Ingrid said to Juniper. "Terrible monsters, those bears. Even our most seasoned hunters struggled with them. I'm glad you survived. You'll be feeling sick for a while. Thankfully, Enna is the best healer in the village. And a warm meal will do wonders for the body!"

"Reid, your room is upstairs." Jarek gestured to the narrow stairs.

"I've tried my best to make it homey," Ingrid added. "It had a good layer of dust. We use it mostly for storage."

"Go on up and see it for yourself," Jarek said. "We'll set the table."

Reid started up the heavy wooden stairs, and Juniper followed. She didn't want to be alone with Jarek and Ingrid, and despite how much she didn't want to, she knew she needed a moment alone with Reid. Sooner rather than later.

The second floor was all one room, and half the size of the hearth room. The ceiling curved above their heads, making the room longer than it was wide. It smelled musty, but also like the earthy cleaner the women in the Great Hall used. It had a wood-framed bed barely big enough for two, a small washing basin with a thick coating of dust, and an old wooden trunk stuffed with blankets and cloaks and old clothing. Of course, these people had had no contact with supply lines in decades—they would have to reuse everything.

Juniper made her way to the window on the far end of the room and pushed open the shutters. Afternoon sunlight poured in, illuminating the army of dust motes she and Reid had agitated. The window overlooked the backyard where what looked like blackberry bushes grew in uneven rows. Beyond the garden, Juniper had a decent view of the village wall and the looming Wylds beyond. Sentries patrolled along the wall. The tips of their spears glinted in the sunlight.

She ran her finger along the windowsill. Dust clung to her skin. Using one of the few useful things she had learned in the Marca, she whisked the dust outside.

"Juniper," Reid spat, low and husky.

"What? It was clogging my lungs. I've just saved Ingrid hours of cleaning."

Reid's unreadable mask became a glare. "You heard Jarek talk about magic. These people do not trust magic. And from what you told me about the bears, we should be cautious."

"I'm cautious."

Truthfully, until that moment, she had forgotten about the second bear. The one that had spawned from her own magic.

A beat passed, and Juniper fought a sliver of fear that another bear would materialize. None did.

"You shouldn't use your magic here," Reid whispered, so low she barely heard him.

She heaved a sigh. She wanted to argue, but Reid had a fair point. She did not have an equally fair counterpoint. She meandered around the room, taking in how the wood creaked and where, and visualizing where she stood in relation to the first floor. The room stood above another room—Jarek and Ingrid's room, if she had to guess—and any conversation on the second floor would likely be heard below.

And the lack of conversation on the first floor implied Jarek and Ingrid were listening to them. She didn't blame them. Jarek would be a fool not to listen when he could. He had allowed strangers into his house.

Reid hadn't started the lecture, so she assumed he had come to the same conclusion.

She sat on the bed. The mattress was hard, the blankets were cold and moth-eaten, and the pillow resembled a stone.

"Not bad," Juniper said.

"Better than sleeping outside," Reid added.

"I don't know about that," Juniper teased. "There's something humbling about the hard ground under your head, the bugs crawling on your skin, and the possibility of being rained on."

Reid didn't respond. After a heartbeat, he started his own lap of the room.

Again, the silence persisted between them.

"There's a creak on the third board from the north wall," Juniper said. "And a loud one on the board beside the bedpost."

His eyes found those boards at once. He stepped on the board by the bedpost, and it gave a loud squeak.

"What do you think?" Reid whispered, looking at the floorboard.

"I think there is something going on in the Wylds," she whispered back. "Our archmage vanished into the Wylds centuries ago. The Shadows appeared centuries ago. Nexon has been more active in the past few decades. The trouble here has increased these past few decades, more so in the past few years. It can't be a coincidence."

"I agree."

Reid meandered from the bedpost and to the dusty washing basin. He ran his finger along the edge, smudging the dust she hadn't removed.

"If the archmage went into the Wylds, we need to go in after her and find out where she went and see if she's still here," Juniper whispered.

"You heard Jarek," Reid warned. "We aren't getting anywhere without his permission."

"We aren't here to please the chief," Juniper said softly enough that even if Jarek stood with his ear to the door, he wouldn't have heard. "We are here to find the archmage and stop Nexon. Besides, when have I cared about rules?"

Reid glanced at the open window, then the closed bedroom door. His gaze went unreadable and dark. "Don't let the chief hear you say that."

"I don't plan on it."

Reid scowled. "We do this slowly. These people can be allies or enemies, and considering they are the only source of civilization for several days, we need them to be our allies. You also need to heal. Gods only know what diseases that…beast might have been carrying."

She tore her eyes away from him and fiddled with the hastily stitched seams on the pillow. She muttered, "Fine."

Reid stepped closer. Juniper pretended not to notice. She heard a subtle intake of breath—footsteps thumped up the stairs. Whatever Reid had been about to say died in his throat.

"Dinner is ready!" Ingrid called.

CHAPTER 24

Ingrid had arranged earthenware bowls on the table and was ladling stew into each as Juniper and Reid took seats. Ingrid talked the majority of the time, telling them about Sinjon. Their druid blood allowed them to grow food and keep minimal livestock alive. Without much farmland, they ate little meat. They had chicken and mutton from time to time, but ate mostly roots, vegetables, and fruit.

Reid and Juniper answered their questions about Delphine. No one from the greater kingdom had risked the Wylds in nearly a century. According to Jarek, the druids strove to stay out of any outside conflict. Neutrality was a druid tradition, as ancient as the dirt.

"How do you two know each other?" Ingrid asked, eyes darting between Juniper and Reid. "You seem like good friends. You would have to be in order to travel through the Wylds together."

Juniper's stomach clenched, though she didn't know why. She started to speak but hesitated. Reid had introduced her as his friend. She met his eyes over the table. He wore his unreadable mask.

"We have known each other for a little over a year," Reid said to Ingrid. "Juniper had recently turned a new leaf and began working for the crown. I was assigned as her guard."

Juniper felt Jarek glaring at her. She chose to ignore it. She had gotten good at both meeting glares and ignoring them.

Had it already been a year?

"We spent a lot of time together," Juniper added, looking at Reid. He met her gaze. He kept his emotions masked, like always. A subtle twitch of his brow—he was letting her make the decision. "We're now engaged."

Jarek's brows rose in surprise, and Ingrid's grin widened.

"We plan to wed once we return to the city," Reid added. She couldn't tell if it was relief or frustration that drifted over his mask.

"Oh, how lovely," Ingrid said. "And romantic!"

Jarek cleared his throat. "Still, engaged is not married. We have rules here. Girls and boys do not share a bed until they are properly wed."

"That is understandable," Reid said first, before Juniper could complain that they had already shared a room and a bed.

After dinner, Jarek invited Reid to see the sentries' barracks, and Ingrid recruited Juniper to stay behind and help with the dishes. Juniper would rather not; her entire body ached and her full stomach made her ferociously sleepy. Luckily, Ingrid did most of the washing and talking. Juniper dried and put away.

Ingrid kept the conversation light, explaining that Jarek oversaw the whole village and made rounds every day to make sure everything was going well. She was also fascinated with how Juniper and Reid had gone from thief and squire to betrothed. Juniper obliged and told Ingrid the little things she remembered most, like how Reid had made an effort to make her feel welcome, but he hadn't let her get away with anything, and how he had studied in her room while she read.

With a few dishes left, Juniper braced herself and asked about the Shadows.

Ingrid's soapy hands slipped, and the bowl she was washing fell into the sink. She paled, her kind smile fell into a straight line, and she pinned her cautious stare on Juniper.

"I'm sorry," Juniper said at once. "I—I didn't mean…"

"Shadows are not something to joke about," she whispered. She stared into the dirty water.

Juniper had seen that look before. "Have you seen one?"

"I can manage the rest on my own," Ingrid said shortly. "You're looking pale. Go on back to Enna's for some rest."

And the conversation had ended.

Juniper let herself out of the house. Ingrid's overreaction only piqued Juniper's interest. Why would she not speak of them? Were these Shadows that terrifying? Or was there something Jarek had not told them?

Rather than go straight to Enna's house, Juniper wandered toward the village market. She passed a candle shop, leatherworker, bottles of wine and tonics, soaps and oils, and anything a city might need. They did not use coin; they bartered. Sacks of grain traded for wine; hide for tea; wool for spices.

The constant buzz of voices worsened her sleepiness. They blended together in a roar.

She felt their stares, though. Gold and amber eyes watched her as she passed, and whispers about the pale girl followed her.

She returned to Enna's hut. The granddaughter, Lilianna, tended to the garden outside. She knelt beside a small bush with bright yellow leaves and milky berries. Enna's garden was a mad scene of color. There were flowers with pink stems and white pedals, a skinny tree with indigo blossoms and spiky gray leaves, and a hundred more colors assaulted Juniper's exhausted vision.

As Juniper approached, Lilianna stood.

"You look tired," Lilianna said flatly. "Grandmother has the room at the end of the hall ready for you. It's the one you woke up in."

Juniper forced her legs to carry her into the house. The bed had been made and another fur had been added. The hearth burned. Incense flavored the air with stout herbs. The bundle of herbs had been exchanged for one with pointed mauve leaves and tiny silver berries. She took off her boots and the woolen dress, then collapsed.

Juniper woke to the sound of water. She blinked her eyes open. Lilianna stood on the other side of the small room, pouring water from a wooden bucket into the washing basin. A mud colored cloth hung over the side. A log had been added to the hearth, and the little room was nauseatingly warm. Juniper sluggishly pushed off the furs.

"It's hot," Juniper whined.

"Because the water is cold," Lilianna said flatly. "It is easier to heat the room than the water."

Juniper disagreed, but she kept her thoughts to herself.

"Grandmother has asked me to check your healing." Lilianna set the bucket aside. She dried her hands on her tunic, then motioned for Juniper. "Up."

Juniper struggled to sit up. Lilianna pulled the soft tunic over Juniper's head and gently pulled the bandages away from her skin. She felt the skin pull, felt the stickiness of blood, and smelled the tang of an open wound.

"Why isn't it healing?" Juniper asked, her voice strained with pain.

"It is," Lilianna said. "The curse makes it heal slower. The medicines have helped. Otherwise, you would be dead."

Lilianna pulled mauve leaves from the bundle and pressed them against Juniper's skin. The rough texture of the leaves glued to her wound, and she winced. Lilianna didn't hesitate; she layered an amber ointment against the leaves. At once, the stinging vanished under a breath of heat.

"I've readied a bath," Lilianna said.

"A bath sounds amazing," Juniper said, her words tight and sticky.

Lilianna helped Juniper to her feet and to the washing basin. The water was freezing. Juniper glanced at Lilianna; she stood by the hearth, eyes on the fire. Juniper dared—she took the worst of the chill out of the water by magic. The curse squeezed her magic, trying to prevent it from working. No bears appeared, no monster fish. Only the subtle metallic scent laced with floral.

The druid girl stood by as Juniper washed. She had long since stopped being bashful about having someone else in the room while washing. Between traveling through the kingdoms and staying in the Marca, privacy had become a luxury.

Between the lukewarm water and the hearth, she was beginning to sweat.

"Could you open the window? It's too hot," Juniper asked.

Lilianna obliged. She opened one of the shutters, and a cool breeze rushed inside. It brushed against Juniper's magic, a touch as soothing and gentle as a lover's.

Juniper decided to test her luck a second time.

"I asked Ingrid about the Shadows," Juniper said carefully. "I think I offended her."

"Most are frightened of them," Lilianna said.

"What are they?"

A pause, a shuffle. Lilianna's gaze had drifted to the half-shuttered window.

"Shadows are born of magic and darkness. Their skin shimmers and flickers as they move," Lilianna whispered. "They lurk in the Wylds. They hate the light, so they don't come to the village very often. We burn torches through the night to keep them away. But there is not enough light in the world to illuminate the Wylds."

Juniper had stopped washing. She held the soapy cloth in one hand, the edge of the basin with the other. Lilianna's somber voice chilled her.

"And these…witches created the Shadows?" Juniper whispered back.

Lilianna nodded. "Some say they were once druids, but they have turned into something darker. More sinister. The witches appeared, and shortly after the Shadows appeared. Or so they say. It happened so long ago, no one remembers what really happened. The witches and Shadows are just…there. The witches live in the Wylds alongside their Shadows. They brew poisons and eat the bark of dead trees. Grandmother once told me that on a still autumn eve, you can hear the crunching."

Lilianna glanced at the window. Beyond the timber wall, the Wylds grew in shades of black, gray, and plum.

"If not the Shadows, then the witches killed your queen's scouts," she whispered.

It took Juniper a heartbeat to catch it—*your* queen.

Lilianna released a calming sigh. Her golden eyes scanned the Wylds. At Juniper's prolonged silence, she turned those golden eyes to her. Unreadable and unassuming.

"Sorry," Juniper said, dunking the cloth back into the water. "I enjoy stories."

"The Shadows are not just stories," Lilianna warned. "They are real."

"Reid and I want to help," Juniper said. "We can help. We have both fought dark magic. But Jarek refuses to allow us near the woods."

Uncertainty leaked into Lilianna's gaze. "Jarek is protective of his people. The Shadows are vicious and the witches are vindictive. Neither takes kindly to strangers trespassing on their grounds. They…lash out."

A moment of silence passed.

Lilianna had so far given her more information than Ingrid.

"The witches," Juniper started. "What are they?"

"Our legends tell of a stranger who appeared on a moonless, cloudless night and offered to teach our ancestors magic," Lilianna whispered. She glanced toward the closed door, as if worried one might appear. "The chief and the elders forbade it, but some of the children defied the chief and sought out the stranger themselves. But instead of teaching them magic, the stranger used the children to create the first Shadows."

Juniper took in those words, the story—*a stranger appeared in the night and offered to teach them magic.*

It couldn't be a coincidence that the Archmage of Air vanished into the Wylds centuries ago, and a witch appeared in the very same woods near the same time, with magic. If the archmage had arrived here to find a village hostile toward magic, she wouldn't have had a choice—either show them that magic was good or leave the village.

And legend suggested she was still in the Wylds.

CHAPTER 25

Jarek led Reid to the southern edge of the village, to the flat structure that served as the barracks. Beside it was a sunken circle of packed earth and sand that served as a fighting ring. Currently, two young druids in mismatched leather armor fought with dulled swords. Their steps were off, their stances clumsy, and neither understood how to shift their balance with the blade. Other young druids sat on the incline of the fighting ring while an older druid instructed.

Reid kept his face blank as he watched. He recognized one of the druids in the ring as the one who had carried Juniper to Enna's house.

"Our older hunters train the younger," Jarek explained. "It's nothing like the training you received, surely. I can't imagine what sort of training one must go through to become a knight."

"It is extensive," Reid said.

"We don't have the luxury of such training here," Jarek said. "The real test comes when they face their first cursed opponent."

"That is a hard lesson to learn," Reid said calmly. "To learn from a master is one thing, but nothing can prepare you for the first battle."

Jarek hummed a curious note.

Reid offered no more. He didn't want to give the story of his own first battle to Jarek. It felt far too personal.

The duel below ended. The winning druid wore his victory proudly and slung his dulled sword over his shoulder. He circled the loser once, then held his hand down to help him to his feet, which he accepted. Another druid jumped into the ring, and the loser joined those sitting on the grassy side. Another fight began, just as clumsily as the one before it.

"Hold your sword like that and you'll snap your wrist," barked the instructor.

"Our armor is scraps, our weaponry scarce," Jarek said.

"Armor and a sword do not make a warrior," Reid said. His uncle had said those same words to him years ago, before he had joined the Royal Guard. "They only make you look like one."

Jarek nodded his approval of those words. "Our hunters split their time between patrolling the walls, working in the village, and braving the Wylds for dwindling resources. They prepare as much as they can for the monsters lurking out there. We must be vigilant."

"Do the monsters pose a threat to the village?" Reid asked, each word careful.

"Not often," Jarek said. His gaze swept over the Wylds. "They normally keep their distance. Winter is worse. Diminished sunlight makes the beasts brave. It makes our hunts dangerous. We prepare as much as we can. Our fortitude is but a fraction of what it once was."

Reid had a suspicion of where this conversation was going. The chief had been particularly interested when Reid had introduced himself as a knight. Even in this forsaken corner of the world, the title of a knight held credence.

Still, Jarek reminded Reid of his uncle. He held the village's safety and well-being on his shoulders, just as his uncle had held Castle Bradburn's safety on his. At the thought of his uncle, Reid's heart squeezed. He fought to hold the dismay and sense of grief from his exterior. He missed his family, the family he had left behind in the Undercity while he and Juniper were *supposed* to be gaining an alliance with Delphine.

Juniper had gone against the wishes of King Bradburn and Queen Myrisha. She had fled into the Wylds on her own selfish whims, and it had almost gotten her killed. Had Reid left Delphine even a moment later, or had he rested an hour longer on his desperate rush to find her, that bear would have killed her. He wouldn't have gotten to her in time, and he would have come across her mangled body. If the bear left anything to be found.

Her recklessness churned his anger like nothing else could. It coursed through his bloodstream with vigor, and he fought to suppress the urge to hit something. If they were in Delphine, he could take his frustration to the training yard.

But now they were stuck in the Wylds. They had little supplies for a journey back to Delphine, and a cold wind blew from the forest. As much as Reid didn't want to admit it, they were at the mercy of the druids.

"Reid, I have something to ask you." Jarek clapped his hands together. He had an expectant look on his face, like whatever he was about to propose was a great honor. "You have been formally trained, whereas our warriors learn as they go. Most have never experienced real combat. I would like you to train with them. Show them what you know. Share some of your talent with them."

Reid had expected as much. While he didn't consider it an honor to train inexperienced warriors, he understood the necessity. These warriors needed instruction to better protect their families. Still, Reid would rather be on the way before their absence in Delphine stirred more panic than it already had.

"When do we start?" Reid asked.

"Tomorrow," Jarek said. "You've had a long journey. The Wylds take it out of you."

Reid fully agreed, but more than the Wylds sat heavy on his thoughts.

After a walk through the bare-bones barracks, pitiful armory, and a chat with the grumpy smith, Jarek went into the village to socialize. He asked Reid to accompany him, to introduce him to the elders, but Reid claimed exhaustion. Jarek didn't press him. Reid wound his way through the village, but rather than go straight to Jarek's house, he went to Enna's. The old woman was pruning her garden, and her granddaughter was nowhere to be seen.

"Last room in the hall," Enna called without looking up from the vine she pruned.

Reid let himself into the house. He found Juniper in the farthest sickroom, staring into the small hearth in the corner. Bags hung under her eyes. Her skin was ghostly pale. Her auburn hair hung over her shoulder in a damp braid. A fresh bandage hugged her middle, and the arms of her baggy tunic revealed a generous view of her breasts.

Her tired eyes shifted to him. He recognized the drowsy look. Enna had given her some herbal concoction.

Reid sat on the cot beside her. She had washed; scents of lavender and lye filled the room and her. "Jarek wants me to train druids to be warriors."

"Will you?"

"I'll do what I can. We don't have long to linger here," he whispered. He didn't want Enna to hear. "We should be on our way as quickly as we can." His eyes glanced at the top of the bandage visible from the arm hole of her tunic, and the smooth curve of her breast. "As soon as you heal."

"What about the archmage?"

He frowned.

"I think the archmage is the…witch they're afraid to talk about," she said. A wince caught on her words. "I'm sorry. Whatever herbs Lilianna put on the wound makes me…not think straight."

And she looked it too.

"It's all right," Reid said. At least if she felt woozy, she wouldn't wander. "We should gather what information we can about the witch. Then we come back with reinforcements from Delphine. Battlemages. Sentinels. We are horribly outnumbered in this place, especially if you can't use magic."

He whispered the last few words. He didn't want anyone in Sinjon to suspect Juniper of being a mage.

She didn't argue like he expected her to. Her bleary eyes bore into the fire.

"I wish you were staying here with me," Juniper said, her words lethargic but warm.

"As do I." Reid started to reach for her face, just to feel her skin against his again, but then he remembered her scream, her pleading, her tangled magic. Shame flashed under his skin. He pulled his hand back.

Juniper winced and leaned forward, like she might be sick. She released a slow exhale, and then said, "Do you really? This way, you won't have to worry about touching me."

Her words and bitter tone struck him worse than his shame. He reached for her, and this time flattened his hand against her back. His palm rested against where Maddox's brand had once been. Through the tunic, he felt the new scars that streaked her flesh. The suddenness of it startled her, pushing her breath from her throat and curling her shoulders upward.

"I am sorry for what I did," Reid said, his voice low. His words trembled. "I didn't mean to hurt you, but I did. I am afraid of hurting you again. I am afraid of waking up with you screaming, because of something I didn't mean to do."

Her heart thudded against his hand.

"Reid," she started.

"I don't like sleeping with you so far away," he whispered. "I want to hold you. But I won't be able to live with myself if I hurt you. Do you know what it felt like to wake up with you screaming? To realize it was my doing?"

"Reid," she started again. Her words came out soggy but fierce. "You know me, I love loving dangerously. I'd rather live in danger in your arms than live safely without you."

His heart skipped a beat at those words. They sounded like a vow, though he doubted Juniper caught it.

"Reid?"

When he didn't respond, she twisted her body around as best she could. Her midnight eyes searched his, and a frown pulled at her lips.

"That night, what were you dreaming about?" she whispered.

He hesitated; his breath stumbled.

Her expression softened. She scooted closer and set her cool hand on his knee. "Do you remember those days in the castle when we just talked and got to know each other?"

He remembered them fondly. "Strange how far away those days seem."

"Let's do it again," she whispered. She flattened her hands against his chest and trailed her fingers along his collarbone and to his face. He hadn't shaved, and stubble lined his jaw. "Let's get to know each other. What were you dreaming about?"

Reid held her stare for several long heartbeats. He wanted to tell her, but the words tangled in his throat. She started to pull away, but Reid grabbed her hands and held them against his chest.

"My parents," he whispered. "I was dreaming about the day they were killed."

Reid held onto her hands as he told her about the dream, about the day he had lost his parents and his brother to apostates, how he had hid as they were tortured and killed. Juniper did not interrupt. She did not look away. As Reid laid his ugliest memory bare, she did not flinch.

"And in the dream, I attacked the apostate that killed my mother," he whispered, his voice weak and beaten.

And he had attacked her by mistake.

He looked down at his hand on hers, seeing his small hand wrapped around the apostate's wrist in a deathly grip. Before he could move away, she curled her fingers with his.

"It's okay," she whispered back.

Reid wanted to argue, but before he could speak, she pressed her lips against his.

"I love you." She loosely threaded her arms around him.

Reid wrapped his arms around her shoulders and buried his face in her hair. He hadn't realized how much he had missed her until that moment, her soft skin, her lips.

"Gods, I love you," Reid said into her neck.

He thought about pushing the romance, but the timing didn't feel right. Juniper was still injured, and he felt as though his heart had been cut open.

Later, he told himself.

"There is something else," Reid whispered. "About magic."

"Hmm?"

"Most in the village fear it."

"I gathered as much."

"I think it's best if you keep yours to yourself," Reid whispered. His fingers brushed against the bare skin of her arm and he released her. "If these people hate magic, they might hate you if they found out."

She gave him a lethargic version of her cocky grin. "Strange how familiar that sounds. Me, pretending not to be a mage, fearful of what those around me would think if they knew."

"Jun."

"I know." She blinked, and it took a long moment for her to open her eyes again. "I will keep it to myself."

Because they needed these superstitious druids to like them.

Reid pressed a kiss to her temple, then left her to rest. He had a long day ahead of him tomorrow, and likely several more. As he started toward Jarek's house, he reached into his pocket and closed his fingers around the moonstone ring. Enna had removed it from Juniper's hand, and in fear someone would steal it, Reid had taken it. He had planned on giving it back to Juniper tonight, but her drowsy state had made him change his mind.

Later, he told himself. He tucked the ring back into his pocket.

CHAPTER 26

Ison woke to a blade at his throat and a growl in his ear.

"Get up," spat a rough female voice.

His heart hammered—he was lying on his back in one of Finn's stone tents, and the stranger stood at the small triangular entrance, the pale dawn light seeping around her dark-clad frame. Ison started to summon his magic, but then realized the blade at his throat was made of fire, not steel.

"I said get up," growled the mage. Her fire dagger pressed closer to his skin. He felt the searing heat of it, but it did not burn him. Not yet.

Ison started to move. The fire blade moved with him.

"One wrong move, and I'll turn you into a pile of ashes," growled the mage.

Ison slowly got to his feet—Finn made the tents just tall enough to stand—and got a better look at the mage threatening him. She wore a mixture of leathers but no weapons. Of course, as a mage she wouldn't need them. A deep hood shadowed her bronze face. A few strands of dark brown hair framed her face. Her deep brown eyes took in Ison's every move. She looked no older than Ison, maybe twenty.

"Out," she growled.

Ison did as she commanded and stepped out of the tent. Several strangers had come into their camp, each hooded and some masked.

Ambushed.

Mages forced the others out of their stone tents, each holding a blade of magic to their throats. Ison met Xavier's blue-gray eyes—they burned with a hated Ison had never seen before. If it weren't for the daggers against Bois, Mabyl, Finn, and Ison, Xavier would have killed his attacker and anyone else, but Xavier wouldn't endanger his friends.

The forest had just begun to glow with dawn. The birds remained asleep and the bugs had already quieted, and it left a strange absence of life—the few moments between day and night.

"You stumbled into the wrong part of the woods," said the fire mage holding Ison.

Another mage went through their saddlebags. "They've got no weapons," he said.

"What kind of a fool doesn't carry weapons?" said the pale mage holding a blade of water to Bois's throat.

"The kind that doesn't need them," said the bulky young man mage holding Mabyl with earth. "They're mages."

"That's right," Mabyl said calmly.

Ison felt a steep jealousy for her confident tone.

The fire mage growled. "What's your business here?" she spat.

"We're searching," said Bois, her voice sweet but startled. "For Baxion."

Their ambushers paused and a knowing glance passed between the mage holding Xavier and the one holding Bois. Ison met Mabyl's eye as the same understanding flashed across her features—these mages knew where Baxion was.

"There is no such place," said the thin water mage holding Xavier.

"We were told to go there if we wanted to change the world," Bois said, undeterred.

The bulky mage holding Mabyl glared at Bois, searching the blind girl's face for the truth. "By who?"

"His name was Clive." Bois worked her lips into a quiver and fear into her features. "He was killed by a mage who thought differently than he did, and without him, we…left to come here."

"From where?"

"Rusdasin," Bois answered.

The water mage's brows rose. "You were in Rusdasin? Why not stay there? You could have helped."

The bulky earth mage hissed, silencing her. Guilt came over the water mage's face—she had revealed something she wasn't supposed to.

"Why would we stay?" Bois asked. "We were being hunted, and with our leader killed, we were told to leave. He told us about Baxion, that we should seek out others there. He said that we would be safe."

"This Clive told you that?" drawled the mage holding Bois.

"Not Clive," Bois said, her voice soft. "The Master told me."

"He talks to you?" the mage gasped.

A collective gasp sounded—each of the ambushing mages had gone wide-eyed. In a blink, the bulky mage regained his skeptical glare. Ison swallowed against the fire blade. Bois had found their way in. These mages not only knew about Baxion, but they knew who the master was. They could lead them right to Baxion.

"Yes," said Bois. Darkness came over her face. "But not since Clive's death."

Ison held his emotions as straight as he could. He felt a steep awe at the way Bois twisted her features into fear and innocence, without uttering a single lie.

"I heard about that," said the air mage holding Finn. "Some bitch came in and disputed the clan in Rusdasin. Scattered them."

"What do you think?" said the bulky earth mage. "Take them or kill them?"

"I say we take them back," said the fire mage. She withdrew her blade from Ison's throat but didn't banish it. "If they're telling the truth, fine. If not, let Horace deal with them."

"Agreed," said the mage holding Bois.

Ison placed a hand against his throat. His skin remained unmarred, but hot to the touch.

The mages released the others. Ison met Xavier's vicious gaze and saw it—the option to fight. Ison gently shook his head. Lying their way into Baxion would get them there faster and without violence or bloodshed. Xavier gave a subtle nod.

"Buck and I will take you to Baxion," said the fire mage, motioning to the bulky earth mage. She nudged her fire dagger into Ison's side. "But any of you give us a reason, we'll kill you before we get there."

"All right," Ison said. He looked pointedly at the others. "We agreed."

No one opposed, though Mabyl looked like she wanted to throttle the mage closest to her.

The mages supervised as Ison and the others struck camp and readied their horses. He spied the bulky earth mage—Buck—and the fire mage whispering heatedly. The argument didn't last long, and he looked away before they caught him. The ambushing mages had hidden their horses nearby, and while the fire mage and Buck remained, the others continued their patrol, as they called it.

Unease tingled from Ison's scalp to his toes. How close were they to Baxion? The seed of doubt that had been growing since they'd left Rusdasin vanished, and with it the fear that they would be wandering the northern Collatian forest for months without finding anything.

"All right, follow me," the fire mage commanded. She and her spotted horse started northwest.

Ison rode slightly behind the fire mage, and the others fell into formation behind him. The earth mage, Buck, rode behind them. Rocks the size of a grown man's fist circled him, waiting for someone to try something.

"I'm Cera, by the way," said the fire mage to Ison. She explained that they were one of the many scouting parties tasked with patrolling the woods around Baxion. More than a few wayward mages had been found by scouts, all looking for the mythical city.

Ison's panic lessened. If other mages were doing the same thing they were pretending to do, then their lies wouldn't be met with as much resistance as he had feared.

"You look relieved." Cera looked at Ison with raised brows.

"I feared we would be wandering for months," Ison said. It was the truth. "We had only a rough idea of where to go."

"And that's one of the reason the scouts exist, besides, you know, mosscats and bears and stuff." Cera waved her hand dismissively.

They continued northwest. The sun gradually rose and banished the chill of the night. They had left the edge of the Wylds behind some leagues before they had stopped to camp, and the forest grew green as far as he could see in every direction. They had traveled far enough north that despite the summer in the trees, the air was almost cold at night.

"You made it closer than most do," Cera said as she and Ison crested a grassy hill around midmorning.

Ison was about to ask how close, when he made it to the top of the hill. His words evaporated. In the valley before them was a city nestled between the hills. A stone wall lined the city's perimeter. Battlements and parapets lined the wall, and Ison could see dots of guards patrolling along it. The city itself looked like any other, with towers of stone and timber, vaulted roofs, chimney smoke, and enough houses and buildings to hold several thousand people.

Baxion.

CHAPTER 27

Juniper slept through the night and woke to Lilianna bringing a tray of tea. The lethargy had worn off, as had the stinging in her side. Lilianna lifted a steaming earthen teapot and poured a greenish amber liquid into a matching earthen mug. Juniper pushed herself into a sitting position. Her side felt immensely better. She no longer felt as though she were going to accidentally rip herself in half.

"Your man is going to train us today," Lilianna said as she handed Juniper the mug. Her tone was dry and calm.

A dry chuckle left her throat. "My man?"

"He is, is he not?" Lilianna raised a brow.

"Yes?" Juniper sipped the tea. Grassy. "Is that what druids call a relationship?"

Lilianna shrugged. "It is a claim."

"I guess you can say it like that."

"So you are?"

"Are what?"

"Claimed."

Juniper sipped her tea. She didn't know if she liked that term or not. "Yes. We're engaged. When everything settles down, we'll marry."

And that idea left a strange pitting in the bottom of her stomach that reached into her toes. She and Reid hadn't talked about marriage in a while. She glanced at her bare ring finger. She also hadn't found the time to mention her missing moonstone. She had woken up without it and assumed it was with her dagger and her clothes. It wasn't.

Changing the subject, Juniper said, "Who is *us*? You said, 'Reid is going to train *us*.'"

"Myself and the other sentries who wish to learn," Lilianna said.

"You fight?"

"I do, though not very well," Lilianna said. "I hear you also fight. Grandmother mentioned you told Jarek you are a mercenary."

"That's not accurate," Juniper said. "Yes, I did learn to fight at a young age. It was necessary to survive. But I am not a sellsword. I was a thief. Now I work for the crown as a…an ambassador."

Lilianna's golden eyes met hers, clever and observant. Juniper feared she might call it a lie, so she broke eye contact with a loud sip of earthy tea.

"You are unsure?" Lilianna asked.

Juniper considered it. Revealing a secret of herself could lower Lilianna's guard, and she might slip a secret of her own, or of the Wylds. She didn't know the druid girl well enough to know if she was trustworthy or if she would repeat every word to her grandmother or the chief. Pulling on those lingering feelings of uncertainty, Juniper let them into her expression. She pinched her face into a faux vulnerability and said lowly, "I suppose I am."

Lilianna's brow furrowed, but before she could speak, quick and purposeful footsteps sounded in the hall.

The curtain swished aside, and Enna entered. She set down a bowl of porridge on the tea tray.

"All right, girl, eat up," Enna commanded. "Lilianna, I've got oil for you to deliver to Gata. It's by the hearth in the other room."

Lilianna nodded and vanished through the curtain. Her footsteps barely sounded against the floorboards.

Juniper ate the porridge under Enna's watchful eye. It tasted like muddied herbs and sweet bread. After eating as much as her stomach allowed, Enna checked the wound. It looked better, and it felt better. She pressed fresh mauve leaves against the wound, smothered them in ointment, and wrapped Juniper in clean bandages.

"It's healing," Enna said, standing. She lifted the tea tray. "I've got a list of things for you to do today so you're not sulking around here. Wash up and meet me in the garden…"

Enna left, and Juniper poured a small helping of water into the basin. She washed her face and hands and other necessities in cool water. She pulled on the wool dress from the day before, tugged on her boots, and hid her dagger within. She checked again for her missing ring. Not finding it, she headed to the garden. The garden was no less an assault of color than it had been the day before. Plants were packed into every plot and flower bed, flowers and herbs and bushes and vines. There were trellises choked with flowering vines; bushes thick with berries of every shade of blue, pink, and green; trees that grew fruit shaped like stars, trees with bright blue leaves, and trees that grew topaz nuts. Juniper found Enna kneeling beside a delicate plant with round sapphire leaves and tiny pearl berries.

The chores were tedious and simple: gathering leaves, berries, and fruits from various parts of the garden. Juniper felt the curse lingering in her body. It cast a blanket over her magic and her senses. It wasn't unlike the strange oppression she had felt in the Wylds, only…danker. She had felt the curse on the outside, and now she felt it on the inside. She no longer felt the curse pressing in against her; that part of the curse had not passed the timber wall.

By midday, Juniper was exhausted. For the midday meal, Enna made porridge.

"I'm no cook," Enna admitted grimly.

"Neither am I," Juniper said.

Juniper ate a measly portion of porridge, and then Enna sent her back to bed. Reid stopped by in the evening, but Juniper barely remembered it. Between her drowsiness and the druid medicine, the conversation blurred.

She spent the next few days in the same routine. The strange medicine gave her even stranger dreams of running through palace corridors while the announcement committee chased her, demanding she put on her solstice dress. No matter how fast she ran, they were always behind her. In her lucid moments, she helped Enna with her chores. She walked with Lilianna to deliver tinctures and ointments to villagers. She washed up. Enna reapplied leaves and ointment to her wound, and then she would pass out after a few bites of Enna's tasteless porridge.

Every day was better than the one before it.

"How long has it been?" Juniper asked Enna one morning.

"About a week, maybe two. I don't keep good track of the days like I used to." Enna continued trimming tiny silver leaves from one of her indoor plants.

Juniper rubbed her temples. Had they been in Sinjon that long?

When Enna had run out of easy chores, Juniper took a walk through the farms. She didn't want to give the cranky old healer reason to find her more tedious tasks. She meandered along a narrow dirt path between a field of green wheat and a field of grape vines. From both sides, druids hummed as they worked. They all hummed a different tune, or a different version of the same tune, and it filled the air with an eerie yet calming disharmony.

She skirted the edge of the village, and after the fields and animal pens, she heard the distant clank and clink of swords. Giving in to her curiosity, she followed the sounds.

She found the training ring. She meandered to the outer edge of the sunken ring, where druids too old or too young to fight had paused to watch. . Down below, twenty or so druids practiced sword play while Reid observed. The oldest looked to be about Reid's age, and the youngest looked too young to grow facial hair. To Juniper's admiration, several girls had come. They fought with just as much vigor as the boys. She spotted Lilianna among them, wearing mismatched leather, her twin braids swinging with her movements.

When all of the practice fights had been won, Reid called attention to himself. He lectured them about where they had gone wrong, popular mistakes, and common errors. He looked and sounded frighteningly like his uncle. Juniper didn't miss the curious stares the girls flashed in Reid's direction, but she shoved them out of her mind. She couldn't blame them; she also enjoyed looking at him. Reid had a warrior's body, all corded muscle and hard planes.

Another round of pretend fighting, then Reid dismissed them for a break. The druids watching dispersed as well. Juniper made her way into the arena, to where Reid stood in the center. She folded her hands behind her back to hide her empty left hand.

"It's not as bad as I feared," Reid said. "They have promise."

"They lack drive," Juniper added.

Reid nodded. "How are you feeling?"

"Much better," Juniper said, forcing a smile. "The royal healer in Rusdasin should take notes."

"History paints druids as accomplished healers and fierce warriors," Reid said, low enough for only Juniper to hear. "A thousand years ago, the sick would seek druid clans for healing."

Juniper hummed. Reid met her eye, and she remembered their talk several nights before. He had confessed his dream, had opened his heart to her. If only she had been in a clearer state of mind. She hadn't been able to fully appreciate it. Should she mention the ring?

Juniper inhaled to explain her empty left hand, when a few of the druid trainees returned to the sunken area. Juniper sucked her words back in. Later, she told herself.

"Who are you supposed to be?" asked one of the younger druid men. He ran his pale golden eyes up and down Juniper. He had a sneer that begged to be punched and a crooked nose that suggested someone already had.

Juniper let out a dramatic sigh. "Normally, I would be the one pummeling your ass." She tilted her head toward Reid. "And then he would tell you all the things you did wrong."

The young man snorted a laugh, looked at Reid, and when Reid did not correct her or laugh, his grin faded.

The druid boy behind him laughed, earning a glare from the first.

Juniper retreated to the grassy incline as the other druids returned. The training resumed. Reid ordered them through simple exercises and footwork. Juniper reclined against the sun-warmed grass as the druids squatted, jumped, dodged, and rolled. Reid moved them into the basics of combat and swordplay—most were terrible. Reid walked around the arena and corrected their stances and footwork and grips.

Juniper spotted Lilianna fighting. She had grace, but she lacked precision. Juniper learned that the sneering boy was Sein Braddock, and his friend was Asher.

Every time Sein opened his mouth, she wanted to punch him. She knew the type: arrogant, brash, and determined to prove himself better than others. The Undercity had had a plethora of mercenaries like that. They rarely lasted.

And Reid had never seemed more like his uncle's nephew. She would have to brag to Captain Sandpiper if they made it back to Rusdasin.

If… What kind of thinking was that? Juniper silently cursed herself for such negative thoughts. Of course they would return to Rusdasin, and then she would tell Roslyn all about this little oasis in the Wylds over tea in a sunny courtyard.

Ison would be thrilled at the idea of so many herbs and plants growing under druid song.

"Why isn't *she* doing any of this?"

Juniper brought her focus back to the arena. Sein Braddock glared at her.

Reid glanced over his shoulder at Juniper, offering her the chance to answer for herself.

"Because I don't want to make you look bad," Juniper said simply.

Sein scoffed and muttered what sounded like *bitch*. Juniper shoved off the grass, grabbed a sword from Asher's weak grip, and came at him. Sein's eyes widened and he pulled his sword up to block—poorly. She knocked her sword into his, hooked her foot around his ankle, and spun. Sein fell face-first into the ground. His sword skittered out of his hand.

The others snickered. Juniper sauntered around Sein and met his eye as she said, "Because I've been fighting for my life since I could walk. And you have a long way to go."

Sein jumped to his feet. "You surprised me," he spat.

"All right," Juniper said, adjusting her grip on the sword. "I'm going to come at you again. Ready?"

Sein growled, but he adjusted his footing like Reid had instructed.

"Loosen your grip on your sword," Juniper said. "Unless you want to snap your wrist. Move your left foot in. Your stance is everything."

To her surprise, Sein listened. Not as stupid as he looked, then.

She came at him again. Sein blocked her initial blow, and she hooked her foot around his ankle just as before. He toppled over, though he didn't land on his face or lose his grip on his sword.

"You fight dirty," Sein muttered.

"You can't expect your enemies to have manners," Juniper said. "When you're fighting with steel, you're fighting for your life. You win however you have to. Especially if you go up against something like a demon bear that wants to rip your throat out."

Reid frowned. He didn't agree, but he didn't openly argue. "Juniper has more experience than all of you combined," he said to the whole group, his tone commanding and flat. "And if you want to survive a battle, you practice. You learn. You get better. Pair off and keep at it."

Juniper tossed the sword back to Asher and strolled back to the arena's sloped side, trying her best not to collapse from the stinging and burning pain radiating from her side.

She hadn't yet made it to the top when Lilianna appeared at her side, eyes wide.

"Are you mad?" Lilianna hissed.

"Oh, I'm not mad," Juniper said. She winced. "I am very much in pain."

She put a hand to her wounded side. The bandage squished with warm, fresh blood.

Lilianna rolled her eyes. "Let's get you back before you start bleeding out." She grabbed Juniper by the arm and pulled her toward Enna's hut.

CHAPTER 28

Enna eyed Juniper with neither disappointment nor surprise. She ordered Juniper into her room, and Juniper laid on her side as Enna peeled away the old bandage and leaves—both bloodied—and applied a layer of grayish leaves the size of a child's palm. An icy sensation needled her raw flesh, radiating through her skin and blood. It sent a chill over her skin and under it.

"This herb isn't as strong," Enna said in a low tone Juniper equated to distraction. "It is better for general wounds, not the curse, but I don't think we have to worry about the curse taking you. It lacks the stout pain relief as the other and shouldn't make you as drowsy. You will have temporary numbness."

After a layer of ointment and tight bandages, Enna allowed Juniper to sit up.

"Now don't go fighting," Enna said. "I don't have enough herbs to patch you up every day. Lilianna has tea ready in the other room."

The needling sensation continued up her back and down her arms and legs. It rolled like a slow chill down her bones. Enna headed out, and Juniper pulled her tunic and wool dress over her head.

She shouldn't have risen to Sein's bait, but she had. She didn't regret it. Some men needed to be knocked on their ass a few times. It taught humility.

She found Lilianna in the main room, pouring tea into two earthen cups. She still wore her mismatched leathers. She set the kettle down and nudged one of the cups closer to Juniper. It smelled like normal tea; it tasted herbal.

"You surpass us, even injured," Lilianna said, eyes on her tea.

Juniper couldn't tell if she'd meant it sarcastically or not. Lilianna's tone reminded her of Reid's mask: neutral and unreadable.

"I hurt myself doing so."

"Still," Lilianna started, her voice small. "You moved with skill. I don't think any of us will ever fight like you or Reid."

"It takes practice," Juniper said. The needling sensation had reached her neck and slowly ran up her scalp. "I started learning to fight when I was a girl. I had no choice. The Undercity was a harsh place, and if you didn't fight for yourself, no one else would. I lost a lot of fights to get to where I am."

Lilianna took in every word. "Undercity?"

"A place under the city where the criminals lived," she explained. "I belonged to a guild. I practiced fighting every day, sometimes for hours, sometimes until I couldn't see straight. I suffered through bruises and a few broken bones."

Lilianna frowned. "I'd rather not suffer."

"Reid's training went much smoother than mine. He had a less…sketchy place to learn and live." Juniper reclined on the stone bench by the wall. The tea warmed her insides, battling with the chilly feeling of the leaves. It left her hanging in the middle, hot and cold.

"Sein should not have provoked you," Lilianna said.

Juniper agreed. However, to be civil, she said, "I shouldn't have jumped on his bait."

"He is…immature, according to my mother and most others, but he does have good intentions," Lilianna said.

"You don't have to defend him."

Lilianna inhaled and held it. Words hung on the tip of her tongue.

"What is it?"

"We are engaged."

Juniper blinked. "Engaged? You and…"

"Sein."

Juniper wanted to laugh. Reserved, stoic Lilianna, and arrogant, loud Sein? Then again, she never would have thought she and Reid would have made a match. Sometimes she still thought that.

"I didn't realize you liked him that way," Juniper said.

At Lilianna's hesitation, Juniper leaned closer.

"You…don't?"

"It was arranged," Lilianna said. "We don't have the advantage of options when it comes to marriage. Sein and I are a logical match. Our families have not married in several generations. We are of similar age. We both have admirable qualities."

Juniper held in what she wanted to say, about how stupid arranged marriages were and how Lilianna and Sein should be able to choose who they marry. Druids had their own culture, and Juniper had no place to condemn it.

"It's not bad," Lilianna said. "We've known for years. Sein tries. We patrol the wall together when we can. When he's not around his friends, he's less…"

"Obnoxious?"

"That is a good word for it."

"He sounds like most men."

"Is Reid the same way?"

Juniper hadn't a ready answer. She had seen Reid around Adrian, Henry, and Penet; he hadn't changed. "I don't think so," she said without certainty. "He rarely drops his stoic exterior."

He had with her, a little warm voice reminded her.

"Sein is accompanying me tomorrow while I harvest rare ingredients," Lilianna said. "If you are feeling well, you should come along."

"I can see the garden just fine from here."

Lilianna's small smile returned. "We are not visiting a garden within the walls. We are running low on ingredients only found in the Wylds."

Juniper's heart jumped. Outside the village. In the Wylds, where the archmage was hiding. Hope blossomed in Juniper's chest. Underneath it, dread coiled. "I will consider it," Juniper said, despite having already made up her mind.

"Better than collecting herbs or watching Grandmother stitch up the odd injury," Lilianna whispered.

From the next room, Enna snorted.

Juniper spent the rest of the day resting. The herbs gave her a strange sense of lethargy, but not in the same way the first had. She was in control and not overwhelmingly tired, yet the world seemed farther away. As if she were dreaming. Colors seemed more vivid.

Laying on her cot, she brought a few flurries to life. Tiny blue snowflakes danced around her palm for a heartbeat, then a painful zap surged along her magic. Her ice vanished. Her magic did not want to be used. The curse yet lingered.

She felt for her magic. It was…healing, she thought. The herbs were coaxing the magic into her skin, her blood, to heal. Amazing. Of course, she knew little about herbs and their uses. Ison would love to get his hands on whatever leaves Enna had, and he would likely love to wander her herb garden.

Juniper sighed and said a silent prayer to Bera to keep Ison and her friends out of death's way. Bera and Hiada, the god of death, were twins, and Juniper liked to think Hiada would listen to his sister.

She retrieved her stolen map of Collatia from her satchel and unrolled it over the floor. She added Sinjon to the dark splotch of the Blackwood Wylds, and she drew a crude little bear to the south of the city. Her gaze trailed over the northern part of the kingdom. Somewhere in those forests were her friends.

Gods willing, they weren't dead yet.

Reid came by Enna's house for dinner with a basket packed by Ingrid, for two.

"She said it would be romantic." Reid sat the basket on the little table in her room.

"It is," Juniper said.

A cool wind hissed at the closed shutters.

"Did you hurt yourself too badly?" Reid began to unpack a dinner of dumplings stuffed with buttery roots and cabbage. It smelled delicious.

"Not at all," Juniper said in a voice that implied the opposite.

Reid's lips turned downward.

"Enna patched me up. She also scolded me and warned me not to hurt myself again."

Reid half-laughed. "As she should."

"How did training go after I left?"

"Good," Reid said. "Not as dramatic, but good."

She chuckled.

Reid told her how he had instructed them to fight each other and he had made his rounds adjusting stances, grips, and footing; and commenting on blind spots and finding an opponent's tells.

"Do I have tells?" Reid asked as he poked a dumpling with his slightly bent metal fork.

"Yes."

A beat passed, and she glanced up from her plate. Reid's curious stare bore into hers. He leaned closer and whispered, "What are they?"

"I can't tell you—it defeats the purpose."

He scowled, but it did not meet his eyes.

After the meal, Reid and Juniper took a stroll through the farms. They came to the timber wall, and Reid led them up to the battlement. Druids patrolled, but none argued with their presence. A few stood straighter in Reid's presence.

On the other side, the Wylds stretched as far as she could see. Twilight streaked the sky in indigo, molten pink, and lavender. Her father, King Balendin, had told her of trouble in these woods, and she suspected it had something to do with the witches and the curse. Juniper suspected the witch likely had something to do with the missing archmage.

A sudden, cool breeze hissed from the Wylds. It slithered through the seams of her cloak, erecting gooseflesh. She closed her eyes as the wind picked up, whipping loose strands of her hair from her braid and lashing them against her cheeks. Though the cold caressed her magic, the dry air stung her lungs.

Reid grimaced. "Jarek said the summers have been getting shorter for years. If not for the druids' affinity for plants, they would not have survived. Feel that wind? Autumn is well on its way."

"I can handle an early winter," Juniper said as she and Reid meandered along the top of the wall.

Winter meant cold fingers and toes, but the idea of long, cold nights appealed to her magic. However, winter also meant her birthday—Isolde's on the solstice, and Juniper's a few weeks after. It didn't feel like that long ago she spent her birthday tucked away in a quiet library alcove in the Marca.

Dread curled in her gut. She hadn't thought about Isolde since arriving in Sinjon.

A cold wind whistled through the deadened trees and scraggly brush, and the sound racked against Juniper's skin worse than the air itself. She could have sworn she heard voices drifting on that breeze, speaking in a language she didn't understand—the same as she had heard by the singing tree, only darker. Cursed.

CHAPTER 29

Ison could hardly believe his eyes as he and the others approached the sprawling city of Baxion. It could hold thousands of mages, maybe tens of thousands. The valley rose on either side, spotted with monstrously tall pines and oaks, and it looked as though parts of the outer city had been built into the cliff sides. Rope bridges, stone walkways, and ladders connected structures along the walls, and he spotted a few tree houses in the ancient trees. All tucked within the valley. Out of sight. Safe.

The city would be impossible to see from a distance, just as Ison had been warned.

If you get close enough to see it, the guards will see you, Silas had said.

"Well?" Cera asked.

"I admit, I thought it would be smaller," Ison said, his voice a whisper.

"They say it used to be a few houses and a lumber mill," Cera said. "But that was a long time ago. Come on."

Cera nudged her horse forward, and she guided them down the hill and toward Baxion. Ison tried his best not to look how he felt, and he felt like vomiting. He tried to imagine this place as a desperate mage might—like a beacon of hope. When that didn't work, he reminded himself that they were running low on supplies, including food. Baxion would have food and beds, and likely a place to wash.

For those things, he felt a spike of gladness.

The valley rose around them and the beaten path leading to the city narrowed, so that no one could sneak up on the city walls. No trees grew around Baxion's outer wall, and the guards would have a clear view of any approaching people or animals. As Cera led them closer, guards gathered on the battlements. The guards wore spring green robes and mismatched leathers; they carried no weapons. Ison's panic returned. He gripped the reins to keep his hands from shaking.

"It's okay," Cera said kindly. She winked at Ison. "You're safe here. We're all mages, and the Order has no place."

Ison nodded. If only the Order was the only thing he worried about. He tried to recall the mage he had been a year ago, trembling at the sight of a knight or Mage's Bane. He conjured a fraction of that old fear and pretended to feel relief at the city of mages. He straightened in the saddle.

They halted before the stone portcullis. The mages on the battlements summoned spears of earth and fire.

A city defended by magic. A part of Ison was thrilled at the idea, and the other part felt a stout fear. He had seen how dangerous magic could be when left unchecked.

"Halt," came a loud voice from the parapet. "Who goes?"

"Cera and Buck from scouting party Elk," Cera called up to the mage. "We found a few newcomers."

Ison felt eyes on him, searching him. He prayed none would recognize him, though he didn't know how they would, unless someone remembered him from the Marca. The only mages who had seen his face and knew his connection to Nexon were those in the Undercity, and they had either died or joined Juniper's cause.

The portcullis rose too smoothly for gears—magic.

Cera started through, and Ison followed. As he passed under, he glanced up at the sharpened spikes that lined the bottom of the portcullis. The others followed, and Buck came last. He had ridden behind for most of the journey, giving Ison the feeling of being trapped.

Baxion looked like any other city, only the stone buildings were magically smooth , cut to fit perfectly. The same stones paved the streets. Magelights, dim for the day, hung in lampposts of dark metal and brass. Ison couldn't look at it all fast enough—Cera guided them down a street that ran alongside the outer wall. They stopped at a large stable of stone where stable hands took the horses, and then continued on foot to a flat stone building.

Cera knocked on the wooden door. A mumbled conversation ended abruptly.

"What?" came a deep and rough female voice.

Cera announced, "I found a few fresh backs."

"All right, come in."

Cera held the door open and motioned them inside. Ison moved first, Xavier close on his heels. It was an office, plain and cluttered. A bearded man sat at a desk, and a tall woman wearing the spring green guards' uniform stood beside him.

They filed in, and Cera shut the door.

The woman scanned them all with bored awareness that reminded Ison of Xavier. She said, "They look well enough."

"This one says the Master told her about this place." Cera motioned to Bois.

The room fell quiet, then the woman spat, "The master spoke to *you*?"

"Yes," Bois said, unfazed. "He told me how to use my magic to see. I lost my sight because of Mage's Bane. Thanks to him, I can see."

"Be that as it may, rules are rules," said the man. He stood. "Let's see some magic. Prove you are mages."

Ison summoned gray air into his hands; Xavier summoned twin daggers of his charcoal colored energy; Bois brought her hands together and summoned a whirlwind of pale pink air; Mabyl brought a sprout of fire to the palm of her hand; and Finn pulled a ball of stone from the wall.

"Very well," said the bearded man. He scanned a ledger, then added, "Cera, take them to Boarding House Five. I will send someone to place them tomorrow morning."

Cera guided them out of the office. She led them along a dirt street that wound through stone buildings. By the sounds coming from within, they were offices or barracks or training grounds. Magic, floral and sweet metallic, filled the air. Underneath it, fresh soil and the mineral stench of stone and the stench of a city. Ison spied green-clad guards wandering the battlements, the streets, and standing at intersections.

They entered a complex of stone buildings. Each looked identical to the next, save for the number etched onto each wooden door. Cera stopped at number five.

"Here we are," she said triumphantly.

"Boarding House?" Ison asked.

"They're not bad." Cera opened the door and motioned them inside.

The house opened to a simple hearth room. The walls were smooth stone, and the floors were worn wooden planks. It smelled like wet minerals, woodsmoke, and magic. Wooden seating angled around an old woven rug. Cera lingered by the door as Ison and the others entered.

"Make yourselves at home. Washing room is in the back. Bedrooms are upstairs," said Cera. "Stay here until the placer comes to talk to you."

"A placer? What does that mean?" Xavier asked.

Cera frowned at the tone. "A placer will place you with a job and a place to live. Uh, let's see… What else do you need to know?" In a bored drawl, she added, "Baxion is divided into quadrants, and each quadrant has a captain. Each quadrant is divided into districts. Each district has a captain. Those captains answer to the quadrant captain who answers to the commander. Don't worry you'll get used to it."

"Who is the commander?" Mabyl asked. At Cera's hesitation, she added, "I want to know whose name to curse out loud when I get stuck with a lousy foundry job."

Buck, who remained outside, chuckled.

"Commander Lora oversees Baxion and reports directly to the master," Cera said, a beat of fear in her voice. "I would advise you not to curse her name."

"She gets testy," added Buck. "She has no sense of humor."

Ison felt a chill run down his spine. Clive hadn't been lying about that. He had said Lora was Nexon's second in command.

"Need anything?" Cera asked, but it sounded like something she had to say, not something she wanted to say.

"No," Ison said. "Thank you. You've done more than most others have."

He meant it. Cera had been a great help, despite their intentions.

"You are welcome." Cera turned to go, then paused in the doorway. "Oh, and someone will bring food in a little bit, so don't worry about that."

"Thank the gods," Mabyl muttered. "I'm sick of dried venison."

The door closed, and Cera and Buck walked away.

Xavier collapsed into one of the wooden chairs, even graceful when he plopped. He stretched his long legs in front of him. "That wasn't as hard as I thought it would be."

Ison sat in the chair beside him. "Are you disappointed?"

"Maybe a little."

Ison chuckled. "Something tells me you'll have plenty of excitement later on."

Xavier tilted his head toward Ison and offered a cocky grin. "There better be."

"While you boys talk, I'm bathing," Mabyl said, strutting toward the bathing room.

"I claim next," Bois said, sitting in the chair across from Xavier.

"Third," Finn chimed, stretching out on the wooden bench.

Ison let his exhaustion pull him further into the chair. With a tendril of air, he lifted the latch on the shutters and pushed them open—sunlight and fresh air poured in. Sounds drifted in—people talking and laughing, doors opening and closing, a city thriving. Ison allowed himself a few moments of rest. They had found Baxion, gotten inside unscathed, and they had half a day of rest before the placer would arrive.

Although he wanted to believe the hard part was over, he had a terrible feeling the trouble hadn't yet begun.

CHAPTER 30

After a breakfast of bland porridge, Juniper went with Lilianna to the village's eastern gate. Sein was already there, armed and fitted in leather. At the sight of Juniper, his straight-line mouth turned into a frown.

"What's she doing here?" Sein demanded.

"She's coming with us," Lilianna said plainly. "Grandmother thinks the exercise would be good for her."

Sein didn't argue. He glared daggers at Juniper—daggers formed in humiliation and anger.

After passing Juniper and Lilianna blades, sentries opened the gates for them to pass. As Juniper followed Lilianna and Sein out of the safety of the village, the change in the air was immediate. The light dimmed, the air cooled, and a blanket smothered her magic. The oppressive air pushed it down, mimicking suffocation, and Juniper's next breath came as a gasp.

Lilianna glanced over her shoulder, brows slightly raised. "Juniper?"

"I'm fine," she said.

Sein looked at her. "You better not slow us down."

"I won't." Juniper spoke with more spite than she intended.

Lilianna and Sein headed along a path that vanished into the Wylds. Juniper followed a step behind.

Sein hadn't argued about Juniper's presence. He had taken Lilianna's word for it without hesitation. Perhaps Lilianna was right about him having a few good qualities, though Juniper wouldn't admit that out loud. He walked with one hand on the hilt of his sword, fingers tensing intermittently.

This time, Sein and Lilianna took the lead and Juniper trailed behind. The forest path wound between ancient, deadened trees, massive boulders and jutting slabs of dark stone, and around and under sprawling roots thicker than all three of them put together. The Wylds rose around them, blocking the view of the village behind thorny brambles. At times, the canopy was so thick that the shade underneath mimicked night.

It might have been Juniper's imagination, but she thought things scurried through the shade more than the dulled sunlight. The darker the Wylds, the more things scurried just out of sight, through the brambles and bushes.

As they crossed over a mossy bridge that arched over a muddy stream, a shriek sounded above. Juniper readied her magic by reflex, though she did not use it. Sein unsheathed his sword and grumbled what sounded like a prayer under his breath. As Juniper's panic rose, a mangy blackbird flew overhead. It let out another shriek before it vanished.

Sein shoved his sword back into the sheath. He stomped the rest of the way across the bridge, but he did not release the hilt.

"Who built this bridge?" Juniper asked. The stones were small but fit perfectly together.

"Ancient druids who once lived in these woods. Before the Wylds were the Wylds, before the curse descended," Lilianna explained. "Roads once led from village to village, allowing trade of resources and stories. Now only Sinjon remains."

"Why?" Juniper asked.

"The curse took the villages," Sein added, as if it were obvious. "Destroyed the walls, the crops, and livestock. Turned the druids into monsters or forced them to flee."

"No, why is Sinjon the only village left?" Juniper clarified. She forced herself to ignore Sein's condescending tone.

Sein frowned. "What do you mean?"

"Why has your village survived while the others have not?" Juniper looked at Lilianna. Her steps had slowed.

"I have no answer for you," Lilianna said. "Jarek would say it is because we are better prepared, or that our location allows natural protection from the curse and its beasts. Grandmother would say it is because our bloodline is stronger." Juniper looked again to the road they followed. Ancient paving stones peeked from the hard-packed earth and snaking vines and blackened tree roots. She imagined the roads were once wider, enough for wagons and traders.

The road curved as it approached a low mountain range. Gray stone jutted from the ground, rising to jagged points of various heights. Harsh brush and scraggly trees grew along the rocks, deadened and barren. At the base of the mountains were the ruins of an ancient arena. Skeletal wooden beams bent over it, as if it were once enclosed. Rock rose on three sides, forming a natural protection from the elements. A single set of stone stairs led down into the arena floor, where brush and vines had grown through the floor.

Lilianna stepped up to her side. "Once, druids gathered here, but since the Shadows have grown increasingly aggressive, we haven't risked coming here. No ceremony has been held here in centuries."

Lilianna crossed to a shallow cave in the stone above the arena. She scraped what looked like moss from the cavern wall into a leather pouch. She tucked it away.

"Shade lichen," Lilianna said to Juniper. "Grandmother has been unable to cultivate it within the walls. It is effective against fever. Our supply is running low, and with the cold winding blowing from the Wylds, we need all we can gather."

She scraped and scrapped from the stone walls, the sound of iron on stone grating on Juniper's ears. Then, at last, the pouch was full and Lilianna retreated.

"Hold on for a moment," Sein said. "I, uh, need to take care of something."

He sheepishly stepped into the Wylds and out of sight. A moment later, the sound of piss striking the ground.

Juniper rolled her eyes and took the chance to climb a pile of massive stones to see the other side of the mountain. The Wylds kept going. The mountain she clung to was part of a short range that curved along a shallow valley. The stone grew in long spikes and spires, crooked fingers and jagged teeth. No brush or trees grew in the craggy mountains, and too many pockets of shadows existed between the cliffs and bluffs and caves. The Wylds had far too many places for monsters to lurk.

"It is easy to get lost," Lilianna said. "There are few roads that the Wylds have not swallowed. To have found our village among all of the dangers, you are incredibly lucky."

"Reid led the way," Juniper confessed. "Any luck was his. To be honest, I'm sure the gods like him more than me."

When Sein returned, they started back to Sinjon.

Something scurried along the side of the path. Juniper jumped and readied her magic; both Lilianna and Sein reached for their swords. Sein moved faster, unsheathing his blade and jumped in front of Lilianna with an obnoxious war cry.

Whatever had scurried never appeared. Quick, small footsteps trailed into the underbrush.

Juniper released her grip on her magic. Lilianna lowered her guard.

Sein huffed and heaved his sword onto his shoulder. "Good thing it ran. It saw me and knew it would lose."

They started walking again, though Juniper kept her eyes on the underbrush. Be it a bear or a squirrel, she didn't want to be caught unaware.

"Soon, I'll be the one training the warriors," Sein said. "I heard Jarek talking to Goddard about it."

Juniper snorted, and before she could stop herself, said, "Judging by the way you fought yesterday, you'll be ready for a real battle in a decade or two."

Sein spit into the brush along the side of the path. "You fight dirty," he growled. "A real warrior would have faced me with honor."

"Reid would love that," Juniper said with a chuckle. And he would. Thieves had little honor. Thieves fought to survive, not to be honorable. "Knights are all about honor and chivalry."

"You were just afraid that I would win," Sein spat.

Juniper's laugh burst from her lips in a snort. "I'm not afraid of anything, least of all getting bested by the likes of you."

Lilianna glanced sideways at her, neither a warning nor surprise.

Sein huffed and wheeled around. "Well, if you're so brave, why not take the shortcut back to the village?"

Lilianna grew still. The air itself grew silent, the kind that came from the mention of something taboo and uncertain.

Without their footsteps, the sounds of the Wylds grew louder.

"Shortcut?" Juniper repeated with little enthusiasm.

"The shortcut back to the village," Sein said. His grimace flickered into a smug grin. "It's an old road we don't use anymore. It cuts through the heart of the Wylds. Only the bravest dare walk it."

"We call it Blood Tree Pass," Lilianna added grimly. She locked eyes with Juniper, heavy with warning and worry. "Our ancestors once walked along it to reach the arena, but the Shadows have made it too dangerous. To walk the pass is certain death, or worse."

"Blood Tree Pass is a strange name," Juniper said. And it sent chills along her spine.

"It is named for the trees that grow in the heart of the forest," said Lilianna. She took a graceful step toward Juniper. "Legends say the blood trees grow out of the thickest magic of the Wylds. Their roots drink the tainted magic in the ground rather than water. The witches feed from the fruit of the blood trees."

"Why do these trees only grow in the thickest part?" Juniper asked.

"They say that is where the evil mage of the Great War met his end and cast a final curse upon the land," Lilianna whispered. "Only evil grows there now."

Juniper kept her face calm and curious, despite the tremor in her gut. *Where the evil mage met his end.* She had her answer—the heart of the Wylds was where Nexon had been defeated.

And Juniper had her chance.

Lilianna blinked. As if she realized what Juniper planned to do, her golden eyes widened. Realization flashed in her eyes, and she shook her head.

It was a terrible, foolish, brash idea, but an idea nonetheless. And they were running out of time to think of good, noble ideas.

Maddox had taught her to never turn up her nose at golden opportunities. *Sometimes you have to work yourself to the bone, and sometimes the perfect chance opens itself up to you like a lover*, he had said.

In Juniper's experience, chances rarely came that easy. She had always had to work for chances, at least a little bit.

"What's wrong?" Sein taunted. He leaned forward, grin stretching at her silence. "I thought you were supposed to be some big thief where you come from? Or was all that just talk?" He added in a baby voice, "Are you afraid the monsters might get you?"

Lilianna turned her warning glare at Sein, but he ignored her.

Juniper's desire to see him bleed intensified. She wanted to beat him to a pulp, but she needed this chance more.

But she couldn't appear too eager.

"All right," she said, sighing. She rolled her neck over her shoulders. "I'm not afraid of your Shadows. I'll venture down this terrible shortcut of yours. And then tomorrow, you can be my partner when I show the class how to break a nose."

"Right, if you live," Sein taunted back.

"Juniper," Lilianna whispered, warning thick on her name. "The pass is forbidden. There is no telling what kind of evil lurks in there."

Juniper rolled her eyes. She'd seen the evil of man. Bears and wolves were dangerous, but they were not evil. Now that she knew how to handle the cursed animals, or more so how *not* to handle them, she doubted any bears would be trouble. She had her steel tucked at her side.

"Let's just get this over with," she said, feigning indifference.

Sein led them to where the pass started. It was nothing more than a notch along the brush, invisible unless one knew to look for it. The path looked to have once been wider, but without feet to stomp down the weeds, the Wylds had slowly encroached upon it until only a sliver of a dirt path wound through the Wylds. It gradually declined into the shallow valley between the mountains and the village.

A valley, as if something had dented the very ground.

As if a great force had been expelled there.

Sein and Lilianna stood a few steps behind her, a safe distance from the pass, as if its proximity could cause them harm. They eyed the path as if monsters lurked behind every tree and rock, waiting to pounce.

Juniper could hear Reid's voice. *I don't like this plan.*

She wasn't overly fond of her plan either. But she needed to see what was in the heart that had the druids so afraid. If Lilianna was right, and this is where Nexon fell, there might be answers as to how.

And, if she found nothing, then she would find nothing. At least Reid wasn't there to talk her out of it.

The ancient pass looked the same as the rest of the Wylds, only…darker. Heavier. A cool breeze rattled the barren limbs.

The deadened heart of the Wylds, thickest of magic. It was the safe in the basement, the reinforced door with the unbreakable lock, the barred window, the iron-walled bank vault. What was hiding in the deepest part of the Wylds? She had gotten past the toughest security Rusdasin had to offer, and no lock, guard dog, or booby trap had yet deterred her.

"Well?" Sein asked.

"A true warrior wouldn't be afraid of something so silly as a forest path," Juniper said, a taunt on every word. "Care to join me? Show your mettle?"

Sein considered it. He moved his gaze from her and onto the pass. For a moment—less than a heartbeat—genuine fear replaced his bravado. He blinked, and his bravado returned in full.

"No," he said. "I don't want to die today."

Juniper felt a fraction of that fear, that dreadful anticipation. She shoved the feeling away. The world rested on her shoulders, and she had to find out how the archmages defeated Nexon. She had to. She didn't have time to be afraid of folktales.

To shake the lingering tension, Juniper laughed. The sound startled a few birds. Caws rang out and wings flapped, hidden in the gloomy canopy. She took the first step onto the bramble-thick path. Age-old twigs and parched vines crunched under her boot. Despite her straight shoulders and high chin, dread wormed through her stomach. She could do this. Easy. All she had to do was walk.

She took another step, and another. She ducked around the first turn and then the next, and then she paused to see if either of them had followed. Neither had. It would take them a while to return to the village, and she would have time to search for clues about Nexon's defeat.

Easy.

CHAPTER 31

The deeper into the Wylds Juniper walked, the stranger the sounds and narrower the path. The wind whispered through the barren trees and brush, like a thousand voices all at once, hissing malicious ways for a lost traveler to die. The very air felt *wrong*. It was not a wrongness she had encountered before. It felt…wilted and bitter and tired.

Something scurried—she jumped. In reflex, she summoned a dagger of ice and angled it to kill, but nothing lashed out at her.

A beat, then two, then three.

She felt the curse tugging at her magic, trying to pull the ice from her grip. She released it before something could spawn from it.

She spat a curse.

Juniper Thimble did not cower from Shadows. She didn't cower from anything. She had grown up in the shadows of Rusdasin, stealing through the dark like a monster herself. She hadn't risen to the top of Maddox's guild by luck. She had done it through skill and determination. She could handle a few measly Shadows. Probably.

A memory floated in her ears—the roar of the cursed bear.

Juniper steeled herself and drew her steel dagger from her side. The heft of a well-made weapon gave her a deep sense of comfort, though not as much as having ice in her hand.

She navigated the pass one step at a time, watching low hanging branches and stretching brambles. The path steadily angled downward into the valley. She assumed the lowest point of the valley would be the heart of the Wylds, the location of Nexon's defeat, and she kept her eyes open for any clues.

And then she spotted the first blood tree. It was a ghastly thing. Its blackened trunk twisted as if the moisture and life had been wrung out of it. The branches stretched without pattern in every direction, crossing one another, growing into each other. Unlike the other trees, the blood tree's branches were not bare. Leaves of blood red sprouted along the black branches.

It looked like a tree that sucked tainted magic from the ground. They gave Juniper a mixture of wonder and dread.

She kept walking. She didn't have all the time in the world to gawk at the Wylds.

The deadened trees became fewer and fewer, and the blood trees increased. Some grew so close together that they appeared as one tree. Some red leaves had already fallen, and they spotted the dirt path. More fell as the breeze whistled through the Wylds. It might have been the sun reflecting on the leaves, but an unearthly glow seemed to warm the narrow path, almost golden.

Magic—but not the magic she had grown to know. A different sort of magic filled the pass. Tainted magic. Wild magic. It was a glimmer of druid magic spliced with something else, something darker and a shade sinister—an echo of what had happened here a thousand years ago.

As the blood trees increased, so did the golden glow. As the path leveled, the glow became specs, splinters of gold. Juniper searched the ground for any sign of those specs, but she saw only dirt, rocks, and fallen red leaves. The specs did not land on her skin or clothes; they evaporated as she got near, only to reappear after she had passed.

The air smelled bittersweet, like autumn, but also like something she couldn't identify—the strange, wilted magic.

The path leveled. She had reached the bottom of the valley, the deepest point.

Only blood trees grew. The golden specs magnified, and that strange otherworldly smell intensified. Almost overwhelming. The whispering wind faded into a murmur. It did not take long to realize why the locals feared this place. It gave Juniper an unsettling feeling, a pitting in her stomach that hitched her breath.

Juniper plucked a bright red leaf from its black branch. The stiff stem snapped under her touch. It looked like a normal leaf, only red. She lifted it to her nose. It smelled like a leaf, but bittersweet and tangy. Juniper touched the leaf itself—her fingers came away bloody. She gasped and dropped the leaf. Red stained her fingertips where she had touched it, yet she felt no pain. She rubbed her bloodied fingers together—her skin remained intact.

Sap? It felt gooey, but it had a consistency frighteningly like blood.

A chill crawled down her spine like the feather-light legs of a spider. She wiped the blood-sap on the trunk and cursed herself again. She would not be afraid of trees or their bleeding leaves!

She started down the path. The blood trees thickened and thickened. They grew taller, their branches stretched and stretched until they laced together over the path and encased her in a bloody shadow of a tunnel. The dulled afternoon sun shone on the other side, illuminating each bright red leaf. She imagined that in the raw sunlight the leaves would be blinding.

Her unease only worsened.

She paused in the middle of the tunnel. On either side, a splotch of sunlight glowed, slightly angled upward. This was it—the bottom of the valley. This is where her answers would be, if she found any.

She didn't know what she expected. A hole in the ground in the shape of a man, a pit, a marker—but she saw nothing. Though, if no one had been through the pass in centuries, she doubted there would be anything of a marker. The Wylds would have swallowed anything from a thousand years ago.

Though, the more she looked, the more she thought she saw.

She *felt* things moving out there, all around her. Through the dense canopy of blood trees, the ground almost seemed to roll, like black fog. Crags and cracks in the stone jutted through the brambles, and those little golden specs issued from those cracks, fluttering into the air. Whatever they were, they were coming from underground, or at least from under the blood trees.

It might have been the lack of light, but *things* scurried through the shade. Maybe it was her imagination running away, but the gentle murmur became the brush of horns on thick skin, padded footsteps on dead brambles, and tree bark crunching between teeth. The wind picked up. It slid through the air in a feminine sigh, an out of tune song of a hundred different voices.

Something scurried along the path, toward her.

In less than a heartbeat, she flung her dagger—a terrible, shrill cry burst through the whispering silence. As the steel sliced into the hard, leaf-strewn ground, a *thing* darted from the impact—dark as a puddle of ink, shifting as sunlight through water.

A Shadow.

It slithered to the edge of the path.

Juniper held her breath. The Shadow was no bigger than a house cat. It hesitated in the underbrush, and two large white eyes blinked at her. The skin shimmered, just as Lilianna had said, shifting like light through water in shades of black and gray. While its body shimmered and undulating, the eyes remained steady.

The Shadow looked far less intimidating than the bear, and far less terrible than the man-eating demons the locals made them out to be. Of course, the monsters Nexon had set loose in Castle Bradburn had jaded her sense of *monster*.

The Shadow blinked and vanished into the forest. Juniper remained crouched, looking after where the Shadow went. Then she heard them. Footsteps. Calm, steady footfalls, one after the other. Bipedal. Unmistakably human.

Juniper, still crouching, froze. From her angle, she couldn't see anyone in the forest. Her heart pounded. Should she run? Attack? Hide? She had the element of surprise, but she had to think fast. And it might be someone from the village. What would they think if they saw her in the heart of the Wylds? Jarek wouldn't be happy. Knowing these backwater fools, they might kill her on sight for it.

Of course, she wouldn't let it come to that.

A single local, she could handle. Kill them quick and pretend not to be any the wiser. Blame it on the bears and wolves and witches.

Juniper inched forward over the fallen leaves. She spotted someone moving through the forest. On two legs. A dark cloak hid the tall, thin body. The stranger walked between the trees without hindrance from the brambles. They walked with a fluid grace that made Juniper uneasy.

The figure paused by a squiggly blood tree. A scurry, and then the little Shadow jumped into the figure's arms. The Shadow rested its head against the figure's shoulder, looking quite comfortable. The figure reached for the Shadow and stroked its back.

The Shadow's white eyes glazed. Juniper adjusted her footing—her heel brushed a bramble and it snapped—the Shadow's eyes snapped open and settled on her.

The hand on its back paused.

The cloaked figure turned, as if the creature had told it where she stood. Underneath the hood, where the face should have been, was a hideous, yellow wooden mask. Where the eyes should have been was only darkness.

A hissing little voice in her mind screamed, *Witch!*

Behind the figure, a greater Shadow emerged with eyes as large as her head. Another appeared behind it, larger still, unfurling itself from the air like fog. Another plopped onto the ground behind it, and Juniper heard another plop behind her.

Fear curled in her gut as if the witch had wrenched through her stomach. Yellow Mask stared at her, and Shadows unfurled themselves from the air. Shadows closed in around her, lumbering through the forest, growling and hissing. Juniper tore her eyes from the witch—white eyes blinked all around her, inching closer. Talons scraped against hard earth and tree roots.

She had never felt such dread—icy, tingly dread. And then she knew exactly why the locals feared this place, these monsters. Their very beings oozed fear. She couldn't fight them all, especially without her magic.

The air thickened and turned heavy, and each breath became harder to take. Juniper took in her surroundings quickly; she had little time to decide. The path toward Sinjon remained clear—she bolted. She lobbed over the back of a Shadow, rolled, and ran as fast as she could. The Shadow let out a hiss, but she ignored it.

She burst out of the other side of the blood tunnel, into the dimmed sunlight, and ran. Along the bottom of the valley and up the other side, over deadened brambles and grasping vines. She ran until she saw no more blood trees, and the long-dead trees took over the forest. Only then did she pause to catch her fleeting breath and ease the stitch in her side.

Juniper looked behind her. No one pursued. No witch, no Shadows.

She gasped for breath. Had she come close to finding the answer to Nexon's demise? She would have to get past those Shadows and the witch. Somehow. Later, after she had something for her parched throat and queasy stomach. After she had stopped trembling.

CHAPTER 32

When in doubt, get the hell out, Maddox had told her before her first solo heist. *Take risks only when you know the risk, never when the risk is unknown.*

Juniper waited until her heart calmed and her breathing evened. Did she imagine it, or had the air gotten colder? Swallowing her residual panic, she continued toward Sinjon. Relief spread through her limbs when the timber wall came into view. Slipping between the patrolling sentries was far easier than she expected—these were not the thief-wary City Watch or Royal Guards of Rusdasin. They watched for obvious monsters, not sly thieves.

She slid between a butcher and a soap maker's hut—the smells threatened to push her nausea into the dirt. The sounds of the village warped together in her mind, stirring her panic and nausea, and making her crave darkness and silence. She stumbled into a wall, earning a few stares from two passing girls who heaved a basket of leather scraps between them.

Juniper ignored them and pushed on toward Enna's house, to her quiet corner, to her cot of furs.

She heard Jarek's booming laugh spilling from the open doors of what smelled and sounded like a tavern. Ducking into the alley, she went the long way around the tavern to avoid anyone inside seeing her. Jarek knew she had gone with Lilianna. She didn't want him to question why she was back before them.

She weaved through the dirt-floored alleys between stone homes, clouds of singing, and strings of foot traffic. A gaggle of old druid women walked out of the Great Hall as Juniper passed, each eyeing her as she carried an armload of stolen goods. She felt their stares all the way down the street and even after she had put stone between them. She passed a courtyard where druids had gathered to do their washing, each dragging soapy clothing over a washboard. At the sight of Juniper, their conversation halted, as did many of their hands. Juniper pushed it all out of her mind. It didn't matter what the druids thought of it.

Right now, she just needed…rest. Warmth.

She started up the incline to Enna's house, and it took more energy than she anticipated. Her legs begged for rest, her lungs ached from the run, and her light sweat had turned cold. She stumbled through the door.

"Juniper?" came Enna's caw. She stood in the doorway to the hearth room, folded linens in her wrinkled hands. She looked Juniper over, and her brows furrowed. "You're pale."

"The walk took it out of me," Juniper lied. "Could I bother you for a cup of tea?"

Enna hummed indifferently. "I hope you aren't catching a cold so early. Go wash up and I'll make tea."

Juniper didn't argue. She returned to her little room and poured water into the washing basin. She added a log to the fire to warm the air, and she used a little bit of magic to warm the water. Both tasks took a tremendous amount of her dwindling energy. As the air heated, Juniper sat beside the water, catching her breath and letting her heart return to a steady rhythm.

Every other beat felt too fast, but the in-between felt too slow. The floor seemed to undulate under her feet.

She held her fingers to the flickering light. The red sap on her fingers still looked fresh. It squished between her fingers.

"Real blood would have dried and flaked. Clearly, it's not blood. It's sap."

Juniper's heart stuttered and skipped, and as she spun toward the voice, she lost her footing. She careened into the hard floor, knocking her shoulder into the wooden stand of the basin. It wobbled but did not fall.

She scanned the room, but it was empty.

Yet she had heard a voice. As clear as if someone stood beside her. The more she thought about it, the more the voice sounded like Maddox. It had his educated and intelligent tenor, graced with subtle viciousness.

Maddox was not in Sinjon.

She looked down at her fingers.

"See? Magic is dangerous, especially the weird kind."

Juniper looked again around her little room. That voice had been Amery's.

"Hello?" Juniper whispered.

No one answered.

She pushed herself onto her feet and dunked her fingers into the basin and washed them off. The blood-sap didn't come off easily, not like real blood that would have washed away. Then she undressed and washed as quickly as possible.

More than once, the world tilted violently. Juniper clutched onto the sides of the basin, heart pounding, until the world returned right-side up. Washed as much as she cared to be, she hastily dried. She twisted her damp hair into a bun. Her hands shook, her knees were weak, and her stomach roiled.

"Tea is on the table," Enna cawed from the hearth room.

Juniper pulled her wool dress over her shoulders and headed to the hearth room. A line of green-tinted steam gently curled from the spout of an earthen teapot. Juniper poured herself a cup while Enna trimmed a potted herb with spiky green leaves.

The tea smelled like herbs, and it tasted like them too. It reminded her of the tonics Ison had once brought her—in another lifetime.

"Drink all of it," came a voice that sounded unmistakably like Ison's soft tenor.

Juniper didn't bother to look around and see if he had snuck into Sinjon. Like Maddox, like Amery, he wasn't here.

A horrible, horrible thought struck—what if she was hearing ghosts? Her stomach dropped. What if Nexon had infiltrated the Undercity and killed her friends? What if Ison had been caught and killed? What if they were dead, and their ghosts had come to her to let her know?

Her hands shook a little more.

"You look sick," Enna said. Her golden eyes examined Juniper's face.

"I'm fine." It came out a whisper.

Enna hummed in disbelief.

"What can you tell me about Blood Tree Pass?" Juniper asked innocently, eyes on her tea.

A beat passed. "Why do you ask?"

"I heard the sentries mention it." Not an outright lie. Sein was a sentry. "He said it was a road no one uses anymore."

Another beat passed, and Juniper stole her eyes from her tea. Enna stood by the hearth, hands tight around the handle of her ancient clippers. Juniper tried her best to look simply curious, not like she was digging.

"Many believe Blood Tree Pass to run through the heart of the Wylds, that it is where the Wylds first sprouted, where the curse began to swallow everything in its path," Enna said, her words cautious and low, almost whispering. "Once, the road took druids into the mountains, and now it lies abandoned like many of the roads and ruins scattered throughout the forest. Shadows stole it from us centuries ago. It is far too dangerous to tread, even for our most experienced hunters."

"Centuries," chimed a voice that sounded like Maddox. "Your archmage vanished around that time. Coincidence?" He half-laughed. "I taught you better than to believe in coincidences."

She agreed. The witch had taken the pass.

Despite the wooziness that wormed through her body, Juniper continued. "What is a blood tree?"

"A tree of blackened bark and bloody leaves." Enna turned her attention to her spiky green plant. "Young spring blossoms are dark. The leaves gradually unfurl into a bloody red. As autumn approaches, those leaves brighten and brighten, until they fall to the earth." She added in a whisper, "According to the stories, the magic is strongest when the blood leaves are brightest."

Juniper took a drink of her tea. The leaves had been very bright and bloody.

Enna released a deep sigh. Something dark and tired passed behind her eyes. "Magic corrupts all that it touches. Twists it. Taints it."

Juniper's next drink did not go down as smoothly.

The door in the hall opened, and heavy boots sounded on the floor. Before Juniper's hazy mind could think of an escape plan, Jarek appeared in the doorway. He started to speak, but his eyes fell on Juniper. The smile faded from his eyes and his lips pursed.

"Juniper," Jarek said, shutting the door behind him. "You're back early. I haven't seen Lilianna or Sein yet."

Enna scowled at Juniper. Thoughts came together behind her eyes, and genuine anger boiled. Her weathered face flushed with it. "Is that why you asked about the pass?"

Jarek took slow, thunderous steps to the table.

"Tell me you didn't," Enna demanded. She squeezed her clippers hard enough to turn her old knuckles white.

Juniper didn't answer.

Jarek leaned onto the table, mouth twisted downward and eyes piercing. "The pass?" His voice hit like low, rolling thunder. "You went down the pass?"

Under his mountainous glare, she felt small.

"Oooh, someone's in trouble now," came the singsong voice of Xavier.

Jarek did not react to the voice. Fear and grief at the possible loss of her brother hit unexpectedly, like a cold hand around her lungs.

"The pass is forbidden for a reason," Jarek said. "It is dangerous. Do you think yourself above the danger? What if something were to happen to you? Think of your family. Think of the boy that would not get to see you grow old. Think of the children you would not have. Think of the family you would rob from him. All because of one misguided mistake. Your life is not worth the risk."

Juniper met Jarek's glare. Her head pounded. She didn't have words to argue with him. She knew he was right, but she had a realm to save.

Enna stood on the other side of the room, holding her clippers far too tight. Her golden eyes bore into Juniper as if she had committed the most atrocious of crimes. Not even Captain Sandpiper had beheld her with such hatred and damnation, not even that night in the dungeon.

"Juniper," he said, his voice low and dangerous and a shade fearful. "Did you see anything in the pass?"

"No," she lied. "Just leaves and trees."

Jarek held her gaze a moment longer, then cast his eyes to the hearth. Something dark passed over his face—a mirror of what had come over Enna's face a few moments before. Juniper glanced at Enna. The old woman still glared.

"My son," Jarek whispered. Pain twisted his words. "We went scouting further into the woods than we ever had, looking for resources, and we stumbled across Shadows inside a shallow den. We frightened them off because we were arrogant and young. Then, my son spotted a figure within the woods. A cloaked figure wearing a mask. We searched for the witch. To kill it because we thought we could succeed where others had failed." Pain wretched over his features anew. "My son wandered too far into the forest. He was barely ten summers old."

Juniper's chest squeezed; she knew the rest of the story before Jarek said it.

"We never found him," Jarek said. "The witch stole him. Swept him away by the Shadows."

And *killed*. He didn't have to say it.

"I'm sorry," Juniper said.

Jarek nodded his acceptance of her words. "Everyone is sorry," he said, starting for the door. "Do not go wandering the Wylds again, unless you have a death wish."

Juniper wanted to say something more, to assure him that she would put an end to the Shadows and the witches, but the words shriveled on her tongue.

Jarek left, and the air turned stifling.

"You made him mad enough he forgot whatever he came all this way for." Enna hummed in disapproval. "Drink your tea and head to bed. You need rest."

Enna said no more, and Juniper finished her tea in smaller sips. She had stepped in something she shouldn't have, then tracked it all over the village and through Enna's house. Guilt and curiosity fought for dominance. If only her pounding heart granted her room to worry about it.

Tea finished, Juniper slunk back to her room.

"It's warm in here," came the disembodied voice of Mabyl.

Juniper crawled under the furs and wools.

"Tuck in your toes," said Roslyn's sweet voice. "Cold feet, cold everything."

Sleep came quick. Strange, dark shapes filled her dreams, scattered with hisses and howls and scurrying. She was running. Trees taller than mountains and thicker than houses rushed by, their canopies glittering with white eyes. She tripped and fell through a rocky underworld, spotted with sparse lights and torches and mangled, petrified corpses.

Juniper woke up in a cold sweat, gasping for breath.

The hearth burned low. Cold air hissed through the shuttered and howled from the Wylds.

She pulled herself out of the furs and added a log to the fire, then collapsed back into bed. The pounding in her head hadn't subsided, and her entire body felt like it was about to shatter.

A voice spoke as she fell asleep, but in her daze state, she couldn't tell whose voice it was or what they said.

CHAPTER 33

Ison was sitting by the open window in his upstairs room when the placer arrived. Barely a day has passed since they arrived in Baxion. They had all washed, eaten, and slept—Ison had spent the majority of the time sleeping. He felt remarkably better, yet a coil of dread remained.

He and the others reconvened on the first floor of the boarding house. The placer was middle-aged and looked like he had a hundred other places he'd rather be. He stomped into the hearth room, and the strong stench of tobacco wafted with him. He carried a well-used leather journal stuffed with notes.

"I'm your placer," he said in a gruff, bored voice. "Let's get this over with."

They sat in the hearth room, and the placer asked them questions about their magic, their previous jobs, and their potential skills. Ison listened to the others list off what they had done without fear—Mabyl had worked in the Marca's foundry; Xavier had worked as an assassin in the Undercity of Rusdasin; Bois had been an apostate all her life, but she had an infallible ability of observation; Finn had worked several jobs in the Marca including the gardens, greenhouses, and kitchen.

The placer set his gaze on Ison, waiting.

Ison couldn't admit to being the court magician's apprentice. It would give him away. All the Dual-Fangs had known him at once by that title—the one the master had chosen for his dirty work in the castle.

He said the first thing that came to mind. "I worked as a stable hand," he lied. "In a little ranch to the south of Rusdasin."

The placer didn't ask any more questions about it, and Ison felt icy relief crawl down his shoulders. He hadn't entirely lied. He had worked occasionally in the Marca stables. He had found the horses there preferable and more agreeable than most people.

Another round of questions ensued, and then finally, the placer snapped his book closed. "All right, here are my thoughts," he said. "Xavier, I'm putting you with the scouts. They can always use watchful eyes and silent footsteps. Bois, I'm putting you at the school. The other air mages could learn a thing or two from you. Mabyl, I'm putting you—" Mabyl took a sharp inhale. "—on Baker's Street."

"What is that?"

"They bake stuff," the placer said plainly. "Those ovens don't heat themselves."

She released a huff and mumbled, "At least it's not the foundry."

"All fire and earth mages with a talent for metalwork take shifts at the foundry," said the placer. "But don't worry about that until you're more settled in. And Ison, you're going to the stables. They go through helpers, though, so watch yourself. Finn, you're going to the masons for now. They're always repairing and building. And that's all of you. Everyone got it?"

Ison nodded. He'd rather be brewing potions and tending to the herb garden, but he wasn't here to be comfortable. They were spies, he reminded himself, and they had infiltrated Nexon's camp to destroy it from the inside.

The placer stood. "I'll arrange things and return tomorrow morning to escort you to your new homes. Until then, eat and rest."

The placer had brought baskets of fresh bread, jars of berry preserves, hard cheese, nuts, and dried meats. He'd also brought a few bottles of table wine and canteens of clean water.

The placer left, and Ison released a sharp breath of relief.

"The stables?" Xavier asked.

"I couldn't tell them the truth," Ison whispered.

"It was a good call," Mabyl said as she meandered to the basket of food. She tore a loaf of brown bread in two. "How bad could the stables be? Odds are, you'll be shoveling horse shit. At least you won't be draining your magic into ovens every day."

"I bet Baker's Street smells fantastic," Bois said, smiling.

"I'd rather smell like bread than shit," Mabyl said with her mouth full.

They ate their fill. The basket also came with a deck of cards, and they played until sunset. The magelights outside brightened in time with the sun's descent, bathing Baxion in varying shades of pale light. Mabyl started a fire in the hearth, and when those flames dwindled into embers, they drifted up to the second floor.

Bois and Mabyl and Finn shut themselves into their rooms, and Ison drifted to the window at the end of the hall. It looked over the street outside. No one occupied the boarding house across, but lights flickered in the one adjacent. Mages had fled to this fabled city in hopes of freedom and safety, both promised by Nexon. No one would take lightly to Ison destroying their sanctuary and bringing their master down.

It had tied Ison's nerves in a knot.

"You're thinking too hard," said Xavier. He stood in the doorway to his bedroom.

"I'm thinking just the right amount." Ison turned from the window and headed for his bedroom. He paused in the hall, within reach of Xavier. "We're risking a lot in doing this," he whispered. "If someone catches on to what we're doing, they will rip us apart."

"I think they're more civilized than that," Xavier said. "They'd just burn us to ashes. Dismemberment is so barbaric."

Ison chuckled. He blinked—between one look and the next, Xavier moved. He had Ison pinned against the wall, catching his gasp with his mouth.

"If we're going to die tomorrow," Xavier said against his mouth, "I expect retribution."

Another kiss, hard with desire.

Ison hesitated. "I can't guarantee anything," he admitted, to himself, to Xavier, to the stone surrounding them.

"I'm not asking for anything," Xavier retorted. "Just you."

"And you'd have someone as worthless as me?"

Xavier's mouth twitched upward. "If you would have someone as worthless and terrible as me."

Ison threw caution to the wind. He grabbed the front of Xavier's tunic and pushed him into the dark bedroom.

The placer returned the next morning with a basic breakfast of stale bread, hard cheese, and tea. He gave them a simple rule: *You don't work, you don't eat.* With that, he led them from the boarding house and into their new homes. He started with Bois; he dropped her off at a grand stone building of three stories. Within, magic flashed and popped and crackled. The air smelled bittersweet, metallic and floral. The placer then took them down Baker's Street, which indeed smelled like fresh bread, sugary treats, and poppy seeds. Then they took Finn to the masonry, which stank of dust and minerals.

Seeing Baxion at work struck Ison. This wasn't a nest for black magic and evil. Mages lived here, thrived here, used their magic to survive the best they could. They had created their own civilization, their own law and order, their own system.

Had Nexon done something right? And Ison had marched in to destroy it.

The placer headed to the stables in the northwestern quadrant. The stables were massive—iron and stone rose in a dome, and more than a few mages wandered in and out. Ison assumed he would be shoveling excrement as Mabyl had predicted, but as they came closer to the dome, another scent tickled his nose.

And it made every hair on his body stand on end.

He knew that smell. Like death, decay, and old blood. A plume of stench from the underworld. Black magic.

Xavier's hand squeezed his arm. The placer walked ahead of them, and he didn't see the knowing look that passed between Xavier and Ison.

Ison swallowed. *No, I'm not all right.*

Nexon was making more of the monsters he had forced Ison to kill for—so many, he needed an arena.

CHAPTER 34

Juniper woke up to a hand on her cheek. Thinking it yet another nightmare, she turned her face away and sought the comforts of the bed.

"Jun," Reid whispered.

The soft rumble of his familiar voice sounded no different than the other voices, but she caught the scent of leather and sweat… She pulled her eyelids apart. Reid knelt by the bed, his hand cupping her cheek. Enna stood beside him. Both were looking at her, one more concerned than the other. Enna looked down at Juniper with clinical disinterest.

"You've been sleeping too long," Enna cawed. "It's midday."

It didn't immediately register that she had slept so long. She didn't feel rested.

"Enna's made you some tea," Reid said. "Do you feel up to it?"

Juniper struggled to sit up. Her body felt weak and rubbery. If she moved too fast, the world spun. Reid grasped her shoulders. His calloused hands were steady and warm and familiar. He helped her to a sitting position and pulled one of the furs around her shoulders.

She took several moments to gather herself, then Reid walked her into the hearth room. Enna put a cup of tea into her hands. It tasted like herbs, but then again it didn't taste like anything.

"Miss the city yet?" Xavier's voice asked from nowhere. "I sure as hell do."

Reid didn't react to the voice. She glanced around the room, just in case. She didn't see Xavier or even a flicker of a ghost. Reid leaned into her line of sight, brow furrowed.

"Make sure she drinks the whole thing," Enna said. "I'll return shortly. I've a few errands to run."

Juniper took a loud sip.

Enna's quick feet sounded across the wooden floor, and then she was gone. Juniper and Reid were alone.

"Are you all right?" Reid whispered.

She didn't answer.

"You're hearing voices," Ison's voice chimed. "That is never good."

"Jarek told me what you did," Reid said. "You went down the forbidden pass. I promised him I would talk to you about it and make sure you see the error of your ways." He sighed. "I doubt it would matter what I said."

She heard the disappointment in those words.

Reid leaned closer. "What happened?"

The tea helped her head, and the world wobbled less. She took another sip, and then in as little breath as possible, she told Reid what Lilianna had told her about the pass. Reid remained silent. He kept his emotions masked.

"But something is bothering you," Reid said. "Did something happen? Did you find something?"

She listened for Enna's return but heard only the creaking of the house in the wind.

"I saw something," she whispered.

In whispers, she told him about the blood trees, the Shadow, the witch, and the strange feel of the place. As the words tumbled from her lips, it felt as though each scraped against the inside of her mind, leaving a throbbing sensation behind.

"Strange," Reid repeated.

"Weird," Amery's voice added.

Juniper blinked and glanced around the room. Amery's ghost didn't add anything else.

"Have you heard of anything like it?" Juniper asked. The words tumbled ungracefully. Her shaky breath and shattered thoughts prevented coherent speech.

Reid shook his head. "I haven't, but I would bet gold someone of the Order has." A shadow passed over his face, turning the guilt she already felt into lead. "They have traveled far and learned much."

"As you are right now," Juniper added.

Reid studied her, mouth a flat line. "Perhaps one day I'll explain this oddity to a young squire."

The glimmer of hope in his eyes vanished as quickly as it appeared.

"Poor boy," Amery's voice chimed. "They're so delicate under their rough exteriors."

A shadow moved on the edge of her vision. Juniper looked but saw nothing. The sudden movement jarred her head, and for a moment she thought she would empty her stomach onto the floor. She set her head into her hand, and Reid quickly fastened his hand on the tea to keep her from dropping it.

She took a shaky, shallow breath. "Reid," she started. "I have no doubt Nexon met his end in those woods. It feels…wrong. The magic there, it's… I—I can't explain it. It feels like the magic…exploded. Scattered. Everywhere. Broken. Cursed."

She whispered the last word.

"Your powers of description are astonishing," drawled a voice that sounded like Crespin's.

Reid sighed through his nose and rubbed his face. "And you want to go back?"

"I have to," Juniper whispered. She paused in case Crespin, or anyone else, had something to add. No one else spoke. "We need answers. The witches, or whatever they are, must know something. If our archmage is hiding somewhere in those woods, and we can't get directions to her house from the chief, then we're going to have to find her ourselves."

Reid frowned. "It would anger the entire village, and not to mention worsen your health. A fever is nothing to fool around with."

She sighed into the steam of her tea. "Like I've never done that before. Half of Duvane still wants me dead, remember? Crespin wanted to throw me out of the palace."

"Life seemed so much simpler then." Reid's gaze drifted toward the hearth. The fire turned his brown eyes molten. "You really think the archmage and the witches are connected?"

"I know they are," Juniper said. "One disappeared into the Wylds and the other appeared in the Wylds. It seems obvious to me."

"And if you're wrong?"

"Then we are out of luck and back to knowing nothing. Then we can go back to Delphine."

"And apologize profusely to the poor committee," Roslyn's ghost added in pretend sympathy.

The proximity of Roslyn's voice started her. She jumped. With the motion, a tickle worked its way up her throat and erupted in a cough.

"That tea ought to take care of that cough," Enna cawed as she entered the hearth room. She tossed her cloak over a chair and marched to the hearth. She set the tea kettle over the fire. She flicked her wrist toward Juniper's half drank cup. "Stop talking and start drinking."

Juniper took a sip, then another. It pushed the tickle back down her throat.

Enna made her another cup of tea, only this time she added a powdered mixture of herbs. The second cup tasted like she had added dirt, but as she reached the bottom of the cup, the strange fog over her mind had ebbed. The voices had subsided. The shadows on the edge of her vision lessened. In exchange, a severe drowsiness overtook her.

Reid took the empty cup from her hands and kissed the top of her head.

"Get her back to bed before she passes out," Enna ordered. "Then I've got an errand for you. I need you to take this to Ingrid." She set down a basket of freshly picked bright green leaves and bundles of spindly blue twigs.

Juniper gave no protest as Reid lifted her into his arms. He carried her back to her cot and gently sat her down. With another kiss to her temple, he left.

She didn't fall asleep immediately. She dozed on and off. Enna worked around the house and in the garden, humming all the while. More than once, Juniper heard the old woman muttering to the plants.

"Is she brilliant or mad?" Amery's voice chimed. She chuckled. "Odd how often those two are interchangeable."

Midafternoon, a storm rolled in. A chilly wind blew in from the Wylds, whistling through the eaves and rattling the shutters. Juniper pulled herself out of bed to relieve herself and peeked out of the shutters. Storm clouds bubbled in the west, and the air had grown thick with humidity. Low thunder rolled in the distance.

"A storm! You love storms," said Amery's voice.

Juniper returned to her cot and wrapped herself in the woolen blankets. Soon, the roar of the rain drowned out the ghosts.

CHAPTER 35

The placer led Ison and Xavier through heavy doors and into the dome of the arena. They entered onto a walkway of stone that circled a massive pit. Bones and blood stains scattered the hard-packed dirt floor. Ison heard little over the pounding of his heart and the thudding of blood through his ears, but he heard the scratching and clawing and howling. It came from underneath them.

The placer led them along the walkway and to offices with stone walls and wooden doors and dank air.

"Mercer," said the placer. "I've got another one for you."

A broad-shouldered man with light brown hair, sunburnt skin, and a vile expression stepped out of one of the offices. He looked over Ison and Xavier, scoffed, and pointed a dirty fingernail at Ison. "It's that one, right? You never send the tough ones. It's always the skinny wimps."

The placer shrugged. "If you don't want him I'll find somewhere else."

"No," said Mercer. "I can always use another tester."

Tester? Ison did not like the sound of that word. Why hadn't he said he'd made potions in the Undercity? Bois would have backed his story.

"All right, he's all yours," said the placer. To Xavier, he said, "Come on, I'll show you to the scouts' quarters."

Xavier cast a glance at Ison. *If they kill you, I'll kill them all.*

Ison gave the assassin a parting nod. Xavier followed the placer out of the office, and something in Ison's chest tore in half.

Mercer leaned against the stone wall, looking every bit like a thug. "Let me guess, you said you wanted to work with animals."

"Something like that," Ison said.

Mercer laughed, a dark and ill-intending sound. "Come on, then."

Ison followed Mercer into a wide stairwell of gray stone. It rose up and down. Mercer started down. With every step, the howls and growls of Nexon's abominations grew louder.

"We don't keep horses or pigs or chickens here," said Mercer. "We've got a much more important job than keeping horses fed and watered. We're here on the master's orders. He calls this one of the most important jobs in Baxion, so remember that when you're regretting this job."

Ison swallowed against the lump in his throat. He tried to look curious despite his overwhelming dread.

"What exactly will I be doing?" Ison asked as they descended another level. He tried his best to not sound disgusted and dreadful.

Mercer paused on a dark landing. He wore no humor. "We've spent the past few decades rebuilding and rediscovering the knowledge lost from the Iluvin purge. We are among the few the master has tasked with rediscovering lost arts."

Dark arts, Ison thought. He said, "That sounds important."

Just then, a high-pitched shriek echoed off the stone. It crawled over Ison's skin like needle-legged spiders.

"It is," Mercer said. "And the most dangerous job in Baxion."

"Lucky me."

Mercer chuckled. He led Ison down several landings and to a set of heavy iron doors. Runes had been engraved in the metal, for strength and barrier protection. The growls and snorts were terrifyingly loud. Ison stuffed his shaking hands into his pockets. Mercer placed his hand against a small rune—the door unlocked. The doors swung inward, and the stench of rotting flesh and decay and excrement shattered Ison's next breath. He coughed several times before it returned. His eyes stung and watered.

"Finished?" Mercer asked, his tone mocking. "Or do I need to send you back with the placer for a cushy job in baking?"

A few gruff voices on the other side of the doors laughed.

Ison saw the chance—he could find another job somewhere else, far away from these abominations. Yet, as he stared down Mercer's arrogant smirk, he knew this was where he needed to be. The gods had given him a chance at redemption, or a poetically justified death.

"I'm fine." Ison straightened. "Just unprepared."

"Well, you best get prepared," threatened Mercer.

The iron doors led into a stone-floored room lined with cells. Thick stone walls separated each cell. Half the cells were empty, but the other half held monsters. They were the same as the demons that had plagued Bradburn Castle, the ones Nexon had unleashed.

The doors closed behind Ison with a powerful, creaking thud; the locking rune clicked back into place. With it, Ison's heart skipped a beat.

The beasts varied in size, some the size of common wolves and others as large as northern bears. They had leathery skin pulled taut over muscle, patchy hair that varied from blonde to brown to red, talons the size of his longest finger, snouts made for snapping, horns that twisted, and sharp eyes.

When these monsters had first infiltrated Bradburn Castle, everyone assumed them to be demons. In Ison's opinion, they were worse.

Mercer strolled down the center of the corridor, and Ison stumbled to catch up with him. The beasts watched them walk by, their bloodshot eyes wide with hunger and hatred. Mercer stopped at the far end of the corridor, in front of an occupied cell. The beast within growled and stood on its thick legs. The corded muscles shifted under its dark leathery skin. Ison met the monster's dark brown eyes. It growled and bared its teeth.

"Not the friendliest," said Mercer. "But every batch of them is getting better."

"Batch?" Ison gasped.

Mercer raised a brow. "These are the master's prized research and the fiercest part of his army. We are in charge of finding the old way to creation. A thousand years ago, these beasts were fierce and intelligent. Now they're nothing more than rabid dogs."

Mercer kept talking about creation and transformation and research, but Ison focused on his breathing, on keeping his heart from thudding so hard it escaped his chest. He met the beast's eyes once more. It huffed.

It knew. All the souls trapped within knew.

Ison knew too. He knew too well.

Nexon was making an army of these beasts. He would unleash them on the world, a terrestrial army of poisoned talons and ripping teeth. It would be Bala's Ball, but a thousand times worse.

"And that's where you come in," Mercer said, putting his hand on Ison's shoulder. He smiled, but it held no warmth or kindness.

"Me?" Ison asked.

"We lack proper…handlers," Mercer said, an uncertain emphasis on handlers.

"Handlers?" Ison's rapid heart silenced. He looked from Mercer to the beast. The beast snorted—as if it understood.

"Well, we can't very well use them if they'll attack us as soon as we open the doors," Mercer spat. "This batch is the best we've done. The first batch attacked us on sight and had to be put down the same day."

Every bone in Ison's body shuddered. He knew how many people went into the creation of one beast. But for a batch of them? How many people had been killed that day? How many people had died for Nexon's research?

And then, realization struck—apostates had been ravaging villages in the north for months, leaving an odd lack of survivors or bodies. Ison's throat closed. They were harvesting people for this vile research, as fodder for Nexon's transformation.

"So?" asked Mercer, doubt painted on his face. "You think you can handle this job, kid? You look like you're about to lose your breakfast."

"I can do it," Ison said to Mercer, and to the beast.

Mercer laughed, a disbelieving sound. "Sure, you can. That's what they all say. Then they get their ribcage ripped out. Don't say I didn't warn you, kid."

Ison knew what he had to do. He would work in the stables, with these beasts, and he would put an end to the research, however he could. If he could.

CHAPTER 36

"This storm will bring in a rush of cold air," Enna said casually that evening. She set the kettle over the hearth.

Juniper sat at the table with her back against the stone wall, a cup of earthy herbal tea in her hands. Rain splattered against the house, and wind whistled through the eaves. The tea eased the pounding in her head, the vertigo, and the voices that drifted in and out. There were no ghosts, she had realized that morning when Reid's voice had greeted her. Reid hadn't been in the room or the house, yet she knew him to be alive and well.

The voices were just that. Voices.

Juniper had slept through the stormy afternoon and woke up to Enna's invitation to dinner which turned out to be muddy porridge. It didn't matter. Juniper had little appetite and she couldn't taste the porridge. Enna had offered Juniper a dozen chores to keep her occupied—she hadn't started any of them. She didn't feel like moving. Her sleep had been marred with strange dreams of unfamiliar faces and strangling sensations.

The strange tickle in her throat continued, and her chest felt…empty, like she couldn't get enough air.

"I don't mind the cold," Juniper said.

"The Shadows prefer the cold," Enna whispered, her tone a snake of fear curling around Juniper's throat, as if that shared preference could somehow cause disaster. She crumbed dry herbs into a cup of water, swirled it around, then poured it into the roots of a small potted plant. "You'd catch your death if you went out in this cold rain."

Juniper started to speak, but a sudden cough tore its way up her throat and stole her breath. She doubled over, coughing and gasping for breath.

Enna appeared at her side, frowning. She pressed the back of her hand against Juniper's cheek. "You're warmer than you were."

Juniper waved away her hand. "I'll be fine."

Enna refilled her teacup, frowning.

The tea helped. It pushed down the tickle in her throat, opened her lungs, and shushed the throbbing headache. Two cups later, she felt better. She didn't feel good, but she no longer felt like the world was twisting sideways.

The rain abated, and Enna saw to the delicate plants in the garden. Juniper remained by the hearth, sipping tea. Enna had been right about the storm bringing cold air—the chilly wind brought gooseflesh to her arms and legs. She couldn't stay warm. The chill came from within, she realized as the hearth's warmth permeated her clothes and settled over her skin. It radiated outward, battling the heat. Juniper shivered—she had not been prepared for the duplicitous sensations.

Enna returned and tossed her rain-spotted cloak over a chair. She made another pot of tea, and the herbs flavored the air in a peculiar scent that made Juniper think of bright yellow.

A cough ravaged her throat and sucked the breath from her lungs. Enna's hand touched her cheek—Juniper jumped. She hadn't seen or heard the woman move.

Enna clicked her tongue. "You're clammy and cold. Your fever is worse." She sighed, refilling the cup in Juniper's hands. "Drink up."

Juniper muttered a thank you.

"I had a client who developed a cough overnight," Amery's voice chimed. "Died the next day. So tragic." Her tone indicated Amery held little sorrow for the sudden death.

Enna stepped out into the garden. In the glimpse of the outside, the rain had become a blurry drizzle. Still, the druid landscape remained vibrantly green and lush with life.

The wind hissed. The rain sighed against the roof. Juniper's head pounded and chills raked across her skin in waves. Juniper shut her eyes and rested against the solid wall behind her while Maddox gave calm yet arrogant comments on Enna's *quaint* interior design.

A footstep fell on the floor, heavier than Enna's.

Juniper blinked, and her awareness returned. A man stood on the other side of the hearth room. He had dark emerald skin and a scruffy brown beard. Rain spotted his cloak. There was no mistaking that sneering face, though.

Enna had not yet returned.

"You must be Juniper," he said, distaste hanging on her name. "I am Stet Braddock. You met my boy, Sein."

It was hard to miss the family resemblance. Father and son both held themselves as tall as possible, in both physical height and mentality and looked down their nose at her.

The garden door opened, and Enna returned. She tossed her damp cloak over a chair by the hearth.

"What do you need, Stet?" Enna asked in the same dry tone she used on everyone.

"Kitchen accident." Stet held up his hand. A bloodied bandage wrapped his palm.

Enna began to gather herbs. "Missing any fingers?"

"No, just some blood."

Enna unwrapped, cleaned, and added a layer of leaves to Stet's palm. Juniper kept her eyes on her tea. Enna mumbled about needing more of something, and she vanished through the back door and into the garden. The hush of the rain came and went as the door opened and closed.

Stet leaned closer to Juniper and whispered, "No doubt your gallivanting through the Wylds brought this sickness upon yourself."

Juniper glared at him over the rim of her cup. "I doubt that," she said, her tone low and menacing.

Stet shrugged. "It's forbidden for a reason. There is dark magic along the pass, and you stirred it. I hope you learned your lesson."

"I'm fine."

"You're *cursed.*"

Enna returned and Stet said no more.

Still, the word stung. Cursed. Between the short time she had spent in the Marca and from life in the Undercity, she knew curses were not to be played with. They were real and dangerous. Stories littered history of unknowing victims stumbling into ancient curses.

"I say bullshit," said a voice that sounded like Mabyl. "But you never know. That dark magic is odd, and much of it is unknown. He could be onto something."

Wrapped, Stet left and Enna returned to her pruning.

"There is much about curses we don't know," Abrielle whispered.

"Dark stories," said Ison's voice.

"Darker magic," added Xavier's.

"Nonsense," Juniper mumbled.

"Hmm?" Enna turned around.

Juniper sipped her tea and ignored the old woman's stare.

The rain thickened as night fell. Soon, the herbs stopped helping. A cough burst from her lungs every few breaths. The voices turned into whispers. Strange voices joined them, whispering words she didn't know or couldn't understand. They lingered on the edge of her awareness, just far enough to be heard without being understood. She couldn't stay warm. Cold permeated her bones, pushing outward, as if her ice had started to grow on her insides.

Juniper didn't notice the darkness at first, not until she felt the strange presence of someone beside her. A hand touched her forehead, then her cheek.

"Juniper?" Enna asked.

Witch in the Wylds

Juniper's eyes fluttered open. "Just a nap," she breathed.
Her eyes fell closed, and the darkness submerged.

CHAPTER 37

Rain pelted the roof in waves, rushed by the wind. Juniper heard the waves, and her mind conjured a picture of a violent sea, steel gray and vengeful.

She had the vague sense of someone beside her.

"You look like a damp weed," Enna cawed.

Juniper managed to crack her eyelids enough to see the old woman at the bedside. Enna began to poke and prod Juniper's scalp, her cheeks, her neck, and her ears.

"Lilianna, make a pot of tea."

Soft footsteps padded away.

"More than a cold," Enna mumbled.

The old druid proceeded to knead Juniper's limp arms and legs, testing each finger and toe, each joint and nerve. Each time Juniper would cough, Enna's hand rushed to her throat—feeling, she realized. Each cough brought a dissatisfied hum to Enna's vocals.

"Can you sit up?" Enna asked, but she did not phrase it as a question.

Juniper worked her way into a sitting position.

"Toss these onto the bedspread between your knees," Enna instructed.

Juniper accepted a small handful of stones. Most were gray, but among them were stones of emerald, topaz, and opalescent blue. With her limp grip, Juniper tossed the handful of stones as asked. Enna studied the stones for a long moment. Juniper knew of fortune tellers who used stones to tell the future, but she had never sought their services. She'd never had interest in knowing vague slivers of her future. Especially as a thief who lived one day to the next.

Enna proceeded through a series of odd tests—she plucked a hair from Juniper's head and held it to the light; she checked her fingernails and toenails; she made her toss tiny chicken feathers over the stones; and she asked Juniper to describe what she saw on the back of her eyelids. After each test, Enna referred back to the stones.

Juniper's breath came in wheezy gasps, and her lungs refused to fill. The hole where her magic used to sleep felt endless and dark.

"Have I been cursed?" Juniper whispered.

Enna responded with a disgruntled harrumph.

"You have done yourself no favors." Enna sighed through her nose and read the stones. "The pale stones are clustered close to the topaz and avoided the emerald."

Juniper looked at the stones. It looked like a mess to her. "But what does that mean?"

The healer didn't answer. "The Wylds have become a mystery, even to us. Centuries ago, our ancestors knew its secrets, its creatures, its dangers. There is much we no longer know."

A gentle knock sounded on the doorframe.

"Yes?" Enna asked, her voice a caw.

"Tea," said Lilianna.

"Bring it in."

Lilianna set the teapot on the table. She made Juniper a cup, and she drank it greedily. It banished the darkness and teetering voices.

"I've herbs for you," said Enna. She set a worn and latched leather satchel on the bed, the same she carried with her when visiting the sick. From within it, she retrieved several corked bottles and pouches. With a calmness that defied her bony hands, she measured a concoction of herbs into an empty bottle that she then corked. "We'll mix a heaping spoon of this into tea or soup three times a day. Then we'll see how you're faring in three days."

Lilianna added a heaping amount to Juniper's steaming tea. An earthy scent filled the air, like an overripe garden, dirt included. Juniper took a sip—it tasted like it smelled—bitter and harshly floral.

"Drink all of it," Lilianna said.

Both watched to make sure Juniper did just that.

By that evening, the entire house smelled like the harsh, bitter herbs. Like a sick house. Another thing Juniper tried to avoid.

The herbal concoction helped. It soothed the tickle in her throat and the squeezing of her lungs. It eased the darkness in her vision enough for her to be aware of the disembodied voices that spoke around her, each reminding her of what Stet had said: cursed.

A sound as vicious as thunder shook Juniper from her herbal-aided slumber and uneasy dreams. The entire house shook, but as quickly as it happened, it ended.

She rolled onto her back. Her head rolled with her, sloshing as if still asleep. A heartbeat after, the dull headache and fuzziness returned in force. The hearth burned low and menacing, flickering umber shadows over the little room.

Thunder crashed—no. She knew the sound of storms, and that strange sound had not been thunder. It had been closer to the earth. Dread threaded through her gut—something worse than a storm approached.

She fumbled from the bed and half-fell to the window. She threw open the shutters in time to see a black mass climbing over the timber wall of the village. Its undulating shadowy skin shimmered with shades of white and orange, moonlight and torchlight. Another followed it, and then another, and another—Shadows from the Wylds.

A terrible creak came from the ceiling. Loosened dust puffed from the seams.

"One is one the roof," Reid's ghost whispered.

She felt a ghost shift, as if Reid had risen from bed. She imagined him reaching for his Mage's Bane. She glanced about the poorly lit room to make sure Reid wasn't really there.

He wasn't.

But his ghost was right. The sound that woke her had been a Shadow jumping onto the roof.

As she stood there, Shadows climbed over the boundary wall, dozens of them, slithering like spiders. They ran over the grassy paths, toward the village.

Panic had already started—screams and shouts and the jittery sound of chaos. Juniper fumbled through her lethargy to pull on her boots and drab woolen dress. She half-fell through the sickroom curtain and headed for the main door.

Enna blocked her way.

"Stay inside," the old druid warned.

"But I can—"

"Not like this," Enna said. "You're sick, still healing from your other injury, and you will only get yourself or others hurt worse. You won't be of any help in your condition."

"She's right, you know," came Abrielle's sweet chime. "I can feel that curse. It's not good."

"Get back to bed," Enna warned. "The Shadows make a fearsome fuss, but it'll be over soon enough."

Enna maintained her place in front of the door. Juniper could barely stand up straight without swaying. Enna and Abrielle's ghost were right. She would be useless if she couldn't stand. Conceding, Juniper trudged back to her sickroom.

The idea of sitting and waiting while chaos spread unnerved her, but what else could she do? From the window, the sounds of chaos surged inside—warriors cried, steel hit leathery flesh, and Shadows whined and yipped and barked. An alarm sounded—a great bell from somewhere in the village. She leaned out of the window to see the farms on either side of Enna's house. Shadows darted in and out of the grape vines, chased by villagers and torches. Another trampled through the wheat field. Druids stood on the edges of the field, shooting arrows. The Shadow swatted the arrows as if they were twigs.

A fierce cry sounded—a wounded Shadow's howl. Something hard thudded against the side of the house, shaking the timber and stone. The impact sent Juniper stumbling over. Her back slammed into the floor, and her feeble breath rushed from her chest. She pushed herself onto her hands and knees and sucked her breath back in, coughing. Smoke began to slither through the window, as flames just outside grew brighter and brighter. The smoke curled around her lungs, gripping like burning barbs.

"Shit," she gasped.

The firewood had caught, and the flames now licked up the side of the house and into the timber eaves.

Juniper stumbled to her feet and went to the window. She gathered her magic to put out the fire or deter it, but another thud shook the house—a Shadow on the roof. By the angry yip, it had noticed the fire licking up the sides of its perch.

And the flames caught on the shutters of her room.

Too late, her gut screamed.

She focused and aimed her ice at the fire—but nothing happened. No ice came to her command, no flurries appeared, no water came to her aid. Panic flared. It was not the hot air of the room or the fire smothering her magic—it was not a lack of water to command, but a lack of *magic*.

She did not feel her magic.

It was *gone*.

CHAPTER 38

Juniper's panic turned white-hot and ice cold, turning her already clammy skin sweaty. The flames licked over the windowsill, mocking her.

If she could not fight the fire, she had only one option. Run.

She tore through the curtain and into the main hall. She heard yelling outside, to put the fire out, to get that beast off the roof, and other things Juniper's rattled mind couldn't catch. She threw herself at the main door, but it smacked against something on the other side. Something had fallen in front of the door.

Smoke spilled through the sickrooms, filling the hallway with thick smoke and flickering light. Flames licked the eaves of the ceiling. The smoke slithered closer—it tickled her nose and clawed at her throat, stealing what pitiful breath she had. She coughed on the airless taste and gagged on the scent of ash; her next breath refused her.

Panic overrode all other thoughts. She threw herself at the door as hard as she could. Whatever was on the other side moved, but only slightly.

The roof creaked dangerously. Juniper screamed as she threw herself at the door again. It barely budged. Her throat closed, and she collapsed to the floor. She shook. Tears pushed against her eyes. Her vision tunneled.

She didn't want to die. She had no time and no magic. If she couldn't get through the door or the hall, that left the window, which was currently on fire. Damn it! She'd have to jump through and pray for the fewest burns. As Juniper fumbled to her feet in the smoky hall, something heavy scraped across the wood of the front door. She'd taken one step toward the smoke-filled hall when the door burst inward. Strong hands grabbed her shoulders and yanked her back.

And then glorious, breathable air and winter's chill washed over her. Juniper took a fragile, gasping breath of the night's air.

"Juniper?" came Reid's voice.

A calloused and careful hand touched her cheek—Reid's hand. She blinked, and through the stinging in her eyes, she saw his worried and relieved face. This stupid man had raced across a battlefield of monsters and barged into a burning house to get to her. She half-laughed and fell into his shoulder. He hugged her close.

"Get that thing off before it ruins the herbs!" Enna demanded, her crow's voice cracking through the night. Her clothes were singed in several places.

A crowd had gathered around Enna's burning house. To Juniper's dismay, several other houses were burning. Smoke billowed into the sky, catching the light of the flames, flickering from red to yellow to orange and back again.

The Shadow on Enna's roof let out a bark like thunder and bared its teeth. It flicked its tail at the flames encroaching its perch.

Sentries circled Enna's house. Some were busy trying to put out the flames while the others distracted the Shadow with arrows. Several sank into its strange magic-flesh, while it swatted others out of the air with ease. One druid threw a spear. The Shadow knocked it out of the air—the spear tumbled end over end, and then landed tip-first in the earth a step from Juniper's feet. Reid pulled her back another several steps, one hand around her shoulders, the other holding his Mage's Bane blade.

Reid's blade was clean, not bloodied. Juniper glanced at the other warriors. No weapon wore blood.

Shadows did not bleed?

"I told you, dark magic," said Ison's voice.

"Creepy magic," came Amery's chime.

Enna looked furious, a contrast to the fear and panic all around her. Her wrinkled hands fisted in her apron, trembling.

"Odd that she isn't afraid," Maddox whispered in her ear. "Unless she is better at hiding it than the others."

A frightful, shrill cry sounded from the Wylds. The Shadow on the roof lifted its eyes to the sky and returned the shriek. The shrill call came from the Wylds again, only much closer. It sent a terrible apprehension down Juniper's spine, and by the horrified looks of the others, she wasn't the only one.

And then it flew from the Wylds—a black mass among the smoke, leathery wings spread wide, skin shimmering in blacks and grays. A winged Shadow flew a wide circle over the village, flapping its massive wings to keep its steady, churning the smoke in all directions.

"What is that?" Reid asked, his steady voice an accusation and a threat. He held Juniper a little closer.

Several people cried out at the sight, weapons pointed to the sky.

The winged Shadow doubled back and flew over Enna's house—it let out a monstrous shriek.

"Gods," someone behind Juniper said. "There's someone riding that beast!"

The flying Shadow circled back around, lower this time. Juniper saw the tall, thin figure on the beast's back. The rider wore dark leathers and bits of metal, and under their hood, they wore a terrible mask of red painted wood.

A witch, riding a Shadow.

The witch looked down, the eyes of their red mask black as a moonless night. That unsettling gaze settled on Juniper.

The winged Shadow called to the Shadow on Enna's roof, circled it, and hesitated in the air with a whoosh of its wings. It growled at the other beast. The Shadow on the roof protested. The winged beast growled, a menacing warning, and let out a bark of a shriek. The Shadow on the roof lowered its head and climbed down from the roof. It jumped over the villagers and headed for the Wylds. It leaped over the timber wall and vanished into the night.

Juniper swallowed her disbelief. The Shadows were *talking*.

"A demon," someone whispered.

"A witch," someone else added lowly.

An arrow shot toward the rider, but the winged Shadow knocked it from the air. The arrow clattered to the ground.

The winged Shadow cried out, baring its teeth at the shooter, and then with a massive flap of its wings, took off over the village. Juniper had little time to watch—she and Enna were ushered to the Great Hall. Its stone walls protected it from the fires and Shadows. Enna walked; Reid carried Juniper. A group of fussy druids greeted them upon entry, chattering over the fires and Shadows and damages.

Reid set Juniper onto her feet, kissed her temple, and returned to the fight. In the same moment, Ingrid appeared before her.

"You likely inhaled smoke," Ingrid said, pressing her hand against Juniper's cheek. "This way."

Juniper didn't protest. She felt the burning in her throat and lungs. Ingrid pulled her across the hall. Someone draped a blanket over her shoulders. Someone else thrust a cup of herbal-smelling tea into her hands. Ingrid brought her to a quiet spot near the back wall where Juniper sank to the floor.

Gods, her head spun, and it felt like something had clawed her lungs to ribbons. The tea helped. Herbs and a bit of the old druid magic, if Juniper had to guess.

Many had come to the Great Hall for protection, mostly the young and the old, and those like Ingrid who took care of the injured and frightened. Juniper kept her eyes on her tea, though she felt unhappy stares. She drew her knees to her chest and pretended not to notice. Around her, children whined and cried; mothers cooed their babies; the elderly circled the burning hearth fire in the center of the hall.

The witch. The winged Shadow. The curse. It all bled together with confusion that she didn't know how to process.

"Did you see it?" an elderly woman asked another. "I saw it when she opened the door. That demon beast with wings. It's helping the Shadows."

"A demon," another elderly woman hissed. She thumped her knobby cane on the ground. "Only an evil soul could command those monsters. It could only have been a witch."

Everyone was whispering about the witch and the winged Shadow, as if speaking too loud might draw its attention.

"They're really wound up about this witch," Amery's playful voice said. It came as if Amery sat beside Juniper, yet the space remained empty.

Juniper finished her tea and buried her head in the darkness of her arms. The voices drifted by, ghosts and druids.

"It's a witch, isn't it?

"It came for the pale girl."

"What do we do? They haven't breached the walls in centuries." "It was going for that pale girl. She is staying in Enna's house."

"She started this when she wandered down the pass, stupid girl."

The battle slowed, the Shadows quieted, and the Great Hall filled with weary warriors. Most were nursing burns and shallow wounds. The healers flitted around the wounded like birds.

Jarek stormed through the Great Hall's doors, and the chatter fell into a murmur. A bit of the chief's beard had been singed.

"Get those fires out," Jarek roared to the able bodies. "The more we do tonight, the less we'll have to do tomorrow."

Jarek's eyes fell on Juniper, and his frown deepened. Reid appeared behind him, unscathed though a bit out of breath and spotted with soot and dirt. He found Juniper at once, and she gave him a quick nod to tell him she was all right.

He nodded back and went with the others to help with the aftermath.

Something had changed tonight. She felt it in the absence of her magic. She felt it in the air of the Great Hall, heard it in the panicked whispers and accusations of the villagers. None of them had seen a winged Shadow or a witch, and seeing them together caused no small amount of unease or apprehension.

And she was no exception.

CHAPTER 39

A hand touched Juniper's shoulder, gentle and cautious.

"I do love the smell of smoke after midnight," Xavier's playful and malicious voice said.

Juniper lifted her heavy head. Lilianna knelt in front of her, ash spotting her cheek and her clothes. Her golden eyes held a stark exhaustion and fear. The Great Hall had calmed considerably, and sleeping bodies gathered along the walls.

"It's over," Lilianna said.

Reid appeared at Juniper's side and lifted her into his arms. He carried her out of the Great Hall and into black and smoky night. The smoke blotted out what few stars dared to emerge between the lingering storm clouds. The voices hissed and jeered and slithered. Her headache throbbed…

Reid carried her back to Enna's. The worst of the damage had been done to the sickrooms. The garden looked a bit wilted, and the entire house reeked of ash and smoke. Lilianna led them to the second floor, to an unused bedroom. It was no bigger than a sickroom, with a vaulted ceiling and a window that looked out over the front of the house. Under the stench of ash, it smelled like dust. Reid set her on the cot, whispered a goodnight against her cheek, and departed with a kiss to the same spot.

Lilianna was talking, but Juniper wasn't listening. Then, Lilianna left too. Juniper fell asleep to a ghostly chime that sounded terrifyingly like Nexon's drawl. In her dreams, that same voice mocked her.

This curse will kill you and save me the trouble.

The rain abated by dawn. From the village came the clattering of hammers, saws, and druids hard at work to repair what had been damaged. Juniper remained in bed. Her sleep had been fitful and restless. Nexon's ghost had drowned the others, and now only his voice spoke, taunting insults and jests.

Lilianna brought up a pot of tea for Juniper and an extra log for the small stove in the corner.

187

"No one has been in here in decades," Lilianna said as she stoked the fire. "This was my mother's room before she married, and my grandmother's room when she was a girl."

Juniper barely listened. Nexon's seething whispers made her hands shake. The tea had no taste, and it did not help.

Is this what it meant to go mad? To lose one's mind?

That is what she felt like—like her mind was slowly slipping into the curse, into a dark fog that could never be lifted.

Lilianna stood to go.

"That witch," Juniper whispered.

Lilianna stilled. She set her golden eyes on Juniper, wary and careful. Juniper hadn't forgotten what she'd overheard in the Great Hall the night before. Nexon's ghost had made sure of it.

"Do you think the attack was my fault?" Juniper asked sheepishly.

Lilianna didn't answer for a long moment. "No, not intentionally. The…witches have never come to the village. People are afraid. No one knows what this means. And no stranger has angered the witches as many believe you have. It is easy for them to blame one on the other, as Grandmother says."

Juniper accepted that answer. Panicked, fearful people made panicked, fearful decisions and came to brash conclusions. They had directed their fear onto the easiest target: Juniper.

"I need to go," Lilianna said. "Grandmother has enlisted my help with the wounded."

She left, and Juniper sipped her tea alone. When the curse lifted enough, she trudged to the window. She spotted druids fixing roofs, hoisting up new walls, patching fences, and tending to the destroyed crops. Juniper had no desire to collect debris or sweep ash. She had little desire to do anything.

She poured a second cup of tea with shaky hands. She tried to warm the tea with her magic, but she couldn't.

Her magic was *gone*.

What sort of dark curse could steal one's magic?

"Serves you right," Nexon's ghost spat. "All you do is get in the way. You cause nothing but problems for everyone."

The day passed in fits of tremulous sleep, useless tea, and Nexon's hateful whispers. Juniper tumbled from one nightmare to the next, often unsure of when she had woken and when she still slept. A chorus of indistinguishable voices joined Nexon's until she could no longer pull his out. They hissed and seethed, too many to make out much more than a few words here and there.

Cursed. Ruined. The end. Her fault. Cursed. Black magic. Dark. Evil. Cursed.

188

She couldn't tell the nightmares apart. Dark figures and whispers assaulted her on both sides of her eyelids.

"Jun?" Reid's voice sliced through the darkness.

She cracked her heavy, sticky eyelids enough to see his concerned brown eyes. The stove flickered warm light over the little room, and someone had shuttered the window. Reid brushed hair from her face and helped her into a sitting position. He handed her a cup of warm tea, and as she took it, he sat beside her. He did not wear his armor, and leaning against him granted her a sense of balance and stability. Reid slid his arm around her middle, securing her more.

The tea's warmth surged down her throat and spread into her limbs, taking the edge of the stinging headache and the blur out of her thoughts.

"Is it better or worse than being poisoned by Nexon's beasts?" he whispered.

"Worse."

His brows rose.

"I could sleep through that," she said, her voice a harsh croak.

Juniper stared into her tea. It wasn't like Mage's Bane that made her magic turn mean and angry, and it wasn't like when Reid had made her magic curl up and hide—this was like her magic itself had vanished.

And that terrified her.

She wanted to tell him about it, and a part of her knew she should, but the words wouldn't come. Speaking about it made it real, and as she tried to push the words from her throat, her gut clenched and her stomach turned over.

How many times had she wished that her magic would go away? Had that wish finally come true? Had the gods finally decided to grant her that request?

"You need to eat something." He gestured to a basket he had set on the narrow table. "Ingrid made it."

Her stomach clenched at the idea of food, but she knew he was right. She needed to eat something.

Reid unpacked a small meal of steamed dumplings. He sat dutifully at her side while she nibbled her way through a dumpling.

"How are you healing?" Reid asked.

"Like I'm losing my mind," she said without thinking.

He frowned. "You'll get better, we'll find out what we can about this archmage, and then we'll get out of here."

He spoke with sincere reassurance, and Juniper desperately wanted to soak it in and feel it in every bone.

"Reid," she started.

"Oh, yes," Nexon jeered. "Tell him you can hear voices. Hopefully, he'll do the wise thing and cleave you in two with that sword of his like he should have done ages ago."

She closed her mouth. What would Reid say? Would he see it as black magic? Evidence of a curse?

Reid touched her shoulder and brought her closer. His brown eyes searched hers, looking for the rest of whatever she'd been about to say.

She swallowed. "Am I cursed?"

He frowned.

"I heard them talking," she confessed.

And everything else confirmed it. Her magic, the voices, the attack. A common fever could not steal magic.

He didn't immediately answer. "Dark magic is…tricky. The Order has been frugal with the subject. Gods only know what sort of dark magic lingers in these woods. I can't rule out the possibility that you stirred an old curse."

Voices sounded from the floor below, one of them Jarek's.

"Repairs are coming along," Reid said. His expression turned grim. "The village isn't fond of you right now. Some blame you for what happened."

"Are many injured?" Juniper asked.

"Too many," he said lowly. "But we will manage."

"Jarek blames me." She had seen it in his face the night before.

Reid kept his emotions masked. "I can't speak for the chief, but others have openly threatened you. They say we should throw you back to the Wylds and let it have you."

Juniper didn't like that idea.

"Some seem to think if the witches want you so badly, we should let them have you," he whispered without flinching. "Few haven't heard of your jaunt down the pass, and now all of this. The sky is gray. Shadows raid. A witch rides in on a winged beast."

Juniper had no defense, other than to call them all ignorant, suspicious, backwater fools—yet her gut agreed with them. She couldn't shove their suspicions aside anymore. She had done something, triggered ancient magic, or incurred the wrath of an old witch.

Reid stayed until Juniper had eaten two dumplings. Food helped. As he packed the basket, she realized just how tired he looked. Bags hung under his eyes, and he smelled of smoke. Soot stained his hands.

"Get some rest," he said as he kissed her temple.

He hadn't, she realized with a sinking heart, kissed her lips in a while. Was he afraid of catching his curse?

Likely he didn't want to catch a sickness.

"Likely," Nexon's voice sneered. "Or he's finally grown tired of your stink."

CHAPTER 40

Juniper found an old wool blanket in the cabinet and greedily wrapped it around her shoulders. Nexon's whispers mixed with a hundred others, hissing and hurling insults and slurs. She added a log to the stove and curled up on the bed. She watched the shadows flicker away from the stove. A cold breeze hissed through the shutters and fought with the heat.

Slowly, the flames dimmed. The air grew colder. The whispers grew louder. Juniper pulled the blankets over her head.

Cursed.

Her breaths refused to fill her entire lungs. She had never been this sick. Winter sicknesses had rarely touched her, and when they did, they never lasted more than a few days. Could the witch in the yellow mask have cursed her that day? It had all started on the pass.

Without her magic, who was she? She'd spent so long hiding her magic, and she had made herself strong without it. Yet she felt empty without it. She had grown used to her magic. She relied on it. With it gone, she felt…lost.

A whisper seethed close enough to her ear that she swatted at it—her hand lashed through chilly air.

Juniper released a huff. She couldn't stay like this.

Nexon's ghost laughed at her, as charming as it was menacing.

If the witch had done this, they could undo it. The witch in the red mask had come to the village for her, and Juniper could go into the Wylds for them.

If the archmage was out there, Red Mask might know more.

Juniper could knock out two birds with one stone. It was better than lying around waiting for a mob of villagers to throw her over the wall or the ghosts to drive her insane.

A sense of direction evaporated any thought of sleep. Juniper rose from the bed, careful not to make any sound. She dressed as quietly as possible. She slipped out the window, down the side of the wooden house, and onto the cold ground. She landed firmly, but the world wobbled—she fell against the soggy grass. She took shallow breaths to steady herself; when the world no longer wobbled, she lifted herself back to her feet.

"Graceful," Nexon mocked, though the word faded behind a wall of hissing whispers.

The storm had left the village a muddy mess. Mud sucked onto her boots and the hem of her cloak, squishing and squelching under each step. Despite her woozy state, she climbed up the wall and slipped through the patrols with ease.

Even mad and sick, she was the best of the Undercity.

She landed in the grass on the other side, the soft ground squelching. Low thunder rolled overhead, and before she reached the edge of the Wylds, the rain started again. It peppered the deadened forest in an incessant roar. Ignoring the gooseflesh that raced across her flesh, she headed for the heart of the Wylds, navigating the brambles and brush and mud. The rain made the ground treacherously slippery. She nearly fell several times, catching herself on deadened tree limbs. She thought she spotted tracks in the mud, but the rain washed them into splotches.

The Wylds felt different at night. Larger things moved through the blur of the rain. Shadows lumbered through the brush and brambles, their skin shimmery and dark, their eyes wide and white. None paid her any mind.

Juniper tripped and caught herself on the large trunk of a dead oak. Thunder cracked above. She righted herself and took only a moment to catch her breath, then she took off again. She pressed on through the never-ending trees. The rain blurred the Wylds into streaks of black and gray, and it hushed all other sound save for Nexon's occasional taunt. She kept going.

She glimpsed bright red through the darkness and the rain—blood trees. The little golden flecks dotted the air, not bothered by the rain or wind, but there seemed to be fewer of them than before. A little further, and she would pin the witch down for answers. About this sickness, about the archmage, and about Nexon.

She kept going, closer and closer—she squeezed between two blood trees and into the darkened tunnel in the middle of the pass. The rain blurred the pass into a bloody mist.

And… It was empty.

Juniper stood for a moment in the rain, catching her breath. Her chest squeezed, each breath harder than the last.

What the hell was she doing? Her lungs ached, her clothes sucked to her skin, and even her socks were wet. Her skin had chilled beyond gooseflesh. The cold penetrated through her skin, to her bones. Even if she could remove the water from her skin and clothes, it would return in a matter of seconds.

Any other time, she would have loved the cold, the dark, the rain. Now, the darkness pulsed at the edges of her vision. The whispers seemed to come from the trees themselves.

She didn't want to stop, but she didn't know how far she could wander into the Wylds. Nonsense, she told herself. She had come this far.

She meandered along the pass, searching for movement, for that humanoid figure. The rain lightened, allowing her to see farther, though even with her night sight the drizzle blurred the shadows.

She weaved in and out of the pass, widening her search, and just when she was about to give up and return to Sinjon, she spotted it: a dark cloak, tall and lean, walking on the edge of her night sight. She followed, her steps not as light or swift as she would have liked. She hurried and jumped over a fall log—her boots slapped the mud on the other side. The figure paused—they turned.

Juniper saw a mask, though she couldn't tell the color. The shadows made it all the more grotesque. The figure stood for a heartbeat—by the way their arms folded toward their chest, they were holding something. Juniper took a step toward them, and then the figure ran.

"Hey!" Juniper shouted over the rain. "Wait! Don't go!"

The figure ran harder.

Cursing, Juniper darted after them. The figure moved with unnatural grace, over and under and around, but their cloak kept catching on branches and bushes. Still, Juniper couldn't catch up. Her feet caught on brambles and roots; thorns caught her arms and legs and cheeks.

The figure slid down a small ravine with ease, sliding through the mud and jumping the gushing stream like a deer. The cloak swished aside, and two long legs landed in the mud on the other side. Juniper slid down the ravine. She could make that jump with ease—she readied her legs—and realized her mistake too late.

A tree root snagged her footing, sending her face-first into the gushing stream. She broke through the water, and something hard struck her—the impact knocked the sense from her mind and sent stars across her vision. The water raged around her, but she couldn't fathom a response against it. She couldn't swim to find the air she needed or use her magic to save herself—she didn't have the mind to think the thoughts she needed.

The world felt too far away for her to be a part of it.

Then the water vanished. In her blurred, drowsy vision, a garish mask of red loomed from the darkness of the Wylds. Behind it, a great black monster blinked a white eye.

She had things she wanted to say, but her voice did not come. Her thoughts sputtered and collapsed. The mask loomed closer and tilted.

She tried to hold onto her reality, to the world, but it fell away from her grip. The whispers evaporated, and then so did everything else.

CHAPTER 41

Ison buried the shovel into the fresh excrement and heaved it into the cart. His arms ached, his clothes reeked, and every muscle had faded into a dull, numb throb. He'd spent the last several days working in the stables—sunrise to sundown. He fed the beasts, watered them, and cleaned their cages when the trainers took them into the arena. The cages were underneath the arena's floor, and Ison heard every failed attempt to tame the beasts.

He heard the yelling, scolding, and commanding, and then the roaring, tearing, and screaming.

And the silence.

Ison kept his head down, his mouth shut, and listened. The trainers were a colorful bunch, and they liked to talk. The beasts were created deep underneath the arena. The fodder, as they called them, were kept somewhere down there too. Ison would have to free them somehow. The beasts were created in batches of five, and all five of the most recent batch remained alive. Two from the previous batch remained. All the others had been killed. Those two beasts rested in their cages while Ison cleaned.

Ison hadn't seen his friends since being placed in the stable. He lived in a house with the trainers and stable hands. Ison hated every second of it. The house smelled like sweat, blood, and unwashed people. Mercer complained that the useless or stupid were sent to the stables, and Ison agreed—silently—that the trainers shared a common personality.

Not that it mattered. Ison wasn't here to make friends.

He heaved another shovel of excrement into the cart.

"Oh, you're still here?" Mercer strolled into the caged corridor, as Ison had taken to calling it. "That's right, you've been doing the easy job."

Ison didn't retort. He'd rather shovel waste than actually train the beasts.

"We've got another batch of five coming up tomorrow night," Mercer said as if he were talking about a shipment of textiles. "They'll be on this side." He gestured to the empty cages. "I want them ready before you leave."

Ison nodded. "They will be."

Mercer marched to the far side of the corridor and vanished through an iron door. A dark staircase on the other side led down into the experimental chamber. Ison had thought about going down there every day, to stop the transformations, but he couldn't force himself to do it. Every time he thought about it, he saw the Death Chamber in Bradburn Castle and the blood and the bones and the people Nexon had forced him to kill.

Even now, he started to shake. His gut trembled. His memory conjured the smell of the caverns, the blood, the beasts.

His knees gave out—rather than fall on his face, he fell backward.

The beast in the cage behind Ison huffed.

"Of course I'm afraid," Ison whispered to the beast. He turned to meet the beast's black eyes. "Do you want to go back down there?"

The beast tilted its head to the side.

"No, I didn't think so," Ison whispered.

The beast snorted, a disgruntled sound.

"As much as I want to, I can't," Ison admitted. "I…can't."

Ison averted his eyes back to the cart. He had five stalls to clean out. As he cleaned, the beast with black eyes watched him, silent and observant.

The door leading to the experimental chambers opened, and Clint—one of the trainers—marched through. He wore blood stains on his pants and his hands. It looked as though he had tried to wipe it off, but Ison knew too well that didn't work.

Ison had avoided the trainers as much as possible. He didn't have time at the end of the day to talk, and most of them were the dangerous sort—the kind of people who felt no regard for the lives of others. They reminded Ison of the old Undercity, lawless and reckless. They all sported scars where the beasts had bitten and clawed. A few had lost fingers. They were in and out of the healer's quarter more than any other worker in Baxion, enough so they had an antidote to the beasts' poison in constant stock.

Ison had no desire to join them in that regard.

"Don't work too hard," Clint teased. "Wouldn't want you to get a blister on those dainty hands."

Laughing, Clint continued through and up to the arena.

The beast snorted.

"I agree," Ison said.

That night, as Ison washed the grime and sweat and smell of excrement off his body, relief and dread fought in his gut. He had the next day off, yet he knew he would have to return to the beasts. He grabbed clean clothes from the community stockpile—the stable hands and trainers went through a large number of clothes, so no one had their own. Ison had managed to protect his only remaining article of clothing, his red scarf.

Ison fell into his bed, thankful for the moderate silence. He slept in a tiny room with a few other stable hands, none as gruff or obnoxious as the trainers. They came to bed as tired as him, and no one had the mind to talk.

Ison woke up to an overcast morning. Before anyone could recruit him, he slipped out of the house and into Baxion. He hadn't yet had the chance to wander the city. He passed through street after street of industry, businesses, and houses. No space in Baxion went to waste. Something was being made or reused. And magic. He saw bakeries with fire mages heating their ovens; water mages cleaning water and making wine; earth mages fixing roofs and streets; blacksmiths working old iron and steel into new creations; air mages lifting crates for easy transportation. It was all incredible.

And it hurt to think about how Ison would bring it all down.

He wandered into an open square. A fountain spouted water in the center, and tables and chairs scattered the colorful stone ground. Ison bought a cup of mead from the counter and sat in the muted sunlight.

Even overcast, it felt great to be in the sunlight.

"You're looking a bit beat up," came a familiar chime.

Ison opened his eyes. Cera stood at the table, frowning at him with her hands on her hips. She wore common clothes, not her scouting gear. Beside her stood Xavier, in common clothes of dark gray and blue. A wave of relief washed over Ison at the sight of them. He hadn't realized how much he had missed familiar faces.

"This seat taken?" she asked, motioning to the one across from him.

"No."

She plopped; Xavier sat beside Ison with the grace of a cat.

"I see the stables haven't eaten you alive yet," Cera said. "You know, everyone else talks about how stupid the trainers are. They end up there because they aren't good at anything."

"Thanks," Ison said dully. He knew.

"I mean, not you," Cera said quickly.

Xavier chuckled.

"You're the quiet type that ends up there because the placer doesn't know what else to do, and the stable goes through people," Cera added. "You should have been a scout. It's more fun. We at least get to wander around."

"It is," Xavier said.

Ison nodded. He would rather wander around the woods, but he needed to be in the stables. He couldn't explain that with Cera listening, so he didn't explain it at all. He let silence be his answer.

"We have the day off, and I'm guessing that's why you're out here?" Xavier said.

Ison tipped his mead toward the assassin, then took a drink.

Cera ordered drinks for herself and Xavier, and in the few moments of her absence, Xavier leaned closer to Ison.

"Everything all right?" he whispered.

"It's as good as it could be," Ison answered. "I don't know what to do from here. How do I start to dismantle a society? *Where* do I start?"

Xavier didn't have the answer.

Cera plopped back down with two tankards. She slid one to Xavier.

"Baxion special," Cera said.

Xavier took a sip. His grimace was short-lived.

"So, what's your story?" Cera asked Ison.

"I don't have one."

"Everyone has a story."

"Mine's not exciting."

"That depends on who's listening," Cera said. "My story isn't exciting. I was raised in the north. I heard about this group of apostates, and everyone says they're bad. Knights came and said I had to go to the Marca. I didn't want to go. Knights said I didn't have a choice. They clamp these Mage's Bane cuffs on my wrist and throw me into the wagon. Then these apostates ambush the knights and ask me if I want to go with them instead. I went with them, and now I'm here. See? Boring. So, what's yours?"

"I lived in the southeast of Rusdasin," Ison said. Ugly emotions squeezed his heart. "I had a brother. Parents. I thought they loved me. When the knights took me, they didn't protest. They didn't even try."

"Knights?" Cera asked. Her brow furrowed. "I thought you worked on a ranch or something?"

His heart thudded hard. He had no lie ready, and when Cera leaned onto the table, he started to sweat. Xavier tensed beside him. His hand clenched as if reaching for steel.

"I—I…"

"Lied." Cera didn't look surprised. "A lot of people here do. Did something bad happen?"

Ison swallowed. "I went to the Marca," he whispered. He looked away, pretending to remember something horrible. He met Xavier's blue-gray stare. "I got out. I ended up in the Undercity. I met Bois there. She told me about this place, and I…wanted out."

Cera nodded. "I get that. That's why most mages end up here. It's a way out of whatever hellhole they're in. It's a place to be a mage without shame or regret. We have magic, so we're going to use it."

"I agree with you," Ison said. He glanced at the counter where a water mage flung ale and wine into goblets with a showman's grace.

"Have you heard from your family since?" Cera asked lowly. Her eyes were elsewhere.

Ison looked down into his mead. Guilt and shame were turning his insides into mold.

"About a year ago," Cera started, "I went with a scouting team into Duvane. We went by my old home, and I talked them into going there. They didn't want to. They tried to talk me out of it. An older scout told me it wouldn't be worth it, but I wouldn't believe him unless I saw for myself. So, I went to see for myself."

"And?" Ison leaned forward.

Cera wore vulnerability. "My mother disowned me. Loudly. She was more worried about the knights punishing her by extension than seeing me alive and healthy again. She told me to never come back."

Ison felt a pitting in his stomach.

"But that's how it is," Cera said with a sigh. She pulled bravado over her vulnerability, but it didn't work. "Mages are outcasts from the moment the Marca finds them. Sometimes before." Her bravado slipped. "I have a sister. My twin. We did everything together. But she didn't want to see me either. My family lived as though I had died, and they shoved me away." Tears gathered along her eyelids, but she quickly blinked them away. She took a long drink of her ale.

"I had a brother," Ison said. "I looked up to him. I adored him. He wrote me when I went away. His letters came every day at first, then every week, then every month. Then every year. Then…they stopped." He paused, the words heavy on his heart. "The last time I saw him, he told me never to come back. My family had moved on without me."

"People can be so…unforgiving." Cera swallowed the contents of her tankard in a large, unladylike gulp, then slammed the tankard onto the table. She belched. "But you're here now and have a new family. We would fight to keep you."

"I doubt the trainers would put up much of a fight," Ison said in a half-laugh.

"I think they would," Cera said. "You're still a mage, and that's one thing the master made clear: we're all mages, and we're all in this together. We're family."

Ison swallowed. He felt the tug toward those words and the belonging they implied, but he knew the kind of family Nexon would stitch together. Ison wanted no part of it.

Cera stood. "I've got to go. I told Buck I'd meet him for cards."

Xavier waved farewell, and then it was just the two of them.

"Care for a walk?" Xavier asked. "It's awfully loud here."

Ison drank the rest of his mead, then followed Xavier away from the square and down a quiet street. Neither spoke. Xavier paused outside a simple brick building, then went inside.

"My new place," Xavier deadpanned.

"At least it doesn't smell like shit," Ison grumbled.

Xavier chuckled. He guided Ison up to the top floor, to an empty room full of cots.

"So," Xavier started. He pinned his unwavering stare on Ison. "You've seen your brother?"

Ison let out a long sight and plopped down onto one of the cots. He hadn't meant to let that information slip, and he'd known Xavier would catch it. "Do you remember, on the way here, we passed through Nulbax?"

"I remember," Xavier said dryly. "You insisted on being the one to go into town for supplies."

"My parents live there," Ison whispered. He slumped onto his knees and stared at the dirty floorboards under his feet. "I went to see them. They weren't there. Idel was, and he said…" Ison took a deep breath. Shame and sorrow pushed against his eyes. His voice quivered. "He married. He has two sons, five and three. And I have a sister. She was born after I was taken."

"What did you brother say?" Xavier asked, his voice stable and calm. An assassin trained to keep it in, to not feel.

"He told me to leave," Ison whispered. "He told me that knights had been there looking for me. My parents knew that I'd fled my job at the castle, that I'd been labeled an apostate. Idel said I would only cause them trouble if they saw me." He paused, unable to put into words how Idel had said those words; he had spoken with bitterness and malice, not like a loving brother at all.

Ison choked on a sob. He fought hard to keep the others down. He pressed the balls of his palms into his eyes to keep it locked in.

All the while, Xavier said nothing. After a moment, he sat beside Ison, calm and steady. When it passed, Ison wiped his damp eyes. Xavier took one of his hands and held it firmly.

"I can't change what happened," Xavier said. He struggled to get the words out. He had mentioned more than once that in his line of work, emotions only got in the way. "But you're not abandoned. You have a new family. Me. Jun. Mabyl. Finn. Bois. And Reid, I suppose. And everyone in the Undercity. Cera was right about being in this together, even if she isn't on our side. *We* are in this together."

"And we'll figure it out," Ison added. It sounded like something Juniper would have said. She would have known what to do, or she would have figured it out on the way. Ison would have to borrow some of her recklessness and luck and hope it didn't kill him.

Ison loosened his hand from Xavier's and reached for his red scarf. He looped it around the assassin's neck and folded it over his collarbone. Xavier went still as stone, but as Ison's fingers grazed the skin of his throat, he swallowed.

"Do you have any plans for today?" Xavier asked casually.

Ison half-laughed.

"Cera told me about the northern gardens where they grow their herbs," Xavier said, standing. "She said it was quite the sight. All the flowers are always in bloom."

Ison stood. "I could use a calm stroll through a garden."

CHAPTER 42

A strange dream plagued Juniper's sleep, of a stone-walled room, a warm golden fire, and wooden mask painted a faded yellow. The mask loomed over her, tilting this way and that way, curious and observant.

A hand touched Juniper's cheek—first a calloused palm, then the bony back.

Something soft and warm flitted over her skin, a featherlight blanket made of starlight and summer air and morning fog.

A voice spoke, soft as summer moss, but the words were lost in the dream.

Juniper was safe and warm, and nothing else mattered.

Juniper woke without realizing it. For a warm, fuzzy moment, she thought about nothing. Her mind was blank. Then she began to realize, to think. The night sky looked down at her, spotted with wispy indigo and plum clouds.

The black and scraggly limbs of the blood trees and their red leaves lined the edge of her vision.

The pass?

Awareness settled slowly.

Silence filled her ears, peppered with the scurrying, pitter-patter of the night forest. No voices hissed or whispered.

The night, the stars, the chill—it tugged on her magic.

Her *magic*.

It had come back to her. The oppression of the Wylds remained, but her magic!

And she could breathe—she took a full, sturdy breath. Her lungs expanded without fuss and expelled the air just as easily. Had her foolish, irrational, impulsive plan worked?

She sat up—a horrible pain shot through her skull. A gasp escaped her throat and she slumped forward onto her knees, burying her head in her hands. The wave of pain ebbed. She found no knot, no wound, not even blood. Her body was sore and tired. And…cold. The warmth she had felt upon waking had vanished, and the chill of the night oozed through her clothes.

Movement caught her eye—the forest around her was empty, save for one fragment of darkness too full to be pure shadow.

"Is that you?" Juniper asked.

The sliver of darkness moved closer, into the moonlight, into her night sight. Under the hood, they wore a red wooden mask. The witch who rode the winged Shadow. Two eyes blinked at her, no more than glints in the dark. Long green fingers poked out of the sleeves. Juniper doubted they knew she could see them as well as she could.

"Who are you?" Juniper whispered.

Whether the witch would respond, Juniper wouldn't know—the silence of the night erupted with a masculine shout.

"Juniper?" Reid called. "Jarek's, she's here!"

She blinked and took her eyes off the witch. She saw a spark of light first, then she saw Reid running toward her. He carried a torch. Jarek ran not too far behind him. Juniper looked back to the witch, but they had already gone.

"Jun," Reid breathed as he knelt beside her. He touched her face. The palm of his hand felt like a hot coal against her cheek. "You're freezing."

"Reid—"

"We need to get you out of here," Reid said.

Jarek took the torch, and Reid lifted Juniper into his arms.

Juniper kept her eyes on where the witch had been, but she saw nothing more of them. Reid felt impossibly warm; had her own coldness gone unnoticed? It reminded her of her dream, of the surrounding warmth and ease. She shut her eyes and let Reid carry her back to the village. She tried to hold onto her dream, to memorize every detail, but by the time they stepped over the threshold to Enna's house, the vividness had faded.

"Juniper?" Enna cawed. "You found her. Is she all right? What happened?"

She pulled her face out of Reid's thick cloak and blinked several times before her eyes focused. Enna stood by the hearth, golden eyes wide and pinned on Juniper. Anger and worry twisted her wrinkled features.

"Can you stand?" Reid asked her, his breath warm on her temple.

"I think so."

Reid set her back on her own feet. She wobbled—his hands rested on her shoulders, and she leaned back against his chest. His warmth seeped into her back, into her bones. Reid gently squeezed her shoulders.

"What happened?" asked a voice she didn't immediately recognize. It was Jarek. He stepped into her view. The relief had worn off his features. Anger burned in his eyes—the kind that got people killed.

Juniper swallowed. She blinked and saw masks.

Truthfully, it still felt like a dream.

"You had us worried near death," Enna spat.

Enna pressed the palm of her hand against Juniper's cheek, then turned her hand over and pressed the back of her hand to the same spot. Just like the hand in her dream.

"You're chilly, but your fever seems to have broken. Do you feel well?" Enna asked.

"Aside from a headache, yes." Juniper quickly evaluated herself. She felt no pain aside from her headache. No strange voices. No bruises or broken bones. Not even scrapes from her run through the Wylds.

Enna sighed and put a hand over her heart. "Thank the gods, child. We thought something horrible had happened to you."

Juniper frowned. "I'm fine. I just—"

"You've been missing for a week," Reid whispered, the words drenched with stoic fury.

Juniper's next thought slammed to a halt. She met Reid's unreadable gaze. "No," she said. "I left just this evening. I couldn't have been gone more than a few hours."

Surely the sun would soon rise.

"You were," Reid said, his voice dark and threaded with emotion she didn't recognize. His eyes were cold and distant. "But we can talk about this in the morning. You need rest."

"And a strong cup of tea," Enna added.

"I agree," Jarek said, his voice final. "We will talk about this in the morning."

Reid escorted Juniper up the stairs and to her small room. He did not leave her with a kiss or kind words; he said nothing at all.

Juniper sat on the bed. Underneath her panic, she felt her magic rejuvenating. She heard no disembodied voices. She saw no shadows darting on the edge of her vision. She saw no strange colors behind her eyelids. All of that gave her the proof she needed. The witch, the archmage, had done something to her, and had reversed it.

Juniper tumbled through an uneven sleep. Dreams came and went, mixed with wooden masks, warm fires, foreign palaces, ancient trees, and Undercity ruins. Enraged druids chased her through a stony maze. She ran, her lungs burning and her side aching. Closer and closer they came, but still she ran. As claws sliced her back, she woke. The sun seeped through the shuttered window, drawing a bright golden line across the room. The air had turned frigid. Frost gathered on her skin, and her breath puffed from her lips.

It took a heartbeat to realize it was not autumn's coldness but her own. She reigned in her escaping magic, hoping no one downstairs had noticed. The hearth crackled, heating the room. With every breath, the cold lessened.

She pulled the blankets tight around her. Her body felt torn apart and stitched back together. Her head ached and her throat was dry, but her lungs expanded and deflated without fuss. The house was quiet, save for the crackle of the stove.

The night before swam back from her sleepy, disjointed memory.

She had fallen into a stream or river—and the witch in the red mask had pulled her out. They had saved her from drowning. Juniper remembered stone walls, a fire, the masks—where had Red Mask taken her? Their home? It couldn't have been far from the stream, and therefore not far from the pass. They lived somewhere within the heart of the Wylds.

Had it even happened? Or had it been a mad fever dream?

No. Her gut told her it had really happened.

It wasn't the mask she remembered most—it was the feeling of warmth all over her body. Healing magic. During her stay at Bradburn Castle, the royal healer had patched her up after each demon attack. Juniper remembered the royal healer's magic as warm and slightly itchy where it stitched the skin back together and tingly where it brought her torn insides together. Abrielle's healing magic had been warm too.

The witch had healed her with a mage's magic, the same magic the druids abhorred. It only solidified her suspicions. The witch was the archmage. Why else would there be a mage in the gods-forsaken Wylds?

The more Juniper thought about her dream, the more she knew she had felt healing magic.

For a week.

That thought didn't settle well. Then again, she had hit her head. Abrielle had told her how dangerous head injuries were. They took special care to treat.

And after the witch healed her, they returned her to the pass where Reid would easily and quickly find her. They had been waiting just out of sight, watching to make sure he found her.

Her cough had vanished, and her magic had returned. She cupped her hands and summoned a few flurries just to make sure. The bright blue flakes glittered in the sunlight. Had the witch accepted her apology? Had she even apologized? Everything between the fall and waking up in the pass was blurry.

Juniper stayed in bed a while longer, then washed in the small basin—with water she heated. She found Lilianna in the hearth room, setting a pot of tea off the hearth. Lilianna did not mention the pass, witches, magic, or Juniper's absence. She spoke of the odd cold snap, of the incoming winter, of the gray skies. Juniper detected the distraction in her words, the aversion of her eyes, the fidget in her fingers.

The front door opened, and Enna shuffled into the hearth room. She shed her tattered and patched fur cloak and set her bright gold eyes on Juniper. They held nothing of judgment or dislike; she looked at her with the same disinterest as she always had.

"You've done yourself no favors, girl," Enna said. "Up with you. I told Jarek I would make sure you didn't pick anything up in the woods."

"I feel fine," Juniper said.

"Up with you," Enna demanded. "I've got a busy schedule today."

Juniper finished her tea in two gulps and followed Enna upstairs where she proceeded through the same strange tests as before. She started with the stone toss, and referred back to the stones after each test.

This time, Juniper was more aware. "How can you read stones?"

Enna shrugged off the question. "It's an old druid test for health. It's too complicated to explain to one who knows little of druid magic."

"I thought magic was bad?"

Enna scoffed. "Druid magic isn't the same as the magic you know." She pulled her eyes from the stones and looked at Juniper—really looked.

Juniper blanched. "You read that in the stones?" she whispered.

"Aye." Enna moved her hand over the stones and feathers. The strand of Juniper's hair lay over the sapphire—where it had fluttered after Juniper had dropped it. "Druid magic is subtle, and it takes years of study and practice to master. There are no fireballs or mind tricks. It is a method, old as the earth and true as stone."

"What else do they say?" Juniper asked, and almost immediately regretted it.

"I can't see the future." Enna gathered the stones in a single scoop of her hand and dropped them into a small leather pouch. "I can read bits and pieces, things that will not change easily and things that cannot be changed. The stones say that you are stubborn but clever, indifferent yet hold the capacity for compassion, and you fear your future."

Juniper bit her bottom lip. "I won't argue with any of those."

Enna chuckled. "I'd know you were lying if you did." She gathered her things a bit haphazardly and returned them to her healer's satchel. "I didn't find any signs of disease. You're as healthy as anyone can be."

"So, it's just gone? Whatever sickness it was, it's gone?"

"Can't you tell that for yourself?"

"I've never known a sickness to just vanish," Juniper said. "Do you think the witch really cursed me?"

Enna secured her satchel on her shoulder. "I won't claim to know what sort of magic the witch commands. It doesn't matter. Your secret is safe with me, girl. Just don't go blasting our walls to pieces." Enna started to leave.

"Wait," Juniper said, jumping to her feet.

Enna turned, brows raised.

"Can you tell me anything more about the witch? Do you know who they were?"

"You are certainly interested in the witch," Enna said darkly.

"I think she is connected to the Wylds," Juniper whispered. "I think she might have the answers I need to stop something horrible from happening to the entire realm."

Enna stood still as stone. In that moment, she reminded Juniper of a tree—calm, still, and ancient.

"I need to know what happened in the Wylds a thousand years ago," Juniper said, barely a whisper.

Enna's eyes narrowed. "That is a dangerous road."

"I know." It had been a dangerous road since she had stepped into the Undercity.

"I know nothing more than anyone else regarding the witch," Enna said lowly, enough to keep their conversation private. "She appeared, her magic terrified the people of the village, and she vanished into the Wylds. She has become a tormentor and beast of myth, regardless of whatever and whoever she was before. I highly recommend you leave the witch be and return to your city and your queen before your death wish catches up to you."

With that, Enna left.

But her words stuck. *She* appeared. *Her* magic. *She* vanished.

Enna knew more than she let on.

CHAPTER 43

Reid had always found it easy to shove his emotions away. Growing up with his uncle, he had focused on swordplay to clear his mind. When he held a sword against an opponent, the thoughts of his dead parents and their murderers had fallen to the back of his mind. When Nanette had shattered his heart, Reid lost himself in his squire studies. When Juniper had vanished into the Wylds, Reid lost himself in training the druids.

That morning, the first thing he noticed was the cold. The air in the village felt like the air in the Wylds, oppressive, ominous, and dank as a tomb. The sky above the village was dingy, dull gray, a shade paler than the heavy clouds above the Wylds. He was not the only one to notice. The entire village noticed, and as he made his way to the arena, many had eyes on the skies. Pointing. Whispering. Their fear was almost tangible.

A few market stalls remained in varying states of opening. A few hadn't opened at all. Fog lingered in the low alleys and ditches.

And they blamed Juniper.

Reid met Jarek by the arena, and the chief led Reid to the timber wall. A few older sentries stood looking over the Wylds and the steely sky.

"Wolves were howling last night," Jarek said to Reid. "And this" —he gestured toward the steely sky— "isn't good."

Reid closed his fingers around his Mage's Bane. "What does it mean?"

Jarek didn't answer. The older sentry scowled at Reid, accusation heavy in his stare. He quickly looked away.

"Reid, I want you out there, patrolling with the hunters," Jarek said. "The air is harsh. We must be vigilant. I want the patrol on the wall doubled. At least until this strange weather blows through."

Reid took Jarek's lack of an answer to mean he didn't know.

As the sun rose on the other side of the thickening gray clouds, Reid joined Sein and Asher on patrol of the eastern road. Reid walked a few steps ahead of them, eyes on the Wylds. In the daylight, they were unfriendly. At night, they were vicious. Juniper had proven time and time again that she could withstand more than most people, yet how had she survived in the Wylds for so long? Even with her magic, it bothered Reid.

It bothered everyone in Sinjon too. Whispers of the pale girl had spread during her absence, of how she had been stolen from her bed in the middle of the night, of how the curse had turned her to ash, of how she had gone mad and fled into the Wylds, of how she would become a Shadow or worse—another witch. Reid hadn't wanted to hear their theories of where Juniper had gone. Each one had been a knife in his heart, wrenching grief and loss deeper and deeper.

He hadn't told Jarek, but that night they had found her, he had been following something through the forest. He couldn't tell what it was, and before he could find out, he spotted Juniper.

It was as if the creature had led him to her.

He didn't know what to think about it, about Juniper, about the strange magic in the Wylds.

Reid watched a large creature move through the Wylds. It lingered on the edge of his visibility. It made no move to attack, but he kept his hand on his Mage's Bane. From what Reid understood of the patrols, it was mostly to frighten away anything that might come too close. Few patrols ended in injury or bloodshed. The older hunters had warned that boredom was just as dangerous as a beast. The worst of the beasts kept their distance from the commotion of the village, yet the occasional stray would wander near the wall.

He hated how things seemed to be constantly moving in the shade of the Wylds, between the web-like roots, behind the thorny brambles.

"…she came back last night," Sein whispered behind him. The two druids walked several steps behind Reid.

"My father saw Reid carry her to Enna's," whispered Asher. "If she was dead, we would know about it. My mother called this the darkening. She says the pale girl brought the curse back with her, and it's taking over."

"She survived the Wylds," Sein whispered. "Twice. No one has ever done that before. She's clearly cursed. How else did the Shadows not eat her?"

"Maybe she's as clever as she says," said Asher. "I heard Jarek talking to Enna about her. She's a thief from Delphine. Now she works for the Queen."

"So, she's got a history of getting out of trouble," Sein added.

"And she's getting married to a knight," Asher added, so low Reid barely heard. "Do you think she married to get out of prison? My grandmother told me stories about how people would get married and get a new name so people couldn't find them."

"Your grandmother also ate dirt and sang to the moon," Sein said.

"It was an old ritual," Asher defended.

Sein laughed. "For madness."

"And it worked," Asher said.

Sein and Asher both laughed.

"You shouldn't talk about your elders that way," Reid said, loud enough for them to hear him.

Both druids inhaled sharply. Reid glanced over his shoulder. They both wore sheepish embarrassment and shame; they hadn't realized Reid could hear them. He schooled his face into a knight's impassive mask, despite how much Sein and Asher reminded him of himself and Henry and Penet during their pledgehood.

Reid opened his mouth to lecture about warriors and awareness, when a snap drew his attention.

From the shade between two ageless and dead trees, a mass of matted brown fur emerged. It snarled, a sound as deep and threatening as thunder, and flashed its yellowed teeth. It lifted its great head and sniffed the intruders; the hot breath puffed from its short snout.

"Bear," Sein said with uncertainty.

Reid withdrew his sword. Sein and Asher mirrored the action, albeit with less confidence. The bear lumbered through the underbrush and onto the path. Its bloodshot eyes took in the three of them. Snarling, it reared onto its hung legs. It stood thrice as tall as Reid. The bear let out a deafening roar, and Reid felt it in his sternum. It rattled down the rest of his bones. He quickly shoved the feeling away. A knight had no room for fear.

"Gods," Sein whimpered.

"Brace yourself," Reid commanded.

The bear lunged, teeth and talons bared. Reid met its incoming blow. Yellowed fangs clanked against his Mage's Bane, the shriek fierce and sharp. The bear swatted at him, he feinted, and as he prepared to strike, the bear shifted its attention.

"Asher!" Sein cried out.

The bear lunged at Asher. He heaved his sword up into a defense position, just as Reid had taught them, but his face exposed his cowardice. The bear swatted the sword out of his hands. Reid dashed forward just as Sein attacked the bear. His steel slashed through the matted hair and thick hide. The bear swatted again at Asher. Its claws sliced through his leather cuirass as if he wore nothing.

Asher screamed. Sein put himself between his friend and the beast, battle cry on his lips. He thrust his blade at the bear, but between his battle cry and contact, he lost momentum. Reid saw it the moment it happened: the blade slowed. Sein's blade struck the bear and left only a shallow cut on its side.

The bear grunted and reared back, readying a swat at Sein like one might swat at a gnat. In one swift motion, Reid grabbed Asher's arm and threw him back and jumped between Sein and the bear—the bear's swat met Mage's Bane. The bear lumbered back, and Reid took the offense. While the bear cradled its bloodied hand, Reid slashed its side. The bear prepared to claw him. Reid feinted, ducked under its secondary swing, and buried his Mage's Bane into the beast's side, aimed upward at the heart and lungs.

Reid sidestepped and withdrew his blade. The blood that covered his blade did not glimmer bright red—it was curdled and viscus, like tar. It smelled far worse, like it had long since been a corpse yet still walked, slowly decaying.

The bear stumbled to the side, angry growl in its throat, and in a swift blow, Reid removed the head from the rest of it.

The dead bear flopped onto the path. Its head rolled into the brush. Sein stood with his bloodied sword in a defensive position. He wore forced determination, yet his eyes showed his fear. He had never been in a real battle, and now he had.

And he had survived.

Behind Sein, sitting on the ground, Asher looked nearly sick. The slice in his cuirass had only nicked the skin, but the slice in his arm bled freely.

"We need to get back," Sein said. He motioned to Asher. "The curse."

"Can you walk?" Reid asked.

Asher shakily got to his feet without taking his eyes off the bear. He cradled his arm against his chest, smearing blood in the claw-marks.

They started toward Sinjon. Asher walked between Sein and Reid.

"A bear," Asher whispered, his voice strained and dry. "They've never come this close."

Sein held his tongue.

The unspoken accusation hung in the air—they blamed Juniper.

Reid had no explanation for what else could have caused the strange darkening. When he and Juniper had arrived in Sinjon, the air had been warmed and clean, the sky bright and open, the grass and leaves lush. The village he approached now was a shade of ash, the trees drooped, the grass had begun to wilt. He felt no change in the air as he and the two druids passed through the gates. He couldn't deny it, and all the druids knew it.

Something had indeed changed, and he feared Juniper had caused it. Knowingly or not.

After taking Asher to Enna's for healing, Reid and Sein returned to the training pit. The sky had darkened into a shade of steel. Vicious caws sounded from the Wylds, like hordes of crows, yet Reid saw no birds above the trees.

"Teach me how to do that fancy step you did," Sein said, jumping down into the pit. He flourished his dulled blade.

"It won't be something learned in a single afternoon," Reid warned.

"Then let's get started."

Sein wore the same determination he had in the pass, only his fear had turned into something stronger. Reid recognized it; he had seen the same expression on the pledges and younger squires after their first real fight. Sein had overcome his first obstacle, and he welcomed the next.

Reid started the lesson. Sein soaked up every word Reid said, mimicked every movement, and copied every step. As they trained, a few other druids slid down into the pit for practice. Despite the lesson having been canceled, it began anyway. Reid made his rounds as the druids practiced. Dulled swords clanked and clinked, filling the chilly air with a familiar sound. Reid meandered through the pairs, adjusting grips and footing and stances. He heard Sein giving pointers to this opponent, the same Reid had just given him.

News of the bear attack had sent a wave of panic through the already suspicious and paranoid village. As he walked around the edge of the pit, he caught whispers between the older druids. Wolves had been seen on the northern road. A mosscat had been seen on the southern road. Other patrols had spotted weasels and cougars.

Sein fought with a broad druid boy, Jona. Both had greatly improved since that first day. Sein no longer flailed the sword, and Jona no longer flinched at the incoming blade. Lilianna and another girl traded blows. Dark circles hung under her golden eyes. Despite her exhaustion, she fought with budding skill.

One by one, the pairs ended their round with pretended fatal blows.

"Trade partners," Reid commanded.

They listened without complaint. Lilianna faced Sein, and the new round began. Reid made a lap of the arena, and this time did not correct stances or footing. He let them figure it out. As the rounds ended with blunted strikes to the throat or the chest, the clinking and clanking lessened.

Finally, only Sein and Lilianna remained. The rest watched as the two traded blows back and forth, seemingly unaware of their audience. Reid watched— Lilianna's footing needed work, but she held the blade properly. Sein needed to work on his defense, but his offense pushed Lilianna on the defense.

Reid saw the mistake as it happened—Lilianna did not adjust her footing as she stepped back. Sein thrust forward, and Lilianna lost her balance. She started to fall, and Sein aimed for the killing blow. However, as Lilianna neared the ground, she rolled. Sein's thrust missed and struck the ground. Lilianna bounced gracefully back to her feet, and she poised her blunted blade at Sein's throat.

"I win," Lilianna said breathlessly.

Sein blinked several times, at his sword, the ground, then at Lilianna.

"Well done," Reid said.

A wind blew from the Wylds, carrying with it the odd scent of tainted magic, rotten leaves, and…magic. Reid inhaled; underneath the rotting and taint, he caught the floral scent of magic as he knew it. He felt the essence of it, the residual magic. There and gone between one breath and the next.

"Again, different partners," Reid commanded.

As the druids fought a third round, Reid kept his eyes on the Wylds. He had had the distinct feeling of being watched.

The rounds ended, one by one. Willon stumbled—Sein tried to dodge the clumsy attack, but the pommel of Willon's sword struck Sein. Blood gushed from his nose, and Sein let out a painful wail.

"I think my nose is broken," Sein mumbled through the blood.

Lilianna released a sigh and motioned him toward the stairs. "Let's go. Grandmother will see to it."

Sein followed her pointed finger, and Lilianna walked a step behind.

Reid allowed Sein's bloodied nose a few moments of distraction, then barked at the others. They stumbled into new pairs. They had gotten better, though could they defend themselves against a bear? Or worse?

"We're at an odd number. Willon, you're with me." Reid picked up Sein's abandoned sword and took a stance. Willon paled considerably, but he mimicked Reid's footing.

And they began.

CHAPTER 44

Juniper woke the next morning and meandered into the hearth room to find it empty. She took it upon herself to make tea. Regular tea, not the nasty herbal concoction Enna had made to battle the curse.

She breathed in the herbal scents of Enna's house. Her lungs filled, yet she felt the oppressive blanket of the Wylds on her magic. She didn't try to use her magic. She didn't want to risk spawning a monster in Enna's house.

She rolled her neck over her shoulders. She felt remarkably better. The more she thought about Yellow Mask, the more certain she was that she had found the missing Archmage of Air. Yellow Mask had cursed her, and she had healed her.

Odd indeed.

Halfway through the first cup, the front door opened and closed.

"First room," Enna barked. Footsteps shuffled down the hall. "Girl, get in here and help me."

Juniper heard no one else move. Assuming Enna had meant her, she set her tea aside and answered the summons. A thin druid boy roughly Juniper's age sat on the cot, clutching a bleeding arm. His leather cuirass had been slashed, and the spacing of the claws indicated something large. His green skin had gone a shade of ghastly ash. He trembled, and his eyes were unfocused. The wound had not been made by a blade; it was jagged and nasty. The blood Enna cleaned away had turned an ill shade of umber.

Juniper did as Enna sharply instructed as she cleaned the wound, applied a muddy ointment that smelled of mint, and layered on the same leaves she had used on Juniper's wound.

Enna made quick work, and then she spooned a tonic into the boy's mouth to ease him into a slumber. They covered him with a blanket and left him to rest.

"What happened?" Juniper asked back in the hearth room.

"Bear," Enna said. "One attacked a patrol."

"Oh," was all Juniper had to say. She remembered the viciousness of a bear. She wouldn't wish an attack on anyone without proper motive.

"Oh?" Enna repeated bitterly. She turned her fierce stare onto Juniper. "That's all you have to say for yourself?"

Juniper blinked. Had she done something wrong? Aside from the other things she had done, that is.

"Step outside," Enna barked. She pointed to the back door.

Juniper took careful steps toward the door and kept Enna in her line of sight. The old druid had a gleam of madness in her eyes. Juniper pushed the door open and stepped over the threshold. She anticipated the brightness of midmorning, the lushness of the garden, and the distant singing of druids in the fields.

Steely clouds covered the sky, churning and murky. The air carried a vicious chill. The garden had dulled, and some of the plants looked like they were wilting. Sinjon felt…darker, dank. Just like the Wylds. The oppression in the air magnified, pulling on her magic. Thunder rolled over the village, low and heavy and menacing. She spotted no lightning.

"The curse has permeated the walls," Enna whispered from the doorway. Fear and disbelief shook her voice. "The sky darkens, and our song no longer feeds the earth."

Juniper felt the accusation. "What does that mean?"

Enna held her stare. "No one knows. It has never happened before. The cursed beasts have never dared get close to the walls. Our songs have always helped the flowers grow big and strong. Yet our gardens are ill and withering. Bears attack our patrols. Thunder rolls at night, though no storm comes."

"And you think it's my fault," Juniper whispered.

"Most in the village do." Enna's fear remained, but her tenor returned to its indifferent cynicism. "I highly recommend you stay inside where few can see you. Man is prone to panic and fear, and neither lead to good things."

Juniper followed Enna back inside. The morning passed with menial chores: harvesting dried herbs, hanging fresh herbs to dry, mixing herbs into powders, and tending as best as possible to the dying garden. Juniper was in the garden, holding the basket while Enna clipped fat thorns from a curling vine, when Lilianna brought Sein to the house. Blood dripped down his chin.

"Stay here," Enna said to Juniper. "Mind the plants. Some are poisonous if harvested wrong."

Juniper sat the basket on a little wooden bench and stretched her back. The clouds above continued to churn. Could the withering in Enna's garden be her fault? The once vivid colors had dulled, as had the fields of wheat and the grapevines. The Wylds seemed darker than they had before. The air whispered of winter.

The answers were in the Wylds, she knew.

Asher, the druid attacked by the bear, left before the evening meal, but another druid replaced him within the hour. This time, a wolf attacked the patrol.

"Lucky more weren't hurt," Enna mumbled as Juniper helped clean the druid's wounded leg. All the while, the druid glared at her under his heavy eyelids.

Reid came by for dinner, along with a basket packed by Ingrid. It smelled wonderful, especially after Enna's questionable cooking. Enna didn't eat with them. Neither did Lilianna. There had been more accidents on patrols. Cougars. Bears. Wolves. Groundhogs. Owls. Hawks. The list of nightmarish creatures continued to grow. Enna quickly ran out of sickrooms and took to making house calls, heavy satchel of herbs and stones at her side.

"You missed a fine training session," Reid said. His words matched his eyes: distant. "Willon slipped and his pommel struck Sein. Right on the nose."

Juniper let out a snort of a laugh. "I saw him hobble up to the house like he'd been gravely injured. I'm sorry I missed it."

Low, threatening thunder rolled against the sky. Full dark had fallen, but no moonlight shone through the steely clouds.

"Juniper," Reid whispered. He looked at her through his stoic mask, cautious and unreadable. It reminded her of her days in Bradburn Castle, when he was the dutiful squire and she the sly thief. Though his face lacked the subtle hatred and disgust he'd worn back then, it still struck a chord of unease in her chest that thrummed into her fingers and toes. "Do you feel better?"

"Yes," she whispered.

Juniper felt the caution in his words and felt it heavy on his tone. He searched her in a way only he could, seeing things she didn't intend to give away or show. She swallowed, suddenly nervous under his clinical stare.

"That's good to hear," he said.

They talked little over the remainder of dinner, and Juniper found her appetite diminished. She didn't like Reid's coldness. It twisted her gut into guilt. Was he still mad? Dinner finished, Reid packed the basket. Wind rattled the shutters. The two of them stood for a long moment, facing each other in the flickering hearth light, neither speaking.

He took a cautious step toward her—a knight approaching a wild apostate. Each step was calculated, and he never took his eyes off her.

"Jun," he whispered. "We need to talk."

Juniper had little firsthand experience with relationships, but from what she had read, those words never meant anything good. Though she couldn't avoid it. She nodded, and Reid led them upstairs to her little room.

Reid sat on the bed and padded the space beside him. "Come here."

She forced her legs to carry her to the bed. She sat. Reid smelled of lye soap, leather, and that woodsy scent that belonged to him.

A beat passed.

He leaned onto his knees and held his calloused hands out in front of him. He wore his thinking face. "You were just gone," Reid whispered. He squeezed his hands into fists. "Lilianna came to the house looking for you, and you were just gone."

He looked at her. His mask cracked. Anger and worry seeped through, chilling his eyes into a burning cold. She felt it to the bone. The look stole any defense she had of herself.

"Why didn't you tell me where you were going?" Reid whispered. "Why did you not say something? I would have gone with you. I would have… Why just leave me here to wonder? I didn't know where you'd gone or even if you were alive."

Under his gaze, her words failed her. They clattered into a blockade in her throat—it barely let air pass.

"We waited until evening, and you still hadn't returned. I didn't know what to do. We told Jarek, and while I trained the hunters, he went looking for you. Lilianna and I took turns looking." Reid swallowed, and a glimmer of betrayal and fear broke through his stoic gaze. "That's when I realized what you'd done. You'd gone back into the Wylds. We waited until dark, and then we looked for you. Every night, we looked for you. We didn't find you along the outskirts. I wanted to go deeper into the forest, but Jarek warned me against it. He said the Wylds would take me too."

Guilt hit her hard, smashing any other feeling she had. Reid had looked for her. So had Jarek and Lilianna.

"You found me," she said, her voice small.

"I refused to let you die out there." Reid tightened his fists. "I went deeper into the Wylds every night. I saw…things. I thought… I feared I wouldn't find you, or that I would, and I would be too late."

That she would have been dead already, either by the cold or by a Shadow.

"And then, last night, I spotted movement. I followed it. It led me to the pass, and that's when I found you," Reid whispered. "Jarek saw the figure. He was terrified. He wanted to turn back, but I refused."

"They led you to me," Juniper whispered. Reid's gaze narrowed. "The witch led you to me. They aren't evil, or I don't think they are. They saved me, Reid."

His gaze turned suspicious. "What?"

"I saw the witch. They ran, I chased, and…I fell and hit my head and landed in a stream," she admitted, though her cheeks blushed with the blunder. "They pulled me out. I… Everything after that is blurry."

Juniper told him everything she remembered from that night—the Wylds, the water, the pain, the darkness, the masks, and the magic. The end of her story brought a silence to the room. A portion of the anger had faded from Reid's expression, but the worry, the caution, the uncertainty—those remained.

"I've been thinking about why Red Mask saved me," she whispered. "Red Mask pulled me out of the river yet took me back to Yellow Mask. It was Yellow Mask who healed me. I think Red Mask couldn't heal me, or didn't know how, so they took me to Yellow Mask."

"And?"

"Yellow Mask isn't a druid," Juniper whispered as low as she could. "I think Yellow Mask is our missing archmage."

Reid didn't say anything for a long moment. "That means you want to go back."

"Eventually," she said. "I'll have to be smarter about it. Have a plan. Take my time. Not run through the Wylds at night, in the rain, with a fever."

Reid sighed. He held his hand out to her, palm up. She slid hers into his. He folded his fingers around hers, as if he thought she might jump from his grasp and run straight into the Wylds.

"Reid," she started. "We need to find her. If she knows how to defeat Nexon, we could stop him before anyone else gets hurt."

"I know," he said. "That doesn't mean I want to let you wander through the Wylds looking for this woman."

"I'm not a fan of the Wylds either." She sighed. "Do you think we should tell Jarek what we're doing? He might help or at least not glare at me so much if he knew we were trying to save his kingdom and ours."

"I don't know," Reid said. "Let's sleep on it. No good decision is made while trying to fall asleep."

"I disagree, Sir Sandpiper. I fell asleep plenty of nights thinking about you."

His anger faded a little more. "When was this?"

"Before you kissed me." Her cheeks burned. She had entertained herself with thoughts of Reid, the noble squire, and her, the worthless thief, far too many times.

Reid released a soft laugh, and pressed a kiss to her temple, lips curved into a smile. "That makes two of us."

She leaned against him and pressed her forehead against his cheekbone. "I'm sorry. I thought I'd be back before dawn. I never dreamed it would end so… It was rash and stupid, and I shouldn't have done it. But I did, and I'm sorry."

"Juniper," he started. He sighed. He leaned away to look her in the eye. "You can't do those things anymore. Not if you want to be in this with me."

Those words, his tone—the chill drove through her bones and punched the breath from her throat. "Reid, I…" She panicked, and her words faltered. "I didn't mean to. I—I—"

"I love you," he interrupted. He squeezed her hand. "Very little can change that now. But, Juniper, you need to tell me what you're thinking and what you're planning. Your decisions no longer affect just you. They affect me too. To an extent, they affect Adrian and Roslyn, and Ison, and all your friends. If something were to happen to you, many would mourn you."

Juniper swallowed. A lump had formed in her throat, and her words came out as scattered as her thoughts. "I've never had to worry about other people when I make stupid decisions. If I messed up and got myself killed, then it was my fault. Maddox hammered that into our brains."

"You no longer belong to Maddox," Reid said firmly. "You no longer wear his brand. You belong to no one."

"Not even you?" She'd meant to flirt, but it came out wispy and weak.

Reid's brow furrowed. "I love you, but you do not belong to me. I don't own you."

"Are you sure? I thought that was part of the marriage vows."

Reid frowned. "What kind of marriage vows have you heard?"

"The ones where the wife must obey her husband and take his name and be his caregiver and clean his house and cook his meals and wash his clothes while he does none of the same," she said a bit bitterly.

Reid chuckled, though it did not reach his eyes. "I will not force you into any vows you don't wish to take. We can write our own, or take none at all, but, Juniper, I need you to trust me. I need to know that I can trust you without a doubt, without worry, without suspicion. And remember you're not alone. You have me, and you have friends. We are here for you, but you have to let us."

She found solidity in his eyes, the same she had sought in times of uncertainty. "I promise," she started. "I want those things, I do, I just… I don't know how this relationship thing works. I've never…been in one. It's always just been me."

"And now you have me."

"And you have me," she added. "And I promise to tell you when I'm planning something remarkably stupid, and to include you in my reckless abandon, and to keep you and my friends in mind when I risk myself."

A small smile turned up his lips, and the rocky unease in her chest subsided. A little. He brought her knuckles to his lips.

The touch was featherlight and sent a shiver across her skin. "I see you're touching me again."

She'd meant to say it as a flirt, but his eyes darkened with guilt. He tried to release her hand, but she tightened her grip around his.

"I didn't say stop," she whispered, panicked.

"Juniper," Reid started. "I… I'm afraid of hurting you again."

"You won't."

"How do you know?"

She didn't. She remembered the pain that morning, like her magic and bones and blood seizing and tearing itself apart—but she remembered his touch too. She missed his gentle hands on her skin, calloused and warm. She missed his lips on hers, on her neck. She missed the warmth of his skin against hers. She missed it enough to risk the pain.

She brought his hand to her heart. "Reid, I've missed you."

His lips parted, but before the words could leave his mouth, Juniper pressed her lips against his. She had her mind set on more, but the front door burst open and slammed close. Enna's caw traveled up the stairs.

"Put him in here," she barked.

Heavy footsteps sounded. A plop followed, one that sounded like a body on a cot.

And the mood vanished.

She released a sigh against his lips. "Another time," she whispered.

He pulled her close, kissed her lips, then left. Juniper watched his departing back from the window until she could no longer see him. Low thunder rolled overhead, and Juniper closed the shutters.

How would things have been had she stayed in Jarek's house with Reid? They hadn't spent much time together since their fight. They might have made up long before now, and they would have crossed a few more things off her list. He also would have kept her company during her temporary case of madness.

She reclined on the bed and recounted all the bedroom things she still wanted to try with Reid, trying hard to ignore the moans of the injured druid a floor below.

CHAPTER 45

The next morning, Juniper woke to thunder. As she rolled out of bed, she expected to feel the rain and hear the wind. Neither came. She pushed open the shutters. The overcast sky rolled in shades of charcoal, plum, and dingy gray. No rain fell. The breeze whisked a cold, withering stench from the Wylds.

She tiptoed down to the empty hearth room. Snoring rumbled from the sickrooms. Juniper added a log to the hearth and set the kettle over the grate. While the water heated, Juniper peeked out the back door. Enna wasn't in the garden.

Thunder rolled, low and angry. Standing in the open door, Juniper realized with a sinking heart that the sound did not come from the sky. It came from the Wylds, within the forest. The curse was spreading.

The front door opened and closed. Soft footsteps padded against the floor. Juniper shut the back door as Lilianna entered the hearth room. She wore the same cynical expression as her grandmother. Bags hung under her golden eyes, and her skin had paled several shades.

"Good to see you're awake," Lilianna said. "Grandmother told me you'd recovered. I apologize for being scarce. Between patrolling, training, and the chores my mother continuously finds for me, I've kept busy. It's almost as if Mother doesn't want me spending time here."

Juniper caught the bitterness in the other girl's tone. Pointing at herself, she said, "Not with the manic cursed girl lurking."

Lilianna didn't correct her. "Have you gotten the tea yet? Grandmother has a special blend of tea for cold weather." She dumped the tea Juniper had gathered back into the jar and instead reached for a cloudy jar on the top shelf. She heaped a generous amount into the teapot. "I meant to come by earlier, but Mother refused me out of the house until the washing had been done, and then the mending."

"She sounds overbearing."

"She's…overprotective." Lilianna heaved a sigh and sat beside Juniper. "I slipped out when Mother wasn't looking."

"How is the training coming?" Juniper said, if only to fill the silence.

"Better than I expected."

"How did you expect it to go?"

"Bogged by tradition and fear." Lilianna added in a bitter mumble, "Just like everything else around here."

A stray drop of water fell into the fire, hissing into steam. A long moment passed. The hearth extended the shadows on Lilianna's sharp features.

"Is the curse really spreading?" Juniper asked.

Lilianna didn't answer immediately. Keeping her eyes on the hearth, she said, "Everyone in the village thinks so. This has never happened before. The Wylds have always stayed in the Wylds. Bears have never dared to go close to the wall or the roads around it. They have never openly attacked or sought us as prey."

Guilt twisted Juniper's stomach. "Have there been more injuries?"

"Since last night, no. The patrols have not gone as far into the Wylds as they usually do, and we go in larger numbers," Lilianna said. "But this cold weather has brought a bout of sickness with it. Grandmother has been busy. She has recruited my little sister to help her deal out herbs."

That guilty twisted deeper, a knife against bone. She thought of the dwindling garden, the wilting leaves and shriveling fruits.

The kettle boiled, and Lilianna poured Juniper a cup of herbal tea. It filled the room with an earthy citrus scent.

"It's a bit harsh if you aren't used to it," Lilianna warned.

Juniper held the steaming cup in both hands, letting the heat seep into her skin. She wanted to cool it with magic—she doubted Lilianna would notice—but didn't want to risk it. She instead blew on the surface, then took a small sip. She promptly spit it back into the cup.

Lilianna laughed. "I warned you."

Harsh was an understatement. The herbal taste was much more potent than the smell, like she had taken a bite of an underripe grapefruit and washed it down with stagnant pond water. She took another sip. It went down easier.

Juniper sipped her bitter tea, and Lilianna stared into the fire.

"Can I ask you something?" Lilianna whispered.

"Of course."

Lilianna's bitterness and exhaustion faded. "What is the world like outside the Wylds?"

Juniper blinked. Of all the questions she'd expected, that had not been one of them. "Compared to this? Endless. Fewer monsters. More people."

Lilianna's gaze looked beyond Juniper, beyond the wall, beyond the Wylds. To the world outside that she had never seen.

"I know what you're feeling." Juniper drew her finger across a shallow gash on the table, like someone had set an ax down too hard. "The desire to see what's out there. I grew up in the Undercity, a cavern under the city. I knew there was more to the world—oceans and mountains and deserts and ruins of lost civilizations. I wanted to see it, but I had no idea how. I figured I would die in the Undercity and never see anything more."

"And now you're here," Lilianna said.

"I left the Undercity." Juniper didn't bother to mention how. "I left the world I knew for places I had never heard of. I didn't go alone. I had friends who I made along the way. Friends who stuck with me despite how many times our lives were in danger."

"Reid?" Lilianna asked.

Juniper nodded. "I only met him because I left the Undercity."

"That is incredible," Lilianna said, her voice soft and filled with wanderlust and remorse.

A few moments passed where the only sounds came from the flickering of the fire and the thunder from the Wylds.

"Can I ask you something sacrilegious and forbidden?" Juniper asked casually.

Lilianna raised a brow. She wore curiosity, not damnation and fear.

"Do you think I did something to entice this…curse to spread?" Juniper whispered.

Lilianna's expression went unreadable. "It seems that way. Everyone thinks you did. You went down Blood Tree Pass, got terribly sick, ran into the Wylds and got better. Then the sky darkened, the crops withered, and the cursed beasts are daring closer and closer to our walls. A lot of strange things have happened since you arrived."

"I don't know much of how curses work," Juniper whispered. "They can outlast the castor, and they can linger for centuries. I'm afraid that I…stepped on the wrong leaf or something and unleashed an ancient curse."

Lilianna didn't say anything. She didn't demand to know how Juniper knew about curses or where she had learned it. Instead, her gaze reminded Juniper of Josephine—stern, but without judgment.

"I suppose anything is possible," Lilianna whispered. "I can't say for certain."

And just like that, the fear returned to Lilianna's golden eyes. The bridge between them threatened to collapse, and Juniper dropped the subject.

"Thank you for the tea," Juniper said. "It has helped."

Lilianna offered her a smile. "You are welcome."

The front door opened, and Enna hurried inside. She looked especially grim. She flung her cloak and scarf over a chair and mumbled under her breath. She spotted Lilianna, and her scowl deepened. "Lilianna, your mother is looking for you."

Lilianna sighed and rolled her eyes. "Of course she is. I'll be on my way."

Juniper sipped the bitter tea as Lilianna left. Enna added a few jars of oils and tonics to her shelf, then she vanished into the garden. Just like that, the momentary distraction ended, and Juniper was again alone.

By late afternoon, Juniper couldn't take the solitude anymore. Enna had been in and out of the house, tending the sick in her rooms and throughout the village. Lilianna hadn't returned. Reid had gone on patrol. Juniper had stayed in the attic room, trying not to lose her mind to boredom. When Enna left to tend to another sick druid, Juniper slipped out of the back door.

The overcast sky had darkened, leaving plenty of shadows for Juniper to cling to. A strange wind blew from the Wylds, stirring the scent of decay with its own bittersweetness. Low thunder rolled. Juniper thought she could feel the ground tremble.

Juniper wandered through the apple trees and the grape vines. Despite hanging onto the branch, the apples had wrinkled and darkened. The grapes had started to shrivel. Druids sang to the fruit before they picked it, and Juniper spied one woman sing an apple back to plumpness, the darkness of its skin faded into juicy red, and before it could shrivel again, she snapped it from the tree. She did the same with the next apple. Another druid sang to the grapes, and another to the root vegetables.

Juniper slithered through the fields and into the village proper. She kept to the alleys, to the puddles of darkness behind each house, to the shadows gathering between the light of torches. It was remarkably easy. Juniper suspected they were avoiding the dark. A blanket of unease had descended over Sinjon. The laughter and chatter she had first heard on these streets had faded. Few talked louder than a whisper. Druids hurried through the streets. Panic and fear tainted the air. Eyes repeatedly looked at the steely sky, wide with worry.

Juniper hated that they lived in fear, and she hated that they blamed her for it. If Jarek would have listened, would have allowed her to venture into the Wylds and seek out this mysterious witch, none of this would be happening.

Juniper wandered to the other end of the village, past a weaver who spun wool into thick thread while another druid spun that thick thread into thinner, usable thread. Juniper was looking at the deftness of their technique, when Jarek's voice sounded from not that far away, "All right, Goddard, what is it?"

"I told you, someone's been rooting around in my supplies!" spat a harsh male voice like gravel against sandpaper.

Curious, Juniper slipped through the alley around the weaver, around the tannery, and to the smithy. The smith, Goddard, a shaggy-haired man with burn scars up and down his sage arms, was wiggling a broken piece of scrap metal at Jarek. The chief looked none pleased. Juniper climbed onto the roof of the tannery, her soft steps hidden in the crackle of the smithy's fire. Crouching, she peeked over the edge of the roof and into the smithy.

"So, you have said," Jarek said. "Have you seen this thief of yours?"

Goddard let out a gruff laugh. "I set a trap last night. Wire set to rattle the chains. Heard them early this morning, before the sun rose. I came running, and I saw someone all right."

"Is that so?"

"It was no human, I can tell you that," Goddard said matter-of-factly. "It wasn't one of the kids either. This thief wore a mask."

Jarek took a step closer to Goddard. He asked lowly, "And you think this masked thief stole your scrap metal?"

"I know so," Goddard whispered. "I caught 'em. Before I could drag the carcass to your door, it ran off. Into the woods, mind you. It was a witch, Jarek. I saw it. Tall and skinny. Hands like vines. Wore a red mask too. Painted with blood."

Juniper sucked in her next breath. Red Mask had been in the village?

Jarek sighed and rubbed his temple. "Okay, Goddard. I will put a sentry on the smithy tonight."

"Good." Goddard crossed his thick arms over his chest. "Also, I've got some schematics for you to look at."

Jarek's entire demeanor changed. "Good, let's see them."

Goddard motioned toward the door at the back of the smithy. The two of them vanished. Juniper lingered on the tannery's roof. A part of her wanted to see what these schematics were all about, but the rest of her didn't care. Besides, the roof of the smith was angled and old. The odds of them hearing her footsteps were high.

Thunder rolled overhead, closer than it had been before. Close enough to rattle the barrel of broken swords in the smithy and to send a ripple across the cooling water's surface.

She continued her jaunt through the village's dark alleys. Druids scurried from building to building as if afraid lightning might strike them. Juniper paused in the dark alley behind a bakery where baking bread and fruit tarts overpowered the bittersweet decay of the Wylds. Twin chimneys puffed white smoke into the steely sky.

She took a deep breath. This is what she had missed: sneaking and eavesdropping, going entirely unnoticed. As if she were a thief again, slipping through Rusdasin like a ghost, when she had no realm resting on her shoulders or friends relying on her, or an ancient mage plotting her demise. Back when she was just Juniper, and Isolde was a name in history.

But…that thief was gone. Juniper hadn't been that thief in a long time, not since she stepped foot in Bradburn Castle that fateful night. She left that selfish girl behind when she sold out the Undercity, when she trekked across two kingdoms to save Prince Adrian, when she fell in love with a squire, when she sought to learn more about her own magic, and when she had vowed to save the kingdom.

She wasn't Isolde either. Isolde was…a princess, someone capable of saving a realm from a vengeful archmage. Isolde was someone smarter and better than Juniper was capable of becoming. When Juniper thought of Isolde, she thought of someone like Adrian or Roslyn. Regal and capable of making kingdom-wide decisions, of rallying people to their cause, of holding a people together. Isolde wasn't the type of girl to linger in the shadows of a dark alley while two kingdoms waited on her to save them.

Juniper didn't know how to be Isolde. She wasn't Isolde, but she wasn't that thief anymore. She…didn't know who she was.

CHAPTER 46

Ison returned to the stables the next day with a gut-clenching sense of dread. It coiled through his toes, the back of his knees, and up his spine. He felt like throwing up; he felt like fainting; he felt like screaming.

When he arrived, the black-eyed beast lifted its head. It blinked at him, then yawned.

"Morning," Ison said.

The beast snorted.

"I see you're as excited about this as I am."

The beast growled in agreement.

The iron doors at the other end opened, and Clint in his bloodstained clothes marched through.

"Oy there, shit-mover," spat Clint. "Get out of the way. The new batch is coming up."

Anxiety clawed down Ison's arms and legs and needled his neck. Clint pulled open the iron doors at the end of the corridor. A chorus of growls echoed up the stone chute. Ison stood on sand-filled legs as the first windowless cage rattled its way up the chute, pushed and pulled by earth magic. The beast inside growled and snorted and stomped. The cage did not offer enough room for it to move freely.

The trainers pulled the cage into the corridor and pressed it against one of the empty cages. The door to the cage slid open, and the beast reluctantly entered the slightly larger cell. It wore stone shackles on its feet and a matching muzzle— an earth mage stood beside the cage, commanding the stone. Only after the cage was moved and the cell door shut and locked did the earth mage remove the shackles.

At once, the beast lunged for the cell door.

Several trainers jumped. Ison jumped, despite the corridor between the beast and him.

"This one oughtta keep Ison company for a while," said one of the trainers. He sneered at Ison. The others chuckled.

"I'd like to see him up there in the arena," said another, who had lost two fingers. "Mess up that pretty face. Maybe a nice scar."

Ison's entire body flushed. The next beast started its ascent. Ison walked toward the other side of the corridor, where the brooms and shovels hung on hooks. Clint stuck his foot out and tripped him. In the moment before he fell, he worried more about impaling himself on the dirty shovel, so he twisted his body. He fell into the bars of the black-eyed beast.

The beast let out a dangerous, threatening growl of surprise and jumped to its feet.

Ison knew it then, as he slid down the bars, he was about to lose a finger or an eye or something worse. The beast pounced. Ison squeezed his eyes closed. A talon sliced through the air. He heard the talons meet flesh.

Clint let out a painful wail.

Ison opened his eyes in time to see Clint stumble backward, clutching his bleeding face. Two of the other trainers grabbed him and hauled him toward the stairwell, toward the healer's room up top. The trainers had grown accustomed to acting in an emergency, as they would have to when dealing with dangerous beasts with deadly poison. It was one of the few things Ison admired about them; they acted quick and without panic.

Ison staggered to his feet and glanced back at the beast. It blinked at him with curious eyes. He saw the hunger there, the malevolent spirit created in the transformation, but he saw something else, something he couldn't identify.

One by one, the next batch of beasts were brought up. They growled and whined and snorted. They paced. Their eyes took in their new surroundings, confused and angry. When all the beasts had been brought up, the trainers shut the iron doors and headed up to the arena. Ison was again alone with the beasts.

He meandered back to the black-eyed beast. It sat like a cat, eyeing him.

"Thank you for aiming at him and not me," Ison said to the beast. "He's not very nice, is he?"

The beast snorted and seemed to shake its head.

"If he's a jerk to me, I can only imagine what he's like to you," Ison said. "Has he tried to train you?"

The beast snorted, jerking its head down and then back up. A nod, Ison realized. These beasts were smarter than those he had helped create. Nexon didn't just want an army of them, he wanted an army that could take orders.

And that gave Ison a terrible, foolish, stupid idea.

The beast stood and made a circle of its cell, showing Ison scars along its leathery hide. It looked as though it had been whipped.

Ison made a painful face as the beast came back to sit.

"I'm sorry," Ison said to the beast.

"What the hell is going on up here?" came Mercer's gruff voice. He stomped into the corridor, wearing murder on his face. He looked between Ison and the beast. "Ha, you were talking to these beasts? I thought the others were just pulling my leg."

The beast growled at Mercer, like it wanted to rip his eyes out too.

Mercer looked at the beast, then Ison. His grin spread from ear to ear, and Ison didn't like it. "I've got a new job for you, boy."

Mercer grabbed Ison's arm and pulled him toward the doors. The black-eyed beast growled and hissed, and the others started howling. The corridor became a madhouse of guttural growls and claws on stone.

Mercer laughed.

He dragged Ison up the stairs and to the mezzanine. Trainers stood along the railing, watching one of their own work with a fresh beast. By the angry shouting and growls, it wasn't going well. The midmorning sun shone through the open roof, letting in the cold air.

"Whatcha have there, Mercer?" one of the older trainers called.

"Change of plans," Mercer announced. He hauled Ison to the opening in the railing and unceremoniously threw him into the arena.

Ison hit the dirt hard. It knocked the breath from his lungs and earned howls of laughter from the railing. He rolled onto his hands and knees, coughing for his breath.

A scream and a growl—Ison's fall had distracted the trainer. The beast lunged, fixing its jaws around the trainer's head. With a meaty snap and twist, the beast ripped the head from the trainer's shoulders. The body slumped to the ground, and the beast spat the head.

The sounds from the mezzanine were of disgust and gory excitement. Ison felt his stomach fall and his heart drop. Had he eaten any breakfast that morning, it would have come back up.

His dry heave resulted in only bile.

The beast fixed its eyes on Ison. Blood dripped from its jaw.

"Get on with it!" Mercer called from the arena's top. "Why don't you whisper sweet things in its ear?"

"Sing it a song," another said.

"Maybe it wants a story," teased another.

The trainers howled with laughter.

The beast stalked closer, his amber eyes pinned on him, hunger raw and rage bright. Ison stumbled backward, his breath ragged. How fitting of an end it would be—ended by a beast. He deserved it.

But he had one last desperate plan.

The odds were in greater favor of him getting his head bitten off.

Ison stood on shaky legs. The beast stalked closer, and Ison made small, cautious steps toward it. They met in the middle of the arena. Ison hesitated, the beast mimicked the motion; its nostril flared. Could it smell the other beasts on him?

He looked into the beast's amber eyes. The beast beheld him coldly. He saw something there—the same something he had seen in the others. He slowly turned his hands palm-up, showing the beast he held no weapon, steel or magic.

"I know what happened to you," Ison whispered to the beast.

The beast snorted in disbelief.

"I know what they did to you," Ison said. "I know what they did to *all of you*."

Those amber eyes looked up and down Ison's trembling body.

"Nexon took control of me," Ison whispered. At the name, the beast shuddered. "He used me. He forced me to hurt people, just like someone hurt you."

Ison inched closer to the beast. It didn't flinch. It kept its eyes on Ison. Within those amber eyes, Ison thought he could see the souls inside. He couldn't imagine the pain they had endured, and the agony of their existence.

"That is why I'm here," Ison whispered. "I want to stop him from doing this to anyone else. I want to stop him from hurting people."

The beast let out a low, curious grumble. It lowered his head and turned up its ears.

"I'm not one of them," he said, in a voice stronger than he'd been able to find since they had arrived. "But they can't know that. I have friends here working with me. I have friends in Rusdasin. I have friends in Delphine. We are working to stop him. This…what I'm doing, this is my part of the plan. This is my redemption. If I can be redeemed at all."

The beast stalked closer. Its paws padded against the blood-stained dirt. Each talon on its front feet could rip through his chest and tear out his heart in a single swat.

It came closer, nostrils flaring. It sniffed him, its amber eyes searching his, deeper than a human's eyes could.

The beast stood within a breath's distance of Ison. He dared not move. It's breath reeked of blood and innards. Each blasted molted air against Ison's face. He swallowed, fighting against his rising nausea.

"But I can't stop him alone," Ison said. "I need help to bring this damned city to the ground. Will you help me?"

The beast blinked, then stared into Ison with frightening clarity. The beasts he had helped make had not had the same eyes. Their minds had been shattered in the transformation, their souls tortured into madness.

The beast leaned in, and Ison shut his eyes, waiting for the maw around his head, the teeth at his throat—

The beast leaned its snout against Ison's temple, smearing blood from its snout against his skin and in his hair. A hot tongue met his cheek and licked the side of his face, smearing the blood into his hair.

"Eww," Ison whined. He wiped the blood and hot saliva off his face.

The beast grumbled—laughed, he realized.

Its eyes shone with something close to humor, acceptance, and bright defiance.

The beast's amber eyes flickered above Ison's head, to where Mercer and the other mages were standing. Ison turned. They stood stone still, eyes wide and mouths gaping. Mercer looked like someone had put something very cold down the front of his trousers.

The beast nudged Ison toward them.

"Bala's breath," breathed Mercer. He kicked down the rope ladder to let Ison back up.

The beast remained where it was, waiting. When the earth mage opened the stone door that led down into the cells, the beast went willingly.

Ison heaved himself onto the mezzanine.

"You did it," Mercer said, slack-jawed. He stared at the dead trainer.

None of the other trainers had anything to say. They had no insults, no jabs, not even a tease. They stared at Ison as if he had ripped the trainer's head from his shoulders.

The stone door closed with a clank, and the earth mages began to lower the beast to the cells.

"Go get yourself cleaned up, boy," said Mercer. Some of the harshness had left his voice. "You've got a busy day ahead of you tomorrow."

"Want to take bets on how long it takes for him to get killed?" said one of the other trainers.

"I say two beasts."

"I say three."

And as the betting started and their astonishment wore off, Ison left the arena for a cold bath. He needed to think without all the voices.

He indeed had a long day ahead of him tomorrow.

CHAPTER 47

Enna didn't say a word when Juniper slipped through the back door. A stewpot bubbled over the hearth.

"There's firewood in need of chopping," Enna barked.

Juniper took the hint. She'd rather chop firewood than dust the spice rack *again*. She lingered by the chopping block, ax in hand, and scanned the Wylds. The sun was setting, and the western edge of thick gray clouds glowed a frightening shade of dark gold. It gave the air a dingy glow. The timber wall blocked much of her view, but the archmage was out there somewhere.

Juniper heaved a sigh into the cold air. Two kingdoms counted on her to stop Nexon, and she was wasting time. She needed to find the archmage before something happened in Rusdasin or Delphine. Something might already have.

That night, after Enna had gone to sleep, Juniper slipped out of the house and into the night. The dark and cold welcomed her. The curse pulsed against her. The clouds had thickened, blocking the moonlight and dousing the village in heavy darkness. Torches flickered along the wall and throughout the village, but there weren't enough torches to burn bright enough to banish every shadow.

Despite the curse, the night and the cold gave Juniper a sense of freedom she had missed, like she could do anything. Her blood rushed, her heart raced, and she loved it. This—the sneaking, the sly movements, the patience, the thrill of going unnoticed—she missed it.

She was Juniper again. She was *herself*.

She climbed up the timber wall, slipped between patrols, landed without a sound on the other side without a sound, and darted into the Wylds.

She had promised Reid she wouldn't go into the Wylds without telling him, but she wouldn't be gone long enough for anyone to notice her absence.

She crept through the tangled roots carefully this time, watching out for any wayward footholds that might trip her or streams that might swallow her. Navigating the Wylds would have been impossible without her night sight. She could see the roots, the gaps between them, the dark holes underneath, the thorny brambles, and the low claw-like branches that would otherwise have taken out an eye or part of an eyebrow.

How had she managed to run through the Wylds that night without maiming herself?

She vaguely remembered the burning scratches on her face and hands. In her delirium, she hadn't cared. Another thing Yellow Mask had healed.

She approached the half-buried paving stones of an ancient druid road. Either side wound into the darkness, though it was better than crawling over the tree roots. She followed the road until the torchlight of a patrolling sentry brightened her in her peripheral. Juniper hurried off the road and behind the trunk of a massive tree, using its trunk as cover. The torch's shadow undulated as it came nearer, flickering between the brambles and branches, striping the Wylds in gold. The light illuminated the treacherous forest floor on either side of the thick tree. Roots and brambles waited for unsuspecting feet to grab, clothes to snare, and hair to pull, jutting up at dangerous angles, twisting upward and out, in an impossible navigation.

As the sentry's light passed, Juniper eased out from behind the tree. The road curved ahead, back toward the village. No, that wasn't where she needed to go. She left the road behind and let her night sight guide her through the trees, over the roots, and around jutting daggers of stone.

Thorny brambles pulled at her cloak and low twigs yanked her hair, but she kept going.

How long she wandered until she spotted the first blood tree, she didn't know. It sprouted in the distance, its red leaves and faint golden glow a beacon in the night. Juniper navigated her way closer to the pass, to the heart of the Wylds. She had the eeriest sensation of being watched, of things moving just beyond her sight. The curse thickened. Its oppressive nature smothered her like air on a humid day midsummer, heavy enough to steal her breath.

"Hello?" she whispered. "Are you there?"

No one answered.

Juniper pressed forward. She had come this far. She wouldn't turn around without trying. Shadows moved in the distance, barely visible even in her night sight, gliding like ghosts over the treacherous forest floor. Juniper scanned the Shadows, but she saw no person-shaped being among them.

Ages ago, before the Order and before Nexon, the realm thrived with magic. Legends told of vengeful fairies that would attack those who harmed their lands, rip them into bits of flesh and bones with tiny needle teeth and claws.

Maybe once, a long time ago, this forest had such protective inhabitants.

Juniper navigated her way to Blood Tree Pass, but she saw no witch. Only Shadows that scurried away like frightened cats. Many of the blood leaves had fallen to the forest floor. In the moonlight, the bloody pass faded into dull crimson and rust. The color of dried blood.

"Hello?" she whispered.

Silence answered her.

A cold wind blew through the pass, whispering through the blackened branches and plucked a few blood leaves from their stems. Juniper searched in and around the pass until her fingers had gone numb from cold, then made her way back to Sinjon.

If she couldn't blindly find the witch in the Wylds, then she would have to think of another way.

Juniper didn't return to Enna's house. Instead, she slipped through the shadows and past the sentries to Jarek's. She climbed the weathered stone to the dimly lit second floor window. She unlatched the shutters with a narrow twig and slipped inside without a sound. She silently latched the shutters behind her.

Reid was sitting on the bed in a drab shirt and wrinkled trousers. His silver armor hung on an ancient wooden stand in the corner. The candle on the bedside table had recently been blown out; a thin trail of smoke snaked toward the ceiling. The amber glow from the corner stove was the only light. Juniper crept toward the bed. Judging by his damp hair and clean smell, he'd just washed. She felt the lingering water on his skin.

Reid reclined on the bed and pulled the heavy quilt over himself. He rubbed his face and heaved a sigh.

She had never seen him like this, unaware of her presence, unguarded. Vulnerable.

"Reid," she whispered as she approached the bed.

His eyes flew open, he lurched into a sitting position, and his right fist reared back to strike. His eyes found her in the golden darkness, and realization calmed his features. His right hand dropped onto the blanket.

"Jun," he breathed.

She climbed onto the bed. She flattened her hand against his chest and pushed him back onto the bed.

"Are you busy?" She whispered as she straddled his hips.

His hands gripped her hips, and he let out an agitated, disgruntled gasp. His body, however, gave her a different answer.

"They can't find you up here," he whispered.

"They won't."

"Juniper," he warned.

"I don't want to be alone," she whispered. She also craved his touch.

234

She ground her hips into his. He released a small exhale as his body responded. One hand pushed the quilt out of the way while the other slid underneath the hem of her shirt, his warm palm and calloused fingers searching over her chilled skin. She bit her lip as his hand caressed over her breast. Their lips met, and their tongues battled for silent dominance. He tugged on her hair and pulled her closer. Their joining was silent, all hands and muffled moans. Juniper grit her teeth to keep her release quiet. Reid bit her shoulder to muffle his own, one hand gripping her hip, the other fisted in her hair. He released a shattering exhale into her neck, then his entire body released. She collapsed against his chest and flattened her cheek against his heartbeat.

Reid toyed with her hair for a moment. "Juniper," he whispered.

She caught the tone. She likely wouldn't like what he had to say. But the lingering ecstasy kept her in place.

"Yes?"

Reid sat up but slid his arm around her so she couldn't move away. In the low light, his eyes were molten. He opened his lips to speak.

"Reid?" Jarek's call boomed through the house. Heavy footsteps sounded on the stairs.

Her panic turned white-hot, and the same mirrored on Reid's face. Juniper kissed him quickly, slid off the bed, grabbed her discarded boots, pants, and cloak, and then slipped out of the window. Her feet hit the hard, frigid ground.

"I'm awake," Reid called.

Juniper wanted to laugh. Anyone would be awake after Jarek's thunderous voice. In the darkness behind the house, Juniper pulled on her pants, boots, and fastened her cloak.

"Good, we've got news," Jarek said. His voice held an excited edge. "Come down."

Curious, Juniper crept to the other side of the house and crouched among the wilted lavender bushes, underneath the shuttered window of the hearth room.

"What's happening?" Reid asked.

"We caught one," came the harsh voice of Goddard. "Just off the southern road."

"You managed to find one?" Reid asked, surprised.

"We'll use the Shadow to lure the witches out and end this curse before it kills us all," Jarek said, his tone threatening and low and edged with desperation.

Juniper's heart skipped into her throat. They had caught a Shadow.

CHAPTER 48

The following day passed in a tense haze. The sky darkened to a stormy steel, casting the village in dismal, cold shade. Thunder shook the stones of Enna's house and rattled the jars and tins. Even the hearth fire seemed to still with every rumble.

Enna came and went, treating the druids in the sickrooms and all over the village. That night, as the sparse gray glow of daylight had faded into inky darkness, Juniper went with the crowd of nervous druids to the sunken pit by the barracks. She walked alongside Reid, and she caught more than one glare in her direction. Ignoring them as best she could, she reminded herself that she could gut or freeze anyone who tried anything.

Enna and Lilianna had opted to stay home. Enna had too many sick druids to look after, and Lilianna had stayed behind to help.

They had erected a wooden dome over the arena, with a patchwork canvas tarp stretched over the beams. It blocked out what little light daytime had brought, and it also kept the darkness inside. Druids marched into the pit. Hunters and sentries carried torches into the arena and arranged themselves around the edge, shedding their flickering light over the main attraction: a cage. It sat in the center of the pit, silent as death. A dirty cloth had been thrown over it.

Goddard had crafted a vicious cage with a claw-like mouth that snapped together with crisscrossing metal fangs. Those fangs tore through the top of the cloth.

Juniper followed Reid and a handful of hunters onto the arena's hard-packed earth floor. Hushed and anxious murmurs grew louder as druids filed into the arena.

"Let us begin," Jarek shouted over the arena.

At once, the murmurs ceased. Reid and the hunters approached the silent cage. Juniper lingered near the edge. Her gut twisted and her stomach threatened to fall into her bowels. She didn't want any part of what was about to happen.

Sein and Asher stood on either side of Reid, this time holding real steel like they knew how to use it.

"Is it sleeping?" Asher whispered. He nudged the cloth's edge with his sword.

Nothing happened.

The hunters circled the cage, tapping the sides of the metal bars, taunting the monster within, yet the cage remained calm. This anomaly only worsened the unease.

"What's wrong?" a druid whispered behind Juniper. "Why is it not reacting?"

"Something isn't right," another whispered, the words trembling.

Juniper agreed.

Jarek marched into the arena with murder in his eyes. Unsheathing steel in one hand, he gripped the cloth in his off hand, and in a dramatic swish, yanked it off. The vicious ripping of fabric silenced the whispering, and then gasps echoed through the pit. Anxious whispers grew into frightening shouts.

The cage was empty. Between its iron claws, nothing.

"Where did it go?" one of the older hunters demanded.

"It was in the cage this morning," Jarek roared, more so to himself than anyone else. "I saw it myself."

Similar questions rang, "Where did it go?" "What's the meaning of this?" "Where's the monster?"

Goddard made his way into the pit. His eyes fell on the empty cage. He looked around the arena as if the Shadow might be lurking. Goddard, brows furrowed, circled the cage.

"Well?" Jarek said to the smith.

"I don't know, Chief," said Goddard. "It was in the cage last night, it was in the cage this morning, and it was in the cage when we brought it here. It was here when I left."

"Then what happened to it?" Jarek pointed at the cage.

"It's gone," Goddard said plainly.

"I can see that," Jarek spat. "Where did it go? Did it break out? You said this cage would hold it."

"It did," Goddard said darkly. He pointed to the door, where the iron bars didn't fit perfectly together, like a door left ajar. "The cage wasn't broken. It was unlocked. Someone let it out."

"What?" Jarek thundered. He eyed the crowd, and lowered his voice so that only those on the arena's floor could hear. "What do you mean?"

"I don't make faulty cages," Goddard said matter-of-factly. "Once this cage is shut, nothing is getting out of but air. Besides, it's not like the beast is smart enough to undo the latches, unlock the door, and then pry the door open without maiming itself. The task is impossible from the inside. Someone, or something, on the outside had to open it. Someone that knew their way around a lock."

"It was the witch," whispered an older druid behind Juniper. A resounding murmur of agreement swarmed through the crowd. Nervous glances were exchanged, whispers turned feverish and frightful.

Jarek fumed. He looked ready to strangle someone. "Hunters, to the Wylds! The witch might not be too far."

The hunters let out a war cry, swords thrust into the air, and then marched out of the arena and toward the gates. The sound of their voices, their steel, their marching footsteps—it gave Juniper a sinking feeling, like an angry mob. Feral and dangerous as any wild animal. She slipped with the retreating crowd of druids and into the cool night. Reid was waiting for her outside the arena. He put a hand on her shoulder and started to speak. By the worry and warning in his eye, she knew what he was going to say.

"I'm headed back to Enna's," she assured him.

It appeased him. He squeezed her shoulder and went with the hunters to the gates.

She did return to Enna's, however, she did not go inside. She headed straight for the timber wall. With the hunters and sentries scattering and panicking, she slipped over without notice. She bolted into the Wylds. The hunters marched along the roads, headed toward Blood Tree Pass, their furious footsteps resounding through the forest. Juniper headed the opposite way. The pass was the most obvious place for the witch to have gone, and anyone with any sense wouldn't have gone there to hide. A good thief would have gone the way her pursuers wouldn't assume.

The forest grew darker. Deadened trees thicker than houses and taller than mountains rose around her, their roots tangled and gnarled. The canopy thickened. The darkness grew impossibly dark. Juniper's night eyes barely saw.

She spotted a flicker of light ahead, small and golden. Too small to be a torch. A candle?

Juniper edged closer to the light, and to her astonishment, tiny flecks of golden magic floated in the air, the same she had seen on the pass. Their light was so faint, it barely glowed against her skin. It did not illuminate the forest floor or the trees. Juniper glanced around, but she saw no blood trees.

A small *snap* sounded behind her.

She turned—Red Mask stood in shadow on the other side of the glowing clearing. The eyes of the mask were black. Underneath the patched cloak, they wore common clothes in drab earthen colors, not unlike those Juniper wore.

The witch tilted their head to the side, questioning, curious.

"They're looking for you," Juniper whispered. "But I'm sure you know that."

The witch said nothing.

Juniper waited for them to do something, say something, but they remained silent and still. As intimidating as they looked, they didn't seem to have a thirst for blood, but she knew far better than to judge someone's capacity for violence on looks.

"I'm sorry about all of this," Juniper said. "For intruding on the pass and for chasing you that day." She took a small step closer. "The druids think you set the Shadow free, but I know you didn't."

Red Mask cocked their head to the side. Moonlight glinted off one eye. "I did," Juniper whispered. She took another step closer. "Because I need to talk to you."

The witch straightened, the motion sudden as a whip. Juniper felt their appraisal crawling over her skin like spiders.

Steeling herself, she continued, "I think your friend cursed me that day in the pass. Then I fell chasing you, and you took me to see her. She wore a yellow mask."

At that, Red Mask stilled.

"She healed me." Juniper took a small step forward. The golden specs fluttered with the movement. "I've felt healing magic before. I didn't tell anyone about that night. They don't think I remember it, but I do. I remember you and her."

Red Mask took a step back.

"It's okay," Juniper said quickly. She brought her hands together and summoned a bright blue ribbon of raw magic. It twirled between her palms, then she released it before something spawned. "I have magic too."

Red Mask stilled, eyes on Juniper's hands.

"The woman who healed me," Juniper whispered, trying not to sound too intent. "She has power over the air, doesn't she?"

Red Mask took a step back. Then another.

Juniper silently cursed herself. She had never been good with interrogations. Her questions were making the witch nervous, so she tried a different tactic.

"Please," Juniper said with as much pleading as she could muster. "It's important. Fate-of-the-realm important. It's about something that happened a very long time ago. She might be the only person alive who knows what happened."

Red Mask took another step back.

"Please," Juniper repeated. "I don't expect you to show me your lair or whatever it is, but I need you to tell her that I need to speak to her. Tell her it's about Nexon."

If the name of the mage inspired any reaction from Red Mask, they didn't show. They stood still as stone, dark eyes beholding Juniper. Then, they extended their hand. Their skin was emerald, their nails short and dirty. Nothing about them seemed malicious or ill-intending.

Juniper had made plenty of wrong choices, what was one more? She put her hand into the witch's. Consequences be damned.

CHAPTER 49

The witch's hand was cold. Calluses dotted their palm, but their skin felt no different than anyone else's. Red Mask pulled Juniper through the Wylds, around the ageless trees and over the protruding roots, farther from the village. They stopped in a grove of blackened trees and boulders. Juniper stood close enough to see the woven texture of their cloak, the worn fabric, the patches, and subtle stains. Red Mask put a green finger to the mask's carved lips, then glided into the clearing.

Red Mask paused before a wall of blackened vines, beckoned Juniper to follow, and then vanished through the vines. Juniper blinked, and upon closer inspection saw a narrow opening in the trees behind the vines, just big enough for a person to fit through.

Of course, there were secret passages in the forest. Why wouldn't there be? Dread twisted in her gut, but thrill twined alongside it. She had followed a masked stranger with unknown magic into a cursed forest at night. Absolutely mad. But she was already here.

She followed the witch. The vines tugged at her hair and cloak. The trees and boulders blocked her night sight from more than the tatters cloak she followed.

It led into a clearing. The Wylds camouflaged the opening, and the blackened trees had been twisted together with vines so tightly they formed a circular wall. The branches came together, shading them all but for a small opening where the dulled moonlight draped through at the very top. Red Mask turned, and the moonlight shaded the mask in a rusted nightmare. The sight sent a shiver through Juniper's chest and down her spine.

And then she heard it—breathing. Her heart stumbled. Red Mask stepped aside, revealing what had previously been hiding the darkness, even from her night sight.

A Shadow lay curled on the ground, sleeping. Its simmering body rose and fell gently with each breath. It was not the winged Shadow; it had no wings against its body. She recognized the shape of the limbs and the head and the feathered tail— it was the Shadow she had set free.

Juniper opened her mouth to speak, but Red Mask held a finger to their lips. Red Mask carefully approached the sleeping Shadow. They lowered themselves onto all fours and made a guttural clicking sound. The Shadow stirred, and Juniper steeled herself as it blinked its white eyes open. The Shadow gazed at Red Mask without malice or surprise. It chirped, a strange sound somewhere between a hawk and a blue bird.

Red Mask paused within a hand's reach of the Shadow. It rolled onto its stomach and nudged its snout against the mask. Red Mask cooed; the Shadow cooed back.

The Shadow stood up without fright and yawned. Its wide mouth stretched impossibly wide, showing small teeth and an endless throat. The Shadow lay back down on its stomach, let out a warble, and a quick breath. A sigh.

Those were not the sounds of a monster, or a cursed beast. Red Mask crawled closer still and stroked the Shadow's head. It cooed.

Red Mask motioned Juniper closer. She took a step, and the Shadow's eyes flickered open, tired and lazy, and then they found her. Its gaze sharpened. Its nostrils flared, and it took several quick sniffs.

It had done the same when she'd freed it. It was analyzing her.

Red Mask stroked the Shadow's head again. The beast settled; but the unease in Juniper's stomach did not. Red Mask motioned to her, and she took a cautious step, then another, and then crouched beside the Shadow. Her heart skipped several beats and turned over. Last time, the Shadow had been too distracted by its freedom to notice her. Now, it pinned her under its gaze.

Juniper set her hand on the Shadow, beside Red Mask's. She'd never felt anything like it. It thrummed under her touch, like darkness folded into silk. Its skin was smooth and cool. Juniper felt the magic holding it together, that thrived within it, that brought it to life. She stroked it like Red Mask had, and the Shadow purred.

"They are not what I thought," Juniper whispered. She looked down at the beast, just in case the no-talking rule still applied, but the Shadow didn't look bothered. "I've never seen anything like them. What are they? Just magic?"

Red Mask shrugged.

"What kind of magic could create such a thing?" she asked. "It would have to be powerful."

An archmage.

She inhaled to ask another question to turn the conversation toward Yellow Mask, but the Shadow jerked away from her touch. Its eyes looked at the ground, cautious and fearful. Red Mask stood and yanked Juniper away from the Shadow. The Shadow pawed at the ground, hissing. It slithered through a crack in the stone floor, no wider than Juniper's thigh.

Of course. Shadows didn't like light. They were nocturnal. What better place to hide from the daylight than underground? Juniper understood that well.

A commotion erupted in the Wylds. Footsteps, thundering against the forest floor. Red Mask grabbed Juniper and pushed her into the dense shade of the clearing as the footsteps approached.

She stood close enough to Red Mask to catch the strange bittersweet scent of the blood trees, and an earthy scent that reminded Juniper of Enna's herbal teas.

A gruff voice drifted from the forest.

"What is it?" asked an irritated hunter.

"We caught another one!"

"What?"

"It got Frederick good, nearly lobbed his arm off, but we got one."

"This one won't get away."

Juniper swallowed her panic. The druids had come this far into the Wylds? If they caught her out here, with Red Mask, there would be no excuse. Red Mask seemed to understand the severity and remained still as stone and silent as death until the footsteps faded into the forest.

Red Mask huffed. Their breath smacked the other side of the mask. They paced the clearing, even their frustrated walk eerily graceful.

"It's the Shadow, isn't it? You want to protect it?" Juniper whispered.

Red Mask nodded.

"The villagers will be more careful with this one," Juniper warned. She didn't know what to say—she hadn't planned on much conversation. She hadn't thought past finding Red Mask, and a part of her hadn't believed she'd actually find them. "I will see if there's something I can do, but I need to get back before someone realizes I'm gone. They already don't like me, and I don't want to give them any more fuel against me."

Red Mask pushed Juniper back through the vines and into the Wylds. A subtle shift of the air, and Red Mask vanished into the Wylds. Juniper headed toward the village with more knots in her stomach than before.

Chapter 50

The next evening, the druids of Sinjon shared a common panic. The captured Shadow hissed and snapped and cried from the pit. Hunters guarded the cage from all angles, leaving no room for even the sneakiest thief to slip in without being seen. As the gloomy daylight faded, many gathered around the pit as they had the night before.

The Shadow clawed at its cage. It growled and snarled and threw itself at the metal bars, rattling the teeth and wheels. Reid and the hunters made their way to the pit. Juniper hung back. Enna hadn't come, neither had Lilianna. Too many sick, Enna had said.

Jarek approached the cage. A nervous energy filled the arena, and even the Wylds seemed to be holding a collective breath. Goddard yanked the tarp from the cage. The Shadow shrieked; its ears folded back against its head, and its wide eyes took in the crowd. Jarek unsheathed his sword. Reid and the closest warriors mimicked the motion. Goddard, ax in hand, reached for the lock.

The cage snapped open. The Shadow jumped, but without anything between it and a dozen swords, it stopped cowering. It unfurled itself. A million shades of black undulated on its skin, reflecting the flickering torchlight. A frightening growl sounded from within its body.

A round of gasps sounded across the pit. Juniper closed her fingers around the hilt of her dagger. Her growing unease fought to empty her dinner. She didn't want to watch the Shadow get slaughtered, but she wouldn't let it hurt anyone—well, not Reid at least. Everyone else could fend for themselves.

"Unholy beast," Jarek shouted above the whispering unease. He brandished his sword at the Shadow. "Call your master—"

His next words never made it out. A great blast shook the arena and sudden gusts of cold air rushed in—tattered pieces of fabric and fresh splinters rained down on the pit. The burst of air put out the torches, dousing the pit in darkness. Through the gaping hole in the tarp was the winged Shadow, wings broad and poised, teeth bared, and white eyes narrowed. Red Mask rode on its back, wearing makeshift leather armor with mismatched metal plating.

The winged Shadow let out a shrill cry. It shattered Juniper's thoughts and focus. As her thoughts reconnected, she blinked in time to see the captured Shadow running out of the pit. It vanished into the night.

Juniper released a heavy breath. She felt a strong admiration for Red Mask's dramatic rescue yet as the pit erupted with war cries and every armed druid unsheathed a sword or an ax, her panic seized.

Jarek had wanted to draw the witch out, and he had.

Arrows flew—the winged Shadow swatted the arrows out of the air with his wing as easily as a child pushes aside a toy.

"What is the meaning of this!" Jarek roared above the commotion. His shout brought the crowd to a silence. Jarek pointed a thick finger at the beast, anger shaking in his voice. "You dare intrude on our ground? This is an act of war! You and your ilk die tonight!"

Juniper swallowed a curse. That had been his plan all along. City Watch had often tried the same trick, like fencing something illegal and then arresting the fence.

Red Mask said nothing. They pulled a short dagger from their side and threw it at Jarek. It landed in the dirt by his feet.

All eyes shifted between Jarek and the silent witch.

Red Mask moved first. They patted the Shadow. It lifted its great wings and pushed off from the arena, into the night, and vanished. Its shrill cry pierced the night air.

At first, no one in the arena spoke. Then, panic erupted. Every hunter and elder spat questions and fear at Jarek, fury and panic staining the air, their voices rising in pitch. Outside the arena, the wind picked up. It tore at the loose edges.

"Enough!" Jarek roared, silencing the jittering panic. He pointed to the arena's entrance. "Prepare for battle. The council will meet in the Great Hall, immediately."

Juniper glanced at Reid. Underneath his stoic mask, he looked as unsure as anyone else. Juniper filed out of the pit and looked first to the sky. The winged Shadow and its masked rider were long gone. Reid appeared at her side, scowling. Many of the druids marched to the Great Hall. Reid didn't move to join them.

"Let's get out of here," he whispered. He took her hand in his and pulled her into the village.

At first, her hopeful heart thought he meant out of the village, but soon she realized he had meant away from the others. He led her toward Jarek's house. As they started up the muddy path, the front door swung open. Ingrid stood in the doorway, eyes wide and hair falling out if its braid as if she had been toying with it. She looked between Reid and Juniper, then at the anxious druids of the village. Murmurs were a haze around them, fearful and worried.

"What happened?" Ingrid asked. "I heard a terrible commotion."

Reid told Ingrid what had happened in the arena. Juniper remained quiet. At the end of the story, Ingrid sank into one of the kitchen chairs, hand on her heart. With every word, Ingrid's expression had grown gloomier.

"This is not good," she whispered fearfully.

Reid glanced at Juniper, and Ingrid's gaze flickered to her and then away.

Juniper felt a rush of heat into her cheeks. She met Reid's gaze. "What? Don't tell me you think this is my fault. Like I could have made the witch burst in like that?"

"I have no doubt some will think so," Ingrid said darkly.

Juniper scoffed. "They're just looking for someone to blame this mess on rather than doing something about it."

"If you have a better plan, let's hear it then," Ingrid said, indignantly.

"Have you thought about trying to reach out to these supposed witches? See if they're as evil and monstrous as you think? By making friends, you might improve your standard of living."

Ingrid and Reid were both staring at her, one guarded, the other livid.

"They are monsters," Ingrid said. Her fists clenched her skirt with pale knuckles. "There is no magic out there that isn't tainted. Magic itself is a taint upon the land."

"Is the druid magic also evil?" Juniper asked, her voice strained.

Ingrid pursed her lips.

"You sing to the plants to make them grow, is that not magic? A human couldn't do the same."

"Juniper," Reid warned.

She barreled on. "Magic is no more deadly in the hands of a mage than a sword in the hands of a warrior."

Ingrid sat up straighter. The fear in her eyes turned hot and fierce. She glared at Juniper as if she'd not seen her properly before. "Is that what you think?"

"It is," Juniper said firmly. "I have numerous reasons to support my belief. Do you?"

Ingrid bristled. She stood so quickly, she shoved the chair backward. It clattered on the stone floor. "You don't know how it is to live here in constant fear of the witches and their Shadows, to hear the calls of the cursed beasts at night, to mourn those who don't come back."

Tears clogged Ingrid's voice, and a fist clenched Juniper's lungs. The child Jarek had lost—he had been Ingrid's child too.

Ingrid stormed into her bedroom and slammed the door. Dread tightened in Juniper's stomach.

"Happy?" Reid asked, glaring at her.

Juniper crossed her arms and didn't answer. "I'm going back to Enna's."

"No, you're not." Reid side-stepped in front of the door. "Jarek told me to bring you here tonight. Enna's got her hands full, and no one will openly attack you if you're in his house."

"*Attack* me?"

"They are panicking and afraid," he whispered. His mask slipped, and his eyes pleaded.

She wanted to argue. She wanted to curse. Instead, she marched up the stairs with Reid a step behind. Juniper occupied herself with drawing a bowl of water for washing. Reid set about removing his armor, and she peeled away her Wylds-smelling clothes and started to wash. She needed a long, thought-calming soak, but this pitiful bowl would have to do.

CHAPTER 51

By the time Juniper pulled her tunic back over her head, the raw edge of her anger had ebbed. Reid stood at the window with his back to her, staring out at the Wylds. Juniper crawled into the bed. Exhaustion settled like silt in her bones, weighing her down and pushing her into the single pillow.

"Don't fall asleep in the middle," Reid warned.

She scooted a tiny bit.

Reid added a log to the stove, blew out the candle, and sat on the edge of the bed. She waited for him to recline. The bed wasn't very large, and he didn't have room to leave any between them. But he didn't.

"Reid?" she whispered. In the dark, his shoulders drooped ever so slightly.

"I have something for you," he whispered back. He twisted his upper body toward hers and held out his closed fist.

Juniper sat up, heart clenching.

Reid uncurled his fingers, and there, sitting in his palm, was the moonstone ring. The moonstone and aquamarines glittered in the muted light of the woodstove.

Juniper couldn't help the gasp that escaped her throat. She cupped her hands around his.

"I took it that first night," Reid said. "Enna removed it, and I didn't trust her not to take it."

Juniper shuddered a breath of relief. She slipped the ring back onto her finger. "I thought I'd lost it, or someone had taken it."

Reid folded his fingers with hers then brought her hand to his mouth. He kissed her knuckles.

"Still want to marry me?" She offered him a tired smile.

"Of course. You are reckless, at times childish, and stubborn, but I love you."

She frowned. He'd said it all with a straight face. "You're suggesting you are none of those?"

"I did not say that."

She felt like laughing and crying, but she was too tired to do either. She threw her arms around Reid's neck and settled into his embrace.

"We need to tread carefully," Reid whispered into her hair. "The druids are panicking and afraid."

She sighed into his shoulder. "I know. I'm just…annoyed that it's taking so long. I would have found the archmage by now if the druids weren't so hellbent on their superstitions."

Reid kissed her temple, then released her. The firelight turned his brown eyes into glinting embers. "We both need sleep, and I will sleep much better knowing you're safe here with me."

"I will, as well," she admitted.

They settled into the narrow bed. Reid's arm draped over her side, and her body tucked perfectly into his. Reid fell asleep first, his body relaxing, his breaths evening against her neck. Juniper watched the stove cast dancing shadows on the wooden walls, thinking of a calm, luxurious future with Reid once they ended Nexon and his tyrannical empire. Sleep took its time, and her dreams were chaotic and silent. Shadows raced across an orange sky, talons and teeth and hisses. Thousands of them.

The dream ended with a great *bang*.

"Gods," Reid breathed in the dark.

At first, Juniper thought she was still dreaming, but as Reid got out of bed and another bang thundered through the village, realization settled like lead in her stomach.

She was not dreaming, and Shadows cried and cawed and shrieked.

Juniper's drowsiness evaporated. She quickly summoned a magelight and set over the bedpost. Reid didn't scold her. In the cool blue light, they dressed as quickly as they could. Reid reached for the bedroom door, and she snuffed the magelight. Reid took the stairs two at a time, and before he reached the bottom, Jarek burst from his room. They rushed out the front door. Juniper caught the door before it hit the frame, and the scene before her stole her breath.

Shadows, hundreds of them, swarmed the village. On rooftops, in the streets, their eyes wide and their teeth barred. They were smashing and clawing and knocking things over, with no intent other than to harm and cause problems.

Reid lingered by the door, his face a warrior's stoic mask.

"Reid," she started.

He silenced her next words with a swift, tender kiss. "Stay here," he asked—not a command, a pleading request.

Then he was off, sword drawn, into the fray.

"Reid!" she called after him.

"Juniper, close the door!" Ingrid called from inside.

Juniper took a step out. Like hell if she was going to let Reid dash off into battle without her to watch his back!

Ingrid clasped a hand around her arm. "What are you doing? Get back in here."

"I can help, I can't let—"

"You will make it worse!"

"Let go—"

Her words were lost as a Shadow jumped from the roof and onto the ground in front of Jarek's house.

The feral Shadow looked at her with madness in its eyes. The undulating shades of darkness of its skin frenzied, trembling and rippling. This Shadows radiated panic—from it, a dark, dangerous magic scented the air like a rotting garden. Ingrid screamed, and Juniper pulled her dagger free. It seemed like such a silly little thing compared to the hissing Shadow. She also didn't want to hurt the Shadow, but she would if it attacked.

The Shadow lunged at Juniper, jaws wide. She countered its teeth with her dagger and twisted her body and the blade as its jaw clamped shut. The blade sank into its gums, and her arm narrowly missed its teeth. Wrenching the dagger free, she expected blood or something, but the dagger was clean. The Shadow howled in pain and pawed at her—she dodged with ease, but as she adjusted her stance for offense, its tail lashed out at her. She hadn't the time to move; the tail smacked the dagger from her hands. It skirted across the ground, out of her reach.

The Shadow didn't hesitate. In her moment of panic, it lunged—teeth barred, claws ready to rip her to pieces, and death in its eyes.

Ingrid screamed. Juniper didn't have the time to think of a better plan—she acted on instinct.

The Shadow crashed into a wall of clear blue ice. Before it could gather its bearings, a dulled spike of ice rammed into its belly and tossed it into the air. It landed on its back and rolled onto its feet. A heartbeat, and its daze vanished.

The unnatural magic that oozed from her ice did not become a bear or wolf. She felt it soak into the Shadow, become a part of it. For a terrifying moment, she felt the Shadow's magic tug on her own, yearning for it, demanding it.

Juniper demanded it back, yanking it from the strange grasp with a violent war cry of her own.

The Shadow came at her again. This time, Juniper went for the kill. She aimed an ice spike. The Shadow dodged, soaking in the magic closest to it. Juniper aimed another and as the Shadow dodged, she rolled to the side—and grabbed her dagger. Another ice spike, and her dagger found a new home in the Shadow's neck. It hissed, and her ice spread from the steel. Her ice sank into its dark flesh, ripping through the simmering magic, and for a terrifying moment, she felt the magic holding it together—razor-sharp and furious.

250

But it was just magic, and she tore it apart.

The Shadow flopped onto the ground. Its white eyes faded to black, and then its body scattered like ink underwater. The magic soaked into the ground, shades of dark gold, black, and green. The magic soaked in and vanished.

"Witch," Ingrid whispered. She stood in the doorway, hand over her heart. Her wide, fearful eyes looked between where the Shadow had died, then at Juniper.

"Mage," Juniper corrected. She added softly, "Not all magic is bad. It can protect, heal, and help."

Ingrid didn't look convinced. She continued to stare at Juniper with wide eyes, filled with terror. She took a trembling step into her house. "You're a witch," she hissed. "Just like them."

Juniper put her hands on her hips. "I just saved you from being chomped, remember that."

"I knew you were strange. I knew." Ingrid shook her head.

"Ingrid?" called Jarek. He came running up the hill to their house. He looked at his wife, then Juniper. "What happened?"

"I protected your wife from a Shadow," Juniper said immediately.

"With magic!" Ingrid shrieked. She clutched her dress. "I saw her do it! She brought ice out of nowhere and killed it."

"Saved you from it," Juniper corrected pointedly. "You'd rather have been bitten in two?"

Jarek looked between them, chest heaving. His gaze settled on Juniper. "You have magic? You're a witch?"

"*Mage*," she corrected.

"You're one of them?" Jarek gripped his ax like he made to throw it at her, and she held her dagger to defend in case he did. She also readied her magic. Despite the dagger's quality, her magic would be more effective.

A scream sounded from the village. Shadows crawled over rooftops, and more crept up the timber walls. The Wylds beyond had darkened with the corrupted magic, teemed with it. Shadows raged in the streets, batting steel and druids aside like a child's toy. Juniper didn't care to argue—Reid was down there somewhere, and his life outweighed every single druid in her opinion. She raced down the hill and into the village, ice surging to her command, impaling Shadows left and right, dissolving them into their inky magic. It didn't seem to matter; for every Shadow she defeated, two more took its place. The druids were gravely outnumbered.

Three Shadows surrounded Sein. Juniper took out two with ice arrows before he had taken down one. He glanced at the fallen Shadows as they dissolved, relieved and confused.

"On your guard," Juniper shouted.

Sein jumped. He hadn't seen Juniper approach.

No one had the spare breath to argue against her help. Every available body defended Sinjon. No one saw her ice arrows shoot from their hidden place against her dagger. They moved too fast. Her magic tore through the furious magic, scattering it. She spotted Reid among the fighting, his silver armor gleaming. His skill rose above the others.

Juniper took out Shadow after Shadow. The magic bled into the ground, seeping out of sight. What blood marred the ground belonged to the villagers. She fought and fought, until a stitch in her side pulled viciously. The freezing air stung her lungs and throat. She didn't know how long the battle lasted, too long. By the time the wave of Shadows ebbed, her legs and arms and shoulders felt like lead, stretched too far and too thin.

The wounded were carried or limped to the Great Hall. Juniper sheathed her dagger, caught her breath, then meandered toward the Great Hall. Most were gathered there, including Reid. She quickly looked him over—he had escaped injury. He kept a hand on the hilt of his Mage's Bane. His eyes remained focused for battle. He looked utterly too much like his uncle, like a commander. Reid noticed her, and he quickly looked her over.

"I'm all right," she said.

"This was worse than before," Reid said grimly.

"Any dead?"

Before Reid could answer, a series of shouts broke the disquiet.

"There she is!"

Villagers hurried down the street. The druid in front pointed a dirty finger at Juniper. "The witch is here!"

Juniper let out an exasperated sigh. She started to speak when a hand grabbed her arm, yanking her away from Reid.

"Juniper?" came Reid's voice.

Someone got between them, and then Juniper hit the ground hard. The impact knocked the air from her chest.

"What are you doing?" Reid roared, but his threat went ignored.

She started to get up, but a boot slammed into her chest, pinning her. She grasped the ankle of the offending leg.

"Get the hell off me!" Juniper demanded.

"She's been enthralling him the whole time," someone spat.

"Witch!"

"She's been using her magic on Jarek and Ingrid!"

"Steel won't kill a witch."

"Burn her, that's the only way to get rid of them for good." The boot pressed harder into her chest, and her ribs threatened to break.

Torches appeared above her, and her anger turned into white-hot panic. They honestly meant to burn her alive.

The owner of the boot lowered a torch toward her head. She felt the heat on her skin—ice shot out from all around her. It doused the torch and threw those closest to her backward. The druid who had pinned her with his boot got an extra boost.

Juniper staggered to her feet. A crowd of villagers had gathered around her. None she recognized. She didn't see Jarek or Reid, or anyone that didn't look ready to kill her.

One foolish villager swung his torch at her like a sword.

"Burn, witch!" he screamed.

A claw of clear blue ice plucked the torch from his hand. The villager stumbled backward, eyes wide at the sight, fear bright. The hand reached over their heads, growing larger and larger, until the claws crashed into the ground and the palm expanded into a dome of cloudy blue, trapping them inside with her. The ice thickened, and tendrils of bright blue raw magic snapped out each torch with a vicious hiss. The ice thickened, blocking the firelight of the village and dousing them in darkness.

She could see; they could not. Their fear soured the air, and their breaths puffed. Not so big and tough when they couldn't see.

"She's an ice witch," someone breathed.

"I am no witch," she snapped, her voice cracking. "What is wrong with you people? I am a mage. Magic is not evil. If you would get your heads out of your asses long enough to see that, your village wouldn't be dying!"

"She's threatening us," shouted another. The speaker threw his mace, but she saw it. Her ice caught it. In her rage, her ice crushed the steel, and dropped the ruined weapon on the ground.

"Get out of our village!" someone shouted. "Leave us alone!"

"You attacked me!" Juniper spat, but her voice was lost over the wave of shouts.

A druid swung a sword at her voice. Her ice grabbed it and threw it. It clanked on the ground, and her ice dome pulled it out of reach.

"Get out!" they screamed.

Steel beat against the dome.

Juniper growled in frustration and shattered the bottom layer of ice—shards peppered the druids. Between their shrieks and the crashing of the ice, she walked through the ice dome and vanished into an alley. She left her ice there to distract them. With the chilly night, it wouldn't melt very fast.

She heard the chaos she'd added to the night. Steel beat against her ice. Without her magic to hold it up, it cracked. She slipped through the darkness and climbed the mossy walls of the Great Hall. She crouched on the shadowed roof. Below, the foolish druids panicked over her ice. They broke the ice into tiny pieces, as if she were hiding within the shards.

Reid had been pushed back. Sein stood with him, holding a hand to his shoulder to keep him back. The druids seemed too struck by her mess to give him much notice.

A booming voice sounded, and the chaos died only slightly. Jarek appeared. The crowd parted for his hulking form. Juniper flattened against the moss and crept closer to the edge. Jarek surveyed the ice as a dozen druids told varying tales of how Juniper had attacked them. She fought the urge to douse them all in freezing water.

"She ran, Jarek!"

"The witch ran!"

"She attacked us!"

Even Jarek couldn't calm the mob. Then the druids remembered Reid, and her panic returned. The druids pulled him forward, to Jarek. Reid had the sense to look worried and confused.

"That girl was a witch!" shouted a villager at Reid.

"What?" Reid asked, his exasperation blending with confusion. "What do you mean, a witch?"

"Juniper," Jarek said. "They say they saw her use magic against the Shadows."

Juniper rallied her magic. She would kill every single one of them if they threatened Reid. Reid's silence added to his confusion, and that silence may have been what saved him.

"She had him under her thrall," said one villager. "I've heard about that. They use their powers to control the mind of another person."

"What say you?" a villager asked Reid.

Reid hesitated, looking at the angry druids, then Jarek. "I didn't know."

Juniper caught the slight inflection at the lie, but she wasn't upset. The druids appeared to relax.

"This has been a long night for all of us," Jarek said over the crowd. "Clean up what you must tonight, then rest. Tomorrow we will discuss this matter. I will alert the sentries to the witch's flight. Reid, you are welcome to remain at my house."

Reid nodded, and his eyes scanned the darkness above the village. At first she thought he might be looking for lingering Shadows, but his gaze was too low. He was looking for her, she realized, on the rooftops.

He wouldn't find her, not when she crouched on the roof above him.

The crowd dispersed, but Jarek remained on the steps of the Great Hall. He set his hand on Reid's shoulder, and said, "Tell me. Honestly. Did you know about her magic?"

Reid hesitated. "No," he lied.

Jarek released a breath of relief. "She's fled to the Wylds. To be with the other magic monsters. Come, you look like you need a rest. Gods only know what enchantments she put on you. Enna will know what to do."

Reid nodded, though Juniper saw the darkness in his eyes.

Juniper scooted away from the edge. She could try to make peace with Jarek and explain, but she needed to find Yellow Mask. Without anyone in the village worrying over her absence, she had all the time she needed.

CHAPTER 52

Juniper wandered into the gloomy Wylds, evading the patrols scouring the roads for her. They stomped through the underbrush and growled threats, cursing the pale girl with all manner of unsavory names. They had left the roads and trudged with their torches through the thick brambles and roots. Juniper had plenty of experience going unseen, and the druids had little experience looking for the unseen; she could have run circles around them. She crept deeper into the Wylds, leaving the patrols behind, and soon their torchlight faded into the darkness.

The Shadows had left the forest, and the Wylds felt empty. As she crept over fallen logs, treacherous tree roots, and through thorny brambles, thunder rolled low and dangerous. It shook the dead ground and the ageless trees. As the thunder rolled away, she heard the whispering of water. Lightning flashed in the spindly gaps above the canopy. Juniper felt the distant storm building, clawing closer.

She followed the whispering to a wide river with pieces of ice floating along its surface. The calm water was muddied and carried the deadened scents of the Wylds. The water within called to her magic, and she felt along the stream. She felt the depths, the lack of healthy fish, the cloudy silt and…wrongness. The curse had seeped into the waters as well.

"There!"

She whipped around. Two druids were running over the tangled forest floor toward her, swords drawn.

She hadn't heard them approach. She'd been focused on the water.

The *water*.

Juniper jumped into the river. Cursed water surged over her head. Tiny needle-pins stuck her from every side, soaking her clothes and filling her boots. The cold went bone-deep, and deeper. She cast ice around her, pushing the water away from her person and forming an air bubble. The druids were blurry images on the other side of the water and the cloudy blue ice. They lingered on the riverbank.

She and her ice bubble glided upstream, toward Blood Tree Pass. When she had put sufficient distance between herself and the hunters, she guided the ice bubble to the bank. She took a gasping breath of the forest air, as dank and cursed as it was. Thunder crashed as she climbed out of the river. Shivers ravaged her limbs, shaking her to the bone. Her ice dissolved and she whisked the water from her clothes and hair, flinging it back into the river. The druids weren't anywhere in sight. With any luck, they assumed she had gone downstream.

The deadened forest surrounded her on every side. Through the shades of charcoal and black, barely visible within her night sight, was the faintest glimmer of red. Juniper started toward it, navigating the treacherous forest floor, and followed it to Blood Tree Pass. The blood trees had lost almost all their leaves, littering the ground in dull crimson and rust. She wandered through the pass, through the blood trees. At the lowest part of the valley, the rocks jutted up from the tangled ground at violent angles. Fissures ran along the stones and the ground. From those fissures, the little golden specs floated upward.

Less than there had been before. Did that have something to do with the Shadows?

Juniper crept to one of those fissures. The strange scent fluttered upward, the same she'd encountered that day in the pass. Like bittersweet autumn and rotting leaves.

A gentle footstep sounded behind her—Juniper pulled her dagger from her side and pun. Red Mask stood within the shadows. Juniper lowered her dagger but didn't put it away.

"Sorry," Juniper said. "I was just chased out of town by an angry mob."

Red Mask tilted their head.

"I saved the chief's wife from a Shadow, so she called me a witch and a mob tried to burn me alive," Juniper explained. "So ungrateful. They saw magic and assumed me some evil, vile creature, but I'm sure you understand how that feels."

Red Mask nodded.

"But that's usually how things go. Things go wrong, I save myself, and then everyone is cursing my name." Juniper let out a dramatic sigh. "Look, I didn't trek through the Wylds for the scenery. I came here because I'm looking for someone. I need you to take me to Yellow Mask. It's important."

Red Mask looked again in the direction of the village. In the distance, druids were stomping through the brush.

"I can't go back there," Juniper said. "So, I'd also appreciate any help you could offer."

They stood still, considering. Then Red Mask released a long sigh. They turned and motioned Juniper to follow. She did. They trekked through the Wylds and came to a rocky clearing beside a smaller stream. The winged Shadow stood by the water, staring at the lightning's reflection in the water. Thunder rolled overhead, low and lazy.

The Shadow looked up. It wore nothing of the maliciousness of the Shadow Juniper had killed. Red Mask skipped over river stones and to the opposite bank, beside the Shadow. They turned to Juniper, masked eyes black as night. Juniper didn't have to see their eyes—she felt it.

"You don't trust me," Juniper said. "Though, I can't blame you."

"If I didn't trust you, you wouldn't be here," said Red Mask in a voice laced with somber moonlight and cynicism.

Juniper blinked. That voice, she knew that voice.

Before she could ask, Red Mask reached a long-fingered green hand to either side of their head. They pushed down the hood of their cloak and pulled the leather ties holding the mask—two dark braids fell on either shoulder, and two bright gold eyes stared at Juniper.

Lilianna.

CHAPTER 53

Juniper stood dumbfounded. Lilianna tucked the red mask into a satchel hidden under her cloak.

"No witty remark?" Lilianna asked. A small smile turned up her lips.

"You're the witch?" Juniper took a step toward the river stones.

Lightning flashed, illuminating the barren treetops and the steely clouds.

"Why didn't you speak to me before?" Juniper asked.

"I promised her I wouldn't," Lilianna said. "Not while I wore the mask."

"Her?"

Lilianna didn't answer. Juniper felt a prickle wash over her skin. Her—Yellow Mask, the Archmage of Air.

"We need to get out of here." Lilianna reached to the winged Shadow, who nosed her palm. "If you are serious about meeting her, then I can take you to her. The best way is by air, and we need to get going before the storm sets in."

Juniper started to question what she meant, but Lilianna climbed onto the back of the winged Shadow. She set her golden eyes on Juniper, who stood frozen on the opposite bank.

"Well?" Lilianna asked, raising a brow. "Unless you'd rather wait for the warriors to find you here."

Juniper made her way across the river stones and approached the Shadow. Lilianna held her hand out. This time, Juniper didn't hesitate. She took Lilianna's hand and climbed onto the Shadow's back.

"Hold on tight," she said. "Take off can be a little rough."

Juniper snaked her arms around Lilianna's thin middle and braced herself. The Shadow unfurled its great black wings, the leathery black flesh stretched with a sound like a whip against tree bark. Juniper tightened her hold on Lilianna, who suddenly seemed far too thin to be of use.

With a great flap of its wings, the Shadow lurched into the air. The motion threw Juniper's heart into her stomach, and her stomach fell into her groin. With each flap of its great wings, she felt like she might get thrown off, and by some magic beyond her comprehension, she remained seated. The Shadow jumped into the trees, using the branches for leverage, its wings beating.

And then, they were above the forest.

They were flying.

Frozen air whipped past her face, whisking her hair in all directions, stinging her eyes. The Wylds stretched for leagues underneath them, jagged black treetops and gnarled roots. Blood trees offered the only spec of color, a bright red wound in the forest. Storm clouds bubbled on the horizon, and lightning danced between the towering clouds of bruised midnight blue, plum, and silver. The mountains rose in a crescent, as if a god had pressed a giant thumb into the land, a wave of ancient stone. Low clouds hung around the tallest peaks of the mountains, and the Wylds grew thick on the valley's floor. Juniper glanced behind them. She couldn't even see Sinjon.

She tried to imagine this forest alive and teeming with druid villages, of tree houses and rope bridges, of towering lavender and apple trees. Lightning flashed, shedding silver light over the dead, cursed forest. Thunder crashed soon after, beating against the sky and sounding in her sternum.

Lilianna angled them toward the crescent mountain range, to the southern edge where great trees had taken over the rocky terrain, their thick roots hugging boulders and slowly splitting the rock apart. The Shadow maneuvered through an opening in the canopy and glided steadily downward toward the forest floor. They landed gracefully in a shallow stream and skidded out of the water and onto a mossy patch of ground.

And the world stopped moving.

Juniper unlatched her shaking arms from around Lilianna, who slid from the Shadow's back with easy grace. Juniper struggled to get her limbs to follow. She stumbled from its back and hit the ground on all fours.

"Gods," Juniper breathed, letting her heart settle. She pushed herself onto shaky legs.

"This way." Lilianna started over the roots of an ancient tree. The roots spread over a boulder the size of Jarek's house.

Juniper tried her best to follow—Lilianna moved with unnatural grace over the curling roots, and Juniper imagined herself clumsy in comparison.

The winged Shadow did not follow. It vanished into the dark forest.

Lilianna guided her down through the roots and to a wooden door set into the stone. Vines hugged the door as if holding it in place. Old carvings on the wood had faded over time, of flowers and thorns and trees. Lilianna let herself in and held the door open for Juniper. It led into a cavern. It looked like someone had tried to make it homey. The walls were smooth and curved, spotted with worn runes.

But the thing that caught her attention was the glittering light that hovered in the center of the ceiling, resting in an old iron lantern. Magelight.

"Come in," Lilianna said. "It's more comfortable."

She led Juniper through an uneven stone archway and into a room that looked starkly familiar. The stone walls, the hearth fire, the smoke that vanished through a slit in the stone ceiling—this is the room she remembered from her dream. Rugs and pelts and furs made the room homey and warm, and she sat on a soft brown fur.

"Look familiar?" Lilianna unclasped her cloak and hung it on the wall. She sat beside Juniper, folding her long legs underneath her. "And now we speak."

"With fewer secrets," Juniper added.

Lilianna offered her a small, knowing smile. "You have the same magic as she does," she said. "The magic the others hate and fear."

Juniper crafted a palm-sized snowflake in the air. "I am. And you're Red Mask. How?"

"It started years ago." Lilianna leaned forward and set her elbows on her knees. "Grandmother used to tell me stories about the strange woman of magic who appeared centuries ago, how that woman was called a witch and driven into the Wylds. Her stories of magic fascinated me. It drove my mother mad. But…" Lilianna bit her lip, then cupped her hands. A greenish swirl of air appeared between her palms.

"You have magic," Juniper said.

"I feared my mother's reaction. Grandmother told me to hide it, and I did for a while. Then…I grew restless. I sought the witch out for myself. And I found her."

"I thought no one could find her?"

Lilianna smiled. "She is found only when she wants to be."

"And she wanted you to find her?"

"She did," Lilianna said. "She added a new layer to the stories my grandmother told me. The strange woman appeared, and she lived in the village for a while. She married. She had children. Then, the Shadows started to appear. They blamed her for it, and she hid in the Wylds. And…she is part of my family."

"You're related?" Juniper repeated.

"My great-great-something grandmother," Lilianna said, waving the *greats* aside.

Juniper paused—that meant Enna was too. Had that been why Enna hadn't been worried about Juniper's magic?

"She found me. She told me who she was, who I was, and I've been sneaking out here to learn magic ever since." A gleam of excitement brightened Lilianna's eyes. It was the most emotion Juniper had seen in her. "Grandmother says druids don't have that type of magic, but I inherited her affinity for the air. She's been teaching me to harness it."

"Does anyone else know?" Juniper asked.

"Just my grandmother." Lilianna frowned. "She covers for me when I'm out here. She tells my mother that I'm working in the garden or helping her with whatever ointment she's crafting that day. It's not all fake. Grandmother has taught me the old druid magic too."

Thunder rolled overhead, closer than before. The cavernous home muffled it only slightly. The rocks still trembled, and even the fire danced.

"What's happening?" Juniper whispered.

Lilianna didn't voice her answer, but she didn't need to. It was written in the doubt and confusion on her face. She didn't know.

"Angyla doesn't like to talk about it," Lilianna whispered darkly. Her eyes darted to the doorway and back to Juniper.

"Angyla…" Juniper repeated. "Yellow Mask?"

Lilianna nodded. "She can be temperamental, though she is wise and full of knowledge."

As much as Juniper wanted to ask about the archmage, she had other questions first.

"What are the Shadows?" Juniper asked. "I've seen a lot of strange creatures, but I've never seen anything like them."

"They are magic," Lilianna said plainly. "Angyla says they are made from the magic that emits from the wellspring."

"The wellspring?" That sounded important.

Lilianna's expression turned grim. "That is another thing Angyla doesn't like to talk about. She…keeps it from getting worse, she says."

Juniper opened her mouth, but footsteps sounded in the hall.

"What's this?" came a sharp and angry feminine voice.

Juniper jumped, and her question vanished. A tall, slender old woman stood in the doorway. She had dark gold skin lined with deep wrinkles. A braid of dull silver hung down her back. She wore an assortment of furs and hides, and Juniper saw no weapons on her person. Her ears were short and round. Dark brown eyes took in Juniper with a livid rage.

"Angyla!" Lilianna jumped to her feet. Her stoic expression widened into uncertainty and surprise.

Angyla's rage faded, and her pursed lips twisted into a scowl. The air around Juniper thickened, and she felt an unseen force steal the very breath from her throat.

She had found the Archmage of Air.

CHAPTER 54

Angyla glided into the room with all the savage grace of a bolt of lightning. Juniper sat tall, even as the archmage prevented her from drawing breath. Angyla's stare bore into her, analyzing.

Maddox had taught her how to hold a breath, how to recognize her own limits, and how not to show weakness. Juniper hadn't done well on her own. The burning of her lungs had scared her. So, Maddox had made Juniper and Xavier train together underwater. The additional completion had made them both work harder, so much that Xavier had once passed out—and a water mage had had to remove the water from his lungs. Juniper had watched the mage work in a mixed sense of shame, revulsion, and fear.

Her lungs began to burn, her throat felt dry, and every fiber in her being screamed for breath. Juniper held Angyla's glare. She wouldn't gasp or dry heave. She wouldn't give in.

Lilianna pleaded, "I can explain."

"Then you best do it soon," Angyla spat.

Juniper felt the darkness creeping over her limbs, the starvation, the deprivation, the weakness.

"The villagers chased her out of Sinjon because she has magic!" Lilianna's words ran together, but upon the word *magic*, the air returned to Juniper. Her instincts got the better of her. She took sudden, gasping breath.

Angyla's expression only slightly changed. Her wild eyes beheld Juniper with surprise, albeit distrust. "You're that girl. The one who fell in the river."

"You healed me," Juniper said.

Angyla stalked closer. Juniper fought against her urge to flinch. Angyla moved like a spider, cautious and creeping, yet capable of terror. She looked Juniper up and down in a calculating way, like she was looking for the best way to take her apart. In that moment, she looked every bit mad.

"What do you want?" Angyla snapped.

"I need to know how to defeat Nexon," Juniper said.

Angyla's entire face changed. Her anger smoothed into surprise—not confusion, but worried surprise. Then, her anger returned. "Why would you ask such a thing?"

"Because I know you're the Archmage of Air, and you are the only person alive who knows how to defeat Nexon," Juniper said, not bothering to hide the pleading in her voice. "He's on the rise again, and we have to stop him."

"No," Angyla hissed. "We made sure he would never come back. We made sure."

"He's back." Juniper said. "I've seen him. He's tried to kill me several times. I need to know how you—"

"You don't need to know." Angyla glared at Juniper with more hatred than Juniper thought possible. "Get out. Get out of my home."

"She's got nowhere to go," Lilianna defended. "The villagers will kill her, or she'll freeze to death or get eaten by something."

Angyla growled something unintelligible. "That is not our problem, Lilianna. I don't know what she told you to coax you into bringing her here, but she needs to leave. Immediately." She marched down the hall and out of sight, her bare feet slapping against the stone.

Juniper didn't move until she could no longer hear footsteps.

The sizzle in the air retreated with the archmage, and she felt lighter.

"I'm sorry." Lilianna glared at the empty doorway. "She needs time to think. She's not good with change or people."

"How can you tell? Was it when she tried to suffocate me or when she told me to get out?"

Lilianna didn't smile. Standing, she said, "Come with me."

She led Juniper back outside and into the chilly night air. The storm had gained on the Wylds, and lightning danced in the clouds far above them. Thunder rolled, low and dangerous and close. It filled the night with a sense of insignificance and cosmic power.

With a short, sharp whistle, the winged Shadow came bounding through the dark forest, nimbly navigating the brambles and tree roots.

"Moss," Lilianna said to the Shadow, "this is Juniper. Angyla doesn't like her, so we're going for a flight while she cools down. Juniper, this is Moss."

Moss warbled, seeming to understand.

"Does he understand you?" Juniper asked as Lilianna climbed onto Moss's back.

"To an extent," she said. "Shadows are intelligent creatures, frightfully so sometimes."

Juniper climbed onto Moss's back behind her.

"Why does he have wings but the others don't?"

"I can't say. The Shadows are another thing Angyla doesn't like to talk about. Moss listens to me better than the others. Most of the time."

Moss warbled, seeming to agree.

They shot into the air, leaving Juniper clenching tight onto Lilianna's middle. They flew low over the valley. A flash of lightning brightened the dead leaves and impossible trees, their dark limbs reaching toward the sky, their roots crisscrossing the ground. The lightning flashed against the building thunderheads, bubbling dark blues and purples.

"Angyla says the rest of the world is as green as Sinjon," Lilianna said with longing.

"Most of it is, save for the deserts, oceans, and ice-peaked mountains."

Lilianna sighed. "I want to see it."

"Which part?"

"All of it."

"You don't have to stay here." Juniper understood that longing, though if someone had said those words to her a few years ago, she wouldn't have believed them.

They flew for several long moments before Lilianna said, "The person you mentioned, Nexon, who is that?"

"He is a monster," Juniper said. "He is the Archmage of Earth, and a thousand years ago tried to conquer the realm. The other archmages stopped him, in these Wylds, and it ended the Great War. They say the expenditure of magic was so great, it created the Wylds. Angyla is one of those archmages, the only one still alive who remembers how they defeated him. Nexon is rising again, and Reid and I came here to find her, to learn how they stopped him before. We have to stop him."

At the mention of Reid's name, her chest squeezed. In the distance, she spotted the glow of Sinjon. If any of those backwater fools hurt him, she would shatter the entire village. Of course, Reid could take on every warrior inside the walls and win.

"Is that what happened?" Lilianna asked. "I've suspected Angyla knows more than she says, but I've never confronted her about it. She says she is the only one who understands the land, that it speaks to her and she speaks back, and… She fears that if she leaves, the Wylds will swallow everything. But she doesn't like to talk about it. She's told me she wants to show me how, so when she is no longer here, I can take her place."

"Take her place?" Juniper didn't like the sound of that. "But…what does she need you to do in her place?"

"Keep the Wylds from expanding," Lilianna said darkly. "Jarek isn't wrong about the Wylds. They are cursed, and Angyla is holding the curse back. She is the only one who knows how, but she says I will be able to with training."

The storm was approaching fast, and Lilianna steered them southeast, away from the village and Angyla's hovel, and to a clearing. Moss landed softly. Juniper slid off first, thankful to have her feet on the ground. Monstrous sounds chittered through the darkness, cursed and rabid animals of the night.

Juniper suppressed a shiver.

"I have questions," Lilianna said, sliding to the ground. "Why must you defeat this Nexon a certain way?"

"He's an archmage, which means he's more powerful than a regular mage. Only the other archmages rival him in power."

"Would a blade through the heart not kill him?"

"I would love to stab him in all his non-vitals and let him bleed out," Juniper said. "But getting close enough without him crushing me is the problem."

And Nexon was looking for the final pieces—whatever that meant.

"But…" Lilianna sighed. She made a graceful lap around the clearing. "If Nexon is still here, whatever the archmages did didn't work."

Juniper had tried not to think about that little problem. Thunder rolled, closer and cracking. Juniper felt the rain in the sky, the ocean above her head. She felt the urge to command it all, the abyss within her that told her she could. She imagined bringing all the water down at once and washing the Wylds away. She doubted it would be enough.

Lilianna paused and looked at the sky. "Can I speak openly with you?"

"Of course."

"No one else knows that I train with Angyla, aside from Grandmother, and she doesn't like to talk about it. I've never had anyone to speak to about it."

"I'm listening." Juniper motioned for her to go on.

"Angyla's been…different this past year. She vanishes for days at a time. She has become ill-tempered, like you saw her today. She is easily upset over small things. And…when she is angry, the Shadows react. They…leech her anger. They cry out and turn into the monstrous beasts the village thinks they are."

"Angyla sent them to attack the village?"

Lilianna shook her head. "Not intentionally. The Shadows feed off her anger, and they go into a rabid frenzy. Her anger has never been enough to send them Shadows over the village wall before. She gets angry over everything these days, more and more often. I…don't know what to do. I fear the first attack might be a combination of your fault and my own. I couldn't stand by while my family and friends were injured because of me, and I acted with foolish bravery. I took Moss and tried to stem the destruction as best I could. I'm not sure if I helped or made it worse."

"Moss listens to you when the others frenzy?"

"He does. He's not like the other Shadows. I don't understand that either," Lilianna said, looking fondly at the Shadow. It flexed its wings like a bird would do, twitching them upward and out, unintentionally revealing their height. "The Shadows are an extension of Angyla's magic, but Moss is mine, or so Angyla reasons."

"Angyla's magic and the cursed air," Juniper said. "It makes sense why they don't bleed. They seep back into the ground."

Lilianna started to speak, then pulled her words back.

"What is it?" Juniper took a step closer to Lilianna. Her own suspicions were swirling together, faster than she could think.

"Angyla let it slip once, months ago, that when a Shadow is slain, it returns to the wellspring," Lilianna whispered. She glanced around the clearing as if she feared Angyla might be listening. "I think that is where the curse is coming from."

"Where—"

"I haven't found it," Lilianna said lowly. "I've not had much time to wander through the Wylds. The trees grow too thick to see anything from the sky. I've been up and down Blood Tree Pass countless times, but I haven't been able to find it. It's there, I think, near the pass. Underground."

"If Nexon met his end in the pass, then it's safe to assume the two are connected," Juniper said.

Thunder crashed close above them, followed by brilliant lightning. Another crack of thunder shattered the air and rumbled the earth. Juniper felt the sky tear, felt the first of the rain. Then, she heard it on the bare trees, the hardened tree roots, and the rocky forest floor.

"This way," Lilianna said, motioning to the safety of the thick canopy.

Juniper followed her over and under massive tree roots. Moss bounced in and out of view, as languid as a breeze and unaffected by the rain. The rain hammered closer. The thick canopy shielded them from the worst of the rain, but stray drops found a way through. Water trickled down the tree trunks and splattered the rocks. Frigid droplets splattered Juniper's face, and she let them.

Lightning flashed, and Juniper spotted a strange color in the air. Lightning flashed again; A mist oozed upward from the rock and roots, almost imperceptible, except when lightning lit it. The ghostly mist filled the air, undulating and thickening. The wind picked up but did not move the mist as it did the trees. Magic, she realized with a start. It oozed from the very ground.

Underneath the rain and the wet, she could smell it. Bittersweet and corrupted, tangy and rotten.

Lilianna led them to a bend in a shallow river. The ground jutted upward on the far side, and a bluff stretched over the river. The girls jumped across flat river stones and took shelter under the bluff. The rain slowly darkened the rock around them, but the stone underneath the bluff remained dry.

Juniper was feeling the rain and the storm, and when a low grumble sounded behind her, a cold panic raced up her spine. A pinch of shame came with it. She hadn't been paying attention. She turned—a Shadow had taken refuge under the bluff as well. It was smaller than Moss and had spiked ears and a long, snake-like tail. Lilianna calmly approached it, and it warbled.

As menacing as a house cat, Juniper thought. Only much more intimidating.

"When they are like this, they are harmless," Lilianna said. She traced her fingers along the Shadow's snout. It purred.

It blinked its white eyes at Juniper, then cooed. She approached it and knelt. She had never been one for animals, but the Shadows weren't animals. They were magic. Juniper stroked the Shadow's head. The leathery fabric of its hide felt like ghostly silk. She felt the magic that bound the beast together, that gave it life. It hummed with power.

"Angyla doesn't like the village," Lilianna whispered, barely audible over the rain. "She says the druids are superstitious fools, which is why they've nearly died out."

"I have to agree with her on the superstitious part, though I think the cursed forest might have had something to do with the dying out part."

"I've pieced together the bits and pieces I've heard from my grandmother and from Angyla," Lilianna said. "I think our ancestors chased her into the woods because she hurt someone, or several people. I'm afraid to ask her about it. I think…I think she killed someone."

The Shadow suddenly went rigid in Juniper's touch. The magic in its skin turned white hot, and zapped like lightning against her touch.

She gasped and jumped back. Had she offended it somehow?

The Shadow unfurled from its resting position, a low growl in its throat. Its eyes widened, it clawed at the stone ground, and its tail slashed through the air.

"Get back," Lilianna warned. She took slow steps away from the Shadow.

Moss hissed from outside the bluff. His dark wings bent inward, and his white eyes narrowed toward the ground. Lightning seared and thunder banged, almost in unison.

"What did I do?" Juniper gasped.

"You did nothing. It's starting again," Lilianna whispered, fear on each word. "They are raging."

The air thickened, like it did on a humid summer afternoon, but different; it didn't feel hot or cold. It sizzled. It compressed. It took more effort to breathe.

Lightning flashed. The golden mist had thickened. Thick as water, but lighter than air.

Not just any magic, Juniper realized with a start. Air magic. Angyla's magic reached through the Wylds. Had she heard what Lilianna was about to say?

The smaller Shadow growled and jumped into the rain. It bounded through the forest.

"That's it," Lilianna gasped. She grabbed Juniper's arm. "I've not been this far north when the Shadows rage. The village is south. That Shadow ran north. Where is it going?" Her golden eyes were wide and wild. "The Shadows are made of magic, they feed on it."

"The wellspring," Juniper gasped.

"Come on!"

Lilianna ran into the rain. Moss stood in the shallow river, and as Lilianna approached, he bent down. She jumped onto his back with ease. Juniper followed. The cold rain soaked her to the bone before she'd reached Moss's side. Juniper had barely enough time to fasten her arms around Lilianna when they shot into the air.

If they could find the wellspring, they could stop the curse of the Blackwood Wylds from spreading.

CHAPTER 55

Moss flew faster than before. The torrential rain pelted Juniper's face and blurred her vision. Lightning seared across the sky, illuminated the jagged Wylds underneath them, there and gone in a blink. Thunder crashed, rattling Juniper's bones and making her heart skip each time. They flew…north? She couldn't be sure. They hadn't flown over the village, or at least she didn't think so.

Moss flew lower, and then Juniper spotted a dark splotch in the Wylds—darker than the rest and devoid of trees. Moss flew lower still, and as they gained on the splotch, it became a cave opening. A straight shot into the earth.

And Moss flew for it.

Lightning flashed—Juniper's gasp vanished in the wind. Hundreds of Shadows crawled into the cavern opening, throwing themselves into the depths, howling and hissing and roaring. The lightning illuminated the thick magic mist as it flowed upward from the cavern, ignoring the rain and wind.

Moss folded in his wings and free fell into the cavern. Juniper's scream was lost in a crash of thunder. They fell down, down, down, and Juniper squeezed her eyes tight. She heard Moss's wings open, felt the sudden jolt, and then they banked right, left, right—her stomach lurched with each turn and flap of wings.

Moss leveled, and Juniper dared open her eyes. The mist illuminated the cavern in pale gold, flowing like light through water. Shadows crawled along the cavern floor, their bodies undulating and flowing deeper like spilled ink. They surged forward, the same direction that Moss flew, deeper into the cavern.

The air was thick with the same putrid magic that filled Blood Tree Pass. Each breath was a chore.

Moss warbled, either a warning or a plea.

It unsettled her to see so many Shadows. They fed on magic; they were magic. And they were heading into the wellspring—the epicenter of magic.

It hadn't occurred to Juniper that the opening to the wellspring might be somewhere else. It made sense. Lilianna hadn't found it because she'd been looking in the pass—but the way into the wellspring was far from the pass and led through a maze of caves. They could have scoured the Wylds for weeks without finding the opening.

The cavern opened up, and all Juniper saw at first was magic. It filled the chamber, thick as water, thick as it had been in the Spirit Gate. She couldn't see the floor or the ceiling or the walls. Stalagmites and stalactites emerged through the mist, daggers and teeth. Moss flew to the edge of the vast chamber and halted. Shadows swarmed within the magic, black masses among the yellow-gold. The Shadows rushed through the cavern and threw themselves into the magic—some dissolved, others formed.

She spotted the specs of gold, like those she had seen above ground. They floated upward and out of sight. This magic felt different than the magic in Delphine. It lacked the somber indifference of the Spirit Gate. This felt agitated, upset, and unhappy. It crawled along her skin and left her feeling anxious and nauseated.

"It's here," Lilianna whispered. "The wellspring."

"If my guess is correct," Juniper said, "we are under the pass."

They were under the heart of the Wylds, where the magic below seeped upward, tainting the forest. Juniper felt the magic in the wellspring, a tangled mess of…emotion. Juniper had no other way of describing it; anger, hate, fear, betrayal—all tied together in a ball of magic twine, impossibly knotted, tangled in a heap of pulsating power. The threads extended beyond the chamber. They reached deep into the earth, into the cave system, and through the ground to the surface. She felt the magic trying to unknot itself, trying to claw its way out of the confines, trying to break through the surface. She felt its need…its hunger. It wanted to devour everything.

At the far end of the chamber, the magic flowed out through natural caverns. A cave system under the Wylds would allow the archmage access to an untold part of the forest. It would also distribute the curse.

The whole mess made her lightheaded. She felt the magic tugging on her own, incessant and stubborn. This, Juniper realized, was where Nexon met his end. This dent in the ground, covered with stone and hidden by a cursed forest. It had been hidden, either by time or magic or both.

Moss growled and stomped impatiently. He had gotten closer to the magic pool. Juniper felt a hot spike of panic. If Moss jumped into the magic, he would throw Lilianna and herself in with him. She had no desire to see who or what greeted her on the other side of the cursed magic pool.

"We need to get him out of here," Lilianna said. Fear lined her voice. She urged Moss away from the mist. The Shadow warbled in reluctance. He inched closer to the pool. "Moss! Let's go!"

Be it the rise in her tone or the fear that echoed off the chamber walls, Moss snapped out of his trance and dashed back the way they had come. He ran along the cavern, then as the space widened, took to the air.

Juniper held on tight as Moss navigated the maze toward the surface. The magic thinned and thinned, and each breath came easier.

The wellspring was huge. What was she supposed to do about it? If she clogged it with rocks, would the magic seep around the stones or devour them? Her gut and her magic told her it wouldn't work, that the magic would find the tiniest crack and find a way through.

She would bet gold Angyla knew.

Moss didn't fly as furiously as before, and Juniper leaned forward to speak in Lilianna's ear.

"If the Shadows are acting this way, does that mean that Shadows attacked the village again?" Juniper asked.

"Yes," Lilianna said darkly.

Juniper's heart squeezed. She knew Reid could defend himself, but it didn't make her feel any better.

Lilianna sighed. "It's her, isn't it? Angyla is causing this."

"Nexon started it," Juniper defended. "The curse originated from him."

"I think I understand," Lilianna said. "Angyla is holding the curse back, and in the process has…become a part of it."

Juniper didn't like the idea of that. Had Angyla spent too long in the curse? Juniper felt the curse tug on her own magic. Maybe Angyla had finally given in and let the curse have its way.

Moss started the steep incline toward the surface. Both girls held onto the Shadow as tight as they could. Lightning and thunder tore across the sky. Cold rain speckled Juniper's face. The storm grew louder as they neared the surface. It struck every rock and barren tree branch, sounding more mechanical than any other storm. Moss flew low over the Wylds, just barely above the trees.

They flew toward Sinjon—it glowed in the distance, a blur in the storm. As they approached, flying low over the forest, they saw Shadows retreating from the village.

"It's over," Lilianna said. "The Shadows are calm."

Lilianna guided Moss back to the ground. They walked the rest of the way and stopped within view of the timber wall. Sinjon looked fine. Nothing burned or smoked, and even if it did, the rain would help.

"I need to return," Lilianna said. "My mother will panic if she can't find me. My grandmother can only stall for so long."

"Go," Juniper said. "I'll be fine. I've done my fair share of surviving in the woods. I'm also used to things trying to kill me."

That didn't mean she liked it, though.

"Moss knows the way to Angyla's house," Lilianna said, more to the Shadow than to Juniper. "You'll take Juniper there, won't you?"

Moss warbled. Lilianna gave him an affectionate stroke.

"I'll be back when I can," she said to Juniper.

Lilianna started toward Sinjon, and Moss and Juniper waited until she had climbed safely over the outer wall. Then Moss nudged Juniper toward the Wylds. They walked for a while before he paused at a massive tree with a tangle of roots. She blinked; they had not gone nearly far enough to have reached Angyla's tree. Moss slithered through the roots and vanished. Juniper climbed down after him and into a narrow, dark cavern.

Her eyes quickly adjusted, and she spotted Moss a few steps down the cavern. He shook off the rain, splattering the cavern walls and floor.

"Lead the way, but not too fast," Juniper said.

Moss warbled and started along the cavern. He led her down one tunnel then another, and finally they emerged back to the surface. She had assumed the tunnels would connect directly to Angyla's house, but they did not. Moss led her through the forest and to the door hidden by tree roots.

Juniper climbed down to the door and let herself in. Moss did not follow. She stood for a moment in the doorway, listening to the constant pitter-patter of rain, on the rocks and trees and brambles. A whoosh—Moss took off through the rain.

The house was quiet. A fire burned in the hearth, and the air was warmer.

"Hello?" she called.

No one answered.

Angyla had stepped out, it seemed. Juniper magicked the water from her clothes and hair and left it outside, then shut the door. She meandered deeper in the archmage's lair. It looked to have started as a natural cavern. Angyla, or someone, had coaxed the tree roots to grow strategically to make rooms and doorways and bridges over cracks and underground rivers. Though the hearth room had been lit with a magelight, most of the cavern remained dark. Juniper used her night sight to see down dark corridors. She followed the gush of water to a large chamber. A waterfall cascaded down the rocky wall and into a deep pool of crystalline blue.

One side of the chamber had been fashioned into storage, and the other was a workstation piled with dusty bottles, cloudy jars, and crumbling books. Old crates and baskets held all manner of things—wool, leather scraps, broken tools, jars, utensils. Things that could only have been stolen from Sinjon. Suddenly, the blacksmith's claims of thievery didn't sound so outlandish.

The waterfall filled the chamber with a wet mineral scent. Underneath it was the familiar floral and bittersweet metallic scents of magic. It smelled, oddly enough, like the Undercity—and a rush of nostalgia crawled down Juniper's spine.

Juniper pulled a thread of water from the falls—it had few impurities. Curious and thirsty, she brought the thread to her lips. It tasted of minerals and magic. She sat by the pool. She could feel the water; it sank deep into the caverns, farther than she could sense. With her magic, would she be able to navigate such a dangerous place as underwater caverns?

She set her head in her hands. Gods, she was tired. Bone tired. What happened to the days when she could stay up all night, sleep until midmorning, and be fine? Were those sleepless nights catching up to her now? A part of her wanted to go back to those days. She knew the rules of the Undercity, knew the people, knew what she had to do to get by. Now, she didn't know what she was doing or what she should be doing.

She had found the wellspring. Now what?

"And you're still here," said a harsh and exhausted female voice.

Juniper jumped—Angyla stood on the opposite side of the deep pool, a small satchel hanging from her shoulder, and a forever flame of sage green in her hand.

"As are you, archmage," Juniper said, sounding as exhausted as she felt.

Angyla did not balk at the title, and Juniper steeled herself. The time for answers had come, and she refused to leave without them.

Chapter 56

Juniper forced herself to stand on shaky legs. She held Angyla's stare. "Lilianna's gone back to Sinjon. It's just us. You don't have to lie to me. I know who you are."

Angyla heaved a heavy sigh.

"And I have questions."

"Of course you do." Angyla scowled, and the shadows of the room deepened the wrinkles on her ancient face. She marched to the workstation, to a cauldron set upon a bed of artfully placed stones. "Everyone has questions." She snorted a wicked laugh. "Before you start nagging, help with this. Fetch a pan of water from the falls. The falls, not the pool. It's important."

Juniper found an empty jug among the junk and filled it halfway with water from the falls. She carried it to the cauldron. Within it, a lightless chartreuse fire burned underneath a suspended pan filled with roots and berries.

"Pour it over, slowly, so as not to slosh," Angyla commanded.

Juniper did as instructed—she could follow a few measly rules if it meant getting her answers.

"Magic demands delicacy, precision, and intent," Angyla said, her voice calm and even, though a bit accusative.

The water flowed over the berries and roots, jostling them gently. The water began to boil almost immediately. Juniper set the pan aside.

"What kind of fire is that?" she asked.

"Cooking fire," Angyla said. "Took me decades to figure out and another to understand the temperature. I doubt you've seen it. The Order has been intent on stomping out any remaining hint of the Iluvin ways."

"They've nearly succeeded," Juniper said.

Angyla's face darkened. "A cooking fire is designed to cook food without heating up the kitchen or burning what it's cooking. It gives off a small glow, and in the moments just before dawn, the market streets glowed as the bakeries set the first rolls into the ovens."

It took Juniper a moment to realize what she meant. She wasn't talking about a world Juniper knew, but a world a thousand years gone.

"What was it like?" Juniper whispered. Angyla's eyes flashed to her. "Iluvin cities."

"They were like any other city," she said. "They had crime and poverty and problems without end, but they took advantage of magic and its endless uses. The good and bad."

"You were alive during the Great War," Juniper said—not a question. "How was it? Before, I mean."

"Before the war?" Angyla chuckled. "I'm old, but not that old. I was born during the first years of the war, and I never knew the Iluvin before Nexon or the Order. The rest of my childhood was spent dealing with the consequences of that war. Now, we come to the real question: why are you here?"

"I came looking for you." Juniper sat down and leaned forward. Maddox had told her that when someone leaned forward, it implied innocence; leaning away implied guilt.

"Why?"

"Because Nexon is rising to power again," Juniper said, watching for any effect on the older woman's face. "And I need to know how the archmages defeated him the first time."

"No," she said.

Juniper blinked. "You don't know? Are you the Archmage of Air that was present?"

"I am."

"Then you are the only living archmage who knows." Juniper hated how her pleading sounded. She composed herself and attempted to stow her desperation. "Aside from Nexon, I suppose."

"No, as in I will not tell you how we did it," she said.

"Why? He's rising to power, and he's tearing Duvane apart. When he's done, he'll march through Collatia."

"Look around you." Something cold flashed behind Angyla's eyes. "Look at what our power did to this land. We stopped one man, and we killed hundreds of others. We destroyed the druids' homeland, and now they can never return. We destroyed the very ground from which life grows."

Juniper heard it in those words—regret.

"We knew no other way to stop him," Angyla whispered. She blinked; dampness clumped her lashes. "I did what I thought I had to. I was too young to question it."

"Is there no other way?" Juniper whispered.

The archmage's eyes flickered from the fire to Juniper. "Who are you?"

At that, Juniper hesitated. "I've asked myself that same question a lot lately. To most, I'm Juniper Thimble. But to others I am Isolde Balendin. Everyone seems to think that I am the princess who will somehow stop Nexon."

The sadness in Angyla's eyes flashed into something bright and dangerous. She remained silent for a long moment. Then, recognition.

Juniper felt a bubble of relief. Maybe now she could get answers.

"I've seen you," Angyla said at last, looking Juniper over. "In the dreams. Your face. Your voice."

"Dreams?"

"The magic gives dreams," Angyla said, stepping closer. "Glimpses of the past and future. I have seen our mistake played over and over, the murder of the land, the spreading of the curse. It showed me Lilianna, and it showed me you. I knew you would come, but I never knew why. You were not a druid, so you would not come from the village. I see now. I understand. You are a disruption. A betrayer."

Juniper blinked. Angyla's sadness vanished, and her curiosity transformed into a cold fury. The suddenness of the change sent a shiver of panic up Juniper's spine. *Mad,* her gut said. *This woman has gone mad.*

"Disruption?" Juniper repeated, blinking.

"The curse is spreading," Angyla spat. "It is our fault. We did this to the land. Every life that was lost that day and after. Our fault. I contain the curse. I keep it from devouring everything in this realm! And you want to unleash it all again!"

Angyla's voice echoed off the stone.

Juniper held her ground, though she wanted to put more space between herself and the mad woman. She swallowed her fear and whispered, "What happened that day?"

Angyla looked on the verge of tears. Regret darkened her eyes, alongside an emotion Juniper knew well—guilt.

"We were desperate," she said. "People were dying. Cities were falling. We were out of options and afraid. We sought the end of war and tyranny. We saw the end goal, and we neglected the path. In our foolish idealism. Enemies and friends, dead, because we sought to be gods. We paved the past with thorns, and our future now reaps the rewards." She motioned to the Wylds. "This is what we did."

Juniper stared at the archmage. She wanted to ask what the hell she was talking about, but she kept her lips closed. This mad woman had magic to rival Nexon, and Juniper did not want to be seen as a threat.

Whatever the archmages did to Nexon had created the Blackwood Wylds, the curse that was slowly eating the forest. What could they have possibly done?

"You cannot do what we did," Angyla breathed, her voice tired and afraid.

"Because it would create another curse?" Juniper asked.

Angyla's fearful and guilty frown gave her the answer.

It sank like stones. If Juniper managed to do what the archmages did, it would create another curse. Dead trees, tainted creatures, and barren land. She couldn't do that. She couldn't defeat him the same way.

"There must be another way," Juniper whispered.

"A sword through the heart should do the trick," Angyla said. Her eyes were ancient and cold. "Your journey here has been in vain. There is nothing for you here. Go back, take your lover and leave this place. You have already done more than enough to mess up all my hard work! The poor Shadows, so many have been slain, my poor dears. A few by your hands too."

Juniper clasped her fingers together.

The archmage pointed at her, the nail short and dirty. "You don't belong here. I've seen you. I've seen what you've done. Thief. Killer. You are no princess, no savior. You are nothing more than a glorified mercenary. The magic here cannot help you. It helps no one. It only listens to me."

"You would cast me out into the storm?" Juniper hated playing the poor, helpless child, but if playing tough didn't work, she would.

Angyla took several short breaths, then huffed. "Fine. Stay here tonight. Tomorrow, you leave. Now eat up before it gets cold."

Juniper sat on the floor beside the pool while she ate. The boiled roots and berries had a strange herbal taste, and Juniper couldn't decide if she liked it or not. While she ate, Angyla fiddled with her workstation, using her magic to patch clothes and crush herbs. After a wash in the pool, Angyla led her to a small chamber with a bed of furs, pelts, and old blankets. Juniper cast a magelight toward the ceiling and nestled into the furs. Exhaustion settled, and she knew sleep wouldn't be hard to find. She snuffed her magelight and darkness fell. Luckily, she had her night sight. The darkness became shades of indigo and charcoal.

And…her mind refused her rest.

She couldn't defeat Nexon the same way as before. Angyla would be of little help. It seemed they would have to end this in a fight. Delmont would be more helpful in a fight. But if they fought, there would be casualties. She had skill in a fight, but Nexon would win against her.

She remembered the feeling of his magic as they fled Bradburn Castle. It felt as if the world had doubled over, crushing her.

And Lilianna was right—the archmages hadn't gotten rid of Nexon for good. He came back, so if she were to defeat him the same way, would he return in another thousand years?

Juniper draped her arm over her face.

And the pieces—Nexon was looking for the final pieces. She would have to ask Angyla what that meant in the morning.

Had she rushed into her plan without thinking things through? Maybe Reid was right. She had sought a way out of the palace, out of being Isolde, and she had jumped on it without a second thought.

CHAPTER 57

Juniper's dreams were filled with gold mist, angry archmages, and furious kings. Nexon had not been defeated. He and his army of apostates had taken over Duvane, slaughtering anyone not of magical talent. Then he had marched toward Delphine, to finish the war he had started, to kill the rest of the pitiful resistance. In her dream, none of her friends escaped. When Nexon had taken both kingdoms, he set his sights on the rest of the world.

Juniper woke with sweat beading on her neck and sticking her shirt to her back. She struggled to sit up amid the furs. It took several moments to calm the pounding of her heart.

The cavern was dark. In her night sight, the cavern looked smaller than it had before. Through the holes in the cloth-door, the hall was empty. Juniper pushed herself onto her feet. She stretched to the ceiling and then to the floor. She tiptoed through the cavern, toward the glow of magelight near the entrance. She pulled the wooden door open.

Dawn had broken. Dull sunlight seeped through the steely clouds of the Wylds, alighting the gloomy Wylds. Specs of golden magic fluttered freely. Juniper climbed up through the roots to the forest floor. The chilly air seeped through Juniper's clothes and down her throat. The Wylds were deathly quiet. Nothing scurried or cawed. The monsters were sleeping.

She tried to remember what sunlight looked like and imagined the sky in layers of lavender, coral, and butter. She opened her eyes and saw only the dull, gray light.

"You left the door wide open," snapped Angyla. She stood in the doorway, glaring up at Juniper. "What kind of rat hole did you grow up in?"

Juniper laughed. "The worst kind."

Angyla did not smile. "Get in here before the cold seeps in, foolish girl."

She hesitated, then climbed back down to the door. Had Angyla forgotten her threat the night before? Had she taken it back?

Lilianna's warning rang in her mind—Angyla hadn't been the same these past few months. Temperamental.

Angyla led Juniper back to the waterfall chamber. They hadn't yet crossed the threshold when Angyla started barking orders for Juniper to gather a particular arrangement of herbs and spices. Angyla filled an old ceramic pot with water from the walls and set it over the chartreuse cooking fire. She instructed Juniper to add the herbs and spices one at a time, which she did. It was a tedious process.

"And the honeyed dust after it begins to boil," Angyla commanded, pointing at the tiny bubbles at the bottom of the pot.

"Why does it matter?" Juniper sprinkled the dust over the boiling water. It shimmered bright yellow for a few moments, then dulled into a honey brown. It smelled like warm honey.

"Some herbs are very delicate." Angyla waved her hand over the pot, and the cooking fire went out. "The tea should be ready. Pour yourself a cup."

Juniper wanted to pass. The tea smelled like dirt and old flowers. But she didn't want to anger the archmage, so she found a teacup, blew off the dust, and poured a cup. It tasted much like it smelled.

Only, she felt a difference. A pleasant warmth filled her body.

Juniper sat at the pool's edge and sipped her tea while Angyla went about chores—mixing herbs and whispering into potions and salves. Juniper watched the old woman work. She mumbled to herself all the while, only pausing when she read from one of her few crumbling books.

"I need more black wart," Angyla mumbled as she headed toward the front of the cavern.

Juniper sipped her tea and waited until she couldn't see or hear the archmage, then she stood and took a look at the book she had been so invested in. The pages had yellowed with time, the leather cover had dried and cracked, and the thread holding the pages together had been replaced several times, leaving the edges uneven.

She couldn't read the curving, angular language. It looked like Iluvin, as mysterious as it was ancient.

Juniper scanned the shelves of junk and jars and piled…things. Among a basket of buttons, loose spools of thread, and broken needles, she spotted a glint. Juniper glanced toward the cavern to make sure Angyla hadn't returned. Then she pulled the glinting object out.

It was a moonstone brooch. The silver casting had tarnished into dull and cloudy gray. The moonstone looked new, polished to reflect the light to give the illusion of self-illumination.

Just like her ring, she thought.

A flick of her wrist, the moonstone brooch vanished into the inside pocket of her cloak.

A warble disturbed her thoughts. Juniper spun, excuse at the ready. But it was only Moss. He crept into the cavern from a dark side passage. She released a sigh. She didn't want to explain why she was snooping to Angyla.

Moss snorted as if he knew.

"I know," Juniper whispered. She retreated from the book. She couldn't read it anyway. She picked up her tea and took a sip.

Moss warbled. He tilted his head at her as if to ask, *What's wrong?*

"Too many things to name just a few," Juniper said to Moss. She sighed and stretched her legs out.

Moss warbled and tilted his head—listening.

"Well, to start, I have kingdoms relying on me to find a way to stop Nexon, and I have no idea how. Then my dead father told me to come here because there was trouble, which I guess is this whole curse business, but I don't know what to do about that either. I might have already messed it up by making the druids hate me."

Moss snorted.

"And then there's Isolde," she continued. "I'm supposed to be her, but how am I supposed to be a princess? I don't want a throne or a kingdom. I'm not the ruling kind. I mean, I like admiration and praise as well as the next girl, but…I don't want the responsibility. I want to go back to the way things were." She thought of the brooch in her pocket. "I want to be Juniper. Just a thief. But I don't think I can go back to that."

Things had changed too much. She looked at the moonstone ring on her finger.

Moss nudged her shoulder with his snout.

She curled her fingers inward, hiding the moonstone from view. "This is going to sound stupid."

Moss scoffed, or he made a sound that she interpreted as a scoff.

"It's Reid," she whispered. "My…betrothed. I love him, more than I knew I could love another person, but I'm afraid we rushed into this engagement. I'm afraid he is starting to see me for the person I really am. I keep dragging him through trouble, and I'm afraid he'll see his mistake and realize there are other girls prettier, smarter, and better than me. I'm afraid he'll leave. He is an amazing person, honorable and kind and just. The world needs more people like him, and less people like me."

Moss warbled in disagreement.

"Easy for you to say." Juniper tried to smile but couldn't. "You've not seen the girls in Rusdasin, talented with music and speech and beautiful beyond natural reason. I'm not one of those girls. I never have been, and I doubt being raised in a palace would have changed that. I would only have infuriated my tutors and trainers. I'm not a puffy dress kind of girl. I'm not the girl that can cook or clean or…" She sighed. "I'm not the wife kind of girl."

Moss sniffed, blinking. *What kind of girl are you?*

"I don't know," she said. "The lying and stealing type, I suppose. I…don't know how to be anything other than what I am."

Moss shook his head. *Is that so bad?*

Angyla's quick footsteps marched back into the chamber. She held a small leather pouch. She narrowed her glare at Moss.

"Take him outside," she snapped. "He'll knock things over in here."

Moss bounced on his feet, and his wing brushed a shelf of cloudy jars.

"Out!" Angyla snapped.

Moss tucked his wings in close and slithered through the house. Juniper felt the crackle in the air. Not wanting to witness another tantrum from Angyla, she ran after Moss. Juniper opened the front door. The Shadow maneuvered up the tree roots with ease. Juniper grabbed a thick cloak by the door and followed.

She and Moss walked for a while, over sprawling tree roots, around boulders larger than houses, and over puddles left from the storm. Moss jumped and bounced and splashed through puddles; Juniper remained a few steps behind. So many thoughts cluttered her mind. Angyla, Lilianna, Reid, the Shadows, the villagers, Nexon, Ison, Myrisha—people counting on her, people she had continually disappointed.

They hadn't yet reached the cusp of the valley when Moss jerked to a pause; his entire body tensed. Juniper nearly ran into him. Her body moved in reflex into a defensive stance.

The distant cadence of voices murmured through the gloomy Wylds.

Moss snorted his dislike.

The druids had come farther into the Wylds than she realized. From the scattered maps she had seen, the roads around Sinjon did not extend this far.

No, they were hunting. It would seem their hatred for her outweighed their fear of the Wylds.

She patted Moss's side, whispering, "Can you fly us away from here?"

Moss flexed his wings, and she climbed awkwardly onto his back. She felt along his skin for something to hold onto but found nothing. Her panic rose white-hot as Moss flexed his wings outward. Her panic became desperation as he flapped once, twice, and she felt for anything along his skin, and as his feet left the ground, she felt something behind his ears, scales or bone or horns—she latched onto them with white knuckles. They emerged on the other side of the canopy, in the gloomy gray daylight.

Juniper released a shuddering breath. In the muted sunlight, Moss's shadowy skin flickered from black to charcoal to silver. The leathery flesh became translucent, utterly beautiful and utterly terrifying, something only magic could create.

Moss let out a warning warble, but it was too late.

Juniper took her eyes off his wing just as a heavy net crashed over them, the weights yanking them out of the sky. She screamed, but it was lost under the sound that Moss made, a shriek of fear and a cry for help. She cast her magic through the thick rope of the net, slicing through it easily, but it didn't help. Moss's wings were tangled in it, and he frantically tried to free himself, making a clear shot at the ropes impossible.

They hit the ground hard. Moss rolled, she fell, and then the world went black.

Juniper woke up with pain all over her body. She tried to move—a cry of pain escaped her lips. Consciousness settled back into her bones. She'd broken at least one rib, and scrapes stung and bruises throbbed everywhere else. A quick assessment of herself told her she still had all her fingers, toes, and limbs. Her memory returned, and it came as a small wonder that a broken rib was the worst of her injuries. A fall like that could have done much worse.

She was lying in a stone room. Three walls of gray stone, one wall of iron bars. On a hard bedroll that smelled like piss and mildew. Prison. A single torch spat flickering light down the prison's center hall. The cell across from her was empty. Footsteps echoed, muffled by stone and distance.

Juniper released a shuddering breath that throbbed in her chest.

A shuffle—a figure stepped up to the bars. She didn't recognize her face, but her emerald skin and sharp ears marked her as a druid. Her grimace marked her as an enemy.

"The witch is awake," the guard spat, dislike dripping on every word.

Heavy footsteps marched through the prison, echoing off the stone and iron. Jarek's formidable form blocked all but a few slivers of flickering torchlight.

"I half thought you'd be dead," Jarek said.

"I don't feel the best, if that counts," Juniper said, her words strained. "I'm fairly certain one of my ribs is broken."

Jarek mumbled something to the guard, and she marched away. Her footsteps were quick.

"Where's Reid?"

"He's fine," Jarek said. "At the house. He's not said it, but he's worried about you."

"I thought you said he was my thrall," Juniper said through gritted teeth.

Jarek didn't say anything to that. "You ran off," he said.

"Because your people were trying to kill me," she spat. "They tried to burn me alive because I saved them with magic."

"Magic has not been kind to this part of the kingdom," Jarek said darkly.

"It's fine everywhere else," Juniper said. "Your people don't understand magic at all."

Jarek didn't argue.

"What happened to Moss?"

"Who?"

"The Shadow you shot down," Juniper growled. "Where is he? If you harmed him—"

A warble sounded from within the prison, sad and unsure. They had locked him in the jail with her. Out of her sight.

"The Shadow is alive," Jarek spat. "As much as it can be. Tonight, we plan to take it to the pit. If the Shadow Master cares for his pet, he will show."

"Because that plan worked so well the first time," she sneered.

Jarek stared down at her with hatred and blame, then marched away.

She tried to sit up, but it hurt too much. She could feel her magic working to heal her, slowly. Word would have spread. What would Lilianna think? If Moss was injured, if they killed him, it would be Juniper's fault.

Juniper reached into her magic, into that pitiful amount of healing she had, and willed it to heal her ribs before it touched anything else. She wouldn't let them hurt Moss or Lilianna, and she needed to be in the best possible state to do so.

CHAPTER 58

Reid was heaving a load of firewood into the house when Jarek returned. The chief had been flustered since Juniper's flight into the Wylds, but now he looked aged by twenty years.

"What happened?" Reid demanded.

"They caught her," Jarek said.

Reid started for the door. Jarek warned him not to go, but Reid didn't listen. Ingrid stood by the drying spices, pretending the argument didn't exist—it was something Reid had noticed her doing often; she avoided what she didn't like or want to hear. It annoyed him. Problems could not be avoided forever. He preferred to meet them head-on.

The storm had ended and the attack was over, and with the calm came a terrible unease. It threaded through the village. They expected the worst—the unknown. Juniper had upset the balance of what they knew and expected, and they hated her for it. Her recklessness had again smacked her.

Why hadn't she listened to him?

Jarek led Reid to the prison. The guards didn't want to let Reid inside, but with a barked order from Jarek, they stepped aside.

"Don't let the witch into your mind," warned one of the guards.

Reid nodded, though he cast the man's ignorant warning aside.

Sinjon's prison had four cells. Two of which were occupied—by Juniper and the winged Shadow. Juniper was lying on her back, eyes closed covered in fading scrapes and purpling bruises. A small twig stuck out of her hair. Her breaths stuttered. That she felt pain squeezed his heart, even though he knew she had brought it upon herself.

"They shot her down," Jarek said. "Her and the Shadow."

The Shadow kept its back to the cell door. In the low light, it appeared as a blob of ink. Reid kept his distance. The shimmery beast reeked of strange magic.

Reid approached Juniper's cell. "Jun," he whispered.

A soft groan was her answer.

"Open the door," Reid told Jarek.

Jarek bristled at the command, but Reid did not back down. The two men stared at one another—then Jarek heaved a sigh and unlocked the heavy lock. Reid hadn't a doubt that Juniper could escape if she wanted to. She remained because she saw no benefit in escaping, or she was in too much pain.

Reid entered the cell and knelt beside her. "Jun," he asked again, a little louder.

Her eyes opened slowly. It took her a moment to find him and focus. He pulled the twig from her hair, then pushed the stray hair out of her face. He wanted to scold her for her foolish and rash actions; he wanted to scoop her into his arms and never let her go.

He had come here with a lecture in mind, but seeing her like this, he held it in.

"I found it," she whispered, her breath hitched. "The wellspring."

His brows rose. "You did? And?"

"I found her," Juniper said. "Archmage of Air. She's a crazy old bitch."

Reid chuckled.

Behind him, Jarek tensed.

"I don't know what to do about it." She closed her eyes and took a deep breath. "She was there when they defeated him, but she won't talk about it."

Reid cupped her cheek, flattening his palms and fingers against her chilled skin. He felt her magic working to heal her. Her hand twitched, and the moonstone ring caught the torchlight.

"She is unstable," Juniper whispered. Another word left her lips, but it had fallen so soft, Reid hadn't caught it.

"Rest." Reid stroked her temple. "You need it. We will talk later."

She looked like she had something else to say, but the pain and her exhaustion held her back. He stroked her cheek.

She closed her eyes. Reid knelt there a long moment, watching her rest. Her breaths hitched, her eyes flinched. Her magic would heal the worst of it, but she wasn't skilled in healing.

"She needs a healer," Reid said to Jarek as he left the cell.

Jarek locked the door back. He glared down at Juniper.

Had they been in Delphine, a healer would have seen her at once. But here, in the middle of these gods-forsaken woods, being Isolde Balendin meant little.

"I will see if Enna is free," Jarek said.

Reid stood guard while Enna and Lilianna entered the prison. Enna looked as irritated as always, but Lilianna had paled considerably. As she entered the cell, her golden eyes found the Shadow. Panic, fear, and dread broke through her usual stoic expression.

"It's all right," Jarek assured her. He set his hand on the girl's shoulder. "Reid will stay here and make sure the Shadow stays in its cage."

Jarek looked at Reid—he had given him an order and a warning. If anything happened—if Juniper escaped, if the Shadow escaped, if something happened to Enna or Lilianna, Jarek would blame Reid.

"Of course." Reid set his hand on the hilt of his Mage's Bane.

Jarek left the prison, and Enna knelt beside Juniper. Lilianna went immediately to the Shadow's cell. Reid tightened his hand on the hilt. If the Shadow tried anything—

"Moss?" Lilianna asked the Shadow. She clicked her tongue in a sound that mimicked birdsong.

At the sound of her voice, the Shadow unrolled and tilted his head toward the bars. His white eyes found Lilianna, and an energy surged through its graying skin. It became a shimmering black once more, and the beast let out an excited warble.

"You're all right," Lilianna whispered. She stuck her hand through the bars, and the Shadow nudged her palm with its snout.

"These events do not bode well," Enna said from within Juniper's cell.

Juniper said something too low for Reid to understand.

"She will be furious," Lilianna said, fear on every word.

Enna glanced over her shoulder at Reid. "I suppose she didn't tell you anything, since you look confused."

"She did not," Reid said. He looked between Enna and Lilianna. "What is going on?"

"The archmage," Juniper breathed. She set her weary gaze on Enna. "You knew it was her."

"Aye," Enna said. "And I knew it was in your best interest to stay away from her. Look what you've done to yourself."

Juniper chuckled. Her midnight eyes fell onto Reid, and regret filled her gaze.

She had tried to talk to him. Several times. And he had only been concerned with her recklessness. He still held himself to that, and she had done things wrong—but she had done them in her way.

"Reid," she breathed. She started to push herself into a sitting position, then winced—she bent the other way and reached into her pocket. Within her clenched fingers was an old piece of jewelry. Juniper glanced at it, then half-laughed. "I forgot about this."

"What is that?" Enna demanded.

Juniper unfurled her fingers. In her palm was a tarnished moonstone brooch. "Luckily I didn't lose it in the fall or get stabbed by it."

Reid opened his mouth to ask where she had gotten it, but his next breath was harder to take. The very air seemed to press down around them, enough to darken the edges of his vision and make his heart skip.

Thunder shook the sky, the ground, the iron bars of the cells. The heaviness in the air intensified, and Reid knew then what it was: magic. Vicious, trembling, ancient magic.

He had felt something similar only once before, when they had escaped Nexon in Bradburn Castle.

The roar quieted, and the following silence was complete.

"An earthquake of fury," Enna said, her words rough.

"She's upset." Lilianna half-stumbled to Juniper's cell. Her gaze fell onto the brooch. "You stole it?"

Reid scowled. "Of all the things."

Juniper gave him a crooked grin.

Thunder sounded again. It pulsed against the sky, against the ground, in the air. The air, Reid realized, because she was the Archmage of Air.

Bells began their terrible peals. Shrieks sounded in the distance.

Shadows were attacking.

"She knows." Lilianna grabbed the lock on the winged Shadow's cage. "We have to get Moss out. Now."

"Wait," Reid said.

"No waiting," Lilianna said with more force than he had ever heard her speak. "I have to get Moss out of here."

The door to the prison burst open. Jarek rushed inside, sword drawn. "The Shadows are attacking, hundreds of them. Reid, escort Enna to the Great Hall. Lilianna, fight or stay with your grandmother."

"Juniper—" Reid started.

"Is a prisoner," Jarek barked. "Take Enna. We can't afford to lose her."

Reid bristled.

"I will fight," Lilianna said darkly. She looked at Reid. Fear had vanished from her face, and stark determination placed it. "Go with Grandmother."

"I will not leave her," Reid said firmly.

"She will be fine," Lilianna said through gritted teeth. Her golden stare bore into his. Behind her, the Shadow pressed its snout to the bars. "Go."

"Go," Juniper repeated. She tucked the brooch back in her pocket. She flashed him that crooked grin that both infuriated him and heated his blood.

"You heard her, boy." Enna smacked Reid's arm. "Let's go."

"Stay safe, both of you," Reid ordered. He drew his Mage's Bane and followed Enna out of the prison. The sky above the village was dark, the air dark and heavy.

Shadows swarmed like locusts. He did not glance back at the prison, and prayed Lilianna knew what she was doing.

Chapter 59

Juniper felt her magic stitching her bones back together and slowly healing the worst of her injuries. She felt the thunder, felt the stone against her back tremble, felt the sky rattle.

She opened her eyes. Enna had left, Reid had left, and Lilianna knelt in front of Moss's locked cage.

Thunder sounded again—no, not thunder.

"An attack," Juniper gasped, pushing herself into a sitting position. Pain pinched her chest, but she pushed through it.

The bells rang, sounding the alarm, warning of the incoming attack. She heard the panicked voices, shouting and ordering, but no fighting. Not yet. She pushed herself to her feet. Her body felt like she'd thrown it down a long set of stairs. Several times. She closed her hands around the iron bars of her door.

"Lilianna?" she asked.

She didn't move at once. She stroked Moss's head.

"They ambushed us," Juniper explained. "I—I didn't mean—"

"I know," Lilianna said. "In my mind, I know you are not at fault. But in my heart, you are. Why couldn't you have just stayed away? Why bring him close to the village?"

"We didn't leave the valley," Juniper said.

Lilianna's eyes widened. "They went that far?" She deflated. She looked so much younger. Vulnerable.

A shout sounded from outside the stone walls, muffled and shrill. Then, a great boom shook the stone. Dust trembled from the ceiling and rattled the iron bars. Something had crashed into the prison. Moss jumped onto his feet, back arched, teeth bared, and he growled at the floor. His claws scraped at the stone.

"The Shadows are raging," Lilianna said breathlessly. "Angyla knows you took her brooch."

Juniper didn't miss the accusation. In truth, she couldn't explain why she took the brooch. She had wanted to feel like herself again, like the nimble and fearless thief, not the cornered and painted princess everyone wanted her to be.

"It's just a brooch," Juniper said bitterly.

Lilianna glared at her. "We'll fight about it later. Right now, we have to get out of here. At least it will be easier to leave with Moss and slip through the chaos unnoticed."

Lilianna reached into her satchel and pulled out the red wooden mask and a dirty cloak. She fastened the cloak around her shoulders and secured the mask on her face. Once again, Lilianna vanished behind the enigma of Red Mask.

Juniper felt the shift in the air, like when she and Lilianna had gotten too close to the wellspring. Thickened with tangled, wicked magic. Outside, the commotion steadily grew. Shadows filled the village, thudding against walls and roofs and fences, their cries and howls filling the air.

"Come on," Lilianna urged Moss. "We need to get out of here."

"I don't think so," Jarek called from the jailhouse doorway, ax in hand. He walked inside and slammed the door shut behind him. He took a fighting stance, and said, "I knew you'd come looking for them. You're not getting out of here alive."

Lilianna blinked between Jarek and his sharpened ax and threw her empty green hands into the air.

Jarek let out a vicious roar. He lifted his ax at a killing angle and dashed toward Lilianna with all the anger and force of a warrior. Lilianna, smaller and more agile than Jarek, dodged the blow. She rolled forward—one of the moves Reid had taught her—and bounced back to her feet.

"Stop it!" Juniper called. She closed her magic around the iron bars, but they did not want to be moved. The iron groaned and creaked but held firm. The iron must have been reinforced with some druid magic, preventing her own from harming it.

Moss tucked his wings in close and threw himself against the bars. They barely moved.

Jarek spun and thrust the ax at her again. Lilianna jerked to the side, barely out of the way; the tip of the ax sliced through her cloak. She dodged—and tripped, which might have been what saved her—as Jarek feinted and swung his ax toward her. Lilianna hit the floor, and the ax sank into the stone floor with a terrible *crack*.

Lilianna staggered to her feet. Jarek held one hand on the ax and reached for Lilianna with the other. She didn't move fast enough. His hand grabbed the edge of the mask, and with a hard tug, pulled it from her head. The leather tie snapped, and Lilianna stumbled backward.

Jarek blanched. The hand clutching the mask trembled. "Lilianna?"

She put her hands to her cheeks, her own surprise bright and fearful. Jarek threw the mask—it smacked against Juniper's slightly bent iron bars. She tightened her magic around them and yanked as hard as she could. A high-pitched creak reassured her.

Lilianna pleaded, "I can fix this! I can—"

"It was you," Jarek roared, his voice raw with betrayal. "You set those beasts on us! You've been helping those monsters!"

Jarek's ax came loose from the floor. He darted toward Lilianna with a madman's gleam in his eyes.

Juniper's hands, clutched on the bars, had gone entirely white. She screamed, "Stop!"

Lilianna jumped at her sudden outburst, but Jarek barely noticed. He used the chance to butt Lilianna's chest with the pommel of the ax. Lilianna's breath left on impact, stunning her. Jarek pinned Lilianna to the ground with his knee and raised the ax high with the other.

Lilianna's golden eyes widened, and her panic electrified the air. Juniper pulled in her next breath, which took more effort than it should have.

A greenish whirl of wind knocked Jarek backward. He thumped on the ground; his ax tumbled up into the air and slammed into the stone beside Lilianna's head. The green of her skin reflected on the steel.

Lilianna stood on trembling legs, fearful eyes on her chief.

Jarek groaned and stood, hand on his chest. He glared at Juniper, then Lilianna. Realization seemed to dawn over his features, and his glare turned vicious. He looked at Lilianna as if he hadn't seen her before.

"You—" he started.

A scream erupted outside, of pain and fear. A human scream, nearly lost in the chaos of hundreds of Shadows' howls.

"We need to act soon," Lilianna pleaded. "Before there is no village left to save."

"You have a plan?" Juniper asked.

Lilianna shook her head.

"My plan is just as thought out," Juniper said, a half-smile on her lips. "I say we go to that wellspring and clog it up anyway we can."

"What?" Jarek said, glaring. "The wellspring? You found it?"

"Yes," Juniper spat. "If you would've listened, I would have told you. Now let me out of here so I can help!"

Moss growled and pushed at the door of his cell the iron bars creaked viciously but remained upright.

A Shadow let out a vicious call from the outside. Another Shadow, farther away, answered. Through the windows, smoke billowed into the sky. Red and orange reflected on the smoke.

"Juniper's right," Lilianna said to Jarek. "We don't have time for this. I—"

"You will do no such thing!" Jarek grabbed Lilianna with one hand and dragged her toward another cell. She tried to summon another gale, but the air only fluttered the dust. Jarek tossed her into the cell, slammed the iron bars shut, and locked it with the key in his pocket.

"No!" Lilianna gasped.

"You have shown your traitorous ways, witch," Jarek barked at Lilianna.

Juniper scoffed. She should have frozen him when she had the chance.

"I will not have you directing those monsters to hurt anyone else," Jarek said, pointing a finger at Lilianna. "You will stay here, and we will sort this mess out later when there aren't lives at stake. I've got a village to protect."

Jarek stormed out of the jail and into the chaos. Once the door slammed behind him, Juniper pushed herself to her feet. She grasped onto her feeble magic and summoned a lockpick of ice. She started to work on the lock.

"You can do that?" Lilianna asked.

"The lockpick is the easy part," Juniper said, listening and feeling for the tumblers. A magic lockpick worked much better than a metal one. She would mold it as she needed to. But it took concentration—an impossible feat with Jarek shouting and swinging his ax toward Lilianna's head.

The lock clicked, and she pushed the door open.

She took the first step toward Lilianna's cell when a thud crashed into the prison. The impact knocked Juniper to her knees. She hit the floor, and pain flared through her body. The stone cracked and gave, iron creaked and groaned. The ceiling gave way as something large crashed through it, sending bits of stone in every direction. Juniper threw her hands over her head and dived as the ceiling crashed inward. Dust erupted and stone shattered as the prison collapsed.

When the prison stopped moving, Juniper blinked her eyes open. She'd been covered in a white coating of dust. Her exhausted, depleted body felt worse, but she was otherwise unhurt. The ceiling of the prison had come down, and her pitiful shield of ice had saved her from the worst of it. Her ice pushed the slab of stone up and off of her, puffing dust from where it landed.

The sounds of chaos flooded into the prison, swords and Shadows and cries of anger and fear and fury. A large Shadow had crashed into the roof, and as Juniper's eyes fell upon it, it dissolved into gold mist. The mist was thicker than it was before, almost viscus, and it did not seep into the ground as easily. It lingered on the surface.

Juniper could almost feel the anger within it, the betrayal, the pain, the torment—built up over a thousand years.

"Lilianna?" Juniper gasped. "Are you okay?"

"I'm here," she answered weakly.

Juniper climbed over the rubble to Lilianna's cell. It had not fared well. The wall had collapsed toward Lilianna, blocking her in a tiny space, pinning her legs under the thick iron bars and chunks of stone. Blood leaked from her temple.

"Moss?" Lilianna asked.

A warble answered her. Juniper climbed over the rubble to where his cell had been. It had been destroyed in the crash, all four walls toppled. From a narrow crack in the rubble, Moss slithered out—his shadowy form moved through the rubble like water, expanding and shrinking as needed. He shook off the dust and flexed his wings. He warbled lowly and crawled over the debris to where Lilianna was.

"He's fine," Juniper said, surprised he hadn't done that trick sooner. She turned back to Lilianna. "What about you?"

"I'm alive."

"You might not be for long." Juniper felt around the debris with her magic. The stone was too big, and there were too many other stones leaning on it. She wouldn't be able to lift it.

"I'm not bleeding out or in," Lilianna said. "I can feel it. Take Moss and go. Stop her. Moss knows the way. I don't care how. Find her. Calm her down. Lie if you have to. Just…stop the fighting."

Moss warbled beside her, a fierce and determined sound.

"It's all right, Moss," Lilianna said, fixing her tired golden eyes on him. "Go with Juniper. Find Angyla."

Juniper climbed onto Moss, and they shot off into the war-stained night. Smoke billowed from all over the village, houses and farms and wood piles, enough that it blocked out the moonlight. Shadows—hundreds of them— swarmed the village. Steel glinted off the firelight. She spotted Reid and his silver armor among them, armed with his Mage's Bane. He remained unharmed.

She could smell the blood in the air, the smoke, the fire, the fear.

"Faster, Moss," Juniper urged. "We have to stop this before someone finds Lilianna." *Or something happens to Reid.*

Before the archmage suffocated them all and fed their bodies to the Shadows.

CHAPTER 60

Moss roared and flapped his massive black wings against the air, pushing them faster. Juniper flattened herself against his back. Her knuckles were white where she held on. The winter wind whipped past her cheeks, numbing her skin, caressing her magic, and yanking hair loose from her braid. The forest rushed by underneath them. Thunder rolled in the heavy clouds, so close Juniper felt it in her bones. The mountains loomed in the black distance, sharpening with every moment into the jagged peaks crags.

Juniper didn't know what she would do or say to the archmage, only that she would stop her.

She had to.

Juniper steeled herself against the unknown, the uncertainty. She had done the impossible before. How many times had she laughed in the face of death and survived?

Moss flew over the low mountain peaks and into the valley, but then he flew over the ancient tree that held the door to Angyla's cavern home. She watched it fly by underneath.

"Moss?" Juniper asked, her voice barely cutting through the wind. "You passed it!"

He let out a quick spat of a warble.

Juniper looked ahead. They flew straight out, toward the bottomless cavern where they'd found the magic well. Juniper's heart flipped.

Moss was taking her back to the wellspring. To the archmage.

Juniper held on tight as he nose-dived straight down into the dark cavern. The magic dust shone with its own ghostly light, brighter than before. Sizzling with violence. Moss flew at a breakneck speed through the twisting cavern tunnels, almost flinging Juniper from his back more than once. She held on so tight her hands began to ache.

At last, they came to the wellspring. The gold mist churned and bubbled with shades of vicious red. Shadows crashed to the violent storm and others crawled out, shimmering anew.

Moss landed on the precipice of the magic pool and let out a growl.

Juniper squinted into the thick mist. Something human-shaped twisted within the mist, like a caught butterfly desperately fighting to free itself from a spider's web. Archmage.

"Of course," Juniper whispered to Moss. He had known where to find Angyla.

Juniper slid from his back. The Magic crashed below her, splashing her boots. It spilled over the leather like ink, clinging to itself, pulling itself back into the horde. Unlike the magic pool in Delphine, this magic was viscous and sticky, and it pulled at Juniper's feet and her magic as it retreated.

How was she supposed to get to her?

Swallowing, trying not to choke on the thick mist in the air, Juniper shouted, "Archmage!"

The magic trembled. The cavern rumbled, and the Shadows within growled.

"Stay away!" Angyla screamed, her voice twisted and no longer her own. Something deeper, more malicious and ancient underlined it. "You should never have come here. Filthy thief. Lair! This is your fault! You will ruin everything! Kill her! Kill her!"

Moss growled and shook his head. He bent down and pawed at his ears, whimpering.

"What's wrong?" Juniper asked.

"Foolish girl," Angela said, pointing at Juniper. A splat of mist crashed against the side of the pool, and Juniper ducked to avoid being splashed in the face. "The Shadows listen to me, to me! Now, *kill her.*"

Moss whined, backing into the tunnel with his wings folded close to his body.

"Insolent beast," Angyla spat. "I gave you an order! Kill the traitor!"

The cavern surged with her anger. The mist shook with her words.

"Fine," Angyla growled. Then her voice became apologetic, even remorseful, as she said, "I will do it myself. For the sake of the world."

Tendrils surged from within the mist, wrapping around Juniper's legs and up her waist. Before she could blink, Angyla yanked her into the wellspring. The mist sizzled on her skin and stole the breath from her throat. The mist entered her nose and mouth, worked its way down her throat and into her lungs. It ballooned in her chest like water.

Juniper knew she would die if it continued. Her panic gave way into fear, and she acted out of that fear—her own magic surged and pushed Angyla's out of her body. The magic holding her captive vanished, and she fell to the bottom of the pit. Juniper took a gasping breath, despite the stinging in her chest. There went the feeble healing she'd managed to do on that broken rib.

Juniper wobbled to her feet. The mist was too thick to see very far. She summoned a dagger of ice and sliced at the mist. A thin wound appeared and quickly healed itself, and the mist leeched the magic from Juniper's hand, evaporating her dagger.

"You think you can hurt me with your fledgling magic? I have had a thousand years to master my own," said the Archmage of Air from nowhere and everywhere at once. "As powerful as your magic is, it will take you centuries to be on my level."

Juniper half-laughed and summoned another dagger and sliced at the mist. It leeched it from her hand just as before. With more confidence than she felt, she yelled, "I don't need centuries to take you down."

Angyla scoffed. "You don't know, do you? You haven't realized it? I realized it when I healed you."

Juniper flashed an arrogant smirk. "That I'm just that good?"

Angyla laughed, patronizing and pitying. "You really don't know?"

Juniper spat, "Know what? Or is this the part where you try to tell me how alike we are?"

"We have a few things in common," Angyla said, her voice teasing.

"I hope you're not including bat-shit crazy on that list." Juniper sliced at a dark splotch that she thought was Angyla, but her ice hit nothing but magic-mist. Her daggers were leeched before she could try again.

"You don't realize what you are," Angyla hissed, amused. "The power you possess."

Juniper rolled her eyes. "Yes, I know about the prophecy."

"Not the old words, but the other. The power. The magic."

"You're losing it."

Angyla appeared in the mist, wild eyed and vicious, and grabbed Juniper's wrist. Lightning zapped up her arm and into her shoulder.

"You are an archmage!" Angyla hissed with mad delight.

Juniper broke the old woman's grip and sliced—she vanished into the mist, laughing. Her heart skipped several beats as Angyla's accusation settled. Her words came out flustered. "What are you talking about? No, I'm not—"

"I know what I felt, when I healed you and just now," Angyla said. "You are the Archmage of Water. You think just any mage could stand up to Nexon? No. He knew it would have to be an archmage, it would have to be someone like you."

Juniper summoned another ice dagger, sliced at the mist, and as that dagger was pulled from her grip, she summoned another in her off hand. She sliced at the mist, again and again, this way and that, left and right, but she found no one within it. She wanted to argue, she wanted to point out the flaw in Angyla's logic, but she couldn't. She didn't have a flaw to exploit, she didn't have a good reason to argue that she wasn't the archmage.

Was she?

Ison and Mason had both shown surprise at her quick grasp of magic, and her raw magic well always seemed deeper than anyone else's at the Marca. She had more than the other water mages. It explained how she had been able to survive the Marca's collapse, and her dramatic rescue of Captain Tinnly. She…

Gods. Could she really be an archmage?

In her hesitation, a force knocked into her chest, sending her backward. Her back hit the stone floor of the pool, and something heavy pinned her down. She sliced at it with her ice daggers, but the thing on her chest refused to move.

"Foolish girl," Angyla spat. "I am air. I am everywhere. You cannot harm me. You will pay for what you've done. Blasted thief."

Juniper tried in vain to release the thing holding her down, but she couldn't see it or touch it. "All of this, over a stupid brooch?"

"Ignorance! Foolishness!' Angyla cried. A fearful, pained shriek pierced the air. "We couldn't have known what we did would have such dire consequences. We couldn't have… None of us knew what would happen. We saw only Nexon and a way to take his archmage powers from him, from his children, so that there would be no Archmage of Earth. We upset the balance, don't you see? We thought ourselves above the laws of magic. We were wrong. But it's too late. We caused this. The burden is mine. We sacrificed too much. Nexon will not win."

Juniper let out a gasp—and the thing on her chest refused it back in. "You tried to take away his magic?"

And he was looking for the *pieces*.

"In their arrogance, the archmages dared black magic to save the world," Angyla cried. "I was not old enough to know better. I was not aware enough to speak out against it. They said it was all right, and I believed them."

Stones fell into Juniper's stomach. The pieces of his magic, torn from him, with black magic.

"And you storm my home and steal from me!" Angyla hissed. "Traitorous filth! You knew what it was, how much he needed it. You stole it for him!"

The magic pressed hard against her, stealing the air from her throat.

"The wellspring is our reward for playing as gods," cried the Archmage of Air. "It thrives. It seeks only destruction and death. The curse will spread until the world is devoured. I have kept it back all these years. I thought it fitting that I should be the one, because I held my tongue. When I am gone, Lilianna will inherit my mistake and take my place. We will yet keep this world safe."

Juniper gasped for her next breath. Underneath her white-hot panic and burning lungs, Angyla's accusation repeated: thief, traitorous filth. All this started when Juniper had shown the stolen brooch to Lilianna and Reid. That is what set Angyla on her rage.

The pieces. Had the brooch been a piece of Nexon's power?

Juniper felt it more than saw it—a blade of air above her neck. She imagined it—an executioner's ax, meant to sever the head in a single, shift blow, like the old execution grounds in Rusdasin, which had haunted her sparse dreams since she had entered the Undercity.

Her panic flexed, and her magic surged.

Archmage, she said to herself.

And she let her magic go.

CHAPTER 61

Shadows overran Sinjon, hundreds of the monsters. For every one Reid gutted, three more appeared before the first had dissolved into the ground. The druids fought with all their might, but it was not enough. The tide of enemies was never-ending. Reid met the incoming teeth of a Shadow with the blade of his Mage's Bane. The magic of the beast whined, and its magical flesh flinched away from the bane. It was too late—Reid's blade tore through the monster as easily as it sliced through the empty air.

Another appeared behind him, and Sein's ax sliced through the Shadow. It collapsed onto the ground, writhing as it dissolved. Neither had time to talk. Another wave of Shadows slithered over the timber wall, crying and hissing.

Reid's breath heaved in his chest, pulling at his lungs, tearing at his muscles. Strain fogged the edges of his mind. All he knew was the battle. A deeper instinct had taken over, switching his mind and body into a calm blankness, a knight who knew only the battle around him. He had no room for doubt, fear, or worry for those he cared for. He could do nothing if he did not survive. So, he fought with no other thought than to fight, to win, to survive.

A great bang sounded against the other side of the timber wall. Another followed. A vicious crack pierced the air.

"Move!" Reid screamed into the battle.

Some listened, others didn't have the time.

Bang. The timber wall exploded inward, showering splinters and chunks of mortar over the battle. Reid fell onto his knees from the blast, shielding his eyes from the dust and debris. The larger bits of the wall thudded onto the hard ground. The beat of silence faded, and panic spread in feverish screams and battle-weary cries. When Reid opened his eyes, his dread coiled tight around his throat.

A beast the size of a small house lumbered through the hole in the wall. It looked to have once been an elk. Curved antlers, sharp as blades, rose from either side of its head. Long, heavy legs ending in rocky hooves clomped over the debris. Mangy brown fur hung in clumps. Tar-black leathery flesh stretched over heavy muscles and too-large bones. Its breaths puffed into white steam from its massive snout. It black eyes settled on Reid, and it let out a whiny snort.

It charged him, and he met its downward swoop of antlers with his Mage's Bane. The impact pushed Reid's heels into the mud and knocked the beast off course. Reid aimed a blow to its side. His blade left a clean slice down its rough hide, and the beast let out a pained shriek. It kicked its back legs, and while Reid dodged the bone-breaking force of the blow, the beast twisted—the beast reared back, front hooves clawing toward Reid's head.

He adjusted his blade for defense.

Not fast enough.

One hoof thrust against the flat side of his blade, the other tore through his leather chaise. He stumbled back. The beast thrust its sharp antlers toward him, and as they came down at him, a blade cut through the air between Reid and the elk. The blade tangled in the antlers, twisting his head and halting its downward thrust. The hunter appeared between Reid and it, and with a mighty grunt and twist of his blade, he sent the beast to the ground.

Before Reid could gather his thoughts, the hunter wrenched the blade free of the antlers and severed the head from the body.

The monster disintegrated into the earth, alongside the Shadows. The hunter straightened, and Reid realized he was no druid hunter. He wore dark silver armor accented with lighter steel. The breastplate bore a stylized half-moon and half-sun surrounded by laurel leaves.

Sentinel armor.

The sentinel faced Reid and lifted the face of his helmet. A dark skinned young man grinned back at him. "Calvex," Reid breathed. He could hardly believe it.

A second sentinel stepped to Calvex's side, and she lifted the face of her helmet.

"No time for chitchat," Rue said, breathless but grinning.

"Talk after we win," Calvex said, tossing the face back down.

He quickly glanced around the battlefield, but he spotted no more Sentinels among the druid hunters. Reid had never felt such a mixture of relief and dread. Relief to see friendly faces with battle skills, and dread that these two had likely trudged through the Wylds to find them. He didn't dwell on it. He didn't have the time.

The battle continued. No more elks appeared, but wolves, bears, and cougars joined the Shadow's onslaught. As suspected, Calvex and Rue fought with superior skill. Beside Reid, they took down three times as many Shadows as the druid warriors.

Reid felt his own exhaustion, but he didn't back down.

He could only hope that Juniper would hurry.

CHAPTER 62

Juniper had felt, on more than one occasion, powerful enough to move entire lakes. The curse of the Wylds had prevented her from using her magic. Now, she let it flow freely. Bright blue magic pulsed from her. Icy tendrils sliced through the mist and dispelled the force pinning her down. Juniper stumbled to her feet as ice grew out from her. It crawled over the floor and up the walls, creaking and chiming as it grew. It slithered through the mist, searching for Angyla.

Angyla pushed against her ice with air. "You will not leave here! I will not allow you to condemn this world further."

Her ice converged on the ceiling. The cavern was not as vast as it seemed. Juniper felt something move behind her, and she slashed at it with an ice dagger. A Shadow hissed and faded into the mist. She formed a bright blue net of her magic around herself. The Shadows hissed on the other side, unable to trespass.

"The mist shows me things. The future. Yours," Angyla taunted, each word twisted in madness.

"The future is not written," Juniper said. Maddox had told her that. He, like Juniper, didn't care for fortune tellers. "If I know I am going to fail, then I will fail. If I know I am going to win, then I will win."

"Foolish, arrogant nonsense."

For a while, neither of them spoke. Juniper countered every Shadow attacked as it came, dancing about the floor she couldn't see. The mist churned around her feet and knees, stealing every other breath, brushing up against her in ways that felt like a phantom hand, an elbow, a footstep.

Heart racing, Juniper inched toward the back of the cavern. "Why are you hiding?"

A menacing chuckle rang through the air.

Something broke through her magic net and wrapped around her middle like a snake. She yelped, and in instinct thrust her ice toward it. It dissolved as her magic cut through where it had been.

"You think you can hurt *me*?" Angyla laughed. "I'm no longer bound by your human laws."

Angyla had indeed gone mad. With power, with magic, with old age.

"Then show yourself," Juniper taunted. "Stop hiding if you're not afraid of me."

"Put away your dagger."

"You're afraid of my magic?" Juniper scoffed. "I thought you weren't bound by my human laws."

The mist thickened rapidly. The shades of gold became violent crimson. It compressed, threatening to crush her. It pulled the breath from Juniper's throat and coated her insides with fire. Something hard slammed into her chest. The impact lifted Juniper from her feet and slammed her into the stone wall of the cavern. Her breath rushed from her chest. She slumped to the ground and gasped for her next breath—it wouldn't come. She couldn't breathe. Angyla had pulled the air from her lungs.

Juniper fought the darkness creeping into her vision, the weakness tugging on her limbs. The mist clawed at her magic, staining the bright blue with crimson, churning into plum at the edges. Juniper called her ice from the floor and walls— the wave of rushing ice crashed into something solid on the far side of the cavern, a knot of magic. Angyla let out a sudden shout of surprise. Juniper sucked in her next breath and barked out a laugh.

Found you.

Juniper sent a volley of ice arrows at Angyla. Most slammed into a cocoon of air, but each one weakened the magic. Juniper felt it—felt the weak points left by the ice arrows in the sliver of time before Angyla fixed them. Juniper focused another volley, but this time in a concentrated area. She felt the first few arrows strike and bounce off, the next sink in but stop—a strong wind brushed it away— but as the next speared the same spot, a panicked shriek followed. A second arrow found its way through, and then a third followed.

Angyla's scream echoed through the air. The mist shook, and the ground trembled. The mist thinned. The cocoon evaporated, and Angyla staggered a step forward. Blood poured from a wound on her chest and seeped into her dirty wools and furs. Too much, too fast. Angyla staggered backward, hands grasping at the wound.

Juniper's next breath tumbled out in an ungraceful curse. Panic surged hot up her spine and into her fingers. She hadn't mean to kill.

"You!" Angyla gasped. Her furious, terrified gaze met Juniper's. Her skin paled with every heartbeat, with every pump of blood her body lost. "What have you done?"

"I stopped a monster," Juniper said firmly, her breath stabilizing. She regained her stance and held the archmage's disbelieving stare with her own. "Just like I will stop another."

Angyla laughed, though the sound was wet and tired. The mist faded from crimson to orange to chartreuse and then to pale gold. As it thinned, it revealed the cavern's far side. The pit opened into a crevasse that fell deep into the earth. Magic steadily flowed upward from it.

Angyla stumbled backward, losing balance and grace with each breath. She mumbled, "No, no, no…this can't… No! I didn't want… Not this. Why? Why? Why?"

Juniper did not think Angyla was talking to her. No, she was talking to someone else, in a different place and time.

The ground trembled again.

"No!" Angyla screamed. "What have you done? What have we done? You've caused the end of this world!"

The trembling cavern rattled rocks loose from its ceiling and walls. The stone shuttered, cracked, and crumbled. Juniper lost her balance and stumbled forward onto her knees. Angyla stumbled, hands clutching her bleeding chest, and with a shriek, the Archmage of Air fell over the precipice.

"No!" Juniper scrambled to her feet, but by the time she reached the edge, she saw only darkness. Magic shimmered as far as she could see into the depths.

For a heartbeat, silence drenched the cavern. Juniper's hands shook.

And then a thunderous roar sounded from deep within the cavern. From within the darkness, magic surged forward. It came too fast for her to move, to dodge, to think—a wave of angry, tangled magic knocked her off her feet. Her back slammed into the cavern floor, knocking the breath from her chest. She swore, but she heard only the gushing of power, the rushing of force. It pressed against every fiber of her being. It sounded worse than a windstorm, a constant roar of thunder.

Juniper fumbled to her feet. This, she realized with no small amount of horror, is what Angyla had been holding back. This tangle of magic. Juniper had never felt anything like it—magic that had rotted and festered with hatred and anger and vengeance.

The mist began to converge and form shapes. As Juniper watched, the cavern transformed. Trees lined the cavern, full of leaves and spotted with weeds. At first, she wondered if the blast had thrown her all the way to the surface, but upon a closer look, the trees were not real. She could see through them and into the cavern behind. She blinked. With every moment, the trees and grass and weeds grew thicker, heavier, and less opaque. Ghostly grass grew over the rocky floor.

The cavern became a grove. Sunlight dappled from the thick canopy, jostled by an unfelt breeze.

A woman was standing in the middle, fidgeting with a pendant. Her dark hair fell past her shoulders, and she wore unease on her heart-shaped face. Her dress was simple and torn at the hem.

"Hello?" Juniper asked.

The woman did not respond.

Juniper stepped in front of her. The woman's eyes were on her pendant, but also elsewhere.

"Hello?" Juniper asked again.

Nothing.

Juniper reached for the girl's shoulder—her hand went right through. The woman's shoulder rippled and reformed like water. Juniper yanked her hand back. The woman didn't give any indication she noticed Juniper's touch or presence.

"Donna?" asked a male voice.

Both the woman and Juniper jumped. The woman's dark eyes snapped over Juniper's shoulder. She turned—a handsome man approached from between trees. He wore old-fashioned clothes of folded silk and braided leather—Juniper had seen such fashion in history books. He wore dark curiosity that sent a chill down Juniper's spine, and it took a few steps to realize why.

The man had ice blue eyes, cruel and clever and arrogant.

CHAPTER 63

"Nexon," Juniper said at the same time as the dark-haired woman, though she sounded far happier to see him than Juniper did.

"You came," the woman added, breathless. She wiped her eye with her sleeve.

"You sounded worried in your letter." Nexon paused within arm's reach of the woman. His voice was the same that had spoken intertwined with Ison's and Penet's and Ron's, only…softer. "You sounded afraid."

"I am afraid." Donna clutched her pendant.

Nexon set his hands on Donna's shoulders and pulled her closer. "Don't be afraid, love. You have nothing to fear when you are with me."

They kissed, and from where Juniper stood, it appeared tender. Donna curled into Nexon's chest with a lover's affection.

"What did you need to tell me?" Nexon asked.

"I…" She swallowed. "I needed to tell you I'm sorry."

Nexon's brow furrowed. "For what?"

Her eyes went misty. Nexon's confusion thickened.

"Donna, you can—" Nexon's words ended in a gasp of pain. He stumbled away from Donna and clasped a hand around the dagger hilt sticking out of his gut. The worried, tender Nexon vanished. He glared at Donna with all the viciousness and cruelty that Juniper knew.

"What is this?" Nexon spat, his voice strained.

"Runed steel," came another voice, this one deep and feminine.

A middle-aged woman stepped from the forest, eyes on Nexon. "Took weeks to figure it out. A lot of late nights went into that rune. It blocks magic, specifically *earth* magic."

"Bitch," Nexon spat.

"I thought it was rather clever," came a male voice. Juniper saw the shadow first, then a well-dressed man walked into the clearing from where Juniper was standing—through her. He was tall, lean, and utterly calm. He beheld Nexon with disinterested deep blue eyes. Balendin eyes. "You should be honored we went to such lengths to stop you."

"Arrogant trash," Nexon spat. He tried to take a step, but his knees gave out. He knelt in the grass.

Donna remained silent despite the tears leaking down her cheeks, despite the white knuckles gripping her skirt.

"Let's get this over with," said another voice, this time an older woman. Beside her stood a young girl with dark golden skin, dark brown hair, and terror on her face. Angyla.

The breath left Juniper's throat as she realized what she was seeing—the archmages!

The archmages as they defeated Nexon.

The four archmages circled Nexon's trembling body. They reached out to him but did not touch him. Donna collapsed to the ground, pale and trembling, unable to take her eyes off her lover.

Juniper watched as the raw magic of four archmages circled Nexon. The ribbons of vibrant color combined in a shimmery gray haze, so bright Juniper had to shield her eyes. Nexon screamed. Juniper had thought hearing him scream in pain would be satisfying, but she hated it.

His screams turned bloodcurdling, and when Juniper thought she could stand no more, his screams stopped abruptly. The light dimmed. Juniper lowered her hand. Nexon had gone still. The ribbons of raw magic hovered over the archmages, each holding a glowing copper nugget—Nexon's *magic*. She felt a ghostly sensation deep within her chest, a memory of when she had willingly divided her magic. Nexon would have fought against it. She couldn't imagine how painful it would have been to have all his magic ripped out of him at once.

And the desperate, incessant need to have them back. That she remembered well.

The memory rippled. Nexon was lying on his back, eyes staring upward. The archmages were gone. And…so was everything else. The leaves had been blasted, the limbs twisted back. Saplings had been twisted and stripped bare. The grass and weeds were dead. The ground itself had been stomped.

The air smelled rotten, festered, and vile—black magic.

This is what Angyla had meant. This is what they had done. They had used black magic and ripped Nexon's magic out of his body. They had created the Wylds. They had cursed this land with black magic.

And…Nexon was looking for the final pieces, the last of his stolen magic.

"We can't do that," Juniper said to the memory. She looked down at Nexon's body. The dagger still stuck out of his middle.

Nexon's words came back—*my body was left for the wolves.*

The forest faded, and the cavern reappeared. The mist hovered in the air, undulating like light through water, twisting and churning like smoke. Juniper felt the raw power within it, the wrongness of it. Hatred, betrayal, fear—the emotions

Nexon had felt as he lay dying on the forest floor. Those emotions had lingered and festered over the past one thousand years, twisting into something far worse than an ancient curse.

The cavern trembled once more, loosening unstable rocks and sending unseen stones crashing to the floor. This is what Angyla had been holding back, the aftermath of black magic and festering darkness, since Nexon's first defeat. This curse had settled into the stones, the trees, and into Angyla, turning her mad. The worst of it lingered far below, deep within the wellspring, knotting and twisted and violently seizing without its keeper to calm it.

Juniper reached a tendril of her magic out to it, but the thick mist leeched it within an instant. A memory surfaced of the feeling in her chest when she had split her magic. Terror gripped her bones, and she held her magic closer.

If she couldn't do something about it…could the Archmage of Air?

Angyla had been training Lilianna to take over the role of keeper. Even if Angyla had been wrong, and Lilianna wasn't the next archmage, she knew more than anyone else.

The cavern trembled, and rock cracked above her head. Juniper threw herself back as the stone crashed into the cavern floor, shattering itself in every direction. She scrambled to the edge of the pool. She had to find Lilianna before the wellspring brought the entire cavern system down, and Sinjon and the Wylds with it.

Moss paced along the edge of the pool, wings folded tight against his body. At the sight of Juniper, he let out a mournful warble.

She climbed up the side of the chamber and gave Moss an affectionate pat as she climbed onto his back.

"Let's go back to the village," she said. And hope that Lilianna had inherited the archmage power. If not, she didn't know what they would do.

Moss flexed his wings and took off through the twisting and turning caverns. More than once he dodged to avoid falling rocks and crumbling stone.

Night blanketed the Wylds. The ground trembled and shook, thunder from below. Magic spewed from the ground in bursts from all over the Wylds, and already a dangerous golden fog hung in the valleys and low points. All other sound had vanished, save for the wind rushing past Juniper and the flap of Moss's wings. It was as beautiful as it was terrifying.

It toyed with Juniper's magic, pushing and pulling. Juniper felt a simultaneous sensation of being able to move entire oceans and not being able to summon a drop—the conflict made her stomach roil.

The tremors continued as the wellspring flooded the forest. Juniper felt the unsteadiness within it, the destructive nature, the unbiased rage. With each tremor, the wellspring spread and grew. If left unchecked, the wellspring would devour the Wylds, Sinjon, and spread until it devoured everything.

She couldn't let that happen.

Moss seemed to understand. He flew as fast as he could, pumping his wings furiously.

She saw the glow first.

There, nestled within the dark of the Wylds, was Sinjon.

Burning.

CHAPTER 64

Juniper cursed.

The flames glowed against the steely clouds, and black smoke billowed from every corner of the village. The market had been destroyed, the stalls collapsed or burned or smashed. Woodpiles burned, thatch roofing smoked, the debris smoldered. As she and Moss circled, a home collapsed, sending embers and smoke spitting into the air.

Homes on the outer edges had fared only slightly better. The southern edge of the village had gotten the worst of the attack, and little remained standing. Most had been reduced to rubble and ash. Fissures had opened up outside of the village and within it, swallowing parts of the timber wall, gardens, and entire houses.

Shadows and cursed beasts were slinking over the wall and through the gaps, vanishing into the Wylds. Moss flew over the wall. Juniper readied her magic for incoming arrows, but they didn't come. No attack came.

Druids left standing were either heaving buckets of water onto the flames or carrying the injured. Few even noticed Moss flying over. Juniper guided Moss to the Great Hall where a crowd of druids had gathered. Somehow, the ancient building had escaped destruction save for scorched marks and what looked like claw marks near the east wall.

As Moss landed, a burning stall collapsed a street away, sending embers and dust and smoke bursting into the night.

"Keep up your guard," Juniper whispered to Moss. She slid off his back and to the ground.

The earth sighed—a sound of ripping roots and cracking stone, as deep as thunder.

"It's the witch!" came a shrill cry.

"Stop," Juniper said, her voice strong despite her quivering gut. She thought of how Crespin spoke like a commander, how Reid spoke like a knight, how Roslyn spoke like a queen. She held her shoulders back and her chin high. She held the stare of the gathered druids. "If you don't stop the wellspring, it will swallow your village. You can either let yourselves, your families, and your village get swallowed, or you can do something about it. I have no problem with flying away and letting this place fall into the bowels of the earth. So, what will it be? Help me save you or perish?"

Several wounded warriors had joined the gathering on the steps, and all talk from within the Great Hall had ceased. One bandaged druid shoved his way through the crowd.

"I'd rather not die," said Sein as he joined Juniper. A bandage covered his left eye, and several burns marked his left arm. By the pallor of his skin, he had lost too much blood to be useful. "I say we help."

A woman with beige skin and caramel hair stepped out from the Great Hall, and it took Juniper a moment to place her and the dark silver armor—Rue Bellamy. She made her way down the steps and paused before Juniper. She wore a stoic mask Reid would be jealous of.

Rue placed her fist over her heart and knelt.

"What are you doing?" Juniper's heart lurched.

"As a Sentinel, I am sworn to the crown." Rue kept her eyes lowered as she spoke. "I will do as you ask of me, Princess Isolde."

A wave of uneasy murmurs washed through the druids. Eyes shifted from Rue to Juniper, wide and curious, furious but tired. More appeared in the doors of the hall, stretching to see over one another. Juniper's stomach fell into her groin and then tumbled into her ankles.

Rue glanced up at Juniper, expectantly.

"What? Am I supposed to say something dramatic?" she asked, though her voice came out rough and raspy.

Smirking, Rue stood. "Yeah, but that's all right. When the scribes ask about this moment, we'll tell them you said something dark and encouraging."

A murmur flashed through the druids, and then an older druid stepped forward. His silver hair fell past his shoulders in a thick braid, and deep wrinkles lined his face and neck. The way the others lowered their eyes marked him as an elder. The old druid paused before Juniper, watery eyes taking her in, his fingers holding his wooden cane steady. Then, he nodded.

"So be it," said the elder in a wobbly voice. "I'd rather not die by falling into my own tomb."

No one openly argued with the old man, though a few looked like they wanted to.

"What's first?" Sein asked.

"I need to speak to Lilianna," Juniper said, her tone calm but assertive. "Immediately."

"She's at Jarek's," answered Sein. Something dark passed over his expression. "I saw him carrying her there during the battle. She looked rough."

Juniper ran through the debris-strewn dirt streets to Jarek's house on the hill. Moss followed, bouncing along the path. Juniper let herself in, prepared to defend

Lilianna and herself—at her sudden entrance, a sword unsheathed on the other side—Reid stood ready to defend, Mage's Bane halfway out of the scabbard.

"Jun," he breathed, at the same time she said, "Reid!"

She looked him over for injuries as he looked her over. He had a few new dents and scratches on his silver armor, but he had otherwise remained unhurt. She wanted to fall into him, but she steeled herself. There would be time to hold him after they saved the Blackwoods.

"Rue is here," Juniper whispered.

"A group of Sentinels arrived," Reid explained. "They turned the tide of the battle."

"What are you doing here?" Jarek asked. He stood on the other side of the hearth, beside a worried Ingrid.

Lilianna laid on a blanket beside the hearth. Enna knelt beside her granddaughter, working a pale red paste into a wound on her temple. At the sight of Juniper, Lilianna sat up.

"Where is—" Lilianna started.

"Moss is fine. Angyla is probably dead," Juniper said in a single breath.

Lilianna's eyes widened, as did her grandmother's.

"She's dead?" Enna asked, brow furrowed.

"I felt it," Lilianna whispered. She put a hand over her chest. "I—I can't explain how, but it did. It was like…a sudden pressure."

"I think you're the new Archmage of Air," Juniper said.

"What?" Reid asked, looking at Lilianna with wide, skeptical eyes.

"What is this nonsense?" Jarek barked.

Juniper held up her hand to silence his questions. "We need—"

Another tremor shook the earth. It rattled the foundation of the house, the timber walls and roof, sending dust and splinters down over them. Juniper cast a shell of ice to protect them. The splinters and bits of stone and mortar pitter-pattered against the ice.

Lilianna staggered to her feet. She placed her green hand over her chest—the mirror of where Juniper believed her magic to be. Lilianna sighed deeply and met Juniper's eyes with steely resolve. She felt the new archmage magic there, and she believed Juniper.

"We have to stop the wellspring." Juniper let her ice dissolve, whisking the dust and debris to the sides of the room. "If we do nothing, it will spread and devour the village and the Wylds and everything else in its path."

Lilianna shook her head, brow furrowed. "The wellspring has never—"

"Our village has always been safe," Jarek argued.

"Because Angyla used her magic to hold it back," Juniper countered. "And she's gone, and the wellspring doesn't care about your wall or your traditions."

"What do we do?" Lilianna asked.

"Angyla said she'd been training you to take her place," Juniper told her.

Lilianna nodded. "She has."

"Then you might be the only one capable of stopping it," Juniper said.

"Just her?" Enna barked, standing.

"I'll be helping," Juniper said. "I am not an air mage like Angyla or Lilianna, and I have no idea what Angyla did to hold it back. But I can help."

"Jun," Reid started. He closed his fingers around her arm, an unspoken question in his worried gaze.

"I can help," she said to Reid. She didn't tell him why. She didn't want to declare herself an archmage in front of Jarek and Ingrid.

He held her gaze, searching. How he came to his understanding, she didn't know, but he nodded. He dropped his hand.

The earth trembled again, but this time, Juniper did not shield them. Splinters and dust rained from the ceiling. Those that hit the hearth fire hissed and popped.

"Time is not on our side," Juniper said.

Lilianna pushed herself to her feet, ignoring her grandmother's offered hand, and started toward the door Juniper had left open. Reid followed.

"Reid—" Juniper started to protest.

"I'm going with you," Reid said firmly, leaving no room for argument. "I know magic. I know ways to stop it."

He was right. His presence also gave Juniper immense comfort. "Okay."

Reid straightened, his features melted into those of the stoic knight. Calm and commanding, cold and ruthless. "Jarek," he said, "Restore order here as best as you are able. Lessen the panic regarding Juniper and Lilianna."

Jarek bristled at the command, but he did not argue. "I will do what I can."

Moss was ecstatic to see Lilianna. The three of them climbed onto the Shadow's back, and Juniper held back a laugh when Reid gasped during takeoff. Moss flew them over the wall and over the Wylds.

"Look!" Lilianna pointed toward Blood Tree Pass.

The tremors had torn open the earth, and magic gushed out.

"The wellspring is underneath the pass," Juniper said over the rush of the wind. "That will get us there faster."

Moss couldn't fly close with the thick blood trees, so they landed in a clearing and trekked closer. The golden fog thickened and made visibility near impossible, even with her night sight. She could barely make out Lilianna's form in front of her. Reid's armor clanked behind her, and more than once she looked back to see his form in the mist.

"Reid, there is something else I need to tell you," Juniper started.

"Good news or bad news?" asked Reid.

"Good, I think." Juniper half-laughed, mostly to ease the panic in her chest. "According to Angyla, I'm also an archmage."

Reid's silence felt worse than the oppressive magic.

"It would explain things," he said.

"Wait." Juniper paused and turned. Reid stumbled to a halt. They stood close enough for her to see his raised brows. "It *explains* things? Did you know?"

"I…suspected," Reid admitted.

She gawked at him. "How long have you suspected?"

"Since I…" He swallowed and glanced at her arm. "Since I knotted your magic by accident. I felt it. It was so much raw magic. I'd never felt anything like it. Combined with the prophecy… It made sense. I just didn't have evidence."

Juniper blinked at him.

"I found something!" Lilianna called from ahead.

Juniper and Reid trekked through the mist and over tree roots. The earth had spilled near the pass, and though the mist spewed high, the gaping crack went deep into the caverns. Juniper inched to the edge and glanced down—it vanished into darkness, deep and thick. The magic flowed upward, thick as water in places.

"How far do you think it goes?" Lilianna asked.

"Deep," Juniper said. "What we found that day wasn't the wellspring. It was the beginning of it. I'm willing to bet this hole will take us right to the heart of it."

"Magic settles into the lowest parts," Reid said. "Like fog. It will be at the deepest part of the cavern."

Juniper harrumphed. Just like the vault in the basement. She opened her mouth to say so when the earth trembled. The ground under their feet shattered, and the earth swallowed a slice of the Wylds. Juniper, Reid, and Lilianna fell into the abyss along with blood trees and their gnarled roots.

CHAPTER 65

Juniper fell. Golden magic rushed around her. Bits of rocks and roots and even whole trees fell along with her. The darkness swallowed them whole, and the nearly nonexistent moonlight narrowed and narrowed until it vanished.

A gush of air pushed against Juniper's shoulders, slowing her fall. She heard the thudding and crashing of trees and roots and rocks against stone, and then she landed on the same ground. A gasp and a thud told her Lilianna had landed beside her.

Gasping, Juniper rolled onto her hands and knees.

"I did it," Lilianna said between gasps. She had used her air magic to soften the fall.

Juniper summoned a magelight. Bright blue light illuminated Lilianna and the strewn debris. Sweat shone of Lilianna's face.

But—

"Reid?" Juniper called. She staggered to her feet. She looked around the trees, the roots, the rocks. She didn't see him. "Reid! Answer me! Reid!"

His answer didn't come.

"I—I didn't…" Lilianna started.

Juniper rounded on the girl. "You didn't what?"

In the blue light, Lilianna's skin looked ashen. She staggered to her feet, eyes bright and sad. The look tore through Juniper's chest worse than any knife.

"He was too far away," Lilianna whispered.

Her heart stopped. Her thoughts crashed into a dark wall. A sharp buzzing filled her ears.

Slowly, those words sank in. Juniper shook her head. No. No. No.

"Reid!" Juniper screamed. Her voice echoed off the stone. The magic echoed her voice, mocking her.

Lilianna caught Juniper's arm. "You saw how far we fell," she whispered. "He did not have magic to soften the fall. Juniper, he would not have survived."

A sob choked her. "No!"

She wrenched her arm from Lilianna's grasp and held her magelight higher. She fumbled over the roots and rocks, searching the cavern until—

She found him.

And everything stopped.

Reid was lying on the stone. Blood darkened the stone around him.

"Reid!" Juniper screamed.

He did not answer.

Juniper fell at his side. Several of his bones were broken. He wore his stoic expression, impassive and knightly. His eyes... They were not bright with intelligence or cleverness. His eyes were empty. Gone.

"Reid?" she begged. "No. No. No. *Reid.*"

She shoved a trembling and desperate hand into her pocket and pulled out the little leather pouch. She fought to remove the vial of magic she'd stolen from Delphine. With fumbling hands, she uncorked it and held it against Reid's still warm lips. She pulled his bottom lip down and emptied the magic into his mouth. The viscus purple mist vanished down his throat.

She waited. And waited.

Nothing happened. Life did not return to his eyes.

"I'm sorry," Lilianna whimpered.

Juniper screamed—it echoed off the walls, through the magic. She set her forehead against his breastplate, against the damned owl of the Marca. A part of her waited for his hand to touch her shoulder, her head, her hair.

Not Reid. Of all the people in the world, not Reid. Anyone but Reid.

The earth trembled, shaking the stone under her feet, threatening to give way again. It jostled Reid's armor.

Still, he did not move.

How dare she allow herself to think she could be happy, to think she could have someone, to have something. How dare she even hope for it.

She didn't bother trying to pull it together or steel herself. She staggered to her feet with hot tears stinging her eyes.

"Juniper—" Lilianna started.

"The wellspring," Juniper said, her voice tight with emotions she refused to face. "We have to stop it."

Though a part of her wanted to let the entire village fall and for her to be crushed by it.

The trek through the cavern blurred. Juniper spent it burying unpleasant emotions before they got the better of her. She buried them down deep in the dark nothingness. She numbed herself. They came to the bottom, where the golden mist had congealed in a trembling knot, threads undulating and trying to wiggle free but only worsening the tangle.

Lilianna lifted her hands to the knot, and Juniper mirrored the actions. The two archmages reached out to the knot with raw magic, ribbons of bright blue and spring green. Juniper felt the twisted, tangled magic, knotted and clotted with dark emotions a thousand years old.

She felt the pathways of the magic, felt the way.

She and Lilianna worked together. As they worked, the tremors lessened and the fog thinned. It would take time to unravel the magic, to undo what had been simmering since Nexon's defeat.

But they would do it.

They would save the village, and Juniper would stop Nexon, one way or another.

Without Reid, it was all Juniper had left.

Acknowledgments

Here we are, the end of book five. There was a point when I fully believed I would never get here, I would never get my books off the ground, and that I was wasting my evenings and weekends typing away this story I couldn't let go. I persisted and kept writing regardless of how few readers I had, regardless of how many times I called a bookstore and never heard anything back.

First and foremost, I wouldn't have gotten anywhere without the amazing team at Authors 4 Authors. I can't express the gratitude necessary for all that you all have done for me, for giving me a chance to prove myself, for helping me level up my own skills and knowledge of the industry, for being friends in the overwhelming mess of publishing.

My parents have always been amazing—especially when they allowed me to stay at home after college and write while working part-time. Now that I'm grown, I realize how incredible my parents are and have been; I don't think I'll be able to ever say thank you enough.

And of course to you, the reader who has stuck with Juniper through all of the ups and downs—without you, this book wouldn't even exist. Thank you.

About the Author

Beatrice B. Morgan lives in southern Illinois. When she isn't reading or writing, she is most likely playing a video game. She is a night owl, caffeine addict, yoga enthusiast, dog person, hopeless romantic, optimistic, and a shameless Ravenclaw.

Follow her online:

www.bbmorgan.com
TikTok: **@beatrice_author**
Twitter: **@BBMorgan_W**
Instagram and Threads: **@BBMorgan_W**
Facebook: **@BBMorganBooks**

Also by Beatrice B. Morgan

Hard as Stone

Seventeen-year-old Raven Thane wants an adventure...and she's going to get one. Just not the way that she expected. Bored and disinterested with a routine life in her remote underground community, she fails to notice a thief during her turn at guard duty. Zander, a charming sharpshooter, tasks her with helping him retrieve the mysterious stolen item. Posing as a couple on the road, they'll face deadly automatons and Gray Elite soldiers, entangle themselves in a complicated world of spies and freedom fighters, and hide secrets of their own. Can Raven fix her mistake and prove herself more than a simple country girl? Or will she create even more chaos?

books2read.com/hardstone

Authors 4 Authors Publishing

A publishing company for authors, run by authors, blending the best of traditional and independent publishing

We specialize in speculative fiction: science fiction, fantasy, paranormal, and romance. Get lost in another world!

Check out our collection at https://books2read.com/rl/a4a
or visit Authors4AuthorsPublishing.com/books

For updates, scan the QR code or visit our website to join our semi-monthly newsletter!

Want more adventure fantasy? We recommend:

The Anatalian Soldier

by Rebecca Mikkelson

Liam Fulton wants to see the world beyond the vineyard his parents live and work on. The only option he sees is the Anatalian army. Shortly after he joins, war breaks out, where he discovers a treasonous plot. Will he come away unscathed, or will his actions during the war irreparably change his life?

Margaret is just learning to fit in at court when her father falls gravely ill. The other courtiers start to pull away from her family, thinking they're cursed by God for reaching too high. Her mother, unable to handle the pressure of scrutiny, abandons them. Can Margaret figure out how to care for her father on her own?

books2read.com/anataliansoldier

9 781644 771891